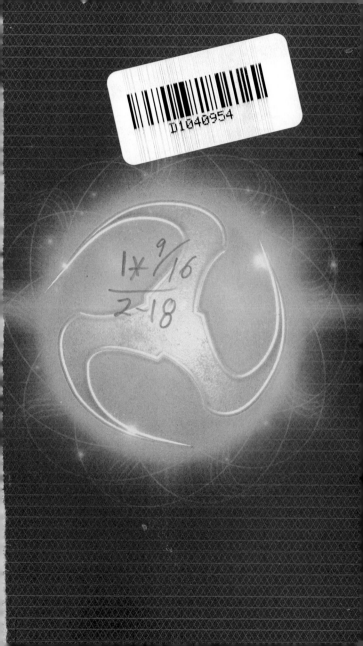

THE
FINISHER

A NOVEL BY

DAVID BALDACCI

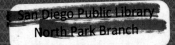
SCHOLASTIC INC.

Copyright © 2014 by Columbus Rose, Ltd.

This book was originally published in hardcover by Scholastic Press in 2014.

This book is a work of fiction. Names, characters, places, and incidents are either the product of the author's imagination or are used fictitiously, and any resemblance to actual persons, living or dead, business establishments, events, or locales is entirely coincidental.

ISBN 978-0-545-88854-7

10 9 8 7 6 5 4 3 2 1   15 16 17 18 19

Printed in the U.S.A.   23
First printing 2015

The text was set in Weiss.
Book design by Sharismar Rodriguez

"You can only come to the morning
   through the shadows."

                              — J. R. R. Tolkien

"Why, sometimes I've believed as
   many as six impossible things before
   breakfast."

                              — Lewis Carroll

"Persons seeking to find scholarship
   herein will be sued; persons motivated
   to discover meaning will be exiled;
   persons hoping to unearth an allegory
   will be summarily ordained."

                              — The Author

A Place Called Wormwood

I WAS DOZING WHEN I heard the scream. It pierced my head like a morta round, doing terribly befuddling things to my mind, as loud and terrifying as though it were all happening right there and then.

After the sound came the vision: the blue, the color blue. It was in a mist like a cloud on the ground. It enveloped my mind, pushing out all other thoughts, all memories. When it finally disappeared, my befuddlement cleared as well. Yet I always believed there was something of great importance that had simply not come back to me.

I suddenly sat up straight on my planks atop my tree, the vision along with my sleepiness struck clean from me. At first light, I was almost always up in my tree — a stonking, straight-to-the-sky poplar with a full towering canopy. Twenty short boards nailed to the trunk were my passage up. Eight wide, splintered boards constituted my floor when I got up there. And a stretch of waterproof cloth I had oiled myself draped over branches and tied down tight with scavenged rope represented my roof. But I was not thinking about that, for a scream was ringing in my ears and it wasn't the scream of the blue mist, which apparently existed only in my mind. This scream was coming from down below.

I hurtled to the edge of my planks and looked down to the ground from where I heard the scream once more. This cry was now joined by the baying of attack canines. The sounds shattered what had been a peaceful first light.

Wugmorts did not, as a routine matter, scream at first light or at any other time of the light or night. I scampered down my tree. My booted feet hit the dirt, and I looked first right and then left. It was difficult to tell from where the screams and baying were coming. Amid the trees, sounds bounced and echoed confusedly.

When I saw what was coming at me, I turned and started running as fast as I could. The attack canine had hurtled from out of a stand of trees, its fangs bared and its hind-quarters lathered in sweat, a testament to the effort it was employing.

I was fleet of foot for a female Wug, but there was no Wug, male or female, who could outrun an attack canine. Even as I ran, I braced for the impact of its fangs on my skin and bone. But it flashed past me and redoubled its efforts, soon vanishing from my sight. I was not its prey this light.

I glanced to the left and saw between two trees a glimpse of black — a black tunic.

Council was about. The attack canines must have been unleashed by them.

But for what reason? Council, with one exception, was comprised of males, most of them older Wugs, and they kept themselves to themselves. They passed laws and regulations and other edicts that all Wugs must obey, but we all lived in peace and freedom, if not in much luxury.

Now they were out in the forest with canines chasing something. Or maybe some Wug? My next thought was that there had been an escape from Valhall, our prison. But no Wug had ever escaped from Valhall. And even if they had, I doubted members of Council would be out trying to round them up. They had other means to collect bad Wugs.

I kept running, following the baying and the racing footfalls, and soon realized that my path was taking me perilously close to the Quag. The Quag was an impenetrable barrier that circled Wormwood like a noose. That's all there was in existence: Wormwood and the Quag. No one had ever gone through the Quag because the terrible beasts in there would murder you within slivers. And since there was nothing beyond the Quag, there had never been visitors to Wormwood.

I neared the edge of this most terrible place that Wugs were repeatedly warned from the age of a very young to avoid. I slowed and then stopped a few yards from where the Quag began. My heart was pounding and my lungs bursting, not simply from my running but from being this close to a place that held only death for those stupid enough to stray inside.

The baying had now ceased, as had the sounds of the footfalls. I looked to the left and glimpsed canines and Council members staring into the depths of the Quag. I could not see their faces, but I imagined them to be as full of fear as was mine. Even attack canines wanted no part of the Quag.

I let out one more long breath and that's when a sound to my right reached me. I looked in that direction and in a stunning moment realized that I was seeing someone disappear into the tangled vines and twisted trees that rose up like a barricade around the perimeter of the Quag. And it was a Wug I knew well.

I looked to my left to see if any of Council or the canines had caught sight of this, but it didn't appear they had. I turned back, but the image was now gone. I wondered if I had simply imagined it. No Wug would voluntarily venture into that awful place.

When something touched me on the arm, I nearly screamed. As it was, I just about collapsed to the ground, but the thing, now revealed to be a hand, kept me upright.

"Vega Jane? It is Vega Jane, isn't it?"

I turned to look up into the blunt features of Jurik Krone. He was tall, strong, forty-five sessions old and a fast-rising member of Council.

"I'm Vega Jane," I managed to say.

"What are you doing here?" he asked. His tone was not stern, simply questioning, but there was a certain repressed hostility in his eyes.

"I was in my tree before going to Stacks. I heard a scream and saw the canines. I saw Wugs in black tunics running, so I . . . I ran too."

Krone nodded at this. "Did you see anything else?" he asked. "Other than the black tunics and canines?"

I peered at the spot where I had seen a Wug run into the Quag. "I saw the Quag."

His fingers gripped my shoulder more tightly. "Is that all? Nothing else?"

I tried to keep calm. The image of the Wug's face before he fled into the Quag slammed into me like a spear of skylight. "That's all."

His fingers released and he stepped back. I took him in fully. His black tunic rode well on his broad shoulders and thick arms.

"What were you chasing?" I asked.

"It's Council business, Vega," he replied sharply. "Please be on your way. It is not safe to be this close to the Quag. Head back toward Wormwood. Now. It is for your own good."

He turned and walked off, leaving me breathless and shaking. I took one more look at the Quag and then raced back in the direction of my tree.

I scampered up the boards and settled myself once more on the planks, out of breath and my head filled with the most dreadful thoughts.

"WO-WO-WOTCHA, VE-VE-VEGA JANE?"

The voice coming from below belonged to my friend. His name was Daniel Delphia, but to me he was simply Delph. He always called me Vega Jane, as though both names were my given one. Everyone else simply called me Vega, when they bothered to call me anything at all.

"Delph?" I said. "Up here."

I heard him scampering up the short boards. I was very nearly twenty yards up. I was also fourteen sessions old, going on a lot older. I was also female.

Being fourteen and female was frowned on here in Wormwood, the village where we both lived. It's never been clear to me why. But I liked being young. And I liked being female.

I was apparently in the minority on that.

Wormwood was a village full of Wugmorts — Wugs for short. The term *village* suggested a communal spirit that just wasn't present here. I tried to lend a helping hand from time to time, but I picked my causes carefully. Some Wugs had neither trust nor compassion. I tried to avoid them. Sometimes it was hard, because they had a tendency to get in my face.

Delph's head poked over the boards. He was much taller than me, and I was tall for a female, over five feet nine inches. I was still growing, because all the Janes were late bloomers. My grandfather Virgil, it was said, grew four inches more when he was twenty. And forty sessions later came his Event and his height became meaningless because there was nothing left of him.

Delph was about six and a half feet tall with shoulders that spread like the leafy cap of my poplar. He was sixteen sessions old with a long mane of black hair that appeared mostly yellowish white because of the dust he did not bother to wash away. He worked at the Mill, lifting huge sacks of flour, so more dust would just take its place. He had a wide, shallow forehead, full lips, and eyes that were as dark as his hair without the dust. They looked like twin holes in his head. I think it would be fascinating to see what went on in Delph's mind. And, I had to admit, his eyes were beautiful. I sometimes went all willy when he looked at me.

He did not qualify to work at Stacks, where some creativity was required. I have never seen Delph create anything except confusion. His mind came and went like rain bursts. It had done so ever since he was six sessions old. No one knew what had happened to him, or if they did, they never shared it with me. I believed that Delph remembered it. And it had done something to his head. It obviously wasn't an Event, because there would be nothing left of him. But it might be a near peer. And yet sometimes Delph said things that made me believe there was far more going on in his mind than most Wugs thought.

If things were a bit off with Delph inside his head, there was nothing wrong with the outside of him. He was handsome, to be sure. Though he never seemed to notice, I had seen many a female giving him the "look" as he passed by. A snog is what they wanted, I'm sure. But Delph always kept moving. And his broad shoulders and long muscled arms and legs gave him a strength that virtually no other Wug could match.

Delph settled next to me, his legs crossed at bony ankles and dangling over the edge of the splintered boards. There was barely enough space for the two of us here. But Delph liked to come up my tree. He didn't have many other places to go.

I pushed my long, dark straggly hair out of my eyes and focused on a dirt spot on my thin arm. I didn't rub it away because I had lots of dirt spots. And like Delph's Mill dust, what would be the point? My life was full of dirt.

"Delph, did you hear all that?"

He looked at me. "H-hear wh-what?"

"The attack canines and the screaming?"

He looked at me like I was wonky. "Y-you o-okay, Ve-Vega Jane?"

I tried again. "Council was out with attack canines chasing something." I wanted to say chasing *someone*, but I decided to keep that to myself. "They were down near the Quag."

He shivered at the name, as I knew he would.

"Qu-Qu-Qu —" He took a shuddering breath and said simply, "Bad."

I decided to change the subject. "Have you eaten?" I asked Delph. Hunger was like a painful, festering wound. When you had it, you could think of nothing else.

Delph shook his head no.

I pulled out a small tin box constituting my portable larder that I carried with me. Inside was a wedge of goat's cheese and two boiled eggs, a chunk of fried bread and some salt and pepper I kept in small pewter thumbs of my own making. We used lots of pepper in Wormwood, especially in our broths. Pepper cured lots of ills, like the taste of bad meat and spoiled vegetables. There had also been a sweet pickle, but I had eaten it already.

I handed him the box. It was intended for my first meal, but I was not so big as Delph. He needed lots of wood in his fire, as they said around here. I would eat at some point. I was good at pacing myself. Delph did not pace. Delph just did. I considered it one of his most endearing qualities.

He sprinkled salt and pepper on the eggs, cheese and bread, and then wolfed them down in one elongated swallow. I heard his belly rumble as the foodstuffs dropped into what had been an empty cavern.

"Better?" I asked.

"B-better," he mumbled contentedly. "Thanks, Ve-Vega Jane."

I rubbed sleep from my eyes. I had been told that my eyes were the color of the sky. But other times, when the clouds covered the heavens, they could look quite silver, as though I were absorbing the colors from above. It was the only change that was ever likely to happen to me.

"Go-going t-t-to see your mum and dad this light?" asked Delph.

I shot him a glance. "Yes."

"Ca-can I c-come t-too?"

"Of course, Delph. We can meet you there after Stacks."

He nodded, mumbled the word *Mill*, rose and scrambled down the short boards to the ground.

I followed him, heading on to Stacks, where I worked making pretty things. In Wormwood, it was a good idea to keep moving.

And so I did.

But I did so in a different way this light. I did so with the image of someone running into the Quag, when that was impossible because it meant death. And so I convinced myself that I had not seen what I thought I had.

Yet not many slivers would pass before I realized that my eyesight had been perfect. And my life in Wormwood, to the extent I had one, would never be the same.

Stacks

A S I WALKED along the now quiet forest path, I calmed and certain things I had been told long ago entered my head. I don't know why exactly; the timing *was* a bit strange, but I have found that these sorts of thoughts come to me at the oddest slivers.

The first one was the most indelible for me.

The most bitterly awful place of all is one that Wugmorts don't know is as wrong as wrong can possibly be.

That's what my grandfather told me before he suffered his Event and was gone forever. I believed I was the only one my grandfather told that to. I never mentioned it to anyone.

I was not, by nature, a very trusting Wugmort. One really couldn't be here.

I was a very young when my grandfather said those words, and he suffered his Event shortly afterward. I had to admit I wasn't sure what he was talking about then. I'm not exactly sure about it now. I agreed that a place could be bitterly awful, but what could be as wrong as wrong can possibly be? That was the conundrum I had never been able to sort out, often though I had tried.

My grandfather had also talked to me about shooting stars.

He said, *Every time you glimpse one making its blazingly haphazard way across the sky, a change is coming for some Wugmort.*

It was an interesting idea for a place that never changed — like Wormwood.

And then these twin thoughts left me like wisps of smoke floating away and I refocused on what lay ahead — another light of toil for me.

As I grew close to my destination, I drew a breath and the smell gobsmacked me. The odor was already in my pores, never to be washed away no matter how many times I stood under the rain bucket or the pipes. I turned the corner on the path and there it was: Stacks. We called it that because it had so many chimney stacks to carry the soot and grime away. Brick piled on top of brick so far into the sky. I had no idea what its original use was, or if it was ever used for anything other than to make pretty things. It was unfathomably large and extremely ugly, which made its current purpose quite ironic.

A shriveled Wug stood at the immense doors with his little ink stamp. His name was Dis Fidus. I had no idea how old Dis Fidus was, but he must have been close to a hundred.

I walked up to him and held out my hand. The top of it was discolored by the collective ink of two sessions laboring here. I could only imagine what it would look like ten or twenty sessions hence. My skin there would be permanently blue.

Fidus gripped my hand with his skeletal one and then stamped my skin. I had no idea why this was done now. It made no sense at all and things that made no sense troubled me to no end. Because, I suspected strongly, it made sense to *someone.*

I gazed at Dis Fidus, trying to detect in his features if he had heard of the chase this light. But he was so naturally nervous-looking that it was impossible to tell. I walked into Stacks.

"I like my charges to be here earlier than three slivers before second light, Vega," said a voice.

Julius Domitar was big and puffy like a plump frog. His skin possessed a curious hue of pasty green as well. He was the most self-important Wug that I knew in Wormwood, and the competition for that title was a keen one. When he said he liked his "charges" to be here earlier than three slivers, he really meant me. I was still the only female at Stacks.

I turned to look at him through the doorway of his office. He stood there at his little tilt-top desk on which rested bottles of ink from Quick and Stevenson, the sole ink purveyors in Wormwood. Domitar held his long ink stick and there were rolls of scrolls lying on his desk. Domitar loved scrolls. Actually, he loved what was on the scrolls: records. Little bits and pieces of our working lives.

"Three slivers early is still early," I said and kept walking.

Domitar said, "There are many worse off than your lot, Vega. Don't forget that. You have it fine here. But that can change. Oh, yes it can."

I hurried on to the main work floor of Stacks. The kilns had long since been fired up. The huge furnaces set in one corner were never turned off. They gave the room a warm, humid feeling on even the coldest lights. The muscle-bound Dactyls pounded away on their metals with hammer and

12

tongs, producing a sound like Steeple bells. Sweat dripped off their brows and sculpted backs, dotting the floor around their feet. They never looked up from their work. The Cutters sliced through wood and hard and soft metals. The Mixers ran their enormous tubs congesting ingredients together.

The Wugs here were just like me, ordinary in all ways and hardworking — simply just trying to get by. And we would be doing this exact same work for the rest of our sessions.

I went to my wooden locker in a room off the main floor, where I put on my work trousers, heavy leather apron, gloves and goggles. I walked toward my workstation, which was located near the rear of the main floor. It consisted of one large, heavily stained wooden table, an old, finicky trolley with metal wheels, a set of both large and small tools that fit my hands precisely, some testing instruments that constituted our quality control and bottles of paints, dyes, acids and other materials that I used from time to time.

Some of my work was dangerous, which was why I put on as much protection as I could. Many who worked here did so with missing fingers, eyes, teeth and even limbs. I would rather not join their lot in having reduced body parts. I liked the ones I had just fine. They were just the right number and matched for the most part.

I passed by the broad stone stairs with marble balustrades leading to the upper floor of Stacks. It was quite an elegant thing to have in a place like this and made me think, and not for the first time, that Stacks hadn't always been a factory. I smiled at the Wugmort guard who stood there.

His name was Ladon-Tosh and I had never heard him

13

speak. Over his shoulder he carried a long-barreled morta. He also had a sword in a sheath and a knife in a small leather casing on a wide black belt. His sole task here was to prevent access by any of us to the second floor of Stacks. With long, coal-black hair, a scarred face, a hooked nose that apparently had been broken several times and eyes that seemed dead, Ladon-Tosh was scary enough even without all those weapons. *With* them, he was pretty much terrifying in all respects.

I heard that, one time, long before I came to work at Stacks, some gonk tried to make it past Ladon-Tosh and up the stairs. It was said that Ladon-Tosh stabbed him with the knife, shot him with the morta, cut off his head with the sword and then threw the remains in one of the furnaces that blazed at Stacks all light and night. I'm not sure I believed that, but I wasn't *that* sure.

For that reason, I was always unfailingly polite to Ladon-Tosh. I didn't care if he never looked at me or spoke to me. I just wanted him to know that he had a friend in me.

When I first started working here, there was a Wugmort named Quentin Herms who helped me on finishing. That's what I was here — a Finisher. I walked in on my first light here, and all Domitar had barked was "You're two slivers late. Never let that happen again."

On that first light, I had looked down at my ink-stamped hand and wondered what it was I was to do at this place. I found my workstation only because it had my name on it. A rectangle of blackened metal with silver letters spelling out VEGA JANE on it and bolted onto the top of the wood. It wasn't a pretty sign.

And the whole time I was thinking, *It's not just my name bolted to this place.*

It's me.

On that very first light as I stood next to my station, Quentin had hurried over and greeted me. He was a family friend and had always been very kind toward me.

"I thought you were starting next light, Vega," he said. "Or else I would have been ready for you."

"I don't know what to do," I said with a touch of desperation.

He went back to his station and returned with a little figurine made out of metal. It was of a very young male petting a canine. He said, "This, or things like this, are what you will finish. This is metal. You will also finish things in wood, ceramic, clay and other materials. The Wug and his canine I will paint in pleasing colors."

"How do you know which colors to use?" I asked.

"There are instructions for each item on your workstation. But you have some leeway to use your own creativity. You will sometimes paint, sometimes carve, sometimes mold and sometimes distress objects to make them look older."

"But no one has taught me how to do this."

"I know you showed artistic ability at Learning," he said. "Or else they would not have sent you here to be a Finisher."

I looked at Quentin. "I just thought there would be some training involved."

"There will be. I will train you."

"What about your work?" I asked, glancing at the unfinished objects at his station.

"That will be part of your training, helping me finish them. I've been looking forward to this light, Vega. I had always hoped you would be assigned to Stacks."

And he taught me. Each light, I had come in with a smile, but only because Quentin was there. I had picked up things quickly until my skill rivaled his.

I was recalling all of this now, not for nostalgic reasons but for a very different cause.

For Quentin Herms had been the very Wug I had seen rushing headlong into the Quag with the canines and Council after him. I knew that he would not be at Stacks this light. I wondered when others would realize this too.

My head filled with more dread than puzzlement, I turned to the one thing I knew how to do: finish pretty things that would be purchased by Wugs who could afford them. I was not among that number.

I lifted up my first task of the light. A small, unfinished porcelain bowl that required painting and then kiln firing. As I held up the bowl, the top slipped and it nearly fell off. I set the top down on the table and gripped the bowl more firmly.

That's when I saw the small piece of parchment tucked in there. I glanced around to see if anyone was watching and then I carefully dipped my hand in the bowl and took out the parchment. I hid it in a work cloth and put the cloth on the workstation and opened it, unfolding the piece of parchment as well. The handwriting was small and precise, the words clear.

I will not be back at Stacks, Vega. Go to your tree this night. What you will find there may set you free from Wormwood, if you so desire. QH.

I balled up the parchment and swallowed it. As it went down my throat, I looked up in time to see four males enter Domitar's office. They were all members of Council, as denoted by their black dress tunics. Jurik Krone was among them, which was not a good thing. He had seen me near the Quag this light. That coupled with the fact that I worked next to Quentin might not bode well for me.

Thirty slivers passed and I lifted my gaze when I heard Domitar's door open. To a Wug, all the black tunics were staring at me. I felt my body stiffen like I'd been poked by one of the hot irons the Dactyls used in their work.

Krone came forward, the other Council members in his wake. He held up an object. When I saw it, my breath caught in my throat. I recognized it immediately, though I had not seen it for many sessions. I wondered how Krone could be holding it now.

"We meet yet again, Vega," said Krone as he and his cohorts encircled me at my workstation.

"Yes, we do," I said, trying to keep my voice steady, but it wobbled badly, like a very young testing out his new legs.

He held out the object in his hand. It was a ring. "Do you recognize this?"

I nodded. "It was my grandfather's." It had a distinctive design etched in the metal that matched a mark my grandfather had on the back of his hand. Three hooks connected as one. I had never known what it meant and he had never talked about it, at least with me, but I had been only a very young when he had suffered his Event.

"Can you explain how Virgil Alfadir Jane's ring came to

17

be found at Quentin Herms's cottage?" Jurik Krone asked patiently, but there was a definite edge to his voice.

I shook my head, my stomach doing tiny flips and my lungs expanding faster than I would have liked them to. "I assumed it had vanished along with my grandfather when he had his Event. As you know, there is nothing left of a Wug after an Event."

Krone tossed the ring down on my workstation. When I reached out to take it, he slammed his knife blade into the ring's opening, pinning it to the wood. I jerked my hand back and stared up at him fearfully.

He slowly pulled his knife blade free and picked up the ring. "You know Herms?" Krone said quietly. "He's a friend of yours, isn't he?"

"He's a friend of my family's. He's the only other Finisher here besides me."

"Why is he not at work this light?"

"I don't know," I said quite truthfully. Still, I was rapturously relieved to have swallowed Quentin's note. "Maybe he's hurt or sick."

"He's neither." He stepped closer. "Let us speak frankly. You were near the Quag at first light. You saw us chasing him."

"I told you, I saw nothing. And you didn't tell me who you were after." I looked up into Krone's face. "But why were you chasing Quentin?"

"There are laws, Vega, laws that Quentin Herms has broken. And for that he will be punished." Krone gave me a searching look that seemed to leave no crevice of my being untouched. "If he tries to contact you, you will inform

Council immediately. The consequences for not doing so will be harsh. This is a serious matter, Vega. Very serious indeed." He paused. "I am speaking of Valhall for those who disobey."

Every Wug there, myself included, drew a sharp breath. No Wug wanted to be locked up in that cage in plain sight and guarded by the brutish Nida and the ferocious black shuck.

He put his hand on my shoulder and lightly squeezed. "I am counting on your help with this, Vega. All of Wormwood needs to stand together on this matter."

Then his hand glided to my face and pulled something free. He held it up. It was a bit of the parchment from Quentin's note that had caught on my skin. With a thrill of horror, I saw that it had a smudge of ink on it.

"A remnant of your work, perhaps?" he said. Krone's gaze once more bored into me. Then he turned on his booted right foot and strode out. His colleagues followed.

I shot a glance at Domitar. I had never seen him so pale and his skin so clammy.

"You *will* cooperate, or it *will* be Valhall," he said to me, and then spun on his heel, almost toppling over in the process, and disappeared into his office.

I turned back to my work and waited for the night to come.

Hector and Helen

AFTER THE BELL rang for the end of work at Stacks, I changed back into my threadbare clothes and left to walk back to Wormwood. I was so full of impatience that I wanted to run the whole way. I wished it were night already so I could go to my tree, but I could do nothing to speed up time.

My route to Wormwood proper did not take long. Wormwood was not sprawling. It was compact, like a small fist waiting to hit something. There were lines of shops set across from each other on the High Street, which consisted of wavy cobblestone. These shops sold things that Wugmorts needed, like clothing, shoes, basic foodstuffs, plates and cups. A chemist's shop sold healing herbs and salves and bandages. There was even a place that would sell you a sense of happiness, which seemed in short supply here. I was told the shop did a brisk business. We knew we had it good in Wormwood, but we apparently had a hard time actually believing it.

As I walked, my mind whirled. Krone and Council had been chasing Quentin, who had fled into the Quag. I had caught a glimpse of him before he had fully disappeared. I had seen the expression on his face. It was one of terror but tinged with relief. Relief at going into the Quag? My mind could hardly contemplate such a thing.

As I trudged along, I passed the Loons. It had been my home for the last two sessions, ever since my mother and father were sent away to the Care. The Loons was a rectangle of warped boards, dirty glass and cracked slate shingles. There were two floors with five small cot rooms on the top floor and six boarders to a room. That added up to thirty Wugmorts with lax hygiene all in close proximity.

That's why I preferred my tree.

I passed by the front door of the Loons, and a Wugmort I well knew stepped out. His name was Roman Picus and he owned the Loons. He was wearing his usual garb: a slouch hat with a dent in the middle; blue, not overly clean dungarees; white shirt; black vest; luminous orange-red garm-skin boots and a long, greasy coat. He had long whiskers running down both sides of his face, curving like fishhooks into his sun-reddened cheeks. A heavy bronze timekeeper suspended by a knotty chain hung across the front of his vest. On the time-keeper's face were the various sections of light and night broken into their respective compartments.

"Good light, Vega," he said grudgingly.

I nodded at him. "Good light, Roman."

"Coming from Stacks?"

"Yes. I'm picking John up from Learning and then we're meeting Delph at the Care."

He gave a loud snort. "Why you waste your time with that great gormless sack-a nothin', I'll never know. But I suppose you don't think too highly of yourself, and I would have to agree with ya there, female."

"If you think Delph is such a waste, why not challenge him in the next Duelum?"

His face reddened. "I'm too old for the Duelum. But in my prime, female —"

"And how many Duelums did you win in your prime, *male*?"

He grimaced. "You best learn, Vega," he growled. "Go along to get along."

"Speaking of going, where are you off to, Roman?"

He looked like I had slapped him. "You're asking me such a question?"

"We're having such a nice conversation, I wanted to keep it going."

"D'ya want to be written up at Council, Vega?"

"Absolutely. I hear that with three or more infractions the offending Wug is eligible for some sort of prize."

"I have no slivers for idle dithering with the poor likes-a you." But then he paused and studied me. "Quentin Herms?" he asked.

"What of him?"

"Hear he's done a bunk."

"Maybe," I said cautiously.

Roman shrugged and looked at his boots. "Maybe a garm got him. Har."

"All lodging fees collected for the quartersession?" I asked, intentionally changing the subject. I did not want to discuss Quentin Herms.

He smiled wickedly and held out a large, grimy hand. "Speaking of, I'll just take yours now, Vega."

22

I held out a small sheet of parchment with writing and a seal on it. "I paid after I walked John to Learning. Your clerk gave me a bit of coin off for bringing it around myself and saving him a trip."

His smile fell away to a frown. "Oh, did he? Well, we'll see about that."

"All mouth and no trousers, Roman."

"And what the bloody Hel do ya mean by that?"

"Your clerk showed me the official scroll you signed authorizing the discount. I like to know things like that before I commit my wages to pay for space in that dung heap you call lodging."

Roman could chuck my brother and me out of the Loons if he wanted to. Maybe part of me desired that. But he simply turned and stalked off, and I hurried on.

Learning was housed in a building located near the other end of the High Street. It could hold a few hundred youngs but now had less than half that. Learning was done in Wormwood, but it was not done with a lot of energy. As I stood on the lumpy cobblestones and waited, it struck me that the top edge of the building's roof was sad-looking. It curved a bit downward like it was frowning.

The door opened and the youngs started to trickle out.

The last Wug out was always my brother.

John Jane was short and skinny and looked far younger than his age. His hair was dark and long, nearly as long as mine. He would not allow me or anyone else to cut it. He was not strong, but he would fight you if you tried to cut his hair. His gaze was downcast. He was seemingly enthralled by his

23

feet, which were disproportionately long and promised great height later. John Jane did not look like much on the outside, but there was a great deal going on inside his head.

I had seen him make observations about things I'd never thought of. And he never forgot anything. It was only in private moments when we were together that I gained glimpses of what was really in his upstairs room. It was quite full, that room, far fuller than mine.

A shy smile crept across his face, and his shuffle picked up. I held up my tin box. On the way here, I had stopped and picked him some berries, and there was also a feather wing I got for him and smoked up earlier in the hearth at Stacks. John liked his meat, though we didn't have much of that at the Loons. He hurried across the cobblestones, opened the box and saw the wing. He looked at me and smiled again. I did not understand John most of the time, but I loved to see that smile. There was no food provided during Learning, although the time spent there was long. They said food distracted youngs. I believed a lack of food distracted everybody. I said so when I was a young. It was a wonder, I realized now, that they let me stay until I was twelve sessions, which was the age when Learning ended. That was far too early, I thought, but I didn't make the rules, did I?

John took my hand with his free one and we walked along. As we did so, I looked around. There were clusters of Wugmorts here and there. They were all talking in hushed whispers. I also saw Council members in their black tunics scurrying around like rats through rubbish.

I had seen Quentin flee into the Quag. It wasn't simply because Council was after him with the canines. His note

24

told me that he had not intended on coming back, and that note had to have been placed in the cup before first light. Clearly, Quentin had planned on going into the Quag, Council and canines or not. But why? There was nothing in the Quag except certain death. And there was nothing on the other side of the Quag at all. Yet Quentin's note had said that what he had left would set me free from Wormwood. My mind leapt ahead to the obvious conclusion.

There was some place beyond the Quag. Or so he believed.

My focus turned back to John.

We had a ritual, John and I. Every other light after Learning, we went to see our parents at the Care, where Wugs who were unwell and for whom the Mendens at hospital could do nothing more were sent. The place was guarded by a huge Wug named Non.

Non knew John and me because we came so often. But each time, he treated us as though it was our first visit. It irritated me terribly and seemed to greatly amuse him.

John had already hungrily begun eating his wing, and the fatty juice from the meat spilled across his small mouth. As we walked up to the Care, I saw Delph step from the deepening shadows of a chestnut tree. He looked nervous. His hair was even whiter from working at the Mill all light, and his face and shirt were sweat stained. He nodded shyly and looked down at John.

"Hello, Delph," said John. He held up his feather wing. "Do you want a bite?"

Delph, I knew, was tempted. But he shook his head. I think I knew why. It was quite obvious how skinny my brother was. I don't think Delph wanted to deprive him this bit of food.

We all turned and walked together to the entrance. I gritted my teeth and told Non we were here to see our mother and father. I let him see the Council parchment that allowed our visits. Non took his time examining the document, although by now he had probably memorized every word on it. He handed it back to me and then glared at Delph.

"But *his* name is nae on there, female."

Delph took a step back, which made Non grin maliciously. He said, "Y'know, for such a great big Wug, you're more like a female, ain't you, Delph? Scared of your own shadow." He made a lunge at Delph, and Delph jumped back.

Non roared with laughter and tossed me the key to my parents' room. "G'on in, then. Don't think the likes of him can do much harm."

I said, "If I remember correctly, Delph beat you in the last Duelum, Non. How long were you unconscious again?"

Non's smile disappeared, and as we passed by, he gave Delph a hard shove in the back that nearly sent him sprawling. I said nothing and didn't look at Delph, because I knew how embarrassed he was. In my mind, I slaughtered Non one thousand times with increasing fervor.

We passed through the doorway and into a long corridor that was dark and cool. Even when it was hot outside, it was cool in here. I didn't know how this was accomplished. At any other place in Wormwood, the only way to get cool was to open a window and hope for a breeze or pour cold water over your head.

We passed a Nurse in the hall. She was dressed in a

gray cloak with a white cap on her head. She nodded, gave a terse smile and hurried on.

There were doors opening off the long hall. They were all locked. I knew this because during past visits I'd tried to open several of them. There were brass plates bolted to the doors of each room with names on them like Judith Frigg, Wolfgang Spriggan and Irin Grine. I didn't know these Wugs, but I had seen some of their families here. They had looked as blank and hopeless as I probably did.

The brass plates were removed only when the Wug whose name was on it "slipped away," as they said in Wormwood. I wondered when our mother and father would slip away. We arrived at the door with two brass plates. I read them out loud for what seemed the millionth time.

"Hector Jane. Helen Jane."

I don't know why I did this. I looked at John. He never read the names out loud; he simply mouthed them.

I pulled out the key Non had given me, turned it in the old lock, and the door opened. I took hesitant steps in. John followed. Delph brought up the rear. I closed the door behind us. It always made a whooshing sound as it sealed shut.

There were two cots in the room with a small wooden table between them. There were no lanterns or torches that I could see. The only illumination seemed to come from the ceiling. I don't know how this was managed. Another mystery. There were no windows. When you're in the Care, apparently sunlight is not required. There were also no chairs for us to sit in. Perhaps they did not like to encourage long visits.

While Delph hung back, I walked up to the first cot.

My father lay small and shrunken under a single dark blanket. I remembered him as tall and strong. He was no longer. His face used to be pleasing to look at. That was also no longer the case. I don't know much about healing or things that make you sick. But it looked to me like what was missing from my father was, well, my father. I don't know how you steal someone from the inside and leave the outside, but it appeared to have been done to him. There could be no sorting out such a thing, I imagined.

John crept next to me and placed his hand on top of our father's. When I looked at John's face, it was scrunched up like he was in pain. I once asked him about this. He merely shrugged and said the hurt wasn't on the outside.

I opened my tuck, which I had brought with me from work, and pulled out a cloth soaked in water from the pipes at Stacks. I put it on my father's forehead. He always seemed hot, even though the room was always cool. I was careful not to let my fingers touch him. I adored my father and I used to love to be hugged by him. But there was something in this room that made me not want to touch him. I have fought against it, but I couldn't seem to break through. It was like a wall of walls separating us.

John lifted out a book from his tuck and began to quietly read to our father.

I glanced over at Delph, who stood like a statue in the corner. "Delph, do you want to come over here and see him?"

Delph stepped forward. "Is he s-s-sleeping?"

"Something like that, Delph."

I left John and Delph and went to the next cot.

My mother too was small and shrunken, though she used to be nearly as tall as I am. Her hair used to be long and light and would catch a breeze and dance across the riled air. Now it was chopped close to her head, almost like a second skull. The dark blanket covered her withered body right up to her neck.

She too had been stolen from the inside. She too could not be sorted out ever again. The Mendens were all in agreement over that. That's why I had never wanted to be a Menden. If you couldn't heal the really sick, what was the point?

I drew closer to her. Perhaps because I was female, I always felt more comfortable around my mother. We talked, kept secrets. She was my friend, telling me things I needed to know to survive here. But I also sensed there was a part of her that was kept from me.

I opened my tuck again and took out a small bottle of water. I sprinkled some on my mother's face and watched it rest there for less than a sliver until it was absorbed into her skin. I don't know why I did this, maybe to convince myself that she really was still alive, that there really was someone still in there.

I looked over at John. He loved our mother too, although there seemed to be a special bond between father and son. But as I looked at him, he glanced up and his gaze drifted to her, lying in the cot. And it seemed to me that John's heart ached even more seeing her lie there than it did watching our father. This surprised me. This had been a light for surprises in Wormwood, where nothing ever happened and the only

29

thing that was certain was that the next light would look just like the previous one.

Delph drifted over and gazed down at my mother.

"She was v-v-very nice t-to me," said Delph.

"I know, Delph. It was her way."

He reached out a hand but didn't touch her. Instead, it seemed like he was tracing just above where the drops of water had been absorbed through her skin.

Twenty slivers later, we walked back down the dark, cool hall and approached the door where Non stood guard. I braced myself for his inane comments. *Why do you bother coming? Do your parents look better this light? How could that possibly be?*

But when I focused on the end of the hall, I did not see Non. My mind seemed to misfire for an instant because Non was always there. Always. Yet, now someone else was.

The figure was tall, looming, substantial. He seemed to fill the broad hall with bulk, with gravitas. His robe was a dull burgundy, denoting his position on Council. He held the top job. There was no one above him.

His name was Thansius. In many respects he *was* Council. By comparison, Jurik Krone was but a gnat on a slep's hindquarters. I had only seen Thansius at a distance. He did not walk the cobblestones. He did not labor at Stacks or at the Mill or as a Tiller. If Wormwood had a leader, it was he.

John and I slowed our walk. John had glimpsed Thansius too and I heard him gasp. And I thought poor Delph was going to faint.

It took us twice as long to walk the hall as it did when we came in. It still seemed far too short a time for me. When we reached Thansius, he did not move. He was just there. He was taller even than Delph. His shoulders seemed to touch each side of the hall. It was said that in his youth, no Wug ever bested Thansius in a Duelum. He conquered all on that pitch. Now that he was older and head of Council, he did not compete. But he looked as though he still could. And win. Up close the burgundy robe seemed like a sheet of blood frozen solid.

When he spoke, the low voice, though deep and dignified, still seemed insubstantial next to the large body. But I was riveted to every syllable.

He said, "A word, Vega Jane. I require a word."

Thansius

JOHN, DELPH AND I dumbly followed Thansius out-side the Care. It was there that we saw the beautiful blue carriage pulled by four magnificent sleps. Their gray coats ran all the way down to their six spindly-looking legs. It was said that sleps used to be able to fly. I have never believed this, although along a slep's withers it's possible to see a slight indentation where something, perhaps a wing, used to be attached.

At the helm of the carriage was a Wug named Thomas Bogle. He sat straight as my tree in the driver's box.

Thansius stood next to the carriage and opened the door.

He looked at Delph. "Get along with you, Daniel. This conversation concerns private matters."

Delph raced away, his long legs carrying him out of sight in half a sliver.

Thansius motioned us inside. We complied. Not because we wanted to but because he was Thansius. He climbed in after us, and the heavy carriage lurched to one side as he did so. The Wug must weigh a great deal to have that sort of effect on a carriage this large. Not that I know a lot about car-riages. I had actually never been in one.

Thansius settled in the seat across from us and smoothed down his robe. He glanced questioningly at John.

I looked at my brother and then back at Thansius.

"This is my brother, John."

"I know who he is," replied Thansius. "I am contemplating whether he needs to be here or not."

I gripped John's hand because I could sense the overwhelming fear in him. "We were just visiting our parents," I said.

"Again, a fact of which I am aware."

Thansius looked older up close than he did from a distance. Even though he sat in the shadows of his seat, I could clearly see his face. It was heavy, lined with worry, the eyes small and the flesh around them puckered. Still, even with his full beard, the face seemed too slight for the body's great bulk. His hair was long and an odd mix of cream and silver, as was his beard. It looked clean and smelled like meadow flowers. Ordinarily, I would welcome that scent. Right now it made me feel queasy.

"I think I prefer him to wait outside," said Thansius at last.

"I would like my brother to stay," I replied, and then I held my breath. I had no idea where that had come from. Talking to Thansius was a once-in-a-lifetime opportunity. Talking *back* to Thansius was unthinkable.

Thansius cocked his head at me. He didn't look angry, simply bemused. I would take bemusement over anger from him.

"And why is that?"

"In case whatever you have to ask me concerns him. Then

I will not have to repeat it because I am certain I cannot match your eloquence, Thansius."

I said this in all sincerity. Thansius was a very learned Wug with prodigious speaking skills. We all loved to listen to him, even if we did not always understand what he was saying.

The bemusement turned to a half smile and then his face became a stone.

"Quentin Herms," he said. "He cannot be located. My deputy, Jurik Krone, has been to see you about this."

I nodded, my heart whacking firmly against my rib cage.

From his pocket Thansius withdrew an object. I knew what it was before he even showed it to me. My grandfather's ring. Seeing it close up, the memories came flooding back to me. I had never seen the image on the ring any other place except on the back of my grandfather's hand.

Thansius held it up so John and I could see it fully. "It is quite an interesting design," he said.

"Do you know what it means?" I asked.

"No, I do not. I doubt any Wug does, other than your grandfather. Virgil kept himself to himself on matters such as these." He pocketed the ring and edged forward, his wide knee nearly scraping my bony one. "But it was found at Herms's cottage."

"He was friends with my grandfather, so he probably gave it to him," I replied.

"Before his own family?" said Thansius skeptically.

"As you said, my grandfather kept such matters to himself. Who knows what he might have thought or done?"

34

Thansius seemed to mull over this for a few moments. Then he said, "Quentin Herms was your mentor as a Finisher."

"Yes, it's true. He helped me learn my job."

"Did you like him?"

This was a strange question, I thought, but I answered truthfully. "I did."

Still, my insides wriggled like worms exposed to light.

He stroked his beard with one large hand. I studied that hand. It was strong-looking, but soft. At one time he might have worked hard with those hands, but not for many sessions now.

He asked, "No mention of anything from him? No indication that he might go off . . . ?"

I chose my words carefully. "Where is there to go *off* to?"

"No message left behind for you?" he asked, ignoring my query.

I could see danger in Thansius's features, the curl of his hand, so close to a fist, the bunched muscles under the blood robe. I furrowed my brow and willed my brain to do the best job of answering without really saying anything of importance. Transparency is fine, if you happen to be a window.

"I don't know what he would have to leave for me." This also was perfectly true. I *didn't* know what he had left for me.

He studied each of my words, it seemed to me, like they were a puzzle that needed solving. He stared at my face so intently it felt like my skin was melting away, allowing him to see into my soul.

He sat back and stared at the floor of the carriage for nearly a sliver. "You and your brother may be on your way."

We should have left right then, but I needed to say something, and although half of me was terrified to do so, the other half of me won out.

"Can I have the ring, Thansius?"

He stared at me. "The ring?"

"Yes. It belonged to my grandfather. And since he's gone and our parents are, well . . . we're the only family left. So can I have it?"

I could sense John holding his breath. I held my own, awaiting Thansius's answer.

"Maybe one light, Vega, but not now."

He opened the carriage door and waved a hand, beckoning us to exit.

We climbed out as hastily as possible, although John could barely move his legs.

Before the carriage door closed, I found Thansius staring at me. It was an enigmatic look, a cross between pity and remorse. I could understand neither end of it. Then the door closed, Bogle flicked the reins and the carriage rumbled off.

I pulled John along in the direction of the Loons.

I had a lot to do, and not much time to do it. My mind whirled with all that lay ahead of me. I was more excited than afraid when a little less excitement and a little more fear would have been far smarter.

By the time we got to the Loons, John had stopped trembling from our encounter with Thansius. I'm not sure I had. At least the inside of me hadn't. But I very much focused on what I would be doing later.

Cacus Loon opened the door for us. He had beetle brows, a low forehead and hair that had not been washed for at least a session or maybe two. His pants and shirt were as greasy as his hair, and he had a habit of forever twirling the ends of his enormous mustache, which seemed to originate inside his flaring nostrils. Though Roman Picus owned the building, Cacus Loon was the lodge keeper.

I nodded at him as he moved from the doorway to let us pass. I could tell he was itching for gossip about Herms. Loon followed us into the main room of the lower floor. It was large and contained a long table where we took our meals. The walls were logs chinked with whatever Loon had found to keep them stuffed with, and the floors were uneven, warped, worm-eaten wooden planks.

A kitchen adjoined it where Loon's wife, Hestia, spent much of her sessions doing the work that Loon told her to do. This included making meals, doing the wash and making sure that Loon had what Loon wanted.

"Stacks," said Loon as he fired up his pipe bowl, and the smoke streamed high from it.

I didn't look at him. I was aiming for the stairs, where our room was. We shared it with other Wugmorts who snored loudly and failed to bathe regularly.

"Stacks," he said again. "Quentin Herms."

I turned to him, resigned that he would simply follow us until his queries were answered.

"They say he has gone off," Loon continued, puffing on his pipe so hard the smoke billowed out, nearly hiding him from our view. It was as if he had suddenly combusted, but I was just not that lucky.

"Where would he go off to?" I asked innocently, taking the same tack I had with Thansius though my heart wasn't really in it. Loon was not nearly the challenge mentally that Thansius presented. He was simply a git.

"You work at Stacks."

"Over a hundred Wugs work at Stacks," I said. "Go ask them."

I pulled John upstairs with me. Thankfully, Loon did not follow.

WE WENT DOWN for last meal when the darkness was gathering across Wormwood. Twenty-eight Wugmorts had beaten us down to eat and were already seated at table. John and I squeezed into the last two seats as Hestia, short and thin, scurried around with trays filled with plates that actually had little food on them. I eyed the other two Loon females, still youngs, who labored in the kitchen. They were also small and skinny, their faces smoky from the kitchen coal fire, just like their mother's.

They didn't go to Learning. This was because they were females and also because Cacus Loon did not believe in education for the most part. I had heard Loon once say that he had never gone to Learning and look how he had turned out. If that was not reason enough to read religiously every book you could possibly get your hands on, I didn't know what would be.

Cletus Loon sat next to his father. Cletus looked more like his dad every light, down to the beginnings of a mustache over his lip. He was only two sessions ahead of me, but his puffy face looked older. He was always maneuvering to get the drop on me. I worried that one time he would wise up and go after John instead. The fact that he didn't told me he feared me too much. Fear was a great thing if it was pointed in the right direction.

After last meal, the light finally gave completely over to dark. John and I went to our room and climbed under our blankets, which had long since given up the notion of providing warmth.

I waited until I heard snores coming from the others, then slipped out of bed and put on my cloak. I also snagged my only sweater and my blanket. A sliver later I was clear of the kitchen and out the rear door.

I would take great pains to make sure I was not followed.

As it turned out, I should have tried much, much harder.

The Way Out

I LIKED THE NIGHT because in darkness I could pretend I was no longer in Wormwood. I don't know where else I would be, but it was inspiring sometimes just to imagine a place other than here.

It was chilly this night, but not cold enough to see my breath as I walked along. I had rolled up my blanket and tied it and my sweater around my waist. If Wugs saw me and wanted to know where I was headed, I was sleeping at my tree.

The path to my tree had been clear enough under the milky ball in the heavens we call the Noc, but then clouds came and blocked it out and the path fell into darkness. I stopped walking and took a sliver to light a lantern I'd nicked from the Loons, using one of the three matches I had brought with me. I lowered the hood and opened its shield, illuminating the way.

That's when I heard it. Every sound in Wormwood needed to be considered, especially at night. Once you left the cobblestones, heightened care was necessary. And there was someone or something else out this night. I turned my lantern in the direction of the sound.

As I waited, my other hand dipped to my pocket and clutched the cutting knife that I took from Stacks a long time ago. The knife fitted neatly into my hand. I could wield it with great skill. I waited, dreading what might be coming and hoping it might simply be Delph prowling around as he sometimes did at night.

Then the smell reached me. That confirmed it wasn't Delph.

I couldn't believe it. This far from the Quag? It had never happened but apparently it was happening right now. I clutched my knife tightly, even though I knew it would be of no use, not against what was coming. It brought back memories to me so fierce, so painfully fresh, that my eyes clouded with tears even as I turned to flee.

I put out my lantern because I knew the light was leading it to me, slung the rope tethered to the lantern over my shoulder and shoved my knife into my pocket, freeing my hands. Then I ran for it.

The thing was fast, much faster than I, but I had a bit of a head start. I followed the path by memory, though I took a wrong turn once and banged off a tree. That mistake cost me precious moments. The thing nearly caught up to me. I redoubled my efforts. I was not going to die this way. I just wasn't. My breaths came in huge clumps and my heart was hammering so badly I thought I could see it thumping through my cloak.

I tripped over a tree root and sprawled to the ground. I turned and there the beast was, barely six feet from me. It was huge and foul and its fangs were not nearly its most fearsome element. It opened its jaws and I had but a moment to live because I knew what would be coming out of that hole. I flung myself behind a thick trunk an instant before the jet of flames struck the spot where I had been. The ground was scorched and I felt the blast of heat all around me as I hid behind the tree. But I was still alive, though maybe not for much longer.

I could hear it taking a long breath in preparation for another blast of fire that would surely engulf me. I had bare moments left. And in those few moments, I found a certain calm, from where I did not know. I knew what I had to do. And I had just a moment left to do it.

I leapt out from behind the tree just as the beast was finishing its replenishing breath. I hurled my knife straight and true and it struck the creature directly in its eye. Unfortunately, it had three more of them.

Then, as blood sputtered from the destroyed eye and the creature howled in fury, I turned and ran. The knife throw had purchased precious moments for me. I made the most of them. I ran like I never had before, not even when the attack canine was after me at first light.

I reached my tree, put one hand on the first rung of my wooden ladder and climbed for my life.

The wounded garm, sensing blood and meat, was coming so fast now, it was as though it were flying. It was said that the garm hunts the souls of the dead. Others say it guards the gates of Hel, where Wugmorts who are bad during life are banished to spend eternity.

Right now, I did not care which theory was right. I just didn't want to become a dead soul this night, headed to Hel or any other place.

I hated garms with all my being, but I could not fight a garm and have any hope of winning. So I climbed with a focused fury driving my arms and legs. Even then, it might not be enough. I knew my tree's trunk as well as I knew the flaws on my face. However, halfway up, my hand struck an unfamiliar object, but I grabbed the next board and kept climbing.

I could feel the garm nearly on me. It was a large beast, easily thirteen feet long and over a thousand pounds in weight. It was a flame expeller from living in Hel, it was said, where all they had was heat and flames and old, moldy death. I did not want to feel its flames on me. It was closing fast, but I was climbing faster. Terror can compel extraordinary physical action. I reached the last board step. Below I heard claws on wood. I thought I felt heat rising toward me. Part of me didn't want to look, but I did.

In the flames down below I saw the hard, armored face of the garm. Its chest was smeared in blood. It had killed nothing to get this. Its chest was always dripping with its own blood as though it were constantly wounded. Maybe that's why it was always in a foul, murderous mood. It looked up at me, its thin, spiky tongue flicking out, its three remaining cold, dead eyes staring up at me, hungry, dangerous, fatal. Its fourth eye was bloody and vacant, my knife still sticking from it.

I screamed at it. I hurled spit from my mouth at it. I wanted to kill it. I wanted another knife to throw, so the point could find its heart and send it back to Hel for all of eternity.

Yet these were hollow thoughts. My only saving grace was that the garm, with all its strength, ferocity and ability, could not climb.

Momentum alone allowed it to get a few feet off the ground, but it fell back and hit the dirt with a thud. It roared and flames leapt upward, scorching my tree and blackening the edges of several of the wooden rungs. Even though the flames could not reach up this high, I jumped back. The garm rammed itself against the tree, attempting to knock it over. My tree shook under the assault and my oilcloth fell down. And then disaster struck. One of my planks was knocked loose, tilted upward and caught me full in the face. I collapsed backward and plummeted downward before my thrashing hands closed around one of my short climbing boards. My plunging weight nearly sheared it off the trunk. As it was, only one nail remained to hold it to the bark.

As my fingers were slipping over the wood, I looked down below. The garm was up on its hind legs, less than fifteen feet from me. Its mouth opened to deliver a blast of flames that would turn me to a blackened husk. With one hand gripping the board, I pulled my sweater and blanket from around my waist, balled them up and threw them directly into the gaping opening. The garm choked and coughed and no flames came out. At least not yet.

I regained purchase with my other hand and fled up the boards as the garm roared again and the flames erupted anew; I could feel them hurtling up the trunk of my tree at me. I leapt over the last short board and threw myself up on the planks. I lay there panting, staring at nothing because my eyes were closed tight.

The garm made one more attempt to reach me and then fell back again. Its innate ferocity was paralyzing.

One sliver later, it turned and headed off. It would look for easier prey. I hoped it would not find any, unless it was Julius Domitar, Roman Picus, or even the smooth-talking Jurik Krone, whom I had decided I could not trust because of that underlying look of hostility in his eyes and because he had said Quentin Herms had broken laws. I would pay good coin to see them encounter a hungry garm. But they possessed weapons the garm feared, particularly a long metal tube that fired out a projectile that would kill anything it hit. We called it a morta. Roman Picus had used one to kill a garm. That's how he got the boots he wore. And it was said that Jurik Krone was the finest morta shot in all of Wormwood. That was, for me, a discomforting thought.

You couldn't do much with a dead garm. Its meat was poison. Its blood was like acid. It was said that the claws could still kill after death and that the flames inside it never truly died. Thus, you only could use the skin.

I sat on my bum in my tree, breathing hard, letting my terror cycle down to mere paranoia. The garm was nearly gone. I could barely see its flames now as it moved in the direction of the Quag. I wondered what had drawn it here this night. Then the Quag made me think of Quentin Herms. He'd said he had left me something that would set me free. And I intended to find it.

I looked in the waterproof tuck I kept hanging from a branch. But inside I found nothing. So where else could he have left anything? There was really no other place.

I looked down my tree. Something was itching at the back of my brain, but I couldn't think what. I went back over my frantic climb up here with the garm at my heels and it occurred to me.

My hand had hit something unfamiliar.

I opened my lantern and peered over the edge of my planks. There was not much to see. Except one thing. I had nailed twenty boards as rungs against my tree's trunk and now I counted twenty-one.

That was what my hand hit. An extra board that shouldn't have been there.

If I was right, then Quentin was brilliant. If I hadn't initially noticed the extra board, who else would have? Probably not even Thansius, as smart as he was.

Trembling with excitement, I climbed down to the board and examined it under my lantern's light. Fortunately, the garm's flames had not touched it. It looked exactly like the other boards. I found this remarkable until I recalled that Quentin was a skilled Finisher.

I scanned the front of the board for a message. There was none. But a message on the front would have been too easily seen. I tugged on it. It appeared firmly nailed into the trunk. Now I began to wonder whether Quentin was actually that smart after all. How was I supposed to pull the board out without falling and killing myself?

But as I looked more closely, I saw that the nail heads in the board were not nail heads at all. They had been colored to look like nail heads. So what was holding the board up? I felt along the top edge of the wood. There was a slender length of metal that hung over the board. I felt along the lower edge of the board and felt an identical stretch of metal there. The metal had been darkened to blend in perfectly with the stain of the board. I put one hand on the end of the board and pulled. It slid out from between the two metal edges. The metal had acted as both a track and a support, to slide the board into place and keep it there. Now, with the board gone, I could see how Quentin had attached the metal to the trunk using stout screws.

The board was light. It was probably a good thing I did not step on it while fleeing the garm. I doubted it would have held my weight.

I scampered back up to the top of my tree and sat on my haunches, the board in my lap. I turned it over and there it was: a small, flat metal box. Inside was a scroll. I unrolled it. It was surprisingly long to have fitted inside such a small space.

I shone my lantern light on it and caught my breath. It was a map. It was a map of something I never thought anyone could have mapped.

It was a map of the Quag.

More than that, it was a map of a way *through* the Quag.

What Quentin Herms had left for me was a way out of Wormwood.

I sat there staring at the parchment like it was both a sack of coins and a bag of serpents. As my eyes ran over the detailed drawings and precise writings, the enormity of what I was holding washed over me. My skin tingled as though I had been hit by a sudden thunder-thrust preceded by spears of skylight.

But when had he placed the board here? I had been here at first light and there had only been twenty boards, of that I was sure. I had seen Quentin flee into the Quag, also at first light. So had he come out of the Quag to place the extra board on my tree after I had gone to Stacks? If so, why? And how could he have survived the Quag in the first place?

Yet this was clearly the message from Quentin Herms. But it was far more elaborate than the cryptic one I had swallowed back at Stacks. This map also could be construed as him contacting me and Jurik Krone had been especially clear on that point. If Quentin contacted me and I did not tell Council, I could be sent to Valhall. For how long, he hadn't said. But even one light and night in that grim place would be far too long. And since it was illegal to enter the Quag, it would most certainly be against our laws to have a map of the place. That would get me in Valhall faster than Delph could say "Wotcha, Vega Jane."

But in truth my curiosity overrode my fear. I raised the wick on my lantern and studied the map. The Quag was an unfathomably large place. Quentin had not marked the map with precise distances, but he had included the footprint of Wormwood within the parchment. I studied the two side by side and saw quickly that the Quag was many times the size of my village. Also telling was the fact that the map ended at the edge of the Quag. If there was anything on the other side, Quentin either did not know or else had not put it down on this parchment for some reason.

My gaze ran down the last bit of the map, and then my dilemma became obvious. Every Wug knew that entering the Quag meant death, and I could never see myself going into it. And even if I survived the Quag, where would I be?

We had always been told that nothing lay on the other side of the Quag. In fact, we had always been told that there was no other side. For all I knew, once I left the Quag, I would fall off a cliff into oblivion. But even if I had been tempted to leave, I could not because of my brother and my parents. In his message, Quentin had said I could escape this place if I had the desire. Well, I wasn't sure if I had the desire, but abandoning my family was not an option. So the easy answer would be to destroy the map since I would never be using it. In fact, I should destroy it right now.

I opened the glass folds of my lantern and held the map up to the flame. But my hand didn't move. It wouldn't dip toward the fire with the parchment.

You can never go through the Quag, Vega, so what does it matter? Just burn it. If you're found with it, your punishment will be Valhall! You can't risk that.

Still, my hand didn't move. It was as though an invisible tether was keeping it in place. I slowly pulled the parchment away from the flame and pondered what to do. I had to destroy the map. But could I destroy the map and yet also keep it?

My gaze moved to my waterproof tuck. I opened it and pulled out my ink stick. I kept it here because I would draw pictures on my boards of things that I would see from this vantage point: birds, clouds, the canopy of massive trees at eye level. But transferring the map from one piece of parchment to another was not an answer to my dilemma.

So I had another solution.

It took some time, a bit of contortion and a fair amount of ink, but when it was done, I held the map up to the spark of my lantern and let its end ignite. I dropped it and watched it descend to the wooden planks as the ends curled up and blackened. In less than a sliver, it had disappeared to ash that floated away in the breeze. And then even the ash was gone.

I slipped down the rungs with the extra board in hand, put it back into its metal slot and continued my descent. My feet hit the dirt and I looked around, suddenly fearful that the garm might return. But I did not smell it. I certainly did not see it. Perhaps it had gone back to Hel. I hoped with all my heart that it stayed there.

I now had a map that I could never use to leave here. But I had something else. A mystery surrounding a ring that had belonged to my grandfather. It wasn't simply curiosity, although I had more of that than most Wugs. This was about my family. This was about my history. Which, in the end, meant it was ultimately about me.

The Delphias

NEXT LIGHT, JOHN and I went downstairs and used the pipe behind the Loons to wash off our faces and hands and under our arms. I was careful with the water on myself so as not to wash off the map marks I had carefully inked on my body while sitting atop my tree. I had been faithful in reproducing them because I knew Quentin to be a methodical Wug. He would have included only necessary details and I desperately wanted to study them more thoroughly, even if I was never going to venture into the Quag. Though I'd always known the Quag was there, seeing details such as were in the map was like learning of a whole new world when I'd thought there was only ours.

Then we ate. Well, John ate. I had already placed my first light meal in my metal tin, which I kept under my cot. I knew most of the clerks in the shops and bartered with them for food and anything else I needed, using nice things that I made out of scraps from Stacks.

A few slivers later, two other Wugmorts joined us at table.

Selene Jones was thirty sessions old but looked younger. She had long blond hair and an unlined face that was wide and mostly vacant at first light. Yet she carried peace in her eyes and seemed wholly satisfied with her life. She ran a shop on the High Street that sold items related to Noc-gazing and predictions of the future.

The other Wugmort at table was twenty-four-session-old Ted Racksport. An industrious and entrepreneurial Wug from his earliest lights, he owned the only shop in Wormwood that sold mortas, along with other weapons. Racksport was a bit taller than me, with broad shoulders, thick legs, a barrel chest, a flattened face, cracked lips, a few whiskers on his weak chin, long, thinning hair tied back with a cord of leather and four fingers on his right hand. It was said that a baby garm had nipped the other one off when Racksport had been hunting it.

He was a hard worker but not a pleasant Wug, and I was glad he slept in a different cot room. He smelled perpetually of sweat, metal and the black powder that gave morta their killing force. I had seen one fired before. It tore right through thick wood and nearly scared me to the Hallowed Ground, where we lay our dead. The way Racksport looked at you, you began to realize that he knew the power he had and he was quite happy that you didn't have it.

I was relieved when John was finished and we left. We parted company at the door to Learning.

"I'll be back to get you after Stacks," I said.

I said this every light so that John would have no worries. And he always replied, "I know you will."

But this light he didn't say that. Instead he said, "Are you sure you'll be back for me?"

I gaped. "Why do you ask that?"

"Where did you go last night?"

"To my tree."

"Why?"

"Just to think. And I left something there I needed."

"What?"

"Just go to Learning, John. I'll be back for you. I promise."

As he walked into the building, his gaze was on me. And I felt painful levels of guilt for lying to my brother. There was nothing else for it, though. To keep him safe, I had to keep him in the dark.

I turned and hurried away. I had something important to do this first light.

I needed to go and see Delph.

The Delphias' cottage was due south of Wormwood and the route ran straight and true until you reached two large trees with permanent red leaves. Here, you turned left down a dirt path that wound in among the forest. As I raced along, I looked down at myself, made sure that every inch of my legs, arms and belly where the map was inked was covered, then doubled my speed, running until my breaths became gasps.

As I drew near to the Delphias', I slowed to a fast walk. Duf was Delph's father and his only living relation. Unlike Delph, Duf was small, barely more than four feet high. Considering Delph's great height, I always assumed that his mother must have been very tall. She died when Delph was born, so neither of us had ever seen her.

Duf's unusual cottage was not made of wood or stone or anything like that. It was made of things that other Wugs had thrown away. It was the shape of a huge ball, with a square door made of rough metal set on fat brass hinges. Next to the cottage was an opening that Duf and Delph had dug into a small hillside. Duf kept the things he used for his work in there.

Duf was a Beast Trainer, one of the best in all of Wormwood. Well, actually, he was the only one in all of Wormwood, but he was still very good. Wugs brought him their beasts and he would teach them to do what you wanted done. He had a large wooden corral with smaller spaces fenced off inside it where the beasts were kept separate from one another.

As I cleared the path and reached the cottage, I paused and studied the beasts Duf had currently. There was a young slep, which made me think Thansius would soon be replacing one that pulled his carriage. There was also an adar, taller than I was, with wings twice my height. They were used to carry things and perform tasks by air for Wugs who owned them. Adars could understand what Wugmorts said, but they had to be trained to obey. And they could also talk back once they'd been trained, which can be both helpful and a great bother. The adar had one leg chained to a peg buried deeply in the ground so it couldn't fly away.

There was a small whist pup, barely ten pounds in weight, with gray fur and a small, scared face. This hound at full size would be larger than me, but it would take at least a half session for that to happen. Whists naturally liked to roam. They could outrun pretty much anything, including garms and their even more vicious cousins, the amarocs.

Then I turned to the largest creature Duf had now. The creta already weighed about half a ton, though it wasn't full-grown. It had horns that crossed over its face, huge hooves the size of meal plates and a face that no Wug would like to see coming at him. It was kept in an inner corral where the wood was much thicker. The space was small too, so the creta couldn't get a running start and crash through this barrier. It would be trained to pull the plow of the Tillers and to carry sacks of flour on its back at the Mill. It seemed to know this would be its plight in life, because it did not look very happy as it pawed the dirt in its small space.

"Wo-wo-wotcha, Vega Jane?"

I turned to see Delph stooping to come out of the hole in the hill. I walked over to join Delph as his father came out of the cottage.

Duf wore boots caked with dirt, and his clothes were not any cleaner. A grimy bowler hat was on his head. Strings attached to it were tied under his chin. I assumed he did this in case of windy lights or temperamental beasts in training. His hands, face and exposed arms were scarred and scabbed from innumerable beast encounters.

"Good light, Vega," said Duf. He pulled a stick bowl from his shirt pocket, stuffed it with smoke weed and lighted it with a wooden match he had stuck behind his ear. He puffed to get the flame set and strong. His face, in addition to the wounds there, was heat- and wind-burned. He was not really that old, but his beard was thick and dotted with gray. It was not easy, his life.

"Hello, Duf."

"What brings you round this early?" he asked curiously.

"Wanted to talk to Delph. Is that slep for Thansius?"

Duf nodded. He pointed his stick bowl at the creta. "Now, that there scallywag is giving me trouble. Aye, he's a stubborn one that. But then cretas always are. Give me an adar any light, though once they learn to talk proper, they carry on like a bunch of females round the washing. But I have a soft spot for 'em. They're good beasts. Loyal they are, if chatty."

Delph said, "I'd be st-stubborn t-t-too if I knew I'd be c-c-carrying stuff me whole life on me ba-back."

"You best be jawing with Delph, then," said Duf. He picked up a leather bridle and marched off to the corral.

I watched for a sliver and then turned to Delph. "I need to talk to you about something important. And you can't tell anybody. Promise?"

He didn't seem to be listening to me. He stared up at the Noc, which was still there in the brightening sky. "How f-far you re-reckon i'tis?"

I looked at the Noc in frustration. "What does it matter? We'll never get there."

"But th-that sh-shows it, right?"

"Shows what?"

And now Delph was about to gobsmack me.

"N-not just us, don't it?"

"Why?" I asked, in what can only be described as a whisper, a *fierce* whisper, for I was feeling things I had never really felt before.

Delph apparently did not notice the struggle going on inside me. He said, "It c-can't be just us. I mean why, y'know? Ju-just Wor-Wormwood?" He shrugged and smiled. "No p-point, really. Just this? No ble-bleeding p-point far as I c-can see."

Since he seemed to be in an introspective mood, I decided instead of talking about Quentin, I would ask a question.

"What happened to you, Delph?" I asked. "When you were six sessions old?"

His shoulders immediately bunched and his face scrunched and he did not look at me.

"I'm sorry," I said. "It's none of my business, really." But I was hoping beyond all hope that he would talk about it.

"I li-liked Vi-Virgil," he mumbled.

"He liked you back," I said, surprised that my grandfather's name had come up.

"His . . . E-Event."

His head suddenly looked far too small to hold all that was going on in there.

"What about it?" I said, quickly thrown by his statement.

"I . . . I s-s-saw it."

That's when it occurred to me that whatever happened to Delph coincided with my grandfather's Event.

"What do you mean you saw it?" I asked, my voice growing louder with fear and surprise.

"S-saw it," he repeated.

"The Event!" I said, more loudly than I should have. "His Event!"

I glanced quickly over at Duf, who was still attending the slep. He had looked my way but then turned back to his task.

Delph nodded mutely.

In a low voice I asked, "What happened?"

"The Event. The Event ha-ha-happened."

57

"No one has ever seen an Event, Delph." I was desperately trying to keep the panic I felt from my voice. The last thing I needed was to scare Delph off.

"I ha-have," he said in a hollow voice tinged with dread.

"Do you remember what happened?" I said as calmly as I could, though I still felt my heart thudding against my chest. It hurt. It actually hurt.

Delph shook his head. "I . . . I don't re-re-remember, Vega Jane."

"How can you not remember?" I demanded.

"It's not good to witness an Event, Vega Jane," he said clear as light. There was an underlying sorrow to his answer that made my heart hurt even more. Though his words were simple, I felt like I had never heard Delph speak so eloquently. He touched his head. "Does no good to you here." He next touched his chest. "Nor here."

My heart went out to him, but my next blunt words came from my head, not my heart. "How can you say that if you don't remember what you saw?"

I had raised my voice again and I caught Duf looking over at us with concern on his small face. I looked back at Delph and lowered my voice. "Don't you see why I have to know? All I've ever been told was that he suffered an Event and there was nothing left."

Delph picked up a spade and struck the ground with it. I could see his huge hands gripping the wooden handle so hard they were turning red.

"Ca-ca-can't say nothin'," he finally replied. He lifted up a spade of dirt and dumped it next to the hole.

"Why not?"

That's when I heard it — the turn of wheels. Thansius's carriage came into view around the curve. The same vile Wugmort was driving it. Thomas Bogle had been Thansius's driver for as long as I could remember. His cloak was black, his hands were huge lumps of bone and his face looked like he had died many sessions ago. The pale flesh hung from his cheeks like shredded parchment as he stared at the shiny flanks of the sleps.

The carriage stopped next to the corral, and the door opened.

I gasped when I saw her.

Morrigone

MORRIGONE WAS THE only female member of Council. In Wormwood she was *the* female. Taller than I was, slender, but not frail, for there was strength in her shoulders and arms. Her hair was bloodred, redder than Thansius's cloak. She strode over to where Delph and I stood.

She was dressed all in white. Her face, her skin and her cloak were all flawless. I had never seen a cleaner Wug in all of Wormwood. Against the white cloak her blood hair was a dazzling sight.

Wugmorts greatly respected Thansius.

Wugmorts dearly loved Morrigone.

I could hardly believe she was here. I glanced at Delph, who looked like he had swallowed the creta whole. I looked at Duf. He still held the rope but appeared to have forgotten about the young slep tied to the other end of it. The slep whinnied as it caught sight of the mature sleps, along with its own future, I imagined.

I did the only thing I could do. I turned to Morrigone and waited for her to speak. Was she here to see Delph? Duf? Or me?

I studied her face. If there was perfection in all of Wormwood, I was looking at it. I felt my face flush under the dirt on it. I felt ashamed I was not better-looking. And more clean.

Most Wugs are much of muchness; it's hard to tell one from another. Not Morrigone. I found her gaze on me and I had to glance away. I felt I was unworthy to share even a look with her.

Morrigone smiled at Duf, who had dropped the rope and walked toward her with hesitant steps. Delph had not moved. His feet could be in the hole he was digging. As big as he was, he looked small, insignificant.

"Good light, Mr. Delphia," said Morrigone in a mellifluous tone. "That slep appears to be a splendid specimen. I look forward to seeing another fine example of your peerless skill once he's in harness."

Her speech was as perfect as she. I wished I could speak like that. Of course it would never happen. I didn't know how old Morrigone was, but I didn't think her Learning had stopped at twelve sessions.

She next walked over to Delph and put her hand on his shoulder. "Daniel, I hear only good reports from your labors at the Mill. We appreciate your prodigious strength so very much. And if it's possible, I think you've grown a bit since I last saw you. I am sure your competitors in the next Duelum will shudder to hear that."

She handed Delph three coins as I looked on in surprise.

"For the work you recently did at my home, Daniel. I believe I forgot to pay you."

Delph nodded slightly, and his big fingers closed around the coins and they disappeared into his pocket. Then he just stood there like a great lump of iron, looking mightily uncomfortable.

Morrigone turned and walked over to me. In her look I knew that I was the reason she was here. And that meant I had been followed. My mind swirled with possibilities and pitfalls. I think she read all this on my face. I looked up at her and tried to smile. But there were so few reasons for Wugmorts to smile I found I was out of practice. My mouth felt lopsided.

"Vega, what a pleasant surprise to find you here so early in the light," she said. The remark was innocuous enough, yet the questioning tone implied the desire for an answer for my presence here.

"I wanted to see Delph about something," I managed to say.

"Really, what was that?" asked Morrigone. Her words were unhurried, but I sensed urgency behind them.

I knew if I hesitated, she would know I was lying. But while Morrigone may have been one of the elites of Wormwood and someone I deeply respected, there were few who could lie as well as I could. The real skill was to weave in something true with a lie. It just sounded better that way.

"I gave Delph my first meal last light. He promised to give me his this light."

I looked over at Delph. Morrigone did the same.

Delph gripped the spade like it was the only thing tethering him to the ground. I braced myself for Delph to say something stupid and ruin my perfectly good lie.

"G-g-got no food for Vega Jane this li-li-light," Delph stammered.

I turned back to Morrigone. "It's okay. I have something to eat before Stacks."

Morrigone looked pleased by this answer. "You have a reputation for making such fine things. As good as Quentin Herms, I'm told."

Morrigone disappointed me with this tactic. It was a little obvious. As I looked closer at her, I saw a slight wrinkle at the left corner of her mouth. Not a smile line; it was going the other way. This calmed me for some reason.

I said, "Quentin Herms has gone. No one in all of Wormwood knows where he is. At least that's what I was told."

"You were at your tree last night," said Morrigone.

My suspicions of being followed were just confirmed.

I said, "I often go there. I like to think."

Morrigone drew a bit closer to me. "Do you think about Quentin Herms? Are you sorry he has left us?"

"I liked working with him. He was a good Wugmort. He taught me how to be a Finisher. So, yes, I am sorry. I also don't understand where he could have gone."

"Do you perhaps have a notion?"

"Where is there to go other than Wormwood?" I said, using the same tactic I had employed with Thansius. However, Morrigone's next words took me by surprise.

"There's the Quag," she said.

Duf snatched a breath and exclaimed, "Quentin Herms ain't no fool. Why in the name of all of Wormwood would he go in the Quag? Load-a bollocks, ask me."

Duf shot an anxious glance at Morrigone and his face sagged. He tugged off his old, stained bowler, revealing a thick spread of dirty, graying hair, and looked thoroughly embarrassed. "Beggin' pardon at me language, uh . . . females," he finished awkwardly.

Morrigone continued to stare at me, apparently awaiting my response to her comment.

I said, "Going to the Quag means death." As I said this, I thought of the look on Quentin's face as he ran into the Quag.

She nodded, but did not look convinced by my statement, which puzzled me. "So you have never ventured near the Quag?" she asked.

I said nothing for a sliver, because while I had no problem with lying, I didn't like to use the skill unnecessarily. It had nothing to do with morals and everything to do with not getting caught.

"Never close enough to be attacked by a beast that lurks there."

Morrigone said, "But my colleague Jurik Krone informed me that you were down by the edge of the Quag at last first light."

"I heard screams and saw the attack canines and Council members. I followed them out of curiosity and also to see if I could help somehow with what they were doing. Before I realized it, we were near the Quag."

"And you told Krone you saw nothing, no one?"

"Because I didn't," I lied. "I know now that it was Quentin they were after, but I still don't understand why." I wanted Morrigone to keep talking. I might learn something important, so I said, "Why were they chasing him in the first place?"

"Good question, Vega. Unfortunately, I cannot answer it."

"Can't or won't?" I said, before I realized I had said it.

Duf and Delph caught breaths, and I thought I heard Delph hiss a warning at me. Morrigone did not answer me. Instead, she motioned with her hand. I heard the creak of carriage wheels. Bogle guided the sleps and carriage back into view.

Morrigone didn't board right away. Her gaze flitted over me.

"Thank you, Vega Jane," she said, using my full name, like Delph did routinely.

"I'm sorry I wasn't much help."

"You were more help than you know."

A bittersweet smile accompanied this comment, which for some reason caused my stomach to do flips.

She disappeared inside the carriage. In less than a sliver, it was gone.

"Har," gasped Duf.

I couldn't have agreed more.

Inside a Book

WHEN I TURNED back to Delph, he was gone. I glanced over at Duf, who still stood there gaping at where the carriage had been.

"Where did Delph go?" I asked breathlessly.

Duf looked around and shook his head. "Mill, most likely."

"So, what sort of work does Delph do for Morrigone that he gets coin in payment?" I asked.

Duf looked at the ground, stubbing a rock with his heavy boot. "Lifting stuff, I 'spect. Delph does that real good. Strong as a creta, he is."

"Uh-huh," I replied, trying to think what Delph really did for the coins.

"What happened to Delph when he was six sessions, Duf?" I asked.

He immediately looked away. He seemed to be gazing at the young slep, but I knew he really wasn't.

"You best get yourself off to Stacks, Vega. If another Wug don't show up for the hand stamp, no telling what Domitar will do, the great insufferable git."

"But, Duf?"

"G'on, clear off, Vega. Nuff has happened. Just let it be."

He didn't wait for another response. He simply strode off. I stood there for a bit, wondering what to do. I kicked a few clods of dirt back into the hole. Delph might be gone, but I did have some time before Stacks. I made up my mind quickly.

I would go to Quentin Herms's cottage.

I looked at the sky to see the clouds had covered it like a cot blanket. I thought the rains would be coming soon. We got them this time of session. When they came, they stayed for a long time. I imagined Quentin struggling through the dark Quag and then feeling the cold pellets of moisture coming down. But perhaps Quentin was already dead. Perhaps the Quag had lived up to its reputation.

I picked up my pace, imagining that Domitar would be on the lookout for anyone who did not come in on time. I hurried along, keeping a watchful eye out for signs of Thomas Bogle and that mighty blue carriage. I thought back to what I might have said to Morrigone that would make her believe I had told her something useful. She was so smart that perhaps it was what I *didn't* say that gave her what she needed.

I slowed down. In another few yards, I would be there. I decided to approach the cottage from not the front or rear, but the right side. This had the most cover, with bushes and a couple of trees nearly as large as my poplar. There was a low fence of piled stone that ran around the small patch of weedy grass that constituted Quentin's property. I jumped this and landed lightly in the side yard. I heard birds in the trees and little creatures roaming the bushes. I did not hear carriage wheels.

This did not make me any less suspicious. Or less scared. But I swallowed my fear and moved forward, keeping as low as possible. I thought of what would happen to me if I were found here. They would believe I was in cahoots with Quentin. Whatever laws he had broken, they would believe I had helped him do so. They would also arrest me for breaking into his cottage. I would be sent to Valhall. Fellow Wugmorts would hurl spit and curses at me through the bars while Nida and the black shuck looked on.

I scampered over another low wall and dropped to the ground. Directly up ahead was the cottage. It was made of stone and wood, with dirty windows. The rear door was only a few feet away. I ran to a window on the side of the cottage and peered through it. It was dark inside, but I could still see if I pressed my face firmly to the glass.

The cottage was all on one floor. From this window I could see most of the inside of the place. I moved to another window, which I judged would let me see into the only other room there. This was Quentin's bedroom, though there was only a cot with a pillow and blanket on it. I looked around but I saw no clothes. And the old pair of boots that he always wore to Stacks was not there either. Maybe that's why Council had assumed he had gone off on his own accord. He had packed his clothes. A Wug didn't do that if he'd been eaten by a garm or suffered an Event. I tried to remember if Quentin had been carrying a tuck with him when he went into the Quag, but I couldn't be sure. I'd really only seen his face.

I took another deep breath and headed to the rear door. It was locked. That was not surprising. I defeated the lock with my little tools. I was becoming quite a cracking law-breaker. I opened the door and moved inside, closing it behind me as quietly as I could manage. Still, it seemed to make a sound like a creta slamming into a wall. I was shaking all over and felt ashamed for being so scared.

I stood up straight, drew another long breath and willed the shakes away. I was standing in the main room of Quentin's cottage. This was also his library, for there were some books on a shelf. It was also his kitchen, for there was a fireplace with a blackened pot hanging in it. And it was also where he ate his meals, for there was a small round table with one chair. On it was a wooden spoon, fork and knife on top of a plate made of copper. All neat and orderly, just like my friend had been.

As my eyes adjusted to the poor light inside, I focused first on the books. There weren't that many, but even a few books were more than most Wugmorts possessed.

I lifted one book out. The title was *Engineering through the Sessions*. I looked inside the pages, but the words and drawings were too much for my feeble mind. I pulled out another book. This one puzzled me. It was a book on ceramics. I knew for a fact that Quentin hated working in ceramics. I did all the fin-ishing on ceramics at Stacks because of that. So why would he have such a book?

I opened it. The first few pages did indeed deal with

ceramics, and I looked at sketches of plates and cups in various colors and styles. But as I kept turning the pages, I found something else. A book inside a book.

The title page brought a chill to my skin: *The Quag: The True Story*.

This inner book was not printed. It was on neatly cropped parchment and handwritten in ink. I turned through some of the pages. There were words and precisely hand-drawn pictures. And the pictures were truly frightening. Some were of creatures I had never seen before. They all looked to be things that would eat you, given the chance. Some made the garm look downright cuddly.

I looked to see if the author's name was anywhere on the book, but it wasn't. Yet surely Quentin must have written this. The conclusion spawned from this was equally shocking: He must have gone into the Quag *before* the time I had seen him do it last light. And come out alive.

I slipped the Quag book out of the other and stuck it in my cloak pocket. What was contained in the pages would fulfill my curiosity but nothing more. Quentin Herms had no one to leave behind. He was free to try his luck in the Quag. I was not, even if I could have mustered the courage. I was Vega Jane from Wormwood. I would always be Vega Jane from Wormwood. At some point, I would be planted in a humble grave in a quite ordinary section of the Hallowed Ground. And life here would go on just like it always had.

The next moment I heard a key turning in a lock to the front door of the cottage.

I slipped behind a cabinet and held my breath. Someone came into the room, and I heard the door close. There were footsteps and low murmurs, which made me realize there was more than one Wug about.

Then a voice grew loud enough for me to recognize and with its rise, my heart sank to the floor.

It was Jurik Krone.

The Reward

I TRIED TO FORCE myself into as small a ball of flesh as possible as their footsteps echoed over the wooden floor.

Krone said, "We have found nothing useful. Nothing! It is not possible. The Wug was not that capable, was he?"

I could not hear the other voice clearly, but what I could discern seemed vaguely familiar.

"The ring is the puzzlement for me," said Krone. "How came it to be back here? I know they were friends, close friends. But why would the accursed Virgil not leave it to his son?"

The other voice murmured something else. It was driving me mad that I couldn't tell what was being said or who was saying it. And why had Krone used the word *accursed* in defining my grandfather?

Krone said, "He's gone into the Quag, that we know. And I believe that Vega Jane knows something about it. They were close. They worked together. She was there that very light."

The other voice said something, in an even lower tone. It was as though the other Wug knew someone was listening. Then Krone said something that nearly made my heart stop.

"We could tell them it was an Event, like the others. Like Virgil."

I had to stop myself from jumping out and screaming, *What the bloody Hel do you mean by that?*

But I didn't. I was paralyzed.

The other voice murmured back in reply but I could not hear the words.

I knew it was risky but I also knew I had to try. Fighting against my seemingly dead limbs, I eased forward on my knees. There was a bit of looking glass on the far wall. If I could just stretch out enough to see if there was a reflection of Krone and the other Wug in —

The door opened and closed before I could move another inch.

Throwing caution to the wind, I leapt up to find the room empty. I raced over to the window next to the front door and looked out. Disappearing around a corner of a hedge was the blue carriage.

How did I not hear the clops of the sleps as they approached the cottage? Or the turn of the wheels? Was it Morrigone in the carriage? Or Thansius?

But who said what paled next to what I had just heard. The words were imprinted on my brain. *We could tell them it was an Event, like the others. Like Virgil.*

That clearly meant that the idea of an Event was a lie to cover something else. If my grandfather had not vanished from an Event, what the Hel had happened to him? Well, Krone knew. And so, I'm sure, did Morrigone and the rest of Council. This destroyed everything I had ever believed in, everything I had been taught. This made me wonder what

Wormwood really was. And why we were all here. I felt so wonky, I thought I might topple over. I relaxed my breathing and slowed my heart. I did not have time for wonky. I had to get out of here.

I was halfway out the window when the front door opened once more. I didn't look back, but the heavy boot steps told me it was Krone. He didn't call out, which meant he hadn't seen me. Yet.

I slid out on my belly and hit the ground hard. I involuntarily yelped.

"Who's there?" roared Krone.

I was over the low wall and out of sight of the cottage probably before Krone had even gotten to the window. I have never run that fast in all my sessions. I didn't slow down until twenty yards from the entrance to Stacks, where I plunked down in the high grass, totally out of breath, my mind reeling from what I had just heard.

A few slivers later, I rubbed my hand after Dis Fidus stamped it. He looked like he had grown a session older since Quentin vanished. His aged chin quivered, making the grayish stubble there appear to be floating against his sallow skin.

"You mustn't be late, Vega. I've set out water for you at your station. The heat is already fierce this light from the furnaces."

I thanked him and hurried in, still rubbing at the ink on my hand.

The book weighed heavily in my cloak pocket. It was stupid to bring it here, but I didn't have time to go anyplace else. Where could I hide it that no one could find it? Yet even though I knew I had to part with it, I was desperate to read the book from beginning to end.

I stuck my cloak with the book in my locker and made sure the door was securely fastened. I put on my apron, work trousers and heavy boots before going to the main work area. With my goggles dangling around my neck, I slipped on my gloves and stared at the high pile of unfinished things next to my workstation. I knew it would be a long light's work. I sipped the cold water that Dis Fidus had left me and began my tasks, working my way through them methodically, reading parchment after parchment of instructions and then improvising when the written directives allowed me to. I worked hard and tried to stay focused even with all the thoughts swirling in my head.

Before I realized it, Dis Fidus was ringing the bell that told us it was time to start packing up.

I was about to change out of my work clothes when we were urgently summoned to the main floor of Stacks. I hurriedly closed my locker and rushed there.

Domitar came out and stood in front of us as we lined up. We all waited as he paced back and forth, while a frightened-looking Dis Fidus hovered in the background. Finally, Domitar grew close enough for me to smell the flame water on his breath. I could only imagine that Council had come down with great force on him. And knowing Domitar as I did, he was about to take whatever pain he had suffered out on us. Thus, I was shocked by his first words.

"Council has ordered that there shall be a reward," he began.

Though we were all knackered from our labors, this got everyone's attention.

"Five quarts of flame water. A pound of smoke weed." He paused for effect. "And two thousand coins."

A gasp went up among us.

I had no use for the flame water or smoke weed, though I supposed I could barter them for a good deal of eggs, bread, pickles and tins of tea. But two thousand coins represented a vast fortune, perhaps more than I would earn in all my sessions at Stacks. It could change everything about my life. And John's.

Domitar's next words, however, dashed any hope I had of earning that fortune.

He said, "This reward will be paid out to whoever provides sufficient information to Council to apprehend the fugitive Quentin Herms. Or it will be paid out to the Wugmort who personally catches Herms and brings him back."

The fugitive Quentin Herms?

As I looked at Domitar, I found his gaze upon me.

"Two thousand coins," he repeated for emphasis. "You would no longer need to work here of course. Your life would be one of leisure."

I looked around at the males. They all had families to support. Their faces were blackened, their hands gnarled and their backs bent from the toil here. A life of leisure? Unthinkable. As I stared at their hungry, exhausted faces, it did not bode well for Quentin.

Domitar added, "We would prefer that he be taken alive. If this is not possible, so be it. But we will need proof. The body, reasonably intact, will do."

My heart sank and I felt my lips tremble. That was practically a death sentence for poor Quentin. If he had risked everything to escape, I could not imagine him not fighting with all his might to prevent his capture. Much easier to simply put a knife blade in him. I felt tears rush to my eyes, but I shoved them away with my dirty hand.

I once more looked at the males around me. They were now talking in low voices among themselves. I could imagine them all going home, getting whatever weapons were handy and heading out after their meager suppers to hunt down Quentin and get the coins and, with them, their life of leisure. They would probably go in teams, to increase their chances of success.

Domitar said, "That is all. You may leave."

We all started filing out, but Domitar stopped me.

"A sliver, Vega."

He waited until the other Stackers were gone. He looked over at Dis Fidus, who still stood trembling in the background.

"Leave us, Fidus," ordered Domitar, and the little Wug shot out of the room.

Domitar began, "You could use two thousand coins. You and your brother. And your parents at the Care. It's not inexpensive. And you would have a life of leisure."

"But then I wouldn't have the pleasure of seeing you every light, Domitar."

His narrowed eyes grew even smaller. They looked like little caves from which something astonishingly slimy and dangerous would explode. "You have brains, but sometimes you spectacularly fail to exercise them."

"A mixed compliment," I said.

"And an accurate one. Two thousand coins, Vega. And as I said, that includes information leading to Herms's apprehension. You needn't catch him yourself."

"Or kill him. Like you said, that's also acceptable to earn the reward."

His eyes opened fully, revealing pupils darker than I had ever realized. "That's right. That's what I said because that is what Council has said."

He stepped aside, implicitly acknowledging that I could leave.

As I started past him, he gripped my shoulder and jerked me toward him. He whispered in my ear.

"You have much to lose, Vega Jane. Far more than you know. Help us to find Quentin Herms."

He let go of me and I rushed from the room, more scared than I had been in a long time. Including the attack from the garm. At least with the garm, you knew how it could hurt you. With Domitar I wasn't sure. I just knew I was afraid.

I only stopped running when I was nearly a mile from Stacks.

It occurred to me while I was running that the reward was meaningless to the other Wugs. Quentin had gone into the Quag, which meant no other Wug could find him. The idea of the reward had been directed at me. They wanted information on Quentin. And they thought I alone could provide it.

My lungs heaving, my mind jumping from one awful conclusion to another, I suddenly realized that I hadn't changed from my work clothes. Even more catastrophic, I had forgotten my cloak. And in the cloak was the book I had found about the Quag.

I felt like I would vomit.

Would Domitar look in my locker and find it? If he did, would I have to become a fugitive as well? Would the reward for my return dead or alive be two thousand coins? Ten thousand coins?

I had to get the book back. But if I returned now, Domitar would grow suspicious.

Then, in a flash, I suddenly had a plan, one that turned everything upside down.

A Pair of Jabbits

I T WAS THE third section of night and I was on the move again. The sky over Wormwood was not clear. The Noc was gone from sight. Drops of rain plopped on me as I hurried along, my head down, my heart full of dread. There was a rumble across the heavens and they lit up and then boomed. I froze. Every Wug had seen spears of skylight before and then heard the thunder-thrusts. That didn't make it any less frightening. Yet something was scaring me even more.

I had never been to Stacks at night. Not once. Now I had no choice. I had to get the book back now before it was discovered in my locker. For all I knew it might already have been.

I stopped about twenty yards away from my destination and looked up. Stacks rose up out of the darkness like some imperious demon waiting for prey to draw just close enough for it to have an easy meal.

Well, here I was.

I didn't know if they had guards at night. If so, I wasn't sure what I would do. Run like Hel, probably. What I did know was I wasn't going in through the front doors.

There was a side door hidden behind a pile of old, decaying equipment that had been sitting there probably since my grandfather was my age. As I passed the mounds of junk, every nook and cranny seemed to hold a garm, a shuck or even an amaroc. As the skylight speared and thunder-thrusts boomed again, there seemed to be a thousand eyes in that metal pile, and all of them were fixed on me. Just waiting.

The door was solid wood with a large, ancient lock. I slipped my slender tools into the mouth of the lock and did my little magic — the door clicked open.

I closed the door behind me as quietly as I could, licked my lips, drew a long breath, then shook my head clear.

I used my lantern now because if I didn't, I would knock into something and kill myself. I moved slowly along, hugging one wall and peering ahead. I was also listening and sniffing the air. I knew what Stacks smelled like. If I smelled something else, I was going to flee.

A few slivers later, I opened the door to the locker room and slipped inside.

I felt my way along each locker until I reached the seventh one down, which was mine. There were no true locks on the lockers, just simple latches, because no one ever brought anything of value here. At least no Wug had until I stupidly left the book that could land me in Valhall. I slowly opened the door, and that's when it hit me.

I dropped my lantern and nearly shrieked. I stood there hunched over, trying to keep the meager dinner I had eaten at the Loons inside of me rather than on the floor. I reached down and picked up the lantern and the book. The book had fallen out and hit me on the arm. I relit my lantern and leafed through the pages. It was all there. I couldn't believe my good fortune. I never dreamed it would be this easy.

I stopped thinking that when I heard the noise. My good fortune had just turned into disaster.

I put the book in the pocket of my cloak and turned my lantern down as low as the flame would go and still allow me to see an inch in front of me. I stood still, listening as hard as I could.

Okay, I thought with an involuntary shudder, *that was the sound of something large and swift*. I knew of several creatures that would make sounds like that. None of them should have been in Stacks. Ever.

After one more sliver frozen, I sprinted down the hall of the locker room, away from the door I came in. This turned out to be a good idea, because a sliver later, that door crashed to the floor. The sound was inside the room with me. It was clearer now. It was not the clops of hooves, or the scratching of claws on wood. That ruled out a frek, garm or amaroc. That left basically one creature.

I shook my head in disbelief. It couldn't be. Yet as I thought this, hoping beyond all hope that I was wrong, I heard the hissing. And my heart stopped for two beats before restarting.

We had been told about these vile beasts in Learning. I had never desired to see one for real.

They could move incredibly fast, faster than I could run, actually. They did not come into Wormwood proper, and they almost never went after Wugmorts because there was usually far easier prey to be found. To my knowledge, three Wugs had perished by them when they had ventured too close to the Quag. I did not want to be the fourth.

I kicked open the other door and shot through it like I was being propelled from a morta. But the sounds were growing closer still. When I made it to the back hall, I could go one of two ways. The left would take me out of here by the side door from which I had entered.

The only problem was, I saw eyes that way. Big, staring eyes that locked on me. There were about five hundred of them, if I had time to count, which I didn't. My worst fear had just been confirmed and then doubled.

There was a pair of them after me.

I went to the right. That would take me up the stairs. Up the stairs was forbidden. Anyone working at Stacks who tried to go up the stairs would have his or her head cut off by Ladon-Tosh and thrown in the furnace with the rest of the parts. But Ladon-Tosh wasn't here at night. And even if he were, I would take my chances with him over what was coming at me.

I flew up the steps, my knees chugging faster than they ever had. I hit the top landing and sped off to the right. I glanced back once and saw the innumerable eyes barely thirty feet behind me. I told myself I was never going to look back again.

Who the Hel had loosed these things in here?

Something occurred to me as I ran down the upper corridor. These things were the guardians of Stacks, but only at night. That was the only way they could be here. It could be the only reason that no Wug had been attacked during the light. You did not keep these creatures around as pets.

And that meant someone in Wormwood could do the

unthinkable. Someone could control them, when we had always been told they were wildly uncontrollable. Not even Duf would ever attempt to train one.

I reached the only door on the hall. It was at the very end and it was locked. Of course it was locked. Why would I think it would be open? I grabbed the tools from my cloak, my fingers shaking so badly that I nearly dropped them. The creatures were coming fiercely now; they sounded like the rush of a waterfall. The screeches from all those mouths were so high-pitched that I felt my brain would burst with the terror of it all. It was said the screech was always the last thing you heard before they struck.

As I inserted the tools in the lock and worked frantically, all I could think of was John. What he would do without me.

They were right on top of me now.

The screech is the last thing you hear before they strike.

The screech is the last thing you hear before they strike.

I didn't know whether I was brave to keep my back turned in the face of their charge, or else the biggest coward in Wormwood. As my tools turned and the door opened, I assumed it was bravery.

I slammed the door shut behind me and locked it. I ran my fingers over the wood, hoping it was thick enough. I was knocked down when they hit it. One of the fangs actually came through the boards and nearly impaled my shoulder instead of simply tearing my clothing. I slid back along the floor and crashed into the far wall, knocking something over. Metal clanged down all around me.

I looked over at the door as it took another blow. More fangs split the wood.

Less than a sliver later, one of the heads broke through. A pair of eyes stared at me, barely six yards away. The hole was too small for the rest of the bulk to get through, but either the hole would grow or the door would come down.

I groped around in the dark. That was when I noticed the tiny door behind the big metal thing that had fallen. The door was barely three feet tall and the knob was curious. I looked more closely. It was a face, yet not just any face. It was the face of a Wug screaming, cast in brass.

There came another smash against the door. I just had time to look back as the massive portal collapsed inward and the beasts sprang through the opening. Now I could see them both fully. I wished I couldn't.

Jabbits were massive serpents with one key difference. There were at least two hundred and fifty heads growing out of the one body along its full length. And all of them had fangs full of enough poison that one bite would drop a fully grown creta. All of them made the screech. And all of them were, right this sliver, charging at me.

They were a thousand nightmares rolled into a massive, thunderous wall of murderous devilry. And their breath smelled like dung on fire. I was not speculating now. The foul odor made me gag when I needed all the air I had to flee.

I grabbed the screaming-face knob, turned it and threw myself through the opening, kicking the door shut behind me. But I didn't feel the relief of a safe harbor. This door, tiny and thin, had no chance to stop the relentless juggernauts that are jabbits after prey. It was said that nothing could stop them once they were on the blood scent. I stood and backed

85

away. I drew the small knife I had brought with me and waited, my heart thumping, my lungs heaving.

I told myself I would not cry. I promised myself I would strike at least one blow before they killed me. It was said they lingered over their prey. I had also heard rumors that it was possible the poison didn't kill but merely paralyzed, allowing you to stay alive until they were halfway through devouring you. No one knew for sure. No one who had been attacked by a jabbit had survived to tell about it.

I prayed to everything I could think of that this was not the case. Let the poison be what killed me. I did not want to watch myself disappear piece by piece into their gullets.

"Good-bye, John," I said between tortured breaths. "Please don't forget me."

Every Wugmort had a time to die. This was surely mine.

I stood there, chest heaving, my pitiful knife held high in some ridiculous semblance of defense and my gaze on the little door, waiting for it to collapse inward with my death to follow.

Yet the little door didn't come crashing down. There was silence on the other side. I still didn't move. All I could think was the jabbits were being tricky, perhaps waiting for me to let my guard down before attacking. Reason quickly dispelled this idea. I couldn't possibly defend myself against them. They just had to knock down the door and eat me.

Sliver after sliver went by and nothing happened. My breath started to level off and my chest stopped heaving. I very slowly lowered the knife, though I kept staring at the little door. I strained to hear anything. All those awful fanged heads bumping up against that slender piece of wood.

Screeches that made your brain feel as if it were on fire. But there was nothing. It was as if sound from out there could not reach in here.

I put my knife away. I had dropped my lantern back there. On the other side of the door. I was not going out to try and retrieve it. And yet, for some reason, it was not completely dark in here. I could make out things, so I slowly turned in all directions. Because the door was small, I had expected the room to be as well. But it wasn't. It was a vast cavern with walls of rock, seemingly bigger than Stacks. I could not even see the ceiling, so high was it. And then my gaze fixed on the wall opposite me.

There was a drawing on it. I drew a quick breath when I saw what it was — three hooks attached as one. The same design as on my grandfather's hand and on his ring found in Quentin Herms's cottage.

I forgot about the three hooks as I stared around at the other walls. They were suddenly awash in different lights and sounds. I jumped back as I saw what looked to be a flying slep with a rider astride it, soaring across the rock. The rider threw a spear and there was an explosion so loud and real that I covered my ears and dropped to the floor. A million images seemed to flow across the stone as I watched in disbelief, my eyes unable to keep up with them. It was like watching a great battle unfold in front of me. Screams and moans and cries mingled with bursts of light and the sounds and visions of blows landing and bodies falling. And then the images faded and something else took their place. And that something else was even more terrifying.

It was blood. Blood that looked as if it had just

been spilled. As I watched, it started pouring down the cavern's walls.

If I'd had enough breath in my lungs, I would have screamed. But all that came out was a low, pitiable moan.

Then another sound came to push my panicked thoughts in a new direction: a roar that was nearly deafening.

I turned to my right. Where there had been a solid wall was now the opening of a long tunnel. Something massive was heading toward me, but I couldn't see what it was yet. I could only hear the sound. I stood rooted to the spot, attempting to decide if I should try my luck with the jabbits outside the door or stay here. A moment later, I had no decision left to make.

A wall of blood exploded out of the tunnel and engulfed me.

I managed to flip over so I was facing another tunnel where the blood was thrusting me. Up ahead, the tunnel ended. I was hurtling toward a sheer wall and my thought was that I would be smashed against it and die instantly. The roar became so loud I could barely think. And I suddenly saw why. The blood was cascading downward at the end of the tunnel. It just dropped off. How far down it went I wasn't sure, but if the roar I was hearing was any indication, the blood was falling a long, long way. And I was about to plummet over this edge.

I tried to swim against the flow. That turned out to be completely and utterly useless. The current was far too strong. I was maybe fifty yards from the edge, mists of red spray rising up from the abyss, when I saw it — something suspended across the end of the tunnel. I didn't know what it was. But I did know what it could be. My way out of this nightmare. My only way out, in fact.

If I missed, I was going to die. But if I didn't try, I was certainly going to die. There was an outcrop of rock to the left, just below the suspended object and just before the drop-off.

I timed my jump as best I could. I would not get a second chance. I leapt, pushing with my feet off the outcrop of rock, my arms and fingers stretching as far as they could. Only I swiftly realized it was not going to be enough. I hadn't pushed hard enough or jumped high enough. I kicked with my feet as if I were swimming and angled my left shoulder lower and my right higher. I stretched until I believed my arm had popped out of its socket. The abyss seemed to scream at me. I heard the blood crashing on what I supposed were masses of rocks at the bottom.

My hand closed around what turned out to be a chain. The links were small and shiny, and at first I was afraid they would not be strong enough to hold me. Yet they did. For far less than a sliver.

I fell, screaming, down into that awful chasm. When I thought my situation could not get any more terrible, I felt something truly horrible.

The chain was wrapping itself around me, link by link, until I was completely immobile. Now I had no chance of attempting to swim, even if I survived the drop. I closed my eyes and waited for it all to end.

The Chain of Destin

I FELL A LONG way. I don't think I opened my eyes the whole way down. Yet in my mind's eye I could see things in the bloody river as I plunged down past them. Faces came out of the dark depths to peer at me for a moment.

My grandfather, Virgil Jane. He loomed up and stared at me with sad, empty eyes. His mouth moved. He held up his hand and showed me the mark on the back of it, the twin of the one on the ring. He was saying something, something I strained mightily to hear, and then he disappeared.

More figures slid past me as I continued my descent. Thansius. Morrigone. Jurik Krone laughing and pointing at me. He shouted something that I took to be *Your punishment, Vega Jane. Your doom.* Then I saw Roman Picus with his fat, bronzed timekeeper, and Domitar sucking on flame water. John came next, looking lost, followed by my father, holding his hands out to me. And, finally, my mother looking pleadingly as her only daughter fell to her death. Then they were all gone. The swirling blood closed farther in on me, like giant, gripping hands.

I opened my eyes. I wanted to see what was coming. I wanted to face death with the little courage I had left. I hit bottom gently. It felt comforting somehow, like falling into my mother's arms. I was not frightened anymore.

I lay there because, well, actually, I couldn't move. The chain was still wrapped tightly around me. I held my breath as long as I could to keep the blood out. But finally I had to take a breath. I expected the foul liquid to rush inside my mouth and my lungs to fill like a pair of buckets. I closed my eyes because I just had to.

Several deep breaths later, there was no blood in my mouth. I opened my eyes a teeny bit, thinking that if death were really horrible, I would only see a wee slice of the horribleness, at least at first.

I looked straight up. The Noc stared straight down at me.

I blinked and shook my head clear. I looked to the left and spotted a tree. I looked to the right and saw a ragged bush. I sniffed and smelled the grass. But I was inside, not outside, wasn't I?

Then I very nearly screamed.

The chain was uncoiling itself from around me. As I watched, it fell away and then neatly coiled itself up next to me like a serpent. After a sliver of hyperventilating, I slowly sat up and tested my arms and shoulders for injury. I found none, though I was sore. I wasn't even damp. There was not a trace of blood on me. As I stared ahead, I gasped.

Stacks stared back at me, about twenty yards distant.

How did I go from plummeting into an abyss all trussed up ready to drown to being outside and far away from where I had been? At first I thought I had dreamed the whole thing. But you dreamed in your cot. I was lying on the ground!

I thought maybe I had not been in Stacks at all. Yet I had been. There was the chain as proof.

And I felt inside my cloak pocket and pulled out the book that most definitely had been in my locker at Stacks. I *had* been in there. The jabbits had been after me. I had discovered a huge cavern where an immense battle had been displayed on the walls, along with the symbol of the three joined hooks. I had been hit by a wall of blood and plummeted over the edge to my certain death. And on the way down I had seen images of Wugs alive, dead and nearly dead.

And now I was outside and my clothes were not even damp.

I'm not sure that even my brother's impressive mind could have wrapped itself around all that. I had to stop thinking about these events for a few slivers as I stood, doubled over and threw up. My knees shaky, I straightened and looked down at the coiled chain. I was afraid to touch it, but I tentatively reached out a finger.

I kept reaching until my finger grazed one of the links. It felt warm to the touch, even though the metal should have been cold. I gripped the same link between two of my fingers and lifted it up. The chain uncoiled as I drew it upward. It was long. In the light of the Noc, it seemed to pulsate, glow even, as though it had a heart, which of course it could not. I looked more closely and saw that there were letters imprinted on some of the links. Together they spelled —

D-E-S-T-I-N.

Destin? I had no idea what that meant.

I dropped the chain and it instantly curled back up.

But the thing was, it never made a sound. I knew that when metal touched metal, it made noise. But not Destin apparently.

I took a long step away from it, and the most incredible thing happened.

The chain moved with me. It uncurled and glided along the ground until it was once more within an inch of my foot. I did not know what to make of this. It was so unimaginable that my mind simply refused to process it. I decided to focus on my most pressing issue. I put my hand in my pocket and pulled out the book. A book was real, solid. A book I could understand. But because a book was real and solid, it also could be discovered. I pondered what to do.

I had to hide it, but where? I started to walk. I thought it might help me think, but I really wanted to put considerable distance between me and Stacks, and the bloody twin jabbits.

I had walked perhaps a mile, with the mysterious chain slithering next to me, when an idea skittered into my knackered mind.

The Delphias'.

I broke into a run and didn't notice until a sliver later that the chain was flying along beside me. Literally flying, straight out, like a long stick. I was so stunned that I pulled up, breathless. It stopped right beside me and momentarily hovered in the air before falling to the ground and coiling up once more.

Still breathing hard, I stared down at it. I took a step forward. It reared up as though ready to take off. I took another step forward and then a third. It lifted off the ground. I broke into a run. It rose completely off the ground, configured itself like a stick again and flew right next to me.

I stopped and it stopped. It was like having a pet bird.

I looked up ahead of me and then back at the chain. It hovered. Even though I had stopped, it seemed to be sensing my indecision. Could it have a brain as well as a warming heart?

I don't know what made me do it, but I reached out, grabbed the chain, looped it around my waist, tied a knot with the links to secure it and started to run. And that's when it happened. I lifted off the ground maybe six yards and flew straight ahead. I didn't realize I was screaming until I gagged when a bug flew down my windpipe. My arms and legs were flailing around me as I looked down. That was a mistake — the looking-down part. I pitched forward and zoomed right into the dirt and tumbled painfully along until I came to a stop in a crumpled heap.

I lay there completely still. Not because I was scared, but because I thought I was dead. I felt the chain uncoiling from around me. It re-coiled next to me. I rolled over and tested myself for broken limbs and blood gushing out of fresh wounds in my body. I seemed to be all there, just bruised.

I looked at the chain. It seemed remarkably calm for having just driven me into the ground. I stood on shaky legs and sure enough, it rose up with me. I walked, and it hovered next to me with every step. I was afraid to put it around my waist again. I was afraid to even touch it. So I just walked, keeping my distance. Well, I couldn't really do that. Every time I moved away, it moved with me. Finally, I just walked straight ahead and it hovered next to me.

Just over a mile later, I moved around the last bend and saw Delph's cottage. I looked at the sectioned-off corrals and fenced paddocks. The creta's huge silhouette loomed back at me from the far corner of his little enclosure. The young slep was sleeping standing up while leaning against the weathered boards of his home.

The adar squatted in one corner, its foot still attached to the chain and the peg in the ground. Its great wings were pointed downward and it seemed to be sleeping in a cocoon of its own body. There was no sign of the whist hound. I hoped it was in the house with the Delphias. Whists could make a racket when disturbed.

I pulled the book from my pocket and peered around. I needed something to put it in. The answer reached me as I looked over at the door in the little hillside. At the entrance was an old lantern, which I lit with a match from a box next to it.

There was a very odd collection of things inside. There were great piles of salted and skinned dead birds and small creatures, which I assumed were food for the beasts. The enormous skin of a garm hung on one wall. I gave that a wide berth.

There were animal skulls lined up on a large trunk, a creta's and what looked to be an amaroc's. The upper fangs were as long as my arm. On one shelf was a line of old metal boxes. I looked through them until I found an empty one. I slipped the book inside and closed the box tight. I grabbed a shovel from against the wall and went back outside.

I dug a hole behind a large pine tree and put the box in the hole. I covered it back over and then spread pine needles over the earth.

The creta was starting to stir in the corral and the adar's wings were now open and it was staring at me. This was a little unsettling. The last thing I wanted was the thing talking to me.

I hurried off down the dirt path and around the bend. I had decided to wrap the chain around my waist once more in case I met someone along the way. I didn't know how I could explain a chain flying next to me. Now that I had separated myself from the book, I felt both relief and concern. At least no one could take it from me, but I was desperate to read it too. I wanted to know everything that Quentin Herms had collected in the Quag down to the tiniest detail. I told myself that I would come back as soon as I could, dig it up and read it from cover to cover.

When I reached my tree, I climbed up. Settling down on the planks, I set my mind to thinking about things. I hiked my shirt and my sleeves up and my work trousers down and looked at the map again. The marks were still fresh and clear. From the map I could tell that the journey through the Quag would be long and difficult. It was vast and the terrain was harsh. It was fortunate for me, I thought, that I would never attempt the journey. But with that thought came a sudden depression that swept over me like a hunter's net before the kill.

As I slowly pulled my shirt down and my trousers up, I felt a slight tug around my waist. The chain was moving.

I jumped up and tried to pull it off. It wouldn't budge. I kept trying, my fingers digging painfully into my skin. It merely tightened around my waist. Duf had told me of serpents that do that. They squeeze the life right out of you.

Suddenly I stopped panicking. My heart stopped racing. My breath returned to normal. The chain had stopped squeezing and fallen limp. I couldn't believe it, but, well, I think it was simply giving me a . . . hug. A reassuring hug!

I slipped the chain off and held it up. It was warm and my fingers felt good holding it. I went to the edge of my tree planks and looked down. A long way, about sixty feet in fact. I glanced at the chain and then looked around to make sure no one was watching. I didn't think about it one sliver more. Despite what had happened last time, the confidence was there somehow. It wouldn't let me down.

I jumped.

I plummeted down, the ground coming at me way too fast. Halfway down, the chain wrapped tightly around my waist and I landed gently, the heels of my boots barely making a dent in the dirt. The chain was still warm and the links moved slightly around my waist.

I lifted my shirt and covered the chain with it, then drew a long breath and had an impossible thought. I might never take the chain off again. I looked around. I knew I shouldn't do it, but then again, how could I not? I was closer to fifteen sessions now than fourteen. I was female. I was independent and stubborn and headstrong and probably many other things that I didn't yet realize or didn't know enough words to adequately describe. I also had never had much in my life. But now I had the chain. So I had to do what I was about to do.

I took off running as fast as I could; I was light and nimble on my feet even with heavy work boots on. After twenty yards, I leapt into the air. The chain hugged me tight and up I went, straight up. I bent my head and shoulders forward slightly and leveled out into a horizontal plane. With my head up, my arms back by my sides and my legs together, I was like a metal projectile fired from a morta.

I soared over trees and open land. My breath came quick, my hair forced back by the wind. I passed a bird and startled the thing so badly it spun downward out of control for a few feet until it righted itself. I had never felt so free in my life. My whole world had been Wormwood. I had been rooted here, never able to rise above it.

Until now.

A view of the village spread beneath me. It looked small, inconsequential, when before it had loomed so enormous in my life.

And around Wormwood, like a great outer wall, was the Quag. I banked left and did a slow circle in the air. That way I could see the Quag all in one pass. It dwarfed Wormwood. But what I couldn't see, even from this vantage point, was the Quag's other side.

I flew for a long time and then landed. The sky was brightening and I figured it was nearing the first section of light. I needed to get John to Learning and then I would head to Stacks. I flew back toward Wormwood, landed about a quarter mile from my digs and fast-walked the rest of the way. When I got back to Wormwood proper I received a shock.

The cobblestones, which were usually quite empty at this time of light, were full of Wugs talking and walking in large groups.

I stopped one of them, Herman Helvet, who ran a very nice confectionery shop and sold things I would never be able to afford. He was tall and bony with a voice as big as his body.

"Where is everyone going?" I asked in confusion.

"Meeting at Steeples. Special called 'twas," he said breathlessly. "Just got the notice fifteen slivers ago. Got Wugs outta their beds, I can tell you that. Nearly scared me to the Hallowed Ground when they thumped on me door."

"Special meeting called by who?" I asked.

"Council. Thansius. Morrigone. All of 'em, I 'spect."

"What's the meeting for?"

"Well, we won't know that till we get there, will we, Vega? Now I got to budge along."

He hurried on to join what seemed to be all of Wormwood streaming out of the village proper.

A thought hit me.

John!

I hurried to the Loons and found my poor brother sitting in front of it, looking scared and lost.

When he saw me, he rushed forward and took my hand, squeezing it hard.

"Where were you?" he said in such a hurt voice that my heart felt shattered.

"I . . . I got up early and just went for a walk. So, a special meeting, then?" I asked, wanting to quickly change the subject so the shattered look on John's face would vanish.

"Steeples," he said, his face now full of anxiety.

"I guess we best get on, then," I said.

Many reasons for a special meeting crossed my mind as we walked.

None of them would turn out to be right.

The Impossible Possibility

W E CALLED THE place Steeples because it had one. John and I rarely went to Steeples anymore. Before my grandfather suffered his Event, and our mother and father went to the Care, our family would go to Steeples every seventh light and listen to Ezekiel the Sermonizer, always resplendent in his blindingly white tunic. It was not mandatory for Wugmorts to attend Steeples, but most went. Maybe it was simply to see the beauty of Steeples and listen to Ezekiel's voice, which sounded like wind rushing between stands of trees, with the occasional thunder-thrust when he wanted to make a point as fiercely as a mallet introducing itself to a nail.

When we arrived outside Steeples, Thansius's carriage was there. We hurried past it and inside. I had never seen Steeples so crowded with warm bodies. As we took our seats near the back, I looked around. The ceiling was high and laced with beams of blackened, gnarled wood. The windows were fully thirty feet tall and located on both sides of the structure. I counted at least twenty colors in each of them, more than I had to choose from at Stacks. There were Wug figures embedded in them, looking properly pious. And there were beasts represented here too, I guess to show the evil of what was around us. I shivered as I saw a jabbit that took up nearly the entire length of one window. As I stared at it, I could only think that it was far more horrible for real than it was re-created in glass and color and placed in a wall.

There was a high altar at the front of Steeples with a carved wooden lectern in the center of it. Behind the lectern, against the wall, was a face chiseled into the stone of the wall. This was Alvis Alcumus, who was said to have founded Wormwood. Yet if he founded the place, that meant he had come from some other place. I mentioned this once at Learning, and I thought the Preceptor was going to have me committed to the Care.

I could see Thansius and Morrigone seated next to the lectern. As I continued to look around, it seemed to me that all of Wormwood was here, even Delph and Duf near the back on the right. And even those sentenced to Valhall were here, with their hands bound with thick leather cords and with the short-statured Nida standing next to them, fortunately without the great shuck.

The Sermonizer stepped out from behind a screen of embroidered fabric that I had actually had a hand in making at Stacks.

Ezekiel was neither tall nor short. He was not broad-shouldered like Thansius. He did not have large arms or a chest like the Dactyls, and there was no reason he should. I was sure he was quite muscular of brain and sinewy of spirit.

Ezekiel paused to bow deeply to Thansius and then Morrigone before taking his place at the lectern. His tunic was the whitest white I had ever seen. It was like looking at a cloud. It was whiter even than Morrigone's robe.

He raised his hands to the ceiling and we all settled down. John snuggled next to me and I put my arm protectively around his shoulders. His body was hot and I could tell there was considerable fear in his small chest. I could hear his heart hammering.

Ezekiel cleared his throat impressively.

"I thank all my fellow Wugmorts for coming this light," he began. "Now let us incant."

Which of course meant let *him* incant while we sat silently and listened to his practiced eloquence. Listening to a sermonizer who above all loves to hear himself sermonize is about as much fun as having your toes sheared off by an amaroc. All bowed their heads, except me. I didn't like looking down. That gave someone the opportunity to get the drop on me. And Cletus Loon was sitting perilously close by and had already glanced sideways at me twice, each time with a nasty grin.

Ezekiel stared upward at the ceiling, but I supposed far beyond that, to somewhere perhaps only he could see.

He closed his eyes and incanted long streams of words that sounded erudite and polished. I imagined him standing in front of a looking glass, practicing. I smiled at this thought. It gave Ezekiel a feeble dimension that I knew he would neither care for nor appreciate. When he was done, everyone lifted their heads and opened their eyes. Was it just me or did Thansius seem a trifle annoyed that Ezekiel had gone on so long?

Ezekiel looked down upon us and said, "We gather this light for an important Council announcement."

I craned my neck a bit and saw the other Council members

resplendent in their black tunics, sitting in a row in front of the altar and facing us. Jurik Krone was prominent among them. As I looked at him, he suddenly stared back at me. I quickly glanced away.

Ezekiel continued. "Our fellow Wugmort Quentin Herms has gone missing. It has been the subject of much idle talk and fruitless speculation."

Thansius cleared his throat loudly enough for me to hear it in the back.

"And now the Chief of Council, Thansius, will address you all," Ezekiel added hastily.

Thansius walked to the lectern while Ezekiel took his seat near Morrigone. The two did not look at each other, and my instinct told me one didn't really care for the other.

Thansius's voice, in comparison to Ezekiel's, was soothing and less ponderous but commanded attention.

"We have items of knowledge to convey to you this light," he began briskly.

I wrapped my arm tighter around John's shoulders and listened.

"It is now believed that Quentin Herms has been forcibly taken," Thansius continued.

There were instant murmurings. Herman Helvet rose and said, "Beggin' your pardon, Thansius, sir, but couldn't he-a suffered an Event?"

"No, Mr. Helvet," said Thansius. "It is well known that with an Event, there is nothing left of one." His gaze found me in the crowd and it seemed that Thansius was speaking directly to me. "There was *something* left of Herms. We have found clothing that he wore last, a lock of his hair and this." He held up something in his hand that I could not see clearly. But the Wugs in the front rows gasped and turned away. A female covered the face of one of her youngs.

I rose to get a better look. It was an eyeball.

I felt sick to my stomach and then I felt something else that erased the queasiness. Suspicion. Quentin had had both his eyes when I saw him running into the Quag. And I doubted very seriously that any Wug would have gone into the Quag to find these remnants. What was going on?

"And it was not a beast either," added Thansius quickly. He had apparently seen several Wugs start to stand and had deduced they would voice this next logical question.

"He was taken by something else that lurks in the Quag."

"Oi! What be the somethin' else, then?" asked a Wug in the second row. He had a large family, at least five little Wugs next to him and his female.

Thansius stared down at him with a sort of ferocious kindness. "I can tell you that it walks on two legs as we do."

A gasp went up among the crowd.

"How do we know that?" demanded another Wug. He pulled on a long stick bowl clenched between his teeth. The Wug's face was red and creased with worry. He looked like he wanted to hit someone.

"Evidence," answered Thansius calmly. "Evidence that we have discovered during our investigation of Herms's disappearance."

Another Wug stood with his hat in his hands. He said, "Beggin' pardon, but why offer a reward if something took him, see? We'd thought he'd broken laws, what we were told. See?" He looked at other Wugs near him and they nodded back. Several called out with hearty "Hars!"

This, I had to admit, was getting interesting. I settled back farther in my seat and stroked Destin under my cloak. It seemed to be made of ice.

Thansius again raised his hands for calm. "Fresh facts, that is the answer," he said directly to the standing Wug. The weight of Thansius's gaze seemed heavy enough to buckle the Wug's knees and he abruptly sat, though still looking rather pleased for having stood in the first place.

Thansius gave us all another long look as though preparing us for what he was about to say. "We believe there are Outliers who live in the Quag," said Thansius. "We believe that they have taken Quentin Herms."

Outliers? Outliers? What were Outliers? I looked around and found John's wide, scared eyes on me. He mouthed the word *Outliers?*

I shook my head and refocused on Thansius. Outliers? What rubbish was this?

Thansius drew a long breath and said, "These creatures walk on two legs and we believe that they can control the minds of Wugmorts and make them do their bidding."

Every Wug in Steeples turned and looked at his neighbor. Even I felt a chill along my spine. I suddenly realized that while it was true I had seen Quentin run into the Quag, I didn't know what had happened to him after that.

Thansius continued. "We believe that these Outliers are planning to invade Wormwood."

If Thansius had intended to incite a panic, he did not fail.

Wugs jumped to their feet. Youngs and very youngs started yelling and crying. Females clutched the tiniest Wugs to their breasts. Shouts and gesticulations and feet stomping sounded throughout. I had never seen Steeples so chaotic. I glanced up at Ezekiel and saw the deep resentment on his features at these outbursts in his sacred domain.

Thansius's voice boomed so loud I thought the multicolored windows might break under the strain of holding it in. "Enough!"

Every Wug, even the very youngs, grew quiet.

Thansius's gaze was deadly stern now. I had never seen him like this. I had forgotten all about Quentin Herms. I was just concerned about being invaded by the Outliers, whoever the Hel they were.

He said, "As you know, long, long ago there took place the Battle of the Beasts here." We all nodded. Thansius continued. "Our ancestors defeated, at terrible cost, an attack from the beasts that made their home in the Quag. Many Wugmorts were killed valiantly defending their own home. Ever since that time, the beasts have remained, in large measure, within the confines of the Quag."

Thansius let this sink in and then continued. "It has been an uneasy balance at times, but a balance nonetheless. Now, however, I'm afraid that delicate balance has been upset by the emergence of the Outliers. We must take steps to protect ourselves from them."

A Wug called out, "But whence did they come, Thansius, these bloody Outliers?"

Thansius said, "We have every reason to believe that they have been spawned by the unspeakable physical intermingling of vile beasts and other hideous creatures in the Quag, resulting in specimens of complete horror and depravity."

If he thought that would keep us calm, Thansius had seriously overestimated our capacity for terror. More shouts instantly started up. Feet stamped the floor. Young Wugs wailed. Mothers clutched their very youngs and screamed. My heart was beating so hard I thought I could see my shirt moving.

Thansius shouted "Enough!" once more and we calmed, although this time it took nearly a sliver to do so. He said, "We have a plan to protect ourselves. And it will involve each and every one of you." He pointed at us for emphasis. Then he paused again, apparently to gather his strength. "We are going to build a wall between the Quag and us, covering every foot of our border. This and only this will keep us safe. All workers without exception, from the Mills, the Tillers, Stacks especially" — here he looked at me — "will be employed to build it. We do not know how much time we have. While the Wall is being constructed, we will take precautionary measures, which will include armed patrols." He paused and then delivered the next giant morta blast right into our heads. "But there is every possibility that Herms is not the only Wugmort who has been forced to work with the Outliers."

Once more, every Wug turned and looked at every other Wug. Their suspicious glances were clear enough.

"How do we know they ain't about us already, these Outliers?" yelled one old Wug named Tigris Tellus.

"They are not," said Thansius firmly. "At least not yet."

"But how do we *know?*" barked a white-faced Tellus, holding his chest and sucking in one scared breath after another. He seemed suddenly to realize to whom he had raised his voice. He clutched his hat and wheezed, "Beggin' your pardon o'course, Thansius, sir."

However, shouts similar to Tellus's outburst went up. The crowd threatened to get completely out of control. I believed we were one punch or a single accusatory word from a riot.

Thansius held up his hands. "Please, fellow Wugmorts. Let me explain. Please. Quiet down." But there was no quieting us down. Not until it happened.

"We do know," said a firm voice booming above all others.

All Wugs turned their heads to her.

Morrigone was standing now, her gaze not on Thansius but on all of us.

"We do know," she said again. She seemed to look us over one by one. "As all of you know I have been given a gift. This gift has allowed me to see the fate of Quentin Herms. He broke the law and ventured into the Quag, and that is where the Outliers took him. They plucked out his eye and made him tell them certain things of Wormwood and of Wugmorts. After that I saw no more of his fate. But from what we found left of him it is clear that Herms is now dead. My gift has also given me the vision of what we must do to protect ourselves from them. And we *will* do so. We must never let them take Wormwood from us. It's all we have."

I was holding my breath. Along with every other Wug.

We all released our collective breaths at the same time and it turned into a cheer.

Morrigone raised her fist to the beautiful Steeples ceiling. "For Wormwood."

"For Wormwood," we all cheered back.

And despite all my misgivings, I was among the loudest.

Morrigone Calls

OUTSIDE STEEPLES, I saw Cletus Loon and two of his male Wug chums taunting Delph, making moronic faces and talking in the halting way he does.

"D-D-Delph s-s-smelts," cried out one of the gits.

Cletus said, "Seen better-looking faces on the back of a creta."

Duf roared, "Get away from here, you heathens. Right outside Steeples no less. Bloody Alvis Alcumus turning in his box, no doubt. Har!"

He grabbed Delph's arm and pulled him along.

I just happened to walk next to Cletus, and my foot just happened to reach out and trip him. He fell facedown in the dirt. When he rolled over and tried to get up, I put one of my boots squarely on his chest and held him down.

"You try that again, Cletus Loon, my boot will end up in a place the light never sees." I removed my boot and walked on. He and his mates raced past, calling me names so bad that I finally had to cover John's ears.

It had been hot in Steeples, but the air outside was cool and damp. I even shivered as we walked along. I took John to Learning and then worked all light at Stacks. It was a curious light for all Stackers. We did our jobs, but no one's mind, I could tell, was on their tasks. At mid-light meal in the common room, all the discussion was focused of course on the Outliers. I said nothing and listened a great deal. To a Wug, they were all behind Morrigone and the plan to build the Wall. While I had doubts, Morrigone had made a convincing case for protecting ourselves.

When John and I walked to our digs after Learning, the Loons were holding what looked like a war meeting at the table in the main room. Cacus had a knife lying close to hand. Cletus was eyeing it greedily, and then he glanced venomously at me.

As we passed by him, I made a show of taking my cutting knife from my pocket and examining its sharpness. And then I wielded it expertly, making tricky maneuvers with the blade and tossing and catching it in a blur of speed. Then I tossed it ten feet, point first into the wall. As I wrenched it free, I glanced over and caught him watching me, wide-eyed.

While I put my knife away, I noticed something was off. There was no smell of food cooking. And there was no heat coming from the kitchen.

"Aren't we having a night meal?" I asked.

Loon looked at me like I was gonked. "After what we bloody heard this light at Steeples? Outliers coming to kill us? Eat our young? Who can think of food at a time like this, eh, you prat?"

"I can," I exclaimed as my belly gave a painful rumble. "We can hardly put up a fight against the Outliers if our bellies are empty." I looked at Cletus and saw the crumbs of bread on his lip and a smear of what looked to be chicken grease on his chin.

"And it looks like you lot ate," I said angrily.

Hestia started to rise. I was sure she was going to go to the kitchen to make us a meal. But Loon put a restraining hand on her arm. "You sit, female. Now."

She sat, not looking at me.

I glared at Loon and Cletus for a half sliver longer and then led John back outside, slamming the door after us. On the cobblestone, other Wugs were standing around talking in small groups. John and I found a private spot and sat down. It was raw and clammy out, and a chill settled in my weary bones as if they were being immersed in cold water.

John said, "Outliers?"

I nodded.

John rested his chin on his bony knees. "I'm scared, Vega."

I put an arm around his shoulders. "Me too. But being scared and being paralyzed are two different things. If we work together, we'll be okay. The Outliers will not get to us."

I pulled my tin box from my cloak and opened it. Inside was some food I had bartered for earlier. It was meant to be for next light meal, but that wouldn't work now. "Eat what you want, John," I said.

"What about you?"

"I had my meal at Stacks, so I'm not really hungry. Go on."

This was a lie but there was hardly enough food for him.

I stiffened when I saw the carriage coming. It stopped right where we sat. Despite the chill, the flanks of the sleps were heavy with sweat. Bogle must have pushed them hard. The door opened and I expected to see Thansius step out. Instead, it was Morrigone.

John and I hastily stood. It seemed disrespectful to sit in her presence. Over her white robe she wore a red cloak that very nearly matched her hair. *Blood on blood*, I thought. She looked at me and then at John and then down at the insignificant meal in my tin box. When she looked back up, her cheeks were tinged with pink.

"Would you like to come and take supper with me at my home?"

John simply gaped at her. I did likewise.

"Come, it would be both my desire and privilege." She held open the carriage door and motioned for us to step inside. As we did, I caught the gaze of the many Wugs who were watching us, openmouthed. That included all the Loons, who had come outside. Cletus Loon, in particular, shot a look of pure malice at me.

We already had been inside this carriage once before with Thansius, but our wonderment was still freshly obvious as we gazed at the rich trappings.

Morrigone smiled and said, "It is quite beautiful, isn't it?"

Bogle whipped up the sleps and off we went. We had never actually traveled in the carriage: We had merely sat in it. I was surprised at how fast and smooth the ride was. I looked out at the lantern-lit windows of Wormwood rushing by as the sleps moved in perfect synchronicity with one another.

Morrigone was very private, and no Wug knew very

much about her, but I knew her home was set off the road north of Wormwood proper.

The carriage rounded one last bend, where the road became crushed gravel, and a sliver later there appeared the set of massive metal gates. These parted on their own somehow, and the carriage swept through. All I could see on the wrought iron gates was the letter M.

When I turned back, Morrigone was watching me closely.

"I've seen where you live," I said haltingly. "But just through the gates as I was passing by. It's very beautiful."

She continued to watch me closely. "When you were a very young?" she asked.

I nodded. "I was with my father."

She looked relieved for some reason and nodded. "Thank you. It is a wonderful place to live." She glanced over at John, who was scrunched so far down in the corner of the carriage as to have almost become part of the cushioned seat. "The time grows late," she said. "We will have our meal and then we can talk through matters."

I gaped. What matters needed talking through with Wugs like us?

The carriage stopped and she reached across and opened the door. She stepped out first and we followed, with me last. I actually had to pull John up and push him out.

The house itself was large and magnificent. Compared to what else was in Wormwood, it was like a crystal vase set among rubbish. It was made of stone and brick and timber but it didn't look jumbled; it looked as though there could be no more perfect way to meld these disparate elements together. The front door was large and made of wood as thick as the width of my hand. As we neared it, the door opened. I was startled by this occurrence, although the heavy gates had done the same.

And then I saw a Wug revealed behind the door. I had glimpsed him once before on the cobblestones of Wormwood, although I didn't know his name. He bowed to Morrigone and then led us down a long hallway illuminated by torches set in bronzed holders. There were large paintings on the wall. And a looking glass hung there as well. The wooden frame was of creatures twisted into different shapes.

Then I noticed a pair of silver candleholders on the wall.

"I worked on those at Stacks," I exclaimed.

She nodded. "I know you did. They are extraordinarily lovely. One of my prized possessions."

I beamed at this praise as we continued down the hall.

My feet sank into thick rugs awash in lovely colors. We passed several rooms, including one that I could see through the open doorway. This was obviously the library since it had books from the floor to the ceiling; a fire burned in a massive stone fireplace. It had a large chimneypiece fashioned from what I knew to be marble. A suit of dark armor taller than I was stood next to the door to this room. Morrigone, I realized, was minted indeed.

As I looked at the armor, I said, "Will we need to start making these in preparation for being invaded by the Outliers?"

She gazed at me with far more scrutiny than the

query probably deserved. For my part, I kept my features unreadable.

"I think our plans for the Wall will be sufficient, Vega, but I rule nothing out."

As we reached the end of the hall, Morrigone, her gaze sweeping briefly over our less-than-clean appearances, said, "William will show you where you can, um, tidy up a bit before we take our meal?"

William was obviously the Wug escorting us. Short and amply fed, and wearing overly clean clothes, with skin that was as smooth and pristine as his garments, he motioned for us to follow him as Morrigone set off down another passageway.

William showed us to a door. I stared blankly at it, not knowing what to do. He opened it and said, "Hot water tap on the left, cold water tap on the right. Matters of a personal nature right where it looks to be," he added, pointing at the device set against one wall. "Meal is awaiting, so no loitering about." Then he gave us each a shove into the room and closed the door behind us.

The room was small and well illuminated. There was a white bowl with pipes against one wall. Against another wall was the toilet where you could sit down or stand up to do your personal business, as William had said.

Our personal business was normally done in the loo located in a shack behind the Loons. The pipes we used were next to it. There was no hot water, only the freezing variety that came out most times at little more than a trickle.

Here were thick cloths and a white cleaning bar set next to the bowl. I had seen one of those at hospital. Most Wugs just used the suds flakes you could get cheap at a shop on the High Street.

I looked at John, who did not appear capable of movement. So I stepped up to the bowl and turned on the left tap. Water flowed out with good pressure. I put my hands under it. It was warm! I picked up the cleaning bar and rubbed it across my palms. The grime came off. I wiped my face and then washed it all off with the water. I hesitated and then grabbed one of the cloths and dried myself.

I motioned to John to come and do what I had done.

When I put the cloth down, I could see that it was black with my freed dirt. As I stared at the soiled cloth, I felt shame for having besmirched something so pristine of Morrigone's.

While John was using the pipes, I stared at the looking glass hung above the bowl. Myself looked back at myself. I had not seen my reflection for some time. It was not a pleasing sight. My face was a bit cleaner because of the bar and water, but my hair was all over the place, looking like an untidy stack of hay. I would have to give myself a hack soon.

My gaze then flitted over my clothes. They were filthy. I felt truly embarrassed to be in this remarkable place. I was unworthy to ride in the elegant carriage. I was too unclean even to ride on one of the majestic sleps.

I self-consciously rubbed at a dirt spot on my cheek that the water and cleaner had missed. My nose looked funny too, I thought. And my eyes appeared mismatched, one slightly larger and higher placed than its neighbor. In the light in here, my eyes looked more silver than blue.

I opened my mouth and counted my teeth. My mother used to do this with me as a very young. We would skip over the gaps where my very young teeth had fallen out and continue on. She made a game and a song out of it.

Tap, tap, tap, leap over the gap.

Smile big and wide, as you have nothing to hide.

John pulled on my arm. I looked down at his clean face as both the lyrics and my mum's face faded from my mind.

"I'm done, Vega," he said, his fear obviously gone and replaced with something even more powerful. "Can we go eat?"

A Night of Queries

WILLIAM WAS WAITING for us outside the door. Still ashamed of my appearance, I kept my gaze down as we followed him along another hall. But I couldn't resist snatching a glance here and there. I wondered how large Morrigone's home was.

William opened another door and ushered us in. "Madame Morrigone, your guests," he announced.

The room alone was about six yards long and eight yards wide, far bigger than our digs at the Loons, where six Wugs slept together on tiny cots that had the firmness of a bowl of mush. It was no wonder I always woke with aches and pains.

Morrigone was already seated. She had taken off her cloak. Underneath was the impossibly white robe she had worn at Steeples.

"Please come and sit," she said pleasantly.

We did as she asked, though after seeing how dirty and disheveled I was, I could no longer meet her eye. What occurred next was something I would never forget. A female Wug dressed in crisply ironed black-and-white clothing appeared and put a bowl in front of me with steam rising off it. She did the same with John and Morrigone.

"Hearty soup will help fight off the chill of the night,"

said Morrigone. She picked up her spoon and dipped it into the soup that had been set before her.

We did not, as a matter of course, use utensils at the Loons, but my parents had done so, and John and I knew how to use them. We were a bit rusty, though, and it showed when I dribbled a bit of soup onto the table and looked horrified.

The female merely stepped forward and dabbed it away with a cloth.

After the soup came cheeses. After the cheeses came breads. After the breads came greens. And after the greens came a side of cow that melted on my fork and then in my mouth along with round potatoes, ears of corn and green sprouts that were warm and tasted far better than they looked. Tiller fare rarely made its way to the Loons. We might get a few corn kernels and a bit of potato, enough for a mouthful, but that was all. I had seen ears of corn when the Tillers piled them in their cart. I had never had one on a plate in front of me. I watched Morrigone closely to see how to properly eat it.

John's face was hovering so close to his plate that I could barely spot the food disappearing into his mouth. Morrigone had to show him that the part of the ear in which the corn kernels were imbedded was not actually edible. John was not embarrassed by this. He just kept eating as fast as he possibly could.

Males are males after all.

I too ate as much as I possibly could and then ate some more just in case I was dreaming and the feeling of being full would disappear when I woke. After the cow came plates of plump fruits and sugary confections that I had seen in the window of Herman Helvet's shop but could never hope to buy. I noticed John surreptitiously slipping a few of them into his cloak. I think Morrigone saw this too, though she said nothing.

When we could eat no more, John and I sat back. I had never eaten such a meal in all my sessions. I felt warm and sleepy and good.

Morrigone said, "Do you desire anything else to eat?"

I glanced at Morrigone, again ashamed to meet her gaze fully.

"I think we're fine. Thank you for such a wonderful meal," I added hastily.

"Shall we go to the library, then?"

We followed her down the hall. I marveled at how she carried herself, so tall and straight and graceful, and I found myself trying to walk straighter too. We passed a longcase clock standing against one wall. It gonged the section of time as we passed, causing John and me to jump. Most Wugs don't have timepieces, much less case clocks.

We settled in the library, where the fire was still blazing. I sat, with Morrigone across from me. I felt my eyes grow heavy because of the big meal and the warm fire.

John didn't sit. He walked around the room, staring up at all the books.

Morrigone watched him curiously.

I explained, "John likes to read, but Learning doesn't have many books."

"Then take any that you would like, John," said Morrigone. He glanced at her in disbelief. "Really, John, take whatever books you want. I've read them all."

"You've read *all* of them?" I said.

She nodded. "My parents encouraged reading from an early age." She looked around. "This is the home I grew up in. Didn't you know?"

I shook my head. "No one in Wormwood knows much about you," I said quite frankly. "They know you're the only female member of Council. And Wugs see you from time to time, but that's all."

"Your parents never spoke about my family?"

"Not that I can recall, no." I frowned because I felt I was disappointing her.

"My grandfather was Chief of Council before Thansius. This was many sessions ago of course. He actually served on Council with your grandfather, Vega."

I sat up straight, my drowsiness gone. "My grandfather was on Council?"

"He left before . . . well, before his . . ."

"Event," I finished for her with a frown. And I wondered once more about what Krone had said back at Quentin's cottage. Did Council simply use an Event to explain away some Wug vanishing? If so, where was my grandfather really?

"That's right," she said. "You really didn't know Virgil was on Council?"

I sat back, my frown deepening. I was so ignorant of my birthplace, my own family history. I looked over at John. He had pulled a dozen books off the shelf and looked to be trying to read them all at once.

"I was never told that much about Wormwood," I said defensively. "But I am curious about it. Very curious," I added for emphasis.

"Learning is not what it once was," she replied in a resigned tone. "Things that were taught when I was John's age are no longer taught. That is sad to me."

"It's sad to me too," I said. "Perhaps you can tell me a few things?"

"Alvis Alcumus founded Wormwood long ago, perhaps five hundred sessions or more in the past; no one knows the exact date."

"I knew that. But where did he come from? Because if he founded Wormwood, that means it didn't exist before him. And that also means he had to come from somewhere else." I had asked questions such as this many times at Learning and had never received an answer. I'm sure they were glad to see the back of me when I turned twelve sessions and my Learning experience was officially over.

Morrigone gave me an uncertain look. "It's not all that clear. Some say he appeared one light out of nothing."

"You mean like a reverse Event?" said John.

We both shot him glances. He was on the floor holding a book whose title was *Jabbits and the Jugular*. After nearly feeling their bite, I felt sick reading those words.

Morrigone rose and went to the fire and held out her long, thin hands to the flames, while John turned his attention to another book, entitled *Nefarious Wugs of Wormwood: A Compendium*.

I turned to Morrigone, hoping she would continue the discussion.

"My father suffered an Event when I was only six sessions old," she said.

"Where?" I blurted out before I could catch myself.

She didn't seem to take offense. "He was last seen down by the Quag. He went there to collect a particular mushroom, the *Amanita fulva*, which grows only along the edge there. We never knew if that was where the Event occurred. There is nothing left to tell you the exact location of course. There never is."

I went to stand next to her, gearing up my courage to ask my next question.

"Morrigone," I began, and my tongue seemed thrilled to say her name, as though we were longtime friends. "If there is nothing left, how do Wugs know it was an Event? If your father was down by the Quag, couldn't a beast have attacked him and pulled him into the Quag? If so, no Wug would go in to find him."

I stopped because I suddenly couldn't believe what I was actually saying. I had just spoken about Morrigone's father in a way that could be deemed disrespectful.

"Your question is a perfectly natural one, Vega. I had it myself when I was a young."

"And did you find a satisfactory answer?" John asked.

She turned from the fire and gazed at him. "Sometimes I think that yes, I have. Other times, well, it's not an easy answer to arrive at, is it? Why some Wugs leave us," she added wistfully.

"I guess not," I said doubtfully.

"Now I would like to discuss some matters with you," she said.

My heart started beating faster because I was afraid what she wanted to discuss was Quentin Herms. But once more, Morrigone surprised me.

"What do you think of the Wall?" She stared at each of us. John put a book down and glanced at me.

"Do you believe it a worthy idea?" she said.

"It is if it keeps the Outliers from eating us," voiced John.

"You said your vision had seen the attack on Herms," I said. "And that you could also see the Outliers want to take Wormwood from us."

"That is true."

"So what became of Herms? You said your vision stopped. But you assumed that he was dead because of what was found left of him?"

"My vision did not stop. What I said was a bit of an untruth to spare Wugs the horror." She glanced over at an open-mouthed John. "I have no desire to comment further on his fate. But Herms is no more."

I looked back from John to find Morrigone's gaze full upon me.

"You were there that light, Vega," she observed. "And while I know you told Krone you saw nothing, are you absolutely sure you didn't? Perhaps a glimpse?"

With a start I realized that with her gift of special sight, Morrigone might have seen what I had seen at the edge of the Quag. She might know I had lied to Krone. I thought for a sliver. When I spoke, I did so with great care.

"Everything happened so fast," I began. "The attack canines were making a lot of noise and there were Council members rushing around. Some of them were very near the Quag. Whether they actually entered it or not, I couldn't be sure. Perhaps I glimpsed one of them darting into the place. But surely a Wug would not stay there long, right?"

She nodded. "No, no Wug in his *right mind* would stay in the Quag." She looked directly at me. "It means death, be very certain of that." She glanced at John. "Both of you."

I looked at John, who I knew needed no such admonishment. He looked ready to fall headfirst into the fire, so shaky was he.

But something had occurred to me. "Thansius said that the Outliers can control the minds of Wugs. How?"

"It is not clear. They are foul creatures to be sure, but their minds are advanced. Perhaps more advanced and cunning than our own."

"So they can make Wugs do their bidding?" I asked.

She looked troubled by this question. "Let us hope you never have occassion to find out the answer to that, Vega," she said ominously.

I felt my face grow warm at her response and I looked away.

She said, "I trust you both will give all your effort to help with the Wall."

John nodded vigorously and I did as well, though not quite so energetically. He said, "What will the Wall look like?"

"It will be high, made of wood with guard towers at specified intervals."

"That's all?" said John, looking disappointed.

She focused more fully on him. "Why? What would you suggest?"

He said with great conviction, "A two-layered defense. Height can be defeated in various ways. What would be much harder to overcome is if we combined the Wall with another obstacle that would reduce the effectiveness of any attack against us."

I was impressed and I could tell by her look that Morrigone was too.

She asked, "What would this other obstacle be?"

"Water," he promptly answered. "Deep enough water to slow the Outliers down. If they are descended from beasts, I would imagine they are large and heavy, even if they do walk on two legs. Thus, I would dig moats on either side of the Wall. It would provide us great tactical advantage because it would allow us to control the situation and divide and conquer our opponent."

"That's brilliant, John," I said, marveling at how he had concocted this seemingly out of nothing. We had only just learned this light of the threat of the Outliers and of the Wall solution, and already he had improved upon our defensive plan.

Morrigone nodded and added with a smile, "Brilliant indeed. When did you think of all this?"

"When I was using the pipes in your room to wash my face. I saw how the water collected in the little basin. It gave me the idea for the moats."

My respect for John's intellect, already high, increased a hundredfold. I could only stare at him in awe.

Morrigone rose and fetched a book off the shelf and handed it to John. "This work is on numbers," she said. "I understand from the Preceptor at Learning that you like to work with numbers."

John opened the book and instantly focused on what was there.

However, I was wondering why Morrigone had queried the Preceptor about John.

Morrigone looked at me. "We all must use our strengths in these difficult times. And it is incumbent on Council to determine what the strength of every Wug is."

I looked back at her uneasily. Had she just read my mind?

Later, as we parted company, Morrigone said, "I would very much appreciate if neither of you talked about your trip here. I realize that most Wugmorts don't live at this level of comfort. And I myself find it more and more difficult to remain here when I understand the challenges the rest of Wormwood faces. However, it is my home."

John said, "I won't say anything." I could tell in his voice that he was hoping for an invitation for another grand meal. John was smart, but he was also a young male with a usually empty belly. Sometimes it was simple as that.

The carriage took us back, with Bogle of course at the whip. The sleps moved swiftly and in perfect coordination and we were soon at the Loons, but Morrigone's home would remain a vivid memory for a long time, as would the wonderful meal we had consumed.

As we headed up to our cots, John, who was staggering slightly under the weight of all the books he had brought with him, said, "I will never forget this night."

Well, I knew that I wouldn't either. But probably not for the same reasons.

The Start of the End

NEXT LIGHT, I walked John to Learning. He had stuffed as many of the books from Morrigone's into his tuck as possible. I knew he would spend the time at Learning reading them. I had loved books at his age. I still loved books. But Morrigone had not extended her offer to me.

I struck out for my tree, where I planned to eat my first light meal, which would forever seem trivial in comparison to the one we had enjoyed at Morrigone's. It was no wonder that she kept her living arrangements a secret. Jealousy was not a lost emotion in Wormwood.

As I walked, I touched the chain, which was wrapped around my waist and tucked under my shirt. A sliver later I ran into them.

I first saw Roman Picus in his greasy coat and dented hat. A long-barreled morta rode over his shoulder and a short-barreled morta was in a garm-skin holder on his belt. With him were two other Wugs, both carrying mortas and long swords. I knew both of them, although I wish I didn't.

One was Ran Digby, who worked at Ted Racksport's weapons shop. He was a mess of a Wug, one of the filthiest blokes about, actually. I would wager that he had never held cleaning suds in his hands in all his sessions. Racksport kept him in the back, building the mortas, principally because no one could stand the stench of him.

He looked at me from behind his great, bristly beard that was filled with remnants of meals eaten long ago. When he smiled, which wasn't often, there were only three blackened teeth visible.

The other Wug was watching me in quiet triumph. Cletus Loon carried a long-barreled morta nearly as tall as he was. He was dressed in some of his father's hand-me-downs. Whether this was done to make him feel like a full-grown male, I didn't know. But the effect was comical. My face must have betrayed this because his triumphant look changed to a poisonous scowl.

Roman said, "And where might you be headed, Vega?"

I looked up at him blankly. "To Stacks. And where might *you* be headed, Roman?"

He made a show of checking his fat timekeeper and followed that by an equally impressive gazing up at the sky. "Early for Stacks o'course."

"I'm going to eat my first meal at my tree, then Stacks. That's my routine."

"Naught ru'teen n'more," said Ran Digby, who followed this nearly unintelligible pronouncement with a great wad of smoke weed spit that hit within an inch of my boots.

"Outliers," added Cletus Loon, looking self-important.

"Rii-ight," I said in a drawn-out syllable. "But I still have to eat and, at least until Domitar tells me differently, I still have to go to work at Stacks."

Roman scratched his cheek and said, "Nae up to Domitar. Not anymore."

"Okay, who, then? Tell me!" I demanded, staring at each of them in turn. Cletus wilted under my confrontational gaze. Digby didn't seem to understand my question, so he merely spit again, and I watched in silent amusement as he misfired and the yuck slipped down his beard. My amusement turned to disgust when he made no move to wipe it off.

Roman said, "Council's who."

"Okay, has Council acted yet? Is Stacks closed?"

Now Roman looked like a Wug who had overplayed his hand. When he said nothing, I decided to go on the offensive.

"What are you doing out here with mortas?"

"Patrol. Like was said at Steeples last light," replied Roman.

"I thought that would be for lesser Wugs than you, Roman."

"If ya must know, female, I'm chief of the newly established Wormwood Constabulary. A powerful, high position worthy of a Wug like me. Thansius created it last night and appointed me to head it special." He indicated the others. "And these are my duly appointed Carbineers."

"Well, Thansius might have picked you because you have more mortas than anyone else." Then I looked at Cletus. "Do you even know how to use one?"

Before Cletus could say anything, Roman replied, "If you're going to Stacks, best get on. But after this light and night, every Wug must show proper parchment to the patrols."

"What kind of parchment?"

"Allowing them to go where they're going," said Cletus viciously.

132

"Why?" I asked.

Roman said, "Council orders, female. Way i'tis."

Digby spat to confirm this.

"And where do you get this proper parchment?" I asked.

"Aye, ain't there a brainer?" said Digby with another dollop of smoke weed going splat on the ground.

I drew a deep breath, trying to will my mouth from saying something that might cause a morta to go off in the general vicinity of my head. "What difference will parchment make to a bunch of Outliers?" I asked.

"You ask too many questions," snapped Cletus.

I kept my gaze on Roman. "That's because I get too few answers."

I turned and continued on my way. With all those mortas behind me, I really wanted to take off running before they could fire and later say it was a tragic mistake.

I could hear Roman's excuse now: *"She made a sudden move. Don't know why. Morta went off. She might have grabbed at it, scared-like, being female and all."*

And the great git Digby would have probably added, *"And what be fer me sup this night? Har."* Splat!

Later, as I finally headed to Stacks, someone was waiting for me on the path. Delph looked like he had not eaten or slept for many lights and nights. His huge body was slumped, his gaze on his brogans, his long hair hanging limp.

"Delph?" I said cautiously.

"Wo-wo-wotcha, Vega Jane."

Somewhat relieved by him using his typical greeting, I asked, "Are you okay?"

He first nodded and then shook his head.

I drew closer to him. In many ways, Delph was my younger brother too, though he was older in sessions. But innocence and naïveté had a way of upsetting chronological order. He looked lost and afraid, and my heart went out to him.

"What's wrong?" I asked.

"Steeples."

"The meeting?" He nodded. "There's a plan, Delph. You heard Thansius."

"Heard Th-Th-Tha-Thans — Oh, bollocks," he mumbled, giving up on the name. "Him."

I patted his thick shoulder. "You'll be a great help with the Wall, Delph. You could probably build it all by yourself."

His next words cast away my lightheartedness and riveted my attention. "Virgil's Event."

"What about it?"

"Like I s-s-said, se-seen it, Vega Jane."

"What exactly did you see?" I demanded.

He tapped his head. "Hard to say, all jar-jar-jargoled," he finally managed with enormous effort, and nearly choking in the process.

"Can you remember anything? Anything at all? Something he said?"

Delph pulled on his cheek, mulling over this query. "Re-red li-light," he said.

"What light? Where did it come from? What did it mean?" My mouth wouldn't stop asking questions. It was as if I were firing mortas loaded with words.

Under this verbal assault, Delph turned and walked fast away from me.

"Delph," I cried out. "Please, wait."

And then it happened. I didn't intend it to, but it just did. I leapt twenty yards in the air, clear over Delph, and landed five yards in front of him, my hands on my hips and my gaze squarely on him. It was only when I saw the terrified look in his eyes that I realized what I had done. Before I could say anything, Delph turned and ran.

"Oi! Delph, wait!"

But I didn't go after him. He was scared and he had good reason. Wugmorts, as a generally absolute rule, do not fly. I stood there among the shadow of the trees, my breath coming fast and my heart pumping right with my jangled breaths. Would Delph tell anyone what he had just witnessed? If he did, would anyone believe him? Of course not, this was Delph. No one took him seriously. I mentally chastised myself. *I* took Delph seriously and I didn't want anyone to make fun of him for simply telling the truth.

Delph had come here to tell me about the Event. I couldn't imagine the courage it had taken for him to do that. And I had chased him away with my incessant questions and my ill-timed leap.

"You git, Vega," I said ruefully. "You've ruined everything."

TWO NIGHTS LATER, John and I were eating our meal at the Loons. I glanced up and down the table, sizing up the mood. It wasn't that hard to do. I would classify it as somewhere between terrified and quietly resigned to being doomed.

Selene Jones was one of the happier ones of us, actually. I had heard that this was due to the recent brisk sales at the

Noc Shop. Apparently, Wugs of all ages were now interested in learning their future from Noc-gazing. I believed what they wanted was to be told that the Outliers would not come and eat them.

Ted Racksport also seemed pleased and for a very basic reason. Morta sales had gone quite through the ceiling. His workers were laboring all light and night to fill the avalanche of orders. I supposed that quite a few of the weapons would be going to arm the patrols.

And that brought me to Cletus Loon, who sat gazing at me with ill-concealed contempt. He had cleaned up somewhat and was wearing what looked like a rude uniform complete with a cap of blue. I knew he was trying to think of something to say to me that he thought might qualify as clever. And I was also fairly certain he would be unable to manage it.

"Scared you, didn't we, that light? In the woods? Thought you might start crying like a very young." Cletus snickered and gave his father a sideways glance to see his reaction. However, Cacus Loon was busily stuffing a whole quail into his mouth and apparently had not heard his son.

Racksport put down his mug, which I strongly suspected held flame water, wiped his mouth and said, "Used your morta yet, Clete?"

"Only on these quail for sup," said Cletus.

I was surprised by this and also a little worried. Cletus was apparently a better shot than I had thought he would be.

Racksport snorted. "Don't be wasting your morta on that. You can spit on them things and knock 'em out of the sky. Morta is overkill." He held up his portion of quail. "See, your morta metal ripped out the heart. Here's a wee bit of it here on me fork."

I looked down at the tiny bit of quail meat on my plate, thought about the even smaller heart that had recently been soaring along free and happy in the sky, and I suddenly lost my appetite. I looked next to me to find John having the same reaction.

Racksport looked at us, realized our dilemma and started to laugh so hard he choked. I did not rush to help him start breathing again. He ended up going outside and gagging for a while. In the meantime, I led John up to our room.

I glanced at him as he sat on his cot and opened one of Morrigone's books.

"Good reading, John?" I asked.

He nodded absently and bent lower to the page.

Rain had started coming down so hard I felt wet even though I was inside. I lay back on my cot, turned to the side and stared at John, who was wholly devouring the book he held. His eyes were flying across the page and then he would turn it and greedily search for more knowledge in the printed letters. That was the last image I had before I fell asleep on this wild and stormy night in Wormwood. I did not wake until John touched my shoulder at first light.

And the next lights would bring change I never could have anticipated.

The Taking of John

JOHN SOON FINISHED reading all the books that Morrigone had lent him. He piled them under his cot, and then the most astonishing thing happened. More books appeared. John had to stack them against the wall next to his cot, the column rising higher than I was tall.

"Morrigone," he said simply when I asked him where the additional books had come from. We were up in our room after last meal.

"Morrigone?" I parroted back.

"She sent them to me by Bogle and the carriage."

"How did she know which ones to send?"

"I told her it didn't matter. I just wanted to read."

"You told her?"

He nodded. "She came to Learning two lights ago, to talk to the youngs about the Outliers and the Wall."

"Why didn't you tell me before?" I demanded.

"Morrigone didn't want us to gossip. She just told us about the dangers and what was expected of us in helping to protect Wormwood from the Outliers."

"How did the youngs react?" I asked.

"They were scared, but they understood the part they had to play."

"Which is?" I was feeling more and more left out by the sliver.

"To do what Council expects us to do."

"Okay, what does Morrigone want *you* to do? Come up with more brilliant ideas for the Wall?"

"She just wants me to read, for now. And go to her home," John added quietly.

I gaped at him. "Go to her home? When?"

"Next light."

"When were you going to tell me?"

"I'll soon be twelve sessions and leaving Learning anyway. Morrigone said she was going to talk to you about it."

"Well, she hasn't."

Right then I heard the creak of the wheels. I raced to the window that looked out on the cobblestones. Morrigone was already getting out of the blue carriage as the beautiful sleps came to a full stop and tossed their noble heads. I heard chairs scraping the floor, hurried footsteps, the front door opening. I knew what was going to happen next and I decided it should occur on my own terms.

Cletus Loon was rushing up the narrow, rickety stairs as I was coming down them.

Breathless, he said, "Morrigone is —"

"I know," I said as I pushed past him.

Morrigone stood in the front room, with Ted Racksport and Selene Jones hovering over near one wall. Selene had her head bowed as though she were in the presence of greatness. Racksport looked suitably awed, but I also saw a glint in his eye as he ran his gaze up and down Morrigone's queenly figure.

Morrigone turned her attention to him. "Mr. Racksport, I understand that your workers are laboring very hard to fill the morta orders Council has given."

He smiled, sidled closer to her and tipped his grungy bowler hat that he never bothered to take off at meals. "Doing my best, 'tis true, Madame Morrigone. Now, if Council wants to pay a wee bit more, I could ask me blokes to work even harder, I could indeed. Just a matter of a few more coins is all. Council would never miss it. Seeing as how they were going to pay two thousand of them just to catch Herms. Eh?"

Morrigone's pleasant expression turned to flint. She stretched upward to her full height. "I think, Mr. Racksport, that instead Council will *decrease* the amount of coins it is paying you, and at the same time, we will expect your production to *increase* nonetheless. If there are bonuses to be paid afterward, I will recommend to Council that they be paid directly to your workers."

The smile on Racksport's face evaporated. "Beggin' . . . p-pardon," he stammered. "Did I miss a bitta somethin'?"

"*You* may have, but I can assure you that I have missed nothing about you at all. Attempting to profit off dangers faced by us all is repugnant. I'm sure it will be so to Thansius when I inform him of your disgusting and even traitorous offer."

Racksport's nine thick fingers clutched his seedy bowler as he whined, "I spoke out of turn, Madame Morrigone, truly I did. O'course we will take less coin for more work. Thansius, I'm sure, is busy. We need not trouble him with this bizness, need we?"

"What I need trouble Thansius with is no concern of yours. Thank you, Mr. Racksport, I must now move on to more pressing matters."

As she turned to me, I realized with a start that I constituted the "more pressing matters." The look in Morrigone's eye was now all business.

"Vega," she said briskly. "I require a word about John."

She walked back outside and I quickly followed.

Bogle was up in the driver's box of the carriage, but Morrigone continued past him and motioned for me to follow. We walked down the mostly deserted High Street.

"I trust you have been given your proper parchment to move about Wormwood?"

I nodded and pulled the sheaf from my cloak. It had so many official signatures and seals on it that even if it weren't important, the papers certainly looked it. "Domitar handed these out to all Stackers the other light. I am right glad to have it, with the likes of Roman Picus and his Carbineer lot patrolling and asking stupid questions of Wugs they know fully well."

"They are merely doing their job, Vega."

"That may be. But mortas in the hands of Ran Digby and Cletus Loon is a recipe for a cock-up of grand scale."

She looked at me curiously. "You may be right about that. I'll speak to Council about the proper hiring, training and deployment of authorized Carbineers." She stopped and added, "But now we need to speak about John."

"All right," I said, my chest tightening.

"At times of crisis like this, we must take advantage of everyone's special gifts."

"And what is John's special gift?"

She looked at me in surprise. "His intellect, Vega. I thought it obvious. You heard the ideas he came up with for the Wall."

"So, what about John?"

"Thansius and I want him to come and live with me."

I stopped walking. It felt like the blood had ceased moving inside me.

"Come and live with you?" I said slowly. I looked back at the Loons, and my heart soared. Trading that pit for Morrigone's home was a dream that I had never even dreamt. It was luxurious with plenty of food to eat, towers of books to read and proper fires and hot water in pipes that one did not have to go outside to enjoy. And then there was Morrigone to show us how to be more clean and proper and smart and just . . . *better* than we currently were.

"Your brother has a great many special talents, Vega, talents that need to be cultivated for the good of all Wormwood. That was why I sent him the books. That was why I invited the both of you to my home for a meal. I wanted to observe John for myself."

"When will the move take place?" I said, not really believing our good fortune.

"*John* can come at first light. I will send Bogle for *him*."

I was so excited, seeing all the possibilities of such an arrangement, that I did not quite comprehend her emphasis on the name *John* and word *him* for a sliver. The smile slowly slid off my face. "So only John will be coming to live with you?" I said, as my high spirits crashed back down like my first flight on Destin.

"I will take especially good care of him. I will teach him many things. He will truly blossom under my tutelage, I can assure you, Vega. He will rise to great heights."

I so wanted to say, *"What about me? Can I not blossom? Can I not rise to great heights with your fine tutelage?"* But I could read the answer in her eyes and I suddenly did not want to give Morrigone the satisfaction of seeing even more evidence of my misinterpretation of her offer.

"My brother has never been away from me. That may not be good for him."

"I can assure you that it will be very good for him. For one thing, he can stop living in that slop house that Roman Picus calls lodging. And the Loons are not exactly the ideal role models in Wugmorts, are they?"

"*I* am a good role model for my brother," I cried.

"Yes, of course you are, Vega. And you can come and visit him."

"Have you told John that I won't be going?" I asked dumbly. I hoped that she said no, because John had not seemed overly disturbed about the move. Perhaps he assumed I would be joining him.

"Not yet. I wanted to talk to you first."

That was actually nice of her, though it wasn't like she had asked my permission for John to go. But at least I had my answer. John didn't know.

She gave me a benign smile and added, "May I tell John I have your good wishes for this arrangement?"

I nodded, my mind largely blank and the lump in my throat and the ache in my chest so profound that I thought this must be what an Event felt like.

"Thank you, Vega. And Wormwood thanks you too."

She turned and walked back to the Loons, which was apparently too awful for John to live at but perfectly fine for me to while away my sessions.

I watched her tall form glide back to where John was with his books. A chill so deep that I felt I had been dropped into the most frigid of water settled into my skin when I realized fully that I had just lost my brother.

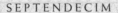

Harry Two

THE WORK ON the Wall had commenced in earnest. Whole forests of trees had been felled. Involved in this process were long saws and axes and cretas and sleps and backbreaking Wug work. All able-bodied males were recruited to do these tasks, while other less physically fit Wugmorts and some females started digging out the foundation on the ground where the Wall would be erected and also the deep moats on either side. Council had wholeheartedly embraced my brother's idea of a double-layered defense.

I continued to work at Stacks, but I stopped finishing pretty things. I was helping to build metal straps that would hold the logs and placement posts together once they were laid into place as part of the Wall.

Delph worked harder than anyone, his great muscles pulling and pushing and his lungs near to bursting as he dragged or carried heavy objects where they needed to go. I watched him do this when I was helping with the logs. We did not speak. Neither of us had the breath.

His father, Duf, led teams of sleps in bringing the felled trees from the forest to the Wall. His trained cretas were employed to pull on the stout ropes attached to strong pulleys that lifted the logs into place, their huge chests and muscled withers straining with the immense effort. I eyed the elaborate pulley systems and figured it might be one of John's creations. I had also glimpsed the setting up of what looked to be a complicated digging machine that I assumed John had invented as well.

The youngs brought food and water to the workers and did some of the tasks that required nimble fingers instead of muscled arms. The females kept the stoves burning and the meals coming for the hungry Wugs. All of us were driven to work hard by the idea that Outliers of incomprehensible evil might turn up any sliver and devour the entire village. And every seventh light we would go to Steeples because it was now required. Ezekiel warned us in a booming voice filled with fiery brimstone that to not complete the Wall in the shortest possible time would spell our absolute doom, and the bones of our youngs would reside in the bellies of the evil Outliers.

I'm sure that provided much-needed pious comfort and solace for many a Wug's frazzled nerves. I had never been at war, but I could sense that that's what Wormwood was becoming: a place waiting to be struck by the enemy. It gave me a better understanding of my ancestors who had lived during the Battle of the Beasts.

I set about my work with great zeal. Perhaps it was to show Morrigone that John was not the only capable member of the Jane family. Maybe it was to demonstrate to myself that I had some worth to Wormwood.

I rose before first light most times and was on my way to my tree with my tin of food slivers after eating a morsel or two at the Loons. I suppose as some sort of token of gratitude for John going to live with Morrigone, the Loons had been instructed by Morrigone to increase my ration portions, including a first meal.

"More food for the likes-a you and why's that, I ask," Cletus Loon had barked at me one night as I was heading up to my cot. "We males are out there killing ourselves felling them trees. And you're at Stacks probably skiving off most of the time. 'Tain't fair. Wugs are brassed off, I can tell you that."

"I don't skip work at Stacks. Do you really think Domitar would allow that?" I added with a malicious smile, "And I thought you were patrolling with your morta, shooting little, tiny quail before they can swoop down and get you."

"I work the trees at light and they expect me to patrol at night," he snapped.

"Well, it's good to keep busy," I told him and then headed up the stairs.

I didn't care about the fairness of the extra ration. I had been hungry for most of my sessions. I was not going to feel bad for a couple more mouthfuls of something in my belly.

TWENTY LIGHTS AFTER John had gone to live with Morrigone, I arrived very early at my tree. Our parting had been sad for both of us. John clearly had mixed feelings. What Wug wouldn't want to live like Morrigone? Plenty to eat, a comfy, clean place in which to live, books that he could read until his eyes and brain could take in no more. And to have a mentor like Morrigone?

Yet I knew that John did not want to leave me. It wasn't just the tears he spilled and the soft cries he let escape as Morrigone escorted him out to the carriage. It was the look on his face that spoke loudest to me. My brother loved me and I loved him and that was really all there was to it. But go he did. He had no choice.

On my first visit to John, he hadn't changed all that much. Well, he was scrubbed clean and his clothes were new and his body looked a bit more filled out. He had been both sad that we had parted and thrilled with the potential of his new life. John confirmed that the pulley and digging machine were of his invention. I marveled at how quickly he had been able to do such a thing. He had shyly accepted my praise, which made me even prouder of him. As I was leaving, he gave me a crushing hug. I finally had to gently pry myself free.

At my second visit seven lights later, a definite change had taken place. John was far less sad; his excitement about his new life and his important work for Wormwood was now paramount. He wore his new clothes easily and didn't seem the least bit awed by his luxurious surroundings. Morrigone fed me, but she didn't leave me and John alone this time. When I took my leave, John gave me a brief hug and then bounded up the stairs to his room to, as he said, "Finish up some important work on the Wall."

As Morrigone opened the front door for me, she said, "He is thriving. I hope you can see that."

"I can," I had said.

"Be happy for him, Vega."

"I am happy for him," I had replied truthfully.

She looked me over and then held out a handful of coins. "Please take these."

"Why? I have done nothing to earn them."

"As a means of thanking you for allowing John to come and live with me."

I had looked at the small pile of coins. Part of me wanted to snatch them out of her hand. "No thanks," I had said, and then turned and walked back to the Loons.

I now looked down from my high perch in my tree. It was still dark technically, although the last section of night always held edges of light creeping in. I gazed around. I had not seen any patrols on my way here and I strongly suspected that many Wugs were unable to carry out both hauling trees during light and acting as Carbineers at night. They simply wouldn't have the energy.

Thus, I felt it was as good a time as any. I backed up to the very end of my boards, took off running and leapt into the sky. The air enveloped me as I soared upward. I flew straight for a few yards and then I did a barrel roll, not once but three times, making myself a bit dizzy in the process. Still, it felt wonderful. So free, unlike down on the ground where virtually every sliver of my time was dictated by others.

I had gotten to the point where I could look down while flying without going into a dive and crashing. It was as though Destin and I had reached an understanding. Maybe it could read minds, or at least my mind.

I landed smoothly and stood there for a sliver or two, breathing in the cool night air. It was hard for me to be without John. I had looked forward to waking him up. I enjoyed walking him to Learning, and then bringing him food when I picked him up after Stacks. Though it was not pleasant for either of us, the time we spent at the Care with our parents had been a significant part of our lives. But that part of my life was over and I could sense it would never return.

I heard it before I saw anything. Four legs, moving rapidly. But I was not afraid, not this time. I had Destin, so I could take to the sky in an instant. I was also unafraid for another reason. The footfalls were not those of a garm, a frek or an amaroc. They were light, barely making an impression on the ground. I stood there waiting.

It came around one tree, slowed and then stopped. Its haunches went up and its long nose came down close to the dirt. I took a few halting steps forward, hardly able to believe my eyes. It rose up and then sat back on its tail.

"Harry?" I said.

But of course it was not Harry. Many sessions ago, I'd had a canine I had instantly loved. I called him Harry because he *was* hairy. He was not too big and not too small, with beautifully soft dark eyes topped by long eyelashes, and a mingling of brown, white and rust fur. He walked into my life one light and instantly loved me with all his heart. He trusted me. And I missed him terribly.

I was also the reason Harry was dead. I had walked too close to the edge of the Quag with him, and a garm had come after me. Harry had gotten in between us, and the garm had killed him as Harry defended me and gave me time to escape. I will never forget the image of my dead Harry in that foul creature's jaws as it carried my beloved canine into the Quag to devour. Even now, as I recalled this terrible memory, tears filled my eyes. When Harry had left me that light, I had screamed and screamed and cried more tears than I could have thought possible. It had been my job to take care of

Harry and I had let him down, costing my canine his life. I would never forgive myself for it. I would have done anything to bring Harry back, though I knew that was not possible. Death was irreversible.

Yet this canine, I swear, could have been Harry's twin. I took a few more steps forward and it rose up on all fours, its tail sweeping back and forth and its tongue hanging out of its snout.

"Harry?" I said again because I could not help myself.

The canine came forward hesitantly and then it broke into a run before skidding to a halt inches from me. Light was just breaking as the sun began its rise and the Noc retreated to wherever it went in the sky when its far bigger sibling woke. And in that first wash of illumination I took this canine fully in.

I touched its head. The fur was soft. It slipped between my fingers like the sort of exceptional cloth I had used in Morrigone's loo. It was warm and its eyes were mismatched, right blue, left green. Harry had had the same, but their order had been reversed. I had always loved the confluence of those two colors on his face, and I loved their looking-glass twins on this canine's.

I knelt next to it and took one of its front paws. It allowed me to do so with a hint of mild curiosity on its face. The paws were large and promised that the little canine would one light be large. Harry had grown to over seventy pounds, still far smaller than the hideous garm that had claimed his life.

Then I noted that its coat was dirty and I could see its ribs through the fur. It also had a cut on its left front leg that needed some sorting out. I scratched its ears and thought about what to do. I knew that Loon was not keen on beasts at the digs. At the very least, he would demand more coin, which I did not have. Harry had been killed a short time before my parents had been taken to the Care, thus I had never needed to face such a choice. It seemed that I was out of options. I would have to let him carry on without me. And it *was* a male, as certain parts of it I could see confirmed.

I rose and started to walk away. But he followed me. I picked up my pace, and so did he. On sudden impulse I took off running and soared into the air. I thought that would be the end of it. But when I looked down, he was right there, running hard and keeping up with me somehow. I swooped lower and landed, and he skidded to a stop at my feet, panting and his tongue hanging out. His blue and green eyes were fully on my face. He seemed to be wondering why I had just done what I had.

I opened the tin in my tuck and held out a knob of bread for him. As hungry as he no doubt was, I expected him to snatch it from between my fingers. But he slowly lifted his snout, sniffed at it and then gently eased it from my hand before devouring it.

I sat next to him and pulled out the bit of meat, a slice of hard cheese and the one egg that, along with the bread, was supposed to constitute my first meal. I laid them on the ground. Again, he sniffed at them before gobbling them up. His breaths lengthened and then he rolled over so I could scratch his belly, which I did.

When he turned back over, he nudged my hand onto the top of his head. Harry used to do that too. But maybe all canines do. Harry was the only one I ever had. I stumbled onto him in much the same way as this, walking in the woods and seeing him darting between the trees, chasing a rabbit. He didn't catch the rabbit, but he did capture my heart when there weren't many things in Wormwood that possibly could.

I pondered what to do.

"I can call you Harry Two," I said. His ears peaked and he cocked his snout at me. Adars can understand Wugmorts, but I knew that canines really could not. Still, Harry Two seemed to know that I had just bequeathed him a name.

I looked to the sky. First light was here. Soon, second light would be toddling along and it would be time for me to go to Stacks. I rubbed Harry Two's ears, letting my fingers slide up and down each one. Harry had liked that and I figured this one would too. He did, licking my hand in appreciation.

I came up with a plan. On the way to Stacks, I threw sticks for Harry Two to chase. And he brought them back each time. I scratched his ears and when we reached Stacks, I paused, bent down, pointed to Stacks and told him to wait.

He immediately sat down. I put down a small tin cup pulled from my tuck and poured some water into it from the cork-stoppered pewter bottle I carried. There was a tree above to provide shade. I figured if he were still out here when I finished work, I would worry what to do about him.

Domitar watched me walk into Stacks. He was now perpetually drunk on flame water every light. It was a wonder to me that the Wug could even stand. I think he wanted to say something to me, but apparently the dexterity of his tongue failed him, because he remained silent and simply tottered off.

After I put on my work clothes, I walked out to the main floor and approached my workstation. I eyed the stairs up. Ladon-Tosh was no longer guarding them. He was probably felling trees along with all the other hardy Wugs. I was one of the few Wugs left at Stacks. All but three of the Dactyls were gone, using their muscle to bring down the great trees and strip them of their bark. The ones who were left had to do the work of many Dactyls, to whack and gong metal into the requisite shapes and thickness for straps. There were a few Mixers left who were using all of their energy to ready the metal for the Dactyls. From the Dactyls the still-hot metal moved to the Cutters, who made the strips into the necessary lengths and widths. And then it was left to me to finish them. There seemed to be an infinite number of straps required for the Wall. That was testament enough to the enormity of the project.

During my meal break, I looked down at my right hand. Along with the scars was the ink stamp of Dis Fidus. That protocol had not been dispensed with even with the urgency of the Wall. I wondered why, but I had many things to wonder about and in my rough pecking order, the ink stamp maintained a lowly place.

I had two slivers left of my mealtime, so I went outside and was heartened to see Harry Two still lying in the grass where I had left him. I went to him and petted him.

"No beasts in Stacks," barked a voice.

I turned to see Domitar behind me. His face was flushed and his speech a little jargoled. I thought it a trifle ironic that he would not allow a canine in Stacks when jabbits were permitted to run freely.

"He's not *in* Stacks, is he?" I countered.

Domitar drew closer. "Is he your canine?"

"Perhaps. We'll see."

Domitar came to stand next to me. I moved away a few paces because the stink of flame water was so strong.

"I had a pet once," said Domitar. I was stunned when he squatted down next to Harry Two and rubbed his ears.

"*You* had a pet, Domitar?" I wondered if it was a jabbit.

He looked embarrassed. "When I was a very young of course. It was also a canine."

"What did you call him?"

He hesitated, perhaps afraid that I might consider him soft by naming a beast.

"Julius," he finally answered.

"Your given name?" I said.

"Yes. You think that's peculiar, do you?"

"No. You can name a canine whatever you want."

"What is yours called?"

"Harry Two."

"Why Two?"

"I had a canine named Harry when I lived with my parents, but a garm killed him."

Domitar looked down. "I am sorry for that." And he indeed did look truly sad.

"And Julius?"

"He died when I was still a very young."

"How?"

"It doesn't matter, does it? Not much matters anymore, not really."

When I looked down into his face, I was surprised to

155

see his eyes gazing out listlessly over the terrain in front of Stacks. He didn't seem a bit squiffy from flame water right now. He was a Wugmort who seemed totally lost, when I would expect Domitar to be as secure in his future as any Wug could be.

"Times are changing and Wugmorts must change with them, Vega," he said in what sounded more like a general pronouncement than specific advice. "But we must carry on here. No budge jobs ever at Stacks. Quality work through and through. 'Buck up right and proper' is our motto so long as I'm in charge here." He hiccupped, covered his mouth and looked embarrassed.

I looked over my shoulder at the entrance to Stacks, my curiosity, always close to the surface, compelling me to ask a question. "Domitar, what did this place used to be?"

He didn't look at me, although I saw his body stiffen with the query.

"It has always been Stacks," he said.

"Always?" I said skeptically.

"Well, since I have been alive."

"But you haven't been alive as long as this place has been here, Domitar. I bet it's hundreds of sessions old, maybe more."

"Then what good would an answer to your query be?" he replied.

The words seemed harsh, though truthfully his tone was one of resignation.

"Do you think the Wall will hold the Outliers back?"

Now he glanced up at me. "I am *certain* it will."

The way he said it troubled me greatly. Not because I didn't think he believed his own words. It's because I could tell he absolutely believed them to be true.

"Mealtime is over," he said, his normally harsh tone back in full force.

I headed back to Stacks. But when I turned around, I saw Domitar was still squatting next to Harry Two and petting him. I saw him pull out a piece of bread and cheese and feed it to my canine. I even thought I saw Domitar smile.

Times indeed were changing in Wormwood.

Home Again

WHEN I ARRIVED at the Loons with Harry Two, Cacus Loon met me at the door. He took one look at my canine, and his response was as coarse as it was predictable.

"That ugly, foul beast is nae comin' in these proper digs," he cried out in a voice made hoarse by his smoke weed habit.

I looked down at Harry Two, who was by far the most handsome creature of the three of us, his face far cleaner than Loon's, his coat far more reputable than mine.

I said, "He's a canine and they are acceptable inside Wug homes. I'll take care of him, and his food, water and cleanliness will be my responsibility."

"There ain't a chance in Hel of that beast staying in me home."

"It's not *your* home. It belongs to Roman Picus." I knew this would provide me no help, but Loon made me mad just by breathing.

He swelled up his chest. "Oh, so you think Roman Picus will allow that disreputable thing inside his digs, do you? Well, you clearly don't know the Wug as I do."

"I can talk to Morrigone about it," I ventured.

"You can waggle to any Wug you want, and the bloody answer will be the same."

He slammed the door in my face. I looked down at Harry Two, who gazed up at me with complete adoration, unaffected by Loon's brutish tirade. I stood there thinking for a few slivers and then decided that perhaps a silver lining had appeared unexpectedly from out of the darkness.

I went inside, marched up the stairs to my kip, collected my few belongings and stamped back downstairs. Loon looked at me dumbfounded, while a puzzled Hestia gazed at me from the kitchen doorway, wiping her coarsened hands on her dirty apron.

"Where you be going?" Loon asked when he saw the bundle representing all my posessions slung over my shoulder.

"If my canine isn't welcome here, I have to find other lodgings."

"'Tain't none," he barked. "Full up other digs, they are. Every Wug knows that. Stupid prat!"

"I know of a place," I shot back.

"Not on the High Street, not a kip to be found."

"On the Low Road there is," I countered.

Loon gazed at me darkly. "Are you meaning what I think you're meaning?"

Hestia meekly came forward. "Vega, you can't go back there. You're too young to live on your own. You're not yet fifteen sessions. That's the law."

"Well, I'm not giving up my canine, so I don't really have a choice," I said. "And I'll be fifteen sessions soon enough." I aimed a warm smile solely at her. She was totally under her male's rule, but she had always treated John and me decently. "I thank you for your hospitality over these last sessions."

Loon spat on the floor and Hestia turned and went back into the kitchen.

He said, "We'll see what Council says about this."

I stared him down. "Yes, we will."

I walked out and Harry Two obediently followed me down the cobblestones. Wugs here and there watched us go. I guess with a bundle holding all my possessions over my shoulder and a young canine playfully nipping at my heels, I made an unusual sight.

I reached the Low Road and we turned down it. It was so named because it was apt to flood when the hard rains came and it was also old and worn down. Its few shops were not as well perused and what they sold was inferior to what one could purchase on the High Street.

The plain wood-fronted home was tiny, nondescript and weathered, but to me it would always be beautiful and warm and inviting. I knew it well. I used to live here with my mother and father and John. We only left and moved to the Loons when our parents were taken to the Care.

I stopped and looked at the small front window. There was a crack from when John was a baby and threw his cup of milk against it. Glass was hard to come by in Wormwood, so we had never fixed it. I moved closer and looked through the window. Now I could see the table where I ate with my family. It was scuffed and covered in cobwebs. In a far corner was a chair I used to sit in. In another corner was a stack of family belongings that we never took with us because we had no room for them. Against another wall was a cot. The cot I used to sleep in.

I tried the door. It was locked. I took out my pieces of slender metal, and the lock was quickly sorted out. I opened the door and Harry Two and I went inside. I was immediately cold, colder than I had been outside. This surprised me, but only for an instant.

It was said that the spirits one leaves behind are always cold, because they are alone, with nothing to warm them. We had left much behind here. Here, we were a family. Here, we had something together that we would never have apart. That we would never have again, in fact.

I shivered and pulled my cloak closer around me as I walked the space. I squatted down and picked up some things in the pile while Harry Two sniffed around his new home. In the stack were odd bits of clothes that would no longer fit my shrunken mother and father. They wouldn't fit me for that matter, for I had grown much in the last two sessions. I passed over the clothes and turned to some drawings that I had done as a young. There was a drawing I did of my brother.

Then I saw the self-portrait I had sketched. I could see my breath in the air as I looked down at the picture. I was maybe eight sessions old, which meant my grandfather had been gone for half my life at that point. I did not look happy. In fact I was frowning.

I unpacked, found some wood out back and managed to build a decent fire using one of my two remaining matches. I opened my tin and had my meal at the small table. I shared my food with Harry Two, who gobbled his share down. Now that meals were my responsibility, I would have to work harder on collecting, bartering, selling and hoarding, especially with Harry Two and John —

I stopped my thought. It was just my canine and me. There was no John in the equation.

I ran some water into a bowl for Harry Two from the set of pipes out back. At first the water came out dark, but it quickly cleared. That was good because this was the water I would drink as well. After Harry Two gulped down nearly the entire bowl, I let him out to relieve himself in the dirt behind my new lodgings.

I pulled a chair up close to the fire and stared into its flames as Harry Two settled next to me, his snout on his front paws. This place had belonged to Virgil Jane, and on his passing, it had gone to his son, my father. We had abandoned it when my parents went into the Care, but I felt I had more right to it than any other Wug.

A knock on the door disrupted my thoughts. I turned to it with trepidation. Was I about to find out that our old home had been confiscated by Council? Or that because I was too young to live on my own, I would have to leave?

I opened the door to see Roman Picus standing there.

"Yes?" I said as casually as I could.

"What's got into ya, female?" he said as he rolled a lighted stick of smoke weed from one side of his mouth to the other.

"What's got into me about what?" I asked innocently.

"Loons to here is what, o'course."

"Loon wouldn't take my canine, so I had no other choice."

Roman looked down at Harry Two, who stood next to me. His hackles were up and his tiny fangs were bared. I could see he had excellent taste in Wugs.

"Givin' up good digs over *that* beast? What rubbish."

"Well, at least it's my rubbish."

"You're too young to live on your own."

"I've been living on my own ever since my parents went to the Care. Do you really think Cacus Loon looks after me? And John doesn't live with me anymore. I can take care of myself. If Council doesn't think so, they can take it up directly with me."

Roman appraised me with a cunning look. "Speaking of, ya heard 'bout your brother?"

"He's living with Morrigone now."

"Old news. Talkin' 'bout his promotion o'course," he added triumphantly.

"Promotion?"

"Oh, ya mean you didn't know?" he said gleefully.

I wanted to know what Roman was talking about of course, but I wasn't going to give him the satisfaction of begging for it. He ground his smoke weed stick with his boot heel into the cobblestones outside my door and made a show of pulling his pipe from his greasy coat. He packed it with more smoke weed and lit it, puffing contentedly on his stem until gray smoke curled into the night air.

"So his promotion," Roman began. He took two more puffs while he kept me waiting. If I had possessed a morta, there was no telling how many times I would have shot him. "His promotion to be special assistant to Council o'course."

I felt like someone had just struck me in the belly. But I swiftly regrouped. "He's a young. He can't hold a position with Council until he's much older."

Roman replied in a condescending tone. "Well, now, Vega, that's why they term it *special*. Parchment done and everything. Oh, it's official all right. Thansius pushed it through with Morrigone's blessing. Council had no choice, did they? Not with them two Wugs behind it. Up and down vote with all yeas, or so's I heard. Even Krone went along, and that bloody Wug don't agree with nothin'."

"And what does a 'special assistant' to Council do?" I asked, scowling. I did it because I knew he would keep talking and giving me details just so he could continue to see me upset.

"Well, you musta seen John going over plans for the Wall with the both-a them."

"I haven't really been involved in the Wall other than making straps."

"Oh, is that so?"

"Yes, that's so," I retorted.

Roman drew a bit closer but retreated slightly when Harry Two started to growl. "Right you are. Well, now they've enlisted him to oversee the whole blasted thing, haven't they?" he said offhandedly.

I looked askance at him. "I thought Thansius was doing that."

Roman shrugged. "Dunno. I hear it's a right puzzle, lotta obstacles, so they say. My head's too thick to quite unnerstand, but there you are."

"So what is John going to do about it?" I asked.

He pointed his stick bowl at me. "Well, now, that's the question, ain't it? I hear he's thinking 'bout the Wall and such. A great mind, so's I've been told. Good thing one of the Janes ended up with something up here." He tapped his forehead with his pipe.

"You're saying Virgil Jane didn't have a strong mind?"

"That's in the past, Vega. Just down to you and John now. You make a honest living at Stacks, but no more'n that. Reached your limits, haven't you? Now, John, well, he's got possibilities, ain't he? A future, you see. And after this special assistant job, with a bitta spiffin' up, I could see him one light sitting on Council, I could."

"Why would he want to do that?"

Now Roman looked stunned. "Sitting on Council? Why would he want to do that? Are ya out of your bleedin' mind? And you and your brother, the last of the Janes. Sad business. Sad business indeed."

"My mother and father are still alive!" I said through clenched teeth.

He dumped the dottle from his stick bowl onto the cobblestone and stamped out the spark and smoke with the heel of his garm-skin boots, then dipped a thumb into his belt and said, "Show me the difference 'twixt them and the dead. Corpses under sheets I call 'em."

I didn't have to touch Destin to know that it felt like a flame. But it couldn't be any hotter than I was. I could tell that Roman wanted me to take a swing. He had put his thumb in his belt because in doing so, he had drawn back his long coat to reveal a short morta in a leather holder riding on his belt.

I decided not to take the bait. Well, that's not entirely true.

"You know, it might be a good idea for John to sit on Council," I said abruptly.

"Glad you seen the good sense in that. Mebbe you have

a bitta brain after all, though I doubt it." He laughed heartily until he very nearly choked.

I continued, ignoring this. "He told me he thinks Council should run all lodging because there are some Wugs who take advantage and charge too much. I'm sure he'll share that idea with Morrigone, and she with Thansius."

Roman stopped coughing and his jaw fell nearly to his short morta.

John had never said any of this. This was my idea, but since I was female, it never would be taken seriously.

"You have a good night, Roman," I said, closing the door in his face. I smiled for the first time in a long while. But that wouldn't last. I could taste it in my spit, as they said in Wormwood.

I put another small log on the fire and then gazed around my new, old home. My eyes went again to the stack of odds and ends in the corner. I ventured there. The fire lit the room poorly, so I grabbed a small lantern from my bundle, lit its wick using the fire flames and carried it over to the corner.

Harry Two sat next to me on his haunches and watched as time went by while I methodically dug through what amounted to a history of my family. There were colored images of my grandparents, Virgil and his mate, Calliope. They were a handsome couple, I thought. My grandfather's features were vividly distinctive. There was a lot going on behind those eyes. Calliope was kind and bright and seemed to take great pleasure in seeing her family happy. I was quite her pet. And I would do anything for her. Yet her time was to be cut short, as it turned out. Calliope had succumbed to the sick a session before Virgil suffered his Event.

I finally put all of these things away and stared into the dying embers of my meager fire. I envisioned John, now firmly part of Council and, with it, the hierarchy of Wormwood, reading contentedly in front of a blazing fire in Morrigone's beautiful library after having had a sumptuous meal.

"Don't feel sorry for yourself, Vega," I said out loud, causing Harry Two to peak his ears. "Fancy meals and fancier titles do not really matter."

But for the first time, for the very first time, I was seriously contemplating leaving this place. No, *escaping* this place. It had been my home. Now I didn't know what it was. Or what was keeping me here.

Later, unable to sleep, I rose and put on my cloak. Harry Two rose obediently and stood beside me.

I did have *something* left in Wormwood, something of great importance to me.

I was going to see my parents.

Truly Alone

I STARED UP AT the hulking doors to the Care. It was long after visiting time, but I didn't want to be alone. I wanted to be with the family I had left.

I had already looked around for Non but hadn't seen him anywhere. The git was probably off patrolling as part of the Carbineers. I drew my tools from my cloak pocket, inserted them in the lock of the huge door, and I was soon on my way down the corridor.

The light was dimmer in my parents' room at night it seemed, though I could still make them out. Each of course was lying in their cot. They couldn't move. They couldn't speak. That was okay. I planned on doing the talking.

I stood between the cots because I wanted to address them at the same time. I didn't know where the words came from, I really didn't. But I was soon pouring out my heart to them, complaining of wretched injustice, poor Quentin, fiendish jabbits, walls of blood, lost brothers, insufferable Council members like Jurik Krone, vile Outliers, and Wormwood simply going mad on me. I told them I wanted them back. No, I *needed* them to come back to me. I was all alone. Then I ran completely out of words and just stood there, tears running down my cheeks as I stared at the two Wugs who had brought me into Wormwood and who had not uttered a word or moved a muscle for over two sessions.

A sliver later I was rubbing my eyes because I could not believe what I was seeing. My father's cot was vibrating. No, my father was vibrating. In fact, he was shaking so hard that I was afraid he would simply fly apart. When I looked at my mother, the exact same thing was occurring to her. I rushed forward to seize them, to stop whatever was happening to them.

I had to leap back to avoid being killed.

Towers of fire had sprouted from both cots at the same time. They rose together to the ceiling and then started to swirl in a circular motion, like a fierce, fiery funnel of wind trying to escape the narrow confines of whatever was trapping it.

I leapt farther back as the flames threatened to engulf the room, and slammed against the hard wall. My eyes were so wide I felt as if there was no space left on my face to contain them. I screamed. The flames leapt higher. I looked around the room for something to put out the fire. There was a pitcher of water on a stand against the wall. I grabbed it and hurled the liquid against the inferno. It splashed back in my face, repelled by the flames, though I couldn't imagine how.

I screamed, "Mum! Dad!"

They had to be burned to nothing by now, the heat was so intense. But still, I desperately looked around for something, anything, to use to defeat the flames. There was a stack of sheets on another table. I wrapped them in my arms, bent to the floor and soaked them in the spilled water from the pitcher.

I charged the twin maelstroms of fire, whirling the cloths that were now heavy with water. I was going to beat the fire out and save my parents. Or what was left of them.

I got no closer than a foot and a half when I was again thrown back toward the wall. I put out my hands to cushion the collision and they took most of the brunt of it, although my shoulder slammed into the hard wall an instant later. I slid down, dazed and sick to my stomach. As I staggered back up, it happened.

And all I could do was watch.

From out of the flames rose my parents. Into the air, up to the ceiling. They were not burned. They were not hurt in any way that I could see. As I looked at their faces, I fell back stunned. Their eyes were open. They seemed to be awake even as the flames devoured them.

I screamed at them again, trying to get them to notice me, but they never looked at me. It was as though I didn't even exist to them.

And then came a blast of wind and a shriek that was so loud I covered my ringing ears. In a blink of my eyes, they were gone. So were the flames.

I sat there slumped against the wall and stared at two empty cots that were not damaged in any way.

And yet my parents were gone.

I rose on legs that did not feel strong enough to hold my weight. I braced myself with a hand against the wall. My shoulder ached from where I had hit it. My hands were cut and bruised and my face and hair were wet with the water from the pitcher. The doused sheets lay on the floor. All of that had happened. But it was as though the fire had never occurred. I would have doubted that any of it had taken place, except for the fact that I was now alone in the room.

I looked to the ceiling, expecting to see a hole there where my parents had escaped. But it was still simply a ceiling and completely intact.

I bent over and sucked in long breaths. The room did not even smell of smoke. The fresh air quickly replenished my lungs. I kept a hand on the wall as I staggered over to the door, pulled it open and raced down the hall with renewed energy.

I thought I might see my parents soaring through the air and, with the aid of Destin, I could fly with them to wherever they were going.

I reached the front double doors, wrenched one open and hurtled outside. I looked to the sky, desperately hoping to catch a glimpse of them. Then something grabbed me and slammed me down to the ground.

I had no idea how long I had been in my parents' room, but first light was weakly managing to break through the clouds and the rain. Its dim illumination reflected off the rain-drops, making them seem dirty, misshapen.

Then I saw that hulking idiot Non standing there. He was the one who had grabbed me, pushed me down, cost me any chance of following my parents. Waves of rage swept over me, even as Non looked down at me, a malicious grin spreading over his face.

He glittered in the rain, for he was wearing a metal breastplate. Over his shoulder was a long morta. In his belt was a short morta and a dagger. He must have been on patrol.

"Caught you, didn't I? Breaking into the Care. Valhall for you, female. That'll teach you not to break rules."

I tried to get up and he pushed me back down.

"You'll stand when I say you can and not before." He touched the barrel of his morta. "Official Council business, I'm on. Lucky for me I came round here to see that things were okay. What, were you stealing from the sick Wugs in there?"

"You idiot," I screamed. "Get out of my way."

I jumped to my feet and he tried to slam me back down.

That was a mistake. An enormous one on his part.

When I hit him with my fist, I felt the breastplate bend and then crack under my blow. The next instant, Non toppled to the dirt. I looked down at my hand. It was swollen and bleeding. The impact had carried all the way up my arm to my shoulder and borne with it searing pain. But it was worth it, to unleash my rage, because I couldn't contain it any longer.

Yet there was Non lying on the ground. He was injured, perhaps dead even. I turned and ran. And then I took a few steps and my feet lifted off the ground and I was flying. I did not really intend this, it just happened. The winds buffeted me but I kept on my straight course through sheer will.

I searched the skies for my parents but they were not there. Where they had gone after leaving their room at the Care in a vortex of fire, I knew not. I just understood that I had lost them, probably forever. What I had seen was not something a Wug would return from. I sobbed even as I flew.

Slivers later I landed on the outskirts of Wormwood. I didn't want to add flying to my assault against Non. Surely

Council would have me in Valhall for a long enough time as it was.

Yet I was still thinking of my parents. How could two Wugs be engulfed in fire and not die? How could the fire transport them from where they were to somewhere else? And do so through a solid ceiling of stone? I could not think of a single answer to those questions. I just knew that my parents were gone and there was nothing I could do about it.

I set out for Wormwood proper and soon reached the cobblestones. I was not looking where I was going. In truth, I was so wonky that I was unsure whether all I had just witnessed was simply a nightmare.

When I heard a low growl, I froze on the spot. Though first light was breaking, the clouds and rain made it still seem dark and the gloom was thick upon Wormwood. The growl came again and then I heard a sharp voice.

"Who is there? Speak now or suffer the consequences of your silence!"

I stepped forward and saw him. Or rather them.

Nida and his black shuck, from whence the growl had come.

Nida was one of the few Wugs belonging to what are known as the Pech race. He was thus short and thick with heavily muscled arm and legs. For sessions I had thought Duf Delphia was a Pech, but he wasn't. Nida was dressed in corduroy trousers, a leather coat, a wide-brimmed hat to keep both sun and rain away and a pair of amaroc-skin boots. It was said that before he was hired to guard Valhall, he and his shuck had killed an amaroc on the edge of the Quag. If so, I did not want to tangle with either of them, for amarocs are fierce beasts with many ways to kill. Some say they can even shoot poison from their eyes.

"It's me, Vega Jane." I had apparently wandered near the prison in the village center.

Nida gazed up at me while his shuck sat next to him, as tall as Nida. He clenched a wooden club in one thick hand. "Leave here, female, now."

He turned and marched off, his shuck, a canine as large as a calf, obediently following.

When I emerged from the gloom, I could see that only four prisoners were currently being held at Valhall, which had a wooden roof, and bars all around and a dirt floor. Having the prison open to the elements was deemed to make it even more depressing. And being in public, one's shame was complete.

As I passed by the bars, a Wug slid forward on his belly and spoke to me.

"Cuppa water, female. Mouth's so dry, feels like sand, don' it? Please, female, please. Cuppa water. It can be from the rain. Just a cuppa, luv."

A crash came and I jumped back as something shot past my head. Nida had smashed his club against the bars with such force, part of the wood had splintered off and nearly impaled me.

"You'll nae speak to lawful Wugs, McCready," he screeched. "Silence or the next blow will be to your head."

McCready retreated to a far corner of the cage like a wounded beast.

Nida looked at me. "On your way, female. I will not say again."

The shuck barked and snapped its jaws. I ran for it.

And something was running after me. I turned and looked back, prepared to run faster or even take flight. But it wasn't the shuck. It was Harry Two.

I stopped and bent over, panting. Harry Two caught up to me and jumped around my legs, his tongue hanging out. He must have gotten out of my digs somehow and come looking for me. I knelt down and hugged him, and Harry Two calmed as quickly as I did. He licked my face once and then sat on his haunches, gazing up at me.

"You must be hungry," I said.

We walked back to my home and I fed Harry Two with the last bit of food I had. As he ate by the fireplace, where the flames had long since expired, I sat drenching wet on the floor, my knees to my chest, and gazed around the room. This was all I had now. John was gone. And now our parents were gone too. And with a sickening feeling, I realized that I would have to tell John about our parents. How would he take it? Not well, I thought.

And what would happen when Non told what I had done? Would I end up in Valhall like McCready? Begging for a cuppa water?

"Vega Jane!" the voice called out from the other side of my door.

I turned at the sound of my name. I also recognized the voice. It was Jurik Krone.

An Unlikely Ally

I OPENED THE DOOR, revealing Krone standing there. I could see that he was armed with a long-barreled morta and a sword.

"Yes?"

"You were at the Care this light?" he barked, the anger clear on his features.

"Was I?" I said dully.

He drew closer. I felt Destin tighten and turn hotter around my middle.

"You were," he said firmly.

"So what if I was?"

"Non has accused you of attacking him."

"Why would I attack Non? He's three times my size."

Krone looked me up and down. "But that is not all."

I knew what was coming. I waited for him to say it.

"Your parents are gone from the Care."

He leaned in closer so his face was nearer to mine. "What did you see, Vega? You need to tell me. What did you see there?"

I felt my fingers curl into a fist. I squeezed it so hard I felt the blood stop flowing to my fingers.

"I don't have to tell you anything."

"That answer is not good enough," he snapped.

"Go to Hel!"

"Do you want to go to Valhall for this?" he asked with maddening calm. "Or worse?"

He put a hand on his sword. I felt Destin turn ice-cold against my skin.

"Krone," a voice said.

We both turned at the same time.

It was Morrigone.

I looked around for the carriage but did not see it. It was as though she had materialized in our midst on the Low Road.

Krone looked perplexed by her appearance.

"Madame Morrigone," he said stiffly. "I was just about to arrest this female for criminal acts against other Wugmorts."

Morrigone drew closer, her gaze fully on Krone.

"What criminal acts?"

"She has attacked Non outside the Care. He has given evidence of this. And Hector and Helen Jane have disappeared from the Care. These are serious matters that must be brought before Council."

"Have you spoken to Thansius about this?" she asked.

"I have only just been made aware —"

She interrupted him. "What does Non claim she has done?"

"He caught her leaving the Care. He was about to arrest her for that when she attacked him for no reason."

"Attacked him? How?"

"Non says that she struck him a terrific blow and knocked him out."

"A Wug as large as Non was knocked out by a fourteen-session-old female," she said skeptically. "I find that very, very difficult to believe, Krone. And you simply accept Non's word for this?"

"You say that Non is lying?"

"You're saying that Vega is a criminal based only on Non's statement."

"Did you know she has taken up residence here, in her old home? A Wug under the age of fifteen cannot live by herself, but she does not care for rules, do you, Vega?" He glanced menacingly at me.

I didn't answer Krone because I was unsure how to. I looked at Morrigone, whose gaze held steady on Krone.

"I am aware of it, Krone. As is Thansius," said Morrigone in a low, even voice that still managed to carry more menace than his louder words. She stared at Krone for a few moments longer. "Unless there is anything else, Krone, I think you may safely leave us."

Krone stared at me and then Morrigone. He bowed curtly. "As you wish, Madame Morrigone. But I trust this will be followed up appropriately." Then he turned and marched swiftly away.

Morrigone waited until he was out of sight before turning to me.

I started to say something, but she held up her hand. "No, Vega, I do not need to hear anything. I will speak to Non. He will not refer charges." Her gaze dipped to my hand. I looked down and saw that it was swollen and cut from where I had struck Non. I hastily slipped it into my pocket.

"I am sure you had good reason," said Morrigone quietly. Then she added, in a more heated tone, "For Non is a git."

I was about to smile when I found her piercing gaze upon me. Neither of us spoke for at least a sliver.

She finally said, "I know there has been much change in your life, and that this change has been difficult."

"Do you know what could have happened to my parents?" I blurted out.

"I could not possibly know, Vega, since I, unlike you, was not there."

This statement split us like a wall of blood.

"What exactly did you see, Vega?"

"I saw nothing," I lied. "I went to visit my parents."

"At night?" she said sharply.

"Yes. I wanted to see them. I . . . I was . . . sad."

"And?" she said expectantly.

"And when I got there the room was empty. I ran outside and that's where Non grabbed me and pushed me down. I struck him to defend myself."

She considered all this and then said, "I ask you not to tell your brother about your parents, Vega."

"What?" I said, gaping at her. "He has to know."

"His knowing of their disappearance cannot help in any way. And it will distract him from his duties on the Wall."

"His duties on the Wall?" I cried out. "So we keep him ignorant of his mother and father being gone?"

"I can assure you that he is indispensible. I have given instructions to Krone and others on Council to say nothing. And all Wugs involved at the Care have been similarly cautioned. I would ask that you keep this information to your-self as well. Please."

Something struck me. "But if you've done all that, you knew that they had disappeared before Krone told you."

She looked a bit chagrined that I had deduced this, which boosted my spirits just a bit.

"It is my job to know such things, Vega. Will you not tell him?"

I couldn't say anything for a sliver while she and I stared at each other over the width of my doorway.

Finally, I nodded my head. "I won't tell him."

Her next words truly astonished me.

"I admire you, Vega. I really do. I can even say that I envy you."

"What?" I said. "Envy me? But you have so much. And I have nothing."

She said wistfully, "I have things, possessions only. You have nerve and courage, and you accept and take risks like no other Wug I know. All these things come from within you, which is the most important place of all."

I stared at her blankly. She was both looking at me and not looking at me. As though her words were directed at a distant place that only she could see.

Then her gaze settled squarely on me. "You are sure your parents were gone when you arrived at the Care?"

I nodded my head, not confident of my tongue to deliver another lie in a convincing way.

She nodded, sighed and looked away. "I see."

And I could tell that she did see, quite a lot, actually.

She said, "I hope, after all this darkness, that good fortune shines on you, Vega, indeed I do."

Then she turned and walked away.

I watched her until she disappeared from view. Then I looked to the sky. I wasn't sure why. Maybe to find answers I could never hope to discover down here.

Eon and the Hole

I CONTINUED ON TO Stacks, walking, not flying. I didn't care if I was one or even ten slivers late. If Morrigone was right, it seemed that I would stay out of Valhall. But I didn't really care about that. My parents were gone. They had left wrapped in a ball of flames. I had never seen anything like that in all my sessions. I was now really questioning who I was. And who they were. And what really was this place I called home. I suddenly felt that nothing about anything around me was true.

I had promised Morrigone that I would not tell John, that I would not tell anyone. Thus I had no one to help me with the grief and the confusion I was feeling.

At my table I took up the first strap that I would work on this light. It was many feet in length, very rough, and its edges would slice through bark, leather and certainly skin. My job was to smooth out the roughness. Then I would work in holes toward the ends of the metal. That would allow tethers to be used to hold both ends together after the straps were wrapped around a stack of planed timbers. It was difficult, tedious work and I found that even with my thick gloves on, my hands became cut and scarred as the strap's edges on more than one occasion tore through the glove's leather and reached my skin.

Roman Picus's taunting words came back to me. How I would never amount to much. How Stacks was all I would ever have in the way of accomplishments. How John had so much more potential than I. It seemed a trivial, even absurd grievance on my part after what had happened last night with my parents. But I apparently could not will my mind to focus solely on that. Emotions were difficult things to corral, like a herd of cretas with a fierce desire for freedom.

I sanded down the strap's edges and smoothed out the surfaces. I created holes near the two ends of the strap, using my drill punch, hammer and other tools. I knew tethers would be inserted in the holes to tie the ends together for stability. How it would all come together to complete the Wall, though, I didn't know. I was sure no Wugs knew except for a very few like Thansius and Morrigone. And now John.

During my meal break, I went outside and fetched a bowl of water for Harry Two from a nearby stream and then gave him a bit more food I had managed to scavenge, which he wolfed down. I sat on the ground next to him and stared up at Stacks. It was a colossal building and I had only seen a small part of it in my two sessions here. Yet I wagered I had probably also seen more of it than any other Wug who had ever labored here. I counted off the turrets and towers and floors and it suddenly struck me that it was far taller than simply two stories. This was puzzling because when I had headed up the stairs that night, they ended at the second floor. There were no other stairs. But that wasn't exactly right. There were no other stairs that I could *see*.

As I passed back through the double doors, Domitar barred my way. He did not smell of flame water this light. His cloak was reasonably clean and his eyes were clear, with not a hint of the redness the foul drink inspired.

"Just feeding Harry Two. Don't worry. I'll make my work this light. In some ways, the straps are easier than the pretty things."

"Well, there will be many of them," he said. "Very, very many, in fact."

"Perhaps you need to hire another Finisher, then," I said. "To replace Herms."

"There will be no other Finishers," he snarled.

"Well, if that's true, a raise in pay would be nice."

"This work is for all of Wormwood. You should be willing to do it for free."

"So are you forfeiting your wages, Domitar?"

"You will learn your place one light, female."

"I hope so," I said. Under my breath I muttered, "So long as it's not *this* place."

"You were nearly late this light," he noted harshly.

"I had a good reason," I said.

"I can hardly wonder what would be a good enough reason to be late to your job, particularly in times such as this."

I hesitated. Ordinarily, I would not convey personal information to Domitar. "My parents seemed to have taken a turn for the worse at the Care," I replied.

He bowed his head, something that surprised me. But his next words stunned me. "I think of them often, Vega. I pray at Steeples for their recovery. They were good Wugs. And may the Fates be kind to them." When he raised his head, I saw something that was even more shocking than his words.

184

There were tears in his eyes. *Tears in Domitar's eyes?* We locked gazes for an instant before he turned and left.

I felt someone behind me. For an instant I thought it might be Krone come to take me to Valhall despite Morrigone's assurances, but it was simply Dis Fidus.

"It's time to go back to work, Vega," he said quietly.

I nodded and returned to my workstation. As I passed Domitar's office, I could see his silhouette. He was bent over his desk and, unless my ears were deceiving me, the tubby Wug was sobbing.

The rest of my slivers at Stacks that light went by in a sort of blur. I must have worked hard, because when the end-of-work bell rang, all the straps I had been given to finish lay coiled on the trolley with their edges sanded, their surfaces smooth as a baby whist's skin and the requisite holes cut precisely as instructed in the parchment. I went to the locker room, changed into my other clothes and headed out.

Dis Fidus closed the doors behind me and I heard the lock turn. And that's when I made up my mind. I was going back into Stacks. I remembered the vision of the fierce battle and the torrent of blood that had washed me away. I remembered the screaming Wug on the doorknob. I of course remembered the jabbits.

But what I most vividly recalled, as I plunged into the red abyss, were the images of my parents. I needed to find out what had happened to them. I would not find out the truth from the Care. Or Council. Wormwood was not what it seemed to be, this I was learning quite forcefully. It held secrets, secrets I was now determined to discover.

A sliver later, Dis Fidus came out from a side door and walked down a path away from me. A bit later, I saw Domitar emerge from the same door. I crouched down low in the tall grass. Harry Two copied me. Once Domitar was out of sight, I said to Harry Two, "Okay, I'll be back. You stay here."

I got up and started to walk away. Harry Two followed me. I put out a hand. "You stay here, I'll be back." I started to walk again. Once more he followed. "Harry Two," I said. "You stay."

He simply smiled and wagged his tail and followed. Finally, I gave it up as a bad job. It looked like we would do this together.

I accessed Stacks through the same door as before. Harry Two followed me in. I wasted no time and made right for the stairs. I did not want to be in here after dark. I hurried up the stairs with Harry Two right on my heels. I found the door the jabbits had knocked down. It was fully repaired. I opened it and went inside.

I could now see that what had toppled down on me and revealed the little door was a suit of armor. It was all righted and shiny now. I managed to move it aside, again exposing the little door. Harry Two started growling when he saw the screaming Wug on the doorknob, but I told him to be quiet and he obeyed instantly. I closed the door behind us. At the same time, I braced myself for a wall of blood hurtling at me. I had already planned to use Destin to get to my parents' images in that abyss. And I did not intend on drowning Harry Two and myself in the process.

But there was no blood.

As I stood there, the cavernous walls disappeared and an enormous pit was revealed directly in front of me.

I felt woozy at this transformation. How could something that was right there no longer be there? How could one thing change into another thing? Stacks had clearly been something else many sessions ago. There was something in this place, some force that was absolutely foreign to me and every other Wug. Well, maybe not to Morrigone.

I looked at Harry Two. He was no longer smiling and his tail was not wagging. I touched his head and found that he felt cold. I touched my arm. It was as though all the blood had drained from me.

I squared my shoulders and stepped forward until I came to the edge of the pit. I stared down, unable to process what I was seeing. So stunning was it that I felt myself teeter on the edge. That's when I felt Harry Two bite down on my cloak and pull me away from the edge before I might topple in.

I composed myself and once more drew close to the pit and stared down again. What I was looking at filled me with both anger and hopelessness. For what was down there were all the things that Wugs who had long labored at Stacks had made. The ones on the very top, I recognized as objects I had very recently finished: a silver candlestick and a pair of bronze cups. I sat down on the ground, my spinning head between my knees, my stomach suddenly lurching. I felt like I was losing my mind.

How could all these things have ended up here? I had always assumed they were being made for the Wugs who had ordered them. I could never afford any of these things,

but other Wugs could. They were custom-made. They —
Here, my idiotic thoughts broke off. They were made so they
could be thrown into this pit right here. They had never left
Stacks. All my work, my whole existence as a grown Wug,
was in that pit.

Without thinking, I slammed my already-injured hand
against the hard ground, then yelped in pain. I grabbed it
with my other hand and squeezed, trying to stop the pain.
But it only grew worse. What a git I was.

I bent down and, using my injured hand, I picked up a
white stone lying on the floor next to the pit. I wanted to see
if I could form a grip. I could, barely.

I glanced at Harry Two, who stared up at me with a help-
less look, as though he could feel every painful thought of
mine. He licked my hand and I absently patted his head.

I had come here looking for answers about my parents'
vanishing. Instead I had found that my whole working life was
also a lie. The tilt of emotions was crushing, yet I fought
against it. I had labored at Stacks, apparently, just for busy
work and for no other reason. If so, why was it so important
to keep us busy?

I stood. I was here. I had found this pit, but I needed to
find more. Much more.

"Let's go, Harry Two," I said in a determined voice.

We marched around the pit and through a tunnel on the
other side. It eventually opened into a vast cave.

I looked all around. There was no other tunnel out of
here. There were just blank, rock-studded walls.

My frustration boiling up inside, I suddenly screamed, "I
need answers. And I need them now!"

Immediately, a movement came from my left. I wheeled in that direction and called out, "Who's there?" I blinked as a small orb of light glimmered from the part of the cave farthest from me. As I continued to stare, the orb grew and then transformed to a shadow. And then this shadow evolved into a small being holding a lantern. As it came forward and stopped in front of me, I looked down at it and it looked up at me.

"Who are you?" I asked in a quavering voice.

"Eon" came the response.

It had on a blue cloak and carried a brass-tipped wooden staff in its other hand. As the lantern light illuminated the thing calling itself Eon more clearly, I saw a small, wrinkled face that was distinctly male. His eyes were protuberant and took up a far greater proportion of his face than I was used to. His ears were tiny, and instead of being round, they were peaked at the top, like Harry Two's. His hands were thick and plump and the fingers short and curved. He was barefoot. I could just see small toes poking from under his cloak.

"*What* are you?" I asked, for he was clearly not a Pech like Nida, nor was he like Duf Delphia. He almost seemed transparent, as the light appeared to cut right through him.

"I am Eon."

"What are you doing here, Eon?"

"This is where I am," replied Eon.

I shook my head in bewilderment. "And where is this?"

"Where I am," he answered. I felt wonky again. It did not seem that reason applied to this bloke.

I said quickly, "My name is Vega Jane."

I held out my hand for him to shake, but winced with pain.

189

Eon looked at my hand, all battered and bloodied.

He pointed to the white stone I held in my other hand. "Wave that over your injured hand and think good thoughts."

"What?" I was growing convinced that Eon was completely mental.

"Wave the stone over your injured hand and think good thoughts," he repeated.

"Why?"

"It's the Adder Stone. You can tell by the hole through it."

I looked at the rock and sure enough, there was a small hole that ran completely through it. For the first time I also noticed how truly brilliantly white it was.

"What does it do?" I asked warily.

"Just think good thoughts."

I sighed and then did as Eon had asked me to do. My hand instantly healed. No more pain and not a trace of blood. I stared down in utter amazement. I was so stunned that I nearly dropped the Stone. "How did that happen?" I exclaimed.

"The Adder Stone has the soul of a powerful sorceress embedded in it."

I stared at him blankly. "A sorceress?"

"A magical being." Eon fixed his great, bulging eyes on me. "With the power to heal, as you can see for yourself."

I looked once more at my hand and had to admit he was right. I felt a chill soar up my spine at holding something in my hand that could heal wounds with a wave and a wish. Yet I didn't know why I was so astonished. After all, I had a chain that allowed me to fly. I had nearly drowned in a river of blood only to mysteriously vanish from this place and end up outside it. I was coming to learn that Stacks was chock-full of secrets and powers and mysteries. "And yet you just leave it lying around?" I asked.

"It is here, it is there. It is sometimes everywhere," chanted Eon. "Sometimes it is simply where you need it to be."

"It can do anything?" I asked eagerly. "Grant any wish?"

He shook his head. "It can grant the good thoughts of the one holding it. You could be sad and it would make you feel better. You might think that you could use a bit of good fortune, and it might happen. It has its limits, though."

"Like what?" I asked curiously.

"You must never wish ill of anyone with the Adder. Not only will it *not* grant the wish, terrible consequences will befall you in such an attempt." He stopped, looked me over and said, "Are you injured a lot?"

"A bit more than I'd like, actually," I answered curtly. "So what do you do here?"

"My race is the guardian of time."

"Time doesn't need guarding."

"I would expect that response from one who has not seen her past or future from a different perspective. Follow me, Vega Jane."

Before I could say anything, he turned and walked slowly into the cave. I glanced at Harry Two, who looked at me with a curious expression. My past and my future?

I had come to learn that my past was a lie. If I could see it from a different way, would I learn anything useful? I couldn't answer that for sure. But I knew I had to try.

We walked for a long way until we reached the back of the cave. Eon stopped and turned to me, pointing at the wall. I looked where he was indicating, expecting to see only rock.

Instead I saw a pair of enormous iron gates. I had seen some of the Dactyls at Stacks fashion iron like this by beating it with their hammers while it was still molten. The only thing was, this gate looked as if it were still glowing with heat. It appeared so hot, in fact, that it was flaming red.

"Is it on fire?" I asked, keeping my distance from it.

"No. It is actually cool to the touch. You may see for yourself."

I touched it gingerly. It *was* cool.

Eon held up two keys that he had taken from his cloak pocket and handed them to me. "One will take you to the past; the other, your future."

"They're gold!" I said in wonder.

Eon nodded. "Any key used to open something enchanted is made of gold."

I smiled at this strange remark. "Is that a rule?"

"It is more than a mere rule, for rules can be changed. It is truth."

"I think I understand that," I said slowly.

Eon looked at the keys I held and said, "So many fascinating events that might have taken place did not because one lacked the courage to open a certain portal."

"Well, sometimes it might be smarter not to open it," I said stoutly. Then I added, "How do you tell the keys apart? Which is past and which is future?"

"You can't tell them apart, really," Eon replied. "You must take your chances. And you may pick only one, past or future."

"And if I pick the past over the future?"

"Then you will see the past. *Your* past."

"And if I pick the future?"

"You will see what lies ahead of course."

"I'm not sure I want to see what will be coming up for me."

Eon said firmly, "But you *must* choose."

I stared down at the two keys. They were identical. But apparently depending on which one I selected, the outcome would be very different indeed.

"Is there really no way to tell them apart?"

He cocked his small head. "Do you have a preference?"

I had made up my mind. "The past," I said. "Even though I have lived it, I have recently found that it remains as murky as though I had not. I need to understand it fully if I am to have a future. At least I believe that to be true."

Eon considered this. "Then, Vega Jane, I would tell you the vast majority of choosers end up going into the future, because they return here and tell me of their experiences."

"But if there's truly no way to tell, I guess my odds are split right down the middle."

"All I can advise is for you to look at the keys and see if you can feel which is the right one for you, taking into account *all* that I have said to you," replied Eon.

I took a few steps back and held both keys side by side in the palm of my hand. They were identical, down to the teeth. But then something occurred to me. Something that Eon had said. It had been a clue and I had to think it was intentional.

There *was* a marginal difference between the keys. One had more black scratches than the other. I glanced at the heavy iron gates. The lock was irregularly shaped. It would be difficult to insert a key without scratching it against the blackened iron plate. Eon had said that most ended up in the future. So *that* key would have been used far more. And thus have far more scratches. I had my answer.

Grinning, I handed the badly scratched key to Eon. He pocketed it and said, "You have a good mind, Vega Jane." He looked at the gates and then at me. "And now it is time you were off."

Drawing a deep breath, I marched over to the gate and prepared to insert the key. I looked back at Eon. "How exactly will it happen?"

"You will not be seen nor heard and you cannot be harmed. Neither can you intervene in any way in the events you will witness, no matter what happens. That is the law of time and it cannot be circumvented."

"One more question. How do I get back?"

"Through this gate. But do not dawdle, Vega Jane. And do not think yourself mad, though madness you think you may see."

With this disturbing thought in mind, I took a deep, replenishing breath and inserted the key. I gave Harry Two a hopeful smile and opened the gate.

The Past Is Never Past

THE GATES SWUNG open wide and Harry Two and I simply walked through. Everything was fuzzy, as if the clouds had deflated and fallen to the ground for a lie-down. If I was to see my past, it seemed it would be through this filter of fog.

The cry startled me. Eon hadn't said specifically that I would hear things, though I supposed he assumed that I knew I would. Obviously, in the past, folks still talked and things still made sounds. But there was something about the cry that seemed distantly familiar to me. I hurried along, using my hands to push the mist away, although all I really did was muck it up more. Then I reached a clearing in the mist and stopped. My mouth sagged.

I was back in my old home. And the scene I was looking at was remarkable. I had seen it before, only I was a very young and I didn't remember. That was Eon's point, I supposed. Simply because you've lived through something doesn't mean you understand its true significance or even recall the details of it correctly.

I knelt down next to my father as he hovered over the small bed. On the bed was my mother. She looked pale and spent and her hair was slicked back against her head. A female dressed in a white cloak and a domed cap stood next to my father. I recognized her as a Nurse who helped bring new Wugs to life.

My mother was cradling a tiny bundle in her arms. I could just glimpse the small head and thin black hair of my brother, John. The cry had come from him. John and I shared a birthlight, so from this I knew I was exactly three sessions old. When I lifted my gaze from this sight, I was startled to see my younger self peering into the room from the doorway.

I was far shorter and so was my hair. But I was still skinny, although the sinewy muscle I was possessed with now was of course not evident yet. I was smiling as I stared at my new little brother. There was an innocence and hope in that look that brought tears to my eyes. And yet two of my family were now gone. Three if you counted John being with Morrigone. Essentially, I was the only one left.

My father rose, beaming first at John and then at the younger me. He slapped his palms together, and as if on command, I ran and leapt into his arms.

I gasped. I had forgotten that I had done that as a very young. My father hugged me and then held me low enough to see John close up. I touched his little hand. He made a belching sound and I jumped back and squealed with laughter.

With a sudden pang, I realized how long it had been since I had laughed like that. I have had fewer and fewer reasons to laugh as my sessions have piled on top of one another. I looked last at my mother. Helen Jane was beautiful despite her ordeal of giving birth to what would become the smartest

Wug in all of Wormwood. I knew from Eon that she couldn't see me, but I drew closer and knelt down next to the bed. My hand reached out and I touched her. Well, not really, because my hand merely passed through her image. I touched John and then my father, with the same result. They were not actually there with me of course, or I with them. But they were real enough.

I felt my lips starting to quiver and my heart throbbed fiercely. It had been so long since we were a family that I had almost forgotten the joy that came with having one. All the small and large moments, many that I had taken for granted while they were occurring, no doubt bolstered by the certainty that there would be many more.

Yet such endearing and memorable engagements in life are promised to no one. They come and go and one has to be aware that there is no assurance they will ever come again. It made me tremble to think what I had lost.

And then the mists clouded over once more and a new image replaced the old.

They were running hard, the female a bit ahead of the male. I ran too to catch up through the mist that had become my world for now. The trees were towering, though not so towering as I was used to in the present. As I caught up, I saw them more clearly. The female was perhaps four sessions. The male then must be two sessions older, or six. I knew this because the male and female were Delph and I.

He was already tall for his age, as I was. His hair was not that long yet. We jumped a narrow creek and landed on the opposite side, laughing and pushing each other. Delph's face was animated, his eyes bursting with possibilities of the sessions ahead. For the life of me, I had not remembered this part of my past until just now.

Then I realized that Delph would see my grandfather's Event this session, and he would never be the same. And neither would I. Maybe that's why I banished this memory, because it was closely aligned with that terrible time. I wanted to call out to them, to warn of what was coming, though I didn't. There would be no point because they couldn't hear me.

This image faded and I found myself in the Hallowed Ground, where Wugs who had slipped away were laid in the soil. I was staring down at the hole in the dirt as my grandmother Calliope's box was lowered into it. Other Wugs stood around solemnly watching this take place. This was a bit out of order, because she had died from the sick soon after John was born but before me and Delph had been running through the trees.

And then it occurred to me. Calliope going into the ground meant that my grandfather Virgil was here. I found him in the crowd of Wugs on what I now remembered was a miserably cold light full of drizzle and not even a glimpse of warming sun.

He was tall but looked bent. He was not so very old, yet looked aged. Calliope and he had been together for so many sessions that when she left him, my grandfather was reduced to something far less than he had been. My father stood next to him, his arm on Virgil's shoulder. My mother, holding my new brother, stood next to them. And holding my grandfather's other hand was my younger self.

I stood next to Virgil and looked up. It was painful to see his sorrow, etched so heavily across his features. Just as I had been seeing my brother being born, I once more was possessed of an enormous sense of loss. I was still a very young when my grandfather vanished. I could have spent so much more time with him. I *should* have spent so much more time with him. But I had been robbed of that opportunity. My spirits dipped lower than they ever had before.

At the end of a lifetime's worth of lights and nights, it seemed that family was really the only important thing there was. And yet how many of us truly appreciated that significance before our last breath left us? We lost family all the time, and we mourned them and buried them and remembered them. Wouldn't it be better to celebrate family while they are alive to a greater degree than when they are no longer with us?

I put my hand to my eyes and wept quietly. My body shuddered and I could feel Harry Two right next to me, as though he were holding me up.

Once I regained my composure, my gaze settled on the ring on my grandfather's hand. The same ring that had been found in Quentin Herms's cottage. I looked at the back of my grandfather's hand and saw the same design echoed there: the three hooks connected. I had no idea what it meant or why he had such a ring or such a mark. But it was becoming clearer all the time that there was much I didn't know about my family. And it was crystal clear that those were mysteries I had to solve if I was ever going to find the truth. Of my family. Of Wormwood. Even of myself.

I had my ink stick in my pocket and I used it to draw the three connected hooks on the back of my hand.

The crowd of Wugs was large. I wasn't surprised by the size. Calliope was much loved in Wormwood. Near the front of the crowd I saw a younger Ezekiel, and next to him was Thansius, so large and solid. He hadn't really changed at all. But I was startled to see Morrigone in the back of the crowd. She was many sessions younger at that point, but she also looked nearly the same as she did now.

I was just about to go over to her when the mists crowded me out once more. It was frustrating, yet I had no other option but to keep going.

That's when I heard the scream. As the mists cleared once more, I saw Delph. He looked the same age as in my last memory, which meant it was still around the time of my grandfather's Event.

He was running down a hard-packed gravel road that looked instantly familiar to me. I looked up ahead and saw the gates with the large *M* on them. Delph was running from Morrigone's home. As I watched, he looked back in terror and then passed by me. That's when I realized what was happening. That's when I saw her. Or rather me.

I was standing in the lane staring after Delph. I was just four sessions old. I recognized the little dolly I carried. It had been a present from my mother on my fourth birthlight and it still looked new. To my shock, my young self started to walk up the gravel path toward the big gates. They opened at my approach. Harry Two was jumping and growling around my legs as I followed my younger self onto the grounds of Morrigone's home. We arrived at the large wooden door. It was

200

partially open. I heard sounds from inside but I couldn't make out what they were. I drew closer, as did my younger self.

Suddenly, the door flew open all the way and there stood Morrigone, her brilliantly red hair awry and her robes askew. Yet what I was really drawn to were her eyes. They were the eyes of a female who had been struck clean of all reason.

Morrigone caught sight of my younger self standing there clutching the dolly. She took a step forward. There was a blinding blue light. I heard another scream. And then there was a thud. I closed my eyes. When I reopened them, the mists had enveloped me.

I sat down on my bum and gripped my head while Harry Two danced and yipped around me. The blue light seemed burned into my eyes. I couldn't shake it. Morrigone, mad. And then the scream. And the thud. Was that my younger self falling? What had Morrigone done to me?

I rose on quivering legs. I had never felt this wonky before and that was indeed telling, for many recent things in my life had left me woozy. I wondered where Harry Two and I would end up next. I was actually growing a bit weary of my wandering through the past, but I had to admit, I had learned many things I should already have known.

That thought died just about the time the blow struck and knocked me arse over elbows.

Who Must Survive

I FELL HARD TO the ground and rolled over twice from the force of whatever had hit me. I started to rise, but something was holding me down. When I glanced up, I could see it was Harry Two with his paws on my shoulders. He was surprisingly strong.

I finally managed to push him off and sit up. The field was far bigger than the Duelum pitch back in Wormwood, but I could see nothing that would have knocked me down. There were blurs of light racing here and there and emitting sparks and rays of colors. At first it seemed truly beautiful and somehow melodious, though it made no sound. But when a silver ray of light hit one of the blurs that I saw racing across the sky, there was a tremendous explosion. An instant later, a body dropped from the heavens and plowed into the dirt less than two feet from where I sat.

I screamed and scrambled to my feet. Harry Two barked and jumped next to me. I stared down at the body. It was blackened and bits of it were blown off, but I could see the great bearded face and the metal cap and breastplate the male wore. There was liquid all over it, like blood, except instead of red, it was a sparkling green the likes of which I had never seen before. I screamed again and this seemed to rouse him.

For a moment, he stared up at me with the one eye he still had. Then he gave a great heaving shudder, the eye froze and he just died, right in front of me.

I backed away in horror until I heard Harry Two howl. I turned in time to see a steed racing at me. Its size would have put any of Thansius's sleps to bloody shame. And on the steed was a tall, lean figure outfitted all in chain mail. The figure wore a full metal helmet with face shield and was racing right at me. Only when it raised the face shield did I see with astonishment that it was a female. I could only see a bit of her features because the helmet covered most of her, even with the shield up.

She lifted her arm. In her gloved hand was a long, golden spear. She took aim as she rode and hurled it right at me. Only it didn't hit me. It sailed six feet over my head and I whirled in time to see it strike a huge male full in the chest as he was charging me astride another enormous steed. There was a sky burst like I had seen come down from the heavens on stormy nights, and the bloke simply disappeared in a hail of black dust and red fire.

The spear emerged from the ball of fire, turned in the air and flew back into the female's throwing hand. Only now she was right on top of me. I covered my head and waited to be trampled. When I looked up, all I saw was the underbelly of the steed as it rose up in the air, lifted by wings that had seemingly sprouted from its withers. It soared into the sky and I watched in fascination as the rider engaged in battle with another figure perched on a winged creature that looked like an adar, only three times as large.

Everywhere I looked, something was attacking something

else. From the air and the ground, powerful streams of light whizzed by at unfathomable velocities. If the streams managed to hit their targets, they simply exploded. If they missed and hit the ground, the concussive force lifted me off my feet. Suffice it to say, I was off my feet just about every sliver.

Then it occurred to me that this was very nearly identical to the scene I had observed on the wall in the cavern at Stacks before the river of blood had come to nearly hurl me to my death. A full-fledged battle was raging and now I was right in the middle of it.

As I watched, there came a slight lull in the fighting on the ground. I took the opportunity to run full out, with Harry Two slightly ahead of me. Eon had told me that I could not be seen or heard or presumably touched. Well, I had been knocked down and nearly crushed. I knew if I stayed here, I would die. As a silver beam ricocheted off a boulder, it struck the ground a glancing blow barely five yards from me. I was thrown into the air and came down hard on something. When I rolled away, I saw that that something was a body. It was the female rider in the chain mail, the one who had destroyed the male bearing down on me.

She had evidently been blasted out of the sky. Yet even as I started to get up, her hand reached out and gripped my arm. A strange, near-terrifying sensation went through my entire body at her touch. My mind clouded over. I felt cold, then warm, and then cold again. An instant later, my reason cleared, but I felt as heavy as a creta. I couldn't seem to move.

"Wait," she said breathlessly. "Please wait."

As I looked down at her, she touched the side of her helmet. It took me a moment to comprehend what she wanted. I carefully lifted it off and her long auburn hair swirled around her metal shoulders. I could now fully see her face, and her features were beautiful. As I stared down at her, I was certain I had seen her before, somewhere. Then my gaze went lower and I saw the hole in her chain mail dead center of her chest. Red blood just like mine flowed from this wound. She was dying.

I had a sudden thought. I whipped out the Adder Stone and waved it in front of the wound and wished her to be healed. But nothing happened. Then it struck me. I was in the past. This female had died long ago. I couldn't change that.

I slowly put the Stone away and gazed down at her body. She was tall, even taller than I was, and leaner if that was possible. But I had felt the immense strength in her grip when she grabbed my arm. And she must be extraordinarily powerful to have wielded the sky spear the way she had, and to wear the chain mail while astride a steed.

The spear! It was lying beside her. I reached for it. But as I did, she spoke again.

"No, wait," she gasped, but with urgency in her tone. She struggled up a bit and held out her right hand. On it was a glove made of a bright silver material.

"Take . . . this . . . first," she said, each word separated by a gurgling breath.

I hesitated, but only for a moment as the battle raged with increased ferocity all around us. I took the glove off and slipped it onto my own hand. It looked like metal but was as soft as leather.

She dropped back to the ground. "Now," she said breathlessly.

I reached over and picked up the spear. It was lighter than it looked.

"The Elemental," she said in a low voice that I had to bend down to hear.

"What?"

"The Elemental. Take it." She took a long burbling breath that I knew heralded the end of her life. "When you have . . . no other friends . . . it will be there . . . for you."

I couldn't think how a spear could be a friend. "Who are you?" I said. "Why are you fighting?"

She was about to say something in reply when a sound came that shook the very ground. When I looked up, I saw to my horror that advancing upon the battlefield were three gigantic figures, each standing at least twenty yards tall, with huge muscular bodies and small heads. They were grabbing flying steeds and riders out of the air and crushing them in their grasp even as they galumphed across the ground.

I looked back down when the dying female grabbed my cloak. "Go!"

"But —"

"Now." And what she said next shocked me more than anything ever had in my life.

She took a shuddering breath, gripped the back of my head and pulled me so close I could see that her eyes were so brilliantly blue they made the color of the entire sky look insignificant. Those eyes bored into me. "You must survive, Vega Jane." She shook violently and her hand fell away. Her eyes glazed over as she stared upward.

She was gone.

I stared down at her. She had called me Vega Jane. She knew who I was. But who was she? And how did she know my name?

When I looked down at her right hand, my heart nearly stopped. On one of the fingers was a ring, with the same three hooks that my grandfather's held. I reached out to touch it. And then take it. But it would not come off. I would have to cut off her finger to leave here with the ring. And I could not do that, not to a brave female warrior who had saved my life.

I took a moment to close her eyes, gripped the Elemental, scooped up Harry Two in my free hand, looked back once at the giants whose every stride covered a score of yards, and ran for my life.

While the giants were now the focal point on the field, the battle raged on, both on the ground and in the air. As I turned back once to see how close they were growing, a steed and rider swooped low, wielding a great sword nearly as long as I was tall. He ducked under the outstretched arms of one of the giants, and, using both hands, he swung his great blade with incredible force. It sliced the giant's head clean off its shoulders.

"Take that, you bloody colossal!" he screamed before he and his steed swooped safely away.

A colossal? What the bloody Hel was a colossal?

But as the colossal fell, it soon became apparent that he would topple right onto me. And as I estimated he weighed the better part of four tons, there would be nothing left of Harry Two or me.

I ran as fast as I'd ever run, even as I could see the shadow of the colossal blocking out the light and reaching ahead of me by a handful of yards. I was never going to make it, not while carrying both the Elemental and Harry Two. And I was unwilling to sacrifice either one.

And then it occurred to me. "You prat," I told myself.

As the shadow of the falling colossal engulfed me, I lifted off the ground and soared straight ahead, barely a yard in the air. I needed distance now, not height. I half closed my eyes because I was still unsure if I was going to squeak past. The thunderous crash that occurred right behind me jarred my eyes fully open. I glanced back. The dead colossal had missed me by less than two feet.

I soared upward, but this only made me more of a target. Streams of light were coming at me from all directions. Harry Two barked and snapped at them, as though his teeth could defeat the threat they each carried. I used the only tool I had: the Elemental. I did not hurl it because I was not practiced at aiming it while flying. Rather, I used it as a shield. I didn't know if it would block the lights coming at me, but I found out quickly enough.

It did. The lights ricocheted off. One deflected blue streak knocked a rider clean off his steed. A purple streak struck one of the remaining colossals squarely in the chest and he dropped to his knees and fell face-forward, digging a hole ten feet deep in the ground with the force of his impact and crushing a rider and his steed underneath.

All I knew was, I wanted to get the Hel out of here. But to do so, I had to find the gates. And I had no idea where they were.

As I flew, I looked ahead and saw my own death speeding toward me. Six abreast they were. All huge males wearing chain mail. They were riding steeds with withers as wide across as I was tall and they had upraised swords in hand. Yet they didn't wait to get close enough to swing them at me; they brought them down in a slashing move and out of each sword blasted shafts of white light. I gripped the Elemental like I had seen the dead female do. In my head I knew what I wanted the thing to do, but I had no idea how to make it happen.

I hurled the Elemental with all my strength, but I didn't throw it straight at the oncoming shafts of light. I threw it to the right side of the shafts with as much backspin torque as my poor arm could muster. The spear turned to the left, gained speed and shot straight across the air. It hit the first white shaft, then the second, the third, and then the remaining three. It caused them to bounce off and head in reverse, like an orb thrown against a wall.

When the deflected shafts of light struck the wall of riders and their steeds, there came the loudest explosion I had yet seen on the battlefield, even louder than when the first colossal had fallen. Harry Two and I were knocked heels over arse as waves of concussive air pummeled us. When the smoke and fire cleared, the riders and their enormous steeds had vanished. I did not dwell on my improbable victory. I had righted myself in time and had caught the Elemental squarely in my gloved hand as it reversed course and soared back to me.

As I pointed downward and looked toward the ground, I saw them in a valley miles away and partially obscured in a sea of mist. But they were still unmistakable to me: the flaming-red gates. I went into a dive. I had to. For a new peril had emerged from the heavens. Right behind me was a creature I can only describe as a jabbit with wings. And if it were possible, the vile thing was even more terrifying than the dirt-bound variety. And as fast as I could fly, the winged jabbit was swifter.

I looked at the Elemental. I knew I could not throw it as the chain-mailed female had. But she had said that, when I had no other friends, it would be there for me. Well, friends are supposed to be good listeners. I looked back at the jabbit. It was now or never.

I spun in the air, faced the oncoming jabbit and threw the Elemental. In my mind, it flew straight and true at the target.

The jabbit exploded and the Elemental flew in a graceful curve right back into my gloved hand. I landed, set down Harry Two and we ran full tilt toward the gates. I'd had quite enough of the past. As soon as I passed through the gates, everything became black.

I knew where I was. I could feel the grass around me. I heard Harry Two's yips, the impact of his four paws with the ground near me. Part of me just wanted to lie there with my eyes closed for the rest of my sessions. But I slowly sat up and opened my eyes. Stacks was in the distance. I looked to the sky. Hardly any time had passed. It was still light, though growing darker by the sliver. The only things to tell me I had not imagined it all was the glove on my hand and the Elemental gripped in that hand.

And the bulge in my cloak pocket was the Adder Stone.

I rose and held the Elemental tighter. What was I to do with the thing? It was as tall as I was. I couldn't carry it around Wormwood. I couldn't really hide it.

And as though the thing could read my mind, it shrunk down to the size of an ink stick. I stared at it, dumbstruck. And yet it seemed that I was growing accustomed to inexplicable things happening to me as they mounted in number.

It occurred to me that I had not returned to Eon even though he had said time travelers did. Yet then again I was not supposed to be seen, heard or harmed while I traveled back in time. I looked at a burn on my arm. Well, I had been seen, heard, injured and nearly killed.

I touched the burn and pain shot all the way down my arm.

"Oi, Eon," I called angrily out to the air. "You need to rethink your rules of time. They're a bit dodgy."

I took out the Stone, waved it over my wound and thought good thoughts. The pain eased some, but the burn did not heal fully. I sighed resignedly and put the Stone away.

"Figures," I said to myself. "I guess this is a burn from the past that the Stone can't sort out all the way. Thanks loads, Eon."

I walked along, thinking about so many things that I finally couldn't think at all. My head truly felt like it would burst at any moment.

Bloody Hel, Vega. Bloody, bloody Hel.

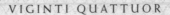
Secrets

I SPENT THE NEXT few nights practicing my flying with Destin and my tossing with the Elemental. During the lights, I kept the Adder Stone and the Elemental hidden under a floorboard at my digs. Destin always rode around my waist. I would never dream of removing it at this point because I never knew when taking to the skies might save my skin.

The next light, I was walking along the forest path to my tree before Stacks when I was confronted by Non wearing his metal breastplate. I looked behind him and there was Nida, who no longer guarded Valhall. The prisoners had been released and then bound into servitude to help build the Wall. But Nida had his shuck with him, and the great beast was growling and snapping its immense jaws.

Harry Two started snapping his jaws and growling right back. My canine had grown surprisingly fast since I had taken him in. His chest, neck and legs were thick and powerful. I put a hand down in front of his face and Harry Two immediately sat on his haunches and grew silent.

Non and Nida paired together were bad enough. But next to Nida was Cletus Loon holding his morta and sporting a malevolent grin.

Non held out a hand. "Pass parchment."

I gave it to him. He flicked a gaze over it and then flung it back at me.

He leaned down and said, "What are you doing, female?"

"What I'm doing is I'm going to my tree to eat my first meal," I said, holding up my battered tin box. "Would you like to see for yourself?"

I shouldn't have made the offer because Cletus snatched the tin from me and opened it.

"Good stuff in here," he said. He pulled out a hard-boiled egg, popped it into his mouth and swallowed it whole. The next instant, he was on the ground holding his belly because that's where I kicked him.

Non snagged my arm to hold me back. "We'll nae have that."

"He just stole my food!" I shouted.

Cletus was on his feet now and appeared to be about to point his morta at me. But Nida smacked him in the head and sent him sprawling again. Nida never said much, but when he hit you, you knew it.

Sprawled on the ground, Cletus moaned in pain and grabbed his head. "What'd you do that for?"

"Simmer down, Loon," advised Non. "Or he'll have the shuck on you next and then you'll be begging for a clubbing on the head 'cause a shuck don't club, it bites."

Cletus stood, looking embarrassed, his cheeks red. I didn't feel sorry for him. I didn't care about Cletus. I snapped, "I'll be coming round and taking that egg from your meal portion at the Loons."

"The Hel you will," he shot back. "I was testing it to see if there was something in it what shouldn't-a been."

I pulled my little knife and smiled wickedly. "You want me to check your belly then, to make sure?"

Cletus leapt back, got his feet tangled and fell on his head. Non roared with laughter and the shuck growled at the sudden noise, but Nida held him back on the chain. I grabbed my tin off the ground where Cletus had let it fall.

Non gripped my arm and leaned in close. "One lucky strike nigh means nothing, female," he whispered in my ear. I glanced at the dent I had made in his breastplate but said nothing. He continued. "Krone has told me the lay of the land. You and Morrigone. She will nae always be there to protect you."

I ripped my hand free. Around my waist Destin felt on fire. "I didn't need her to do *that*, did I?" I shot back, pointing at the dent.

Before he could say anything else, I hurried on my way. I didn't like being stopped by Wugs with mortas. I didn't like having my stuff male-handled and my food eaten. I didn't like that lout Non threatening me. But that seemed how Wormwood was going to be from now on.

I reached my tree, gave a searching look around to make sure no one was watching, picked up Harry Two, gave a great leap and landed neatly on my planks.

We sat and I divvied up our meal. I was parceling out the small harvest from the little garden I kept next to my tree. My crop was not much. A few vegetables, some lettuce leafs, a bit of basil, parsley and witch's ear, which brings heat to any food you might make. But I was supporting myself and living on my own.

Still, I was worried about the fact that Krone so obviously wanted me in Valhall. I had to protect myself from discovery because I intended to keep practicing with Destin and the Elemental. I had studied the map of the Quag on my skin every night. I now knew it by heart. I had to keep the Adder Stone and the Elemental a secret, obviously. It was fortunate that the Adder merely looked like a stone. And the reduced Elemental could have been an ink stick. Destin was a chain. Unless they saw me flying around with it, there was no cause to throw me in prison over it.

That's when I sat bolt upright.

The book. Quentin's book of the Quag. I needed to study it as closely as I had the map. It would give me valuable information about creatures in there, information I would need to survive. I couldn't believe I had neglected it this long. I had to rectify that as soon as possible. Without the book, I could not flee this place. And this place, I now promised myself, I *was* going to flee.

That night after I finished work I snuck from my lodgings, leaving Harry Two sleeping, entered the forest, looked to make sure no Wug was around and then I started sprinting and leapt into the air. I caught an updraft of wind and soared high. The breeze sailed through my hair and over my body. It felt cleansing, like I was taking a long bath under the pipes.

I reached the Delphias' property in record time and dropped to the ground with little sound. The creta Duf had been working on was gone now, taking its muscle to the building of the Wall. The whist hound was nowhere to be seen. The young slep was still here being trained up proper for a place on Thansius's carriage. And the adar was also here and asleep, its leg still attached to a peg in the ground. But its vocal cords and speech capabilities, I was sure, were much enhanced since my last visit.

In the darkness and with very little Noc to guide me, I suddenly realized I had a problem. I couldn't remember where I had buried the book. I walked past each pine tree, examining the ground underneath for the little pile of needles I had placed over the hole I'd dug. Of course, after all this time, the little pile of needles had been blown away by the wind or else carried off by creatures to construct their nests. I was cursing myself again for being so blindly stupid, when I heard it. Or rather, heard *him*.

"Wo-wo-wotcha, Vega Jane."

I turned slowly around and saw Delph standing there. "Hello, Delph," I replied. He drew even closer. He looked tired and while his hair was no longer white because he had not been working in the Mill, it was long and scraggly and right dirty black.

He held up my book.

I stared at it and then at him, unsure whether I should claim ownership.

"C-c-can I c-come t-too, Ve-Vega Jane?"

The Wall of Twiddle Twaddle

I STARED AT DELPH, dumbfounded.

He drew closer and held the book up even higher. "To the Quag, I'm meaning, eh," he said in a too-loud voice.

"I know it's the bloody Quag," I said fiercely, finally finding my voice. "And you don't have to tell every Wug in Wormwood about it. Where did you find it?"

In a far quieter voice, he said, "Box in the ho-hole you d-dug."

"How did you know about that?"

"Wa-watched you, di-didn't I?"

"Have you read it?" I asked in a whisper.

"N-not all. But it don't s-say h-how a Wu-Wug gets th-through it," he said.

He eyed my waist. Rather, he eyed the chain around my waist.

"You ca-can fly," he said. "'Cause-a that thing?"

I felt myself growing angry. "You're sounding very logical, Delph. Was it all an act before? Because if it was, you are the biggest, sorriest git I've ever met."

He fell back a step, his face betraying his hurt feelings. "I ca-can talk, Vega Jane, when I want to. But th-things get mu-mu-muddled up here." He touched his head and sat down on a stump and gazed pitifully up at me, the book dangling between his fingers. My anger faded as I looked at his hurt features.

"Where'd y-you ge-get it?"

"I found it at Quentin Herms's cottage. He was the one who put it together."

"So's he's b-been through the Qu-Quag?"

"I guess so."

"Then th-the Out-Ou — th-the Out —"

We eyed each other for about a sliver but said nothing.

He held the book up to me. "Ta-take it," he said, and I did. "No map-a the Qu-Quag," he pointed out.

"I have one," I replied.

"Where?"

"Someplace safe." I sat next to him on the ground. This actually would be my best opportunity to have my most pressing question answered and I intended to do just that. "I had a vision. Would you like to hear it, Delph?"

"Vi-vision? What, like Mor-Morri . . . gone?"

"Maybe more certain even than that. I went back in time. Do you see?"

I saw him mouth the words *back in time*. But no realization spread over his features. "Wha-what, like when y-you was a ti-tiny thing?"

"Even before that. But when I *was* younger I saw someone, Delph. I saw you."

He looked truly unnerved by this, his face frozen in fear. "The Hel you say."

"I saw you at Morrigone's house."

He shook his head savagely. "You ca-can't ha-have."

"I saw you running away from her home. You were so scared, Delph."

He put his hands up to his ears, covering them. "'Tain't true, 'tain't."

"And I saw Morrigone. She was scared too."

"'Tain't true!" Delph exclaimed.

"And I think I know what you saw."

"No . . . n-no . . . no," sobbed Delph.

I put my hand on his quaking shoulder. "The red light? You remember you told me about the red light? Was it Morrigone's hair you saw? Was that the red light?"

Delph was swinging his head to and fro. I was afraid he was going to jump up and run off. But I swore to myself that if he did, I would fly after him. I would run him down and make him tell me the truth. I needed to know that badly.

"She was there, wasn't she? And my grandfather? At her home? His Event? It happened then and there, didn't it?" I shook him. "Didn't it, Delph? Didn't it!"

He shouted, "I was there, Vega Jane!"

"With Morrigone? And my grandfather?"

He nodded.

"Why were you there? Why? You have to tell me." I shook him again. "Tell me!"

His face was scrunched in agony. He doubled over, but I pulled him back upright. I was out of my mind now. I had to know. I didn't care if I was hurting him. My whole life was apparently a lie. I had to know some part of the truth. I had to know right this sliver.

I slapped him. "Tell me!"

"G-gone to see her new wh-whist hound me dad brung her after he tr-trained it up. H-Harpie. L-loved H-Harpie, I d-did."

"Then what?"

"Th-thought I could h-hear Harpie inside. T-took a peek."

"And you went in?"

He nodded, his face still screwed up in pain, his eyes closed. I kept a grip on his arm. I was willing him to keep going. "D-didn't see no Wug n-n-nowhere. No Har-Harpie neither."

"Keep going, Delph. Keep going."

"H-heard a noise. Still n-no Wu-Wug. So's I w-went up the stairs. I w-was sc-scared."

"You were only six sessions, Delph. I would've been scared too." I was keeping my voice level now, trying to force the same calm on him.

"G-got closer, hear-heard 'em. Argu-arg-arguing." He finally got the troublesome word out of his mouth.

"My grandfather and Morrigone?"

He said nothing. I shook him. "Was it them?"

"C-can't do th-this, Ve —"

"Was it them?" I roared, twisting his face until it was lined up with mine. "Look at me, Delph. Look at me!" I screamed. He opened his eyes. "Was it Morrigone and my grandfather?"

"Yes," he said breathlessly, tears dribbling from his eyes.

"Any other Wug?" He shook his head. "Brilliant. Keep going, Delph."

"Them ar-arguing like that, sc-scared me. But . . . but

220

may-maybe I c-could help, calm 'em down. L-like I'd do w-with the beasts with m-me dad. C-calm 'em down like."

"I would have thought the same thing, Delph. Calm them down. Trying to help."

He let out a little sob and I felt so guilty for making him remember all this, but there was no other way. He put his head in his hands and started sobbing, and I jerked him back straight so he had to look me in the eye.

"You can't stop now. You have to get this out. You have to."

"T-two doors d-down that way. Nothing b-b-behind the first one."

"And the second?" I said, my voice like fragile chips of ice in my throat.

"When I saw . . ." His voice trailed off and he started to whimper. I thought I was going to lose him again. But I didn't yell this time. I didn't hit him.

"You saw something that made you really afraid, didn't you?"

He nodded miserably. "They wa-was f-facing each uh-other."

"Was she mad at him? Was she angry? And he was trying to calm her?"

His response stunned me. "'Twas the uh-uh-other way round, Ve-Vega Jane. 'Twas M-Morrigone, what l-l-looked scared. She s-s-seemed to be tr-tr-trying to calm *him* d-down."

I stared at him in disbelief. "What was she saying to him?"

Delph took deep shuddering breaths, his body twitching with each of them. If I didn't know better, I would have thought he was trying to throw off some sick that had got

221

hold of him. He finally stopped twitching, rubbed his face clear of tears and sat up. He looked directly at me. His expression was clear. There was no more pain there.

"Not to go," Delph said simply. "Please not to go."

"And what did he say?"

"That he had to. He had to try. He just had to. He kept saying it over and over. So terrible-like. Hear him in me dreams . . ." His voice trailed off again.

"Go? Go where?" I said more harshly than I intended.

Delph glanced down at me, his face so pale it looked like the Noc close up.

"Didn't say. And then it happened."

"The red light?"

The look on his face was so fearful, my heart went out to him. "'Twas fire. Fire the likes of which I ain't never seen. It was fire that . . . that was alive. It . . . it flamed up all around Virgil, like a serpent swallowing him whole. And then . . . and then he floated up in the air. And then . . . and then . . . he was gone. Without making a sound." Delph paused, staring ahead. "Not one sound," he added in what was no more than a whisper.

I could barely draw a breath. What Delph had just described was what had happened to my parents. My parents had suffered Events right in front of me. I had seen it! Only I hadn't known that's what it was.

I must have been looking blankly off because I was roused only when Delph gripped my shoulder and shook me.

"Vega Jane, are you all right?"

I still couldn't speak.

"Vega Jane?" he said in a panicked voice.

My mind drifted back to the memory. I could see the fire swallowing them whole. An Event. *Holy Steeples, I had witnessed their Events.*

"Vega Jane?" He shook me so hard I nearly fell over.

I finally focused on him. "I'm sorry, Delph. What happened then?" I asked in a hoarse voice, the terrible image of my parents in flames still firmly in my mind's eye.

He paused, licked his lips. "And then I run 'cause Morrigone saw me."

"What did she look like?"

"Like she would kill me if she could get to me. I run harder than I ever run in all my sessions. But she was faster. She was there, before I got out the door, she was. Then that's when it happened."

"What happened?"

"The red light."

"But I thought the red light happened with my grandfather. It was the flames."

"No. The red light . . . the red light happened to me, Vega Jane."

I thought back to when I had been in the past at Morrigone's home. After seeing Delph run away. She had seen me, waved her hand and there had been a *blue* light.

I looked at Delph. "Delph, are you sure the light wasn't blue?"

He shook his head. "'Twas red, Vega Jane. 'Twas red. Like the fire."

"And what happened after that?"

"My head felt all funny-like. But I was running still. I kept running. And . . . and then that's all. Just running." He turned to me, looking drained by all he had recounted. "Why did you ask if the light was blue?"

"Because that's the color it was when Morrigone waved her hand at me."

He looked nearly petrified by these words. "You were there?"

"But I never remembered it, Delph. It was gone until I saw it again."

"But then why did I just remember pieces of it, then? Until now?"

"Difference between blue and red light, I guess," I said, feeling as drained as he looked. We both seemed to have run countless miles.

But I was also thinking of something else. When I told Morrigone I had visited her home once before, she had seemed immediately tense and suspicious. Now I knew why. She had thought I remembered seeing her all those sessions ago, when she had run out all mad-looking and hit me with the blue light, erasing from my mind what I had seen.

Then something else struck me. I stared hard at Delph.

He finally said, "What is it, Vega Jane?"

"Delph, you're not stuttering anymore."

He looked shaken by this observation; his mouth dropped open and then a smile slowly spread over his features. "You're right." He smiled more broadly.

"But why?" I asked.

"The words ain't jargoled no more, Vega Jane." He touched his head. "In here."

I put a hand on his arm. "The weight has lifted from you, Delph. I don't think you'll ever stutter again. And I'm so sorry

I had to put you through that. So very sorry, Delph, because you're my friend. My only one."

He looked at me and then to the sky. In the Noc light he looked like a very young again, running alongside me through the woods with nary a care in his heart. And the same for me. I couldn't even imagine what that would feel like anymore. Even though we weren't old, we *were* old with all that we carried inside.

He glanced at me, and the look on his face made me want to weep.

He touched my hand with his. "You're my friend too. And I'd take you over all other Wugs put together."

"I'm glad we got through that together, Delph." I paused and then decided to just say it. "My parents had Events. I saw them. They're not at the Care anymore. They're gone."

He looked at me in horror. "What?"

The tears slid down my cheeks as I continued. "The fire swallowed them up. It was just like you described, Delph. I had no idea what had happened to them, but now I do."

"I'm sorry you had to see that, Vega Jane."

"I'm sorry you had to see what you saw too."

I looked down at the book I still held.

"What about Outliers? Are they in the book?" I asked.

He glanced at me and shook his head. "Outliers? Load-a rubbish."

I hiked my eyebrows. I had come to agree with him, but I had seen so much that he hadn't. "Why?"

"If Outliers are out there, what are they waiting for, then? For us Wugs to build this stonking Wall for them to have to get over? Barmy."

"But you're helping to build the Wall," I pointed out.

"And what else can I do?" he said helplessly. "Probably chuck me in Valhall if I didn't."

"That's why they had to put the reward on Quentin's head," I said. The answer had just occurred to me, in fact.

"Why?" asked Delph. "What do you mean?"

"They couldn't simply say he'd had an Event, or a garm had got him. Because that would not have laid the groundwork for the announcement of the Outliers."

Delph seamlessly picked up my line of thought. "And then to the building of the Wall. 'Cause the one made the other happen."

"Right," I said, impressed by his logic. Gone was the mumbly-bumbly Delph with the big heart. He was now strong of both mind and body. And I was pretty sure he would need both. To survive.

What I was about to say might sound to Delph like a spontaneous thought, but I believed part of my mind had been thinking this ever since John left me.

"Delph," I said slowly.

"What?"

"You asked me if you could come with me through the Quag?"

He kept his gaze right on me. "That's right. I did."

"But why would you want to leave Wormwood? It's all you've ever known."

He scoffed. "What is there here, really, Vega Jane? Forty sessions from now, what will be different about here? And who's to say there ain't somethin' out there, beyond the Quag?

If there ain't been no Wug to go there, how do they know there ain't nothin' else? Tell me that. And now they're putting up this bleedin' Wall? Har!"

I was so proud of Delph at that sliver that I wanted to snog him.

"I don't think the Wall is being built to keep Outliers out, Delph. I think it's being built —"

"To keep *us* in," he finished for me.

"Council has lied to us. Krone, Morrigone, even Thansius," I said quietly.

He nodded absently. "I'll go with you through the Quag, Vega Jane. On the grave of me mum, I will go with you."

"Okay," I said. "If we're going to really do this, we have to have a plan."

He glanced at me. "What sort?"

I touched Destin around my waist. "For starters, you're going to have to learn how to fly too."

He looked terrified. "Fly? What, up there?" he said, pointing to the sky.

"Well, that's sort of the point of flying, Delph."

He put his huge hands up in protest. "I never. I couldn't, Vega Jane. I'm . . . I'm too *big*."

I stood and motioned for him to stand too and then I turned my back to him. "Put your arms around me."

"What?"

"Put your arms around me, Delph. And hold tight."

"Bloody Hel," he exclaimed, but his arms encircled me. This close, it was surprising how truly big he was, though I had known him all my life.

"Tighter, Delph, you don't want to fall."

He squeezed me so tight around my middle that I could barely breathe. "Not that bloody tight!" I barked at him. His grip relaxed a bit. "Now together we're going to jump, on the count of three. One . . . two . . . three."

We leapt at the same time, straight up. We shot skyward. I could feel Delph's grip around me tighten. I slowly moved myself forward so that he was now on my back. We raced along only about thirty yards up. The wind whipped over us.

"Bloody Hel!" Delph exclaimed again.

I looked back and up and saw that his eyes were closed.

"Delph, open your eyes. The view is amazing from up here."

He opened his eyes and looked ahead of us. His grip lessened and I felt his body, stiff as a rock before, grow relaxed. "'Tis beautiful," he said in an awed voice.

"Yes, it is. Just don't look down yet. It takes some getting used to and —"

That was a mistake. As soon as I said "don't look down," Delph of course looked down. His grip around my waist became iron, his body tensed and he screamed and rolled. That sent us into a dive. We were heading to the ground far faster than I ever had, but then I realized I had never before flown with a 250-pound Wug on my back.

We were totally out of control. Delph screamed. I screamed. We were a few yards from the ground when I reached back and slapped Delph in the face. He immediately stopped thrashing. I regained control, zoomed upward and then back down in a controlled dive this time and we landed, not smoothly, but we landed. As we sprawled on the ground, I looked over at him.

"You almost killed us," I said hotly. Then my anger faded as I remembered how it had been on my first flight. And at least I had been in control. He was just along for the ride. I stood and helped him up. "That was my fault, Delph. It will be better the next time."

He looked at me like I was asking him to be best mates with Cletus Loon. "Next time?" he said incredulously. "'Tain't going to be no next time, Vega Jane."

"Do you want to get through the Quag?" He sputtered but said nothing. I continued. "Because if we can fly over parts or all of the Quag, we won't have to worry about what's in it." I stared at him expectantly, tapping my boot against the dirt.

Delph blinked, slowly took this in and said, "Let's give it another go, then, Vega Jane. Har!"

Training Up

THE NEXT TWO nights, we practiced our flying. Well, I practiced while Delph hung on for his life. Finally, I slipped Destin off and handed it to him. He turned to run like a frightened Wug facing an amaroc.

"You have to try, Delph," I said.

He turned back. "Why? You can fly the thing. All's I need is to hold on."

"We don't know what might happen. You knowing how to do it by yourself is important." He looked doubtful until I said, "You have to, Delph, if you want to come along with me."

He gingerly took Destin from me. I had uncoiled the chain so that it was longer. Delph was wider at the waist than I was. I helped get it around him and snapped closed a metal hook I had fashioned and added to the chain.

He just stood there. "Now what?" he asked.

"Now what?" I said in amazement. "Delph, you've been flying with me for how long now? What do I do?"

"You either run and take off or you just jump," he replied promptly.

"So don't you reckon that's what you want to do?"

"Should I run or jump?" he asked tentatively.

Males. You have to lead them to the water and then show them how to slurp it.

"I don't care. Pick one."

"And once I get up there, what then?"

"I've shown you, Delph. You know how to steer. You know how to land. Just do it like I did it."

He backed up, got a running start and leapt. He flew straight and fast. Right into a large bush. I ran over and helped him out. He was coughing and his face was scratched from the prickly leaves.

"I can't do this, Vega Jane. I'm no good a'tall. Me feet belong on the ground."

"Yes, you can too do it," I said firmly. "Now, when you run and leap, point your head and shoulders upward. Then you won't hit the bush again. To turn, you point with whichever shoulder is in the direction you want to go. To head higher up, point your head that way. To come down, point your head and shoulders down. Right before you land, swing your feet down and you'll land upright."

"I'll bash my head in."

"You might," I said. "But if you do, I'll put it back together and you can try again."

He looked at me dubiously. "You cannae put no smashed head back together."

I took the Adder Stone out of my cloak pocket and waved it in front of his face and thought good things. The scratches there vanished. He backed away, looking fearful.

"What is that thing?" he exclaimed.

"It heals, Delph. Scratches and smashed heads. Pretty much anything."

"It can do that?"

"Yes, it can," I replied, though I had no actual experience with fixing smashed heads.

On his fourth attempt, Delph soared into the air, flew for about a quarter mile, made a long, if ragged, bank, turned back toward me and landed. On his feet. He was so excited at his success that he snatched me off the ground and whirled me around at such a fast pace I thought I would be sick.

"I did it, Vega Jane. I'm like a bird, I am."

"A very big bird," I replied. "And put me down before I vomit on you."

I decided to show Delph the Elemental. When I first pulled the tiny spear from my cloak pocket, wearing my glove, it was not very impressive to him. And considering it was barely three inches long, I could hardly blame him. But when I focused my thoughts and asked the Elemental to return to its normal state, it grew in my gloved hand to its proper length and assumed its dazzling golden color.

Delph exclaimed, "How in the bloody Hel does it do that, Vega Jane?"

"It doesn't matter to me *how* it does it, Delph," I said. "It's only important that it *does* it when I need it to."

He reached out to take it, but I stayed his hand. "Only with this, Delph," I said, holding up the glove.

"If you touch it without the glove, what happens?" he asked.

"Neither one of us wants to find out, do we?"

He slipped on the glove and hefted the Elemental. I looked over at a tree about thirty feet distant. "Think in your mind that you want the Elemental to hit that tree. Then throw it that way, like a spear."

Delph looked doubtful, but he scrunched up his face — which was a bit comical, though I hid my smile — took aim and let fly.

The Elemental traveled a few yards and then dove into the dirt. Delph looked over at me, smiling. "Cor blimey. Is that all it does? Har!"

I took the glove from him, picked up the Elemental, thought about what I wanted it to do and let it fly. The tree disintegrated in a flash of light when the spear struck it. I held out my gloved hand, and the Elemental flew back to it, like the hunter hawks I had seen Duf training up.

Delph had thrown himself to the dirt when the Elemental hit the tree. When he looked up, I gazed down at him with what I hoped was a sufficiently patronizing look.

"No, *that's* what it does, Delph. Har!"

Soon, Delph could hit just about anything with the Elemental. I didn't know if it would be necessary when we tried to pass through the Quag, but I didn't know it wouldn't be either.

Late that night, Delph and I sat at my digs in front of a meager fire while Harry Two snoozed at our feet. Making up my mind, I stood and said, "Now you need to see something."

"What?"

I slid my trousers down.

"Vega Jane!" he exclaimed, looking away, his face as red as a raspberry.

233

I ignored this and lifted up my tattered shirt and my shirtsleeves, exposing my belly and my arms. "Look, Delph. Look."

"Cor blimey, Vega Jane," he said, his voice shaky. "You gone mental or what?"

"It's not what you think, Delph. I've got my under thingies on. Look!"

He slowly turned his head back. His gaze ran up along my legs to my belly and up my arms. His jaw fell. "What in Noc's name is that, I ask ya?"

"It's the map through the Quag. Quentin Herms left it for me. He had it on parchment. But I was afraid to keep it, so I inked it on my skin."

He drew closer. "The way through?"

"And I've memorized all of it, Delph. But you need to as well."

"I wouldnae b-b-be staring at your . . . at your Wu-Wugness," stammered Delph, turning away once more.

I frowned. "Well, you're going to have to, Delph. If you want to go. We both have to know the way, just in case." I held up the Quag book. "You well know what awaits us in there."

For the next thirty slivers, Delph studied the marks on my skin as I walked him through the map of the Quag. I would do this for as many nights as possible until the directions were firmly entrenched in his brain. As the slivers passed, Delph's eyes slowly closed. Soon he was snoring in his seat. I lowered my shirt and drew up my trousers, sat in my only other chair and looked through the book on the Quag.

Harry Two whimpered a bit at my feet. I looked down and thought he might be having a bad dream. I wasn't sure if canines could dream, though I didn't see any particular reason why not. And anyway, Harry Two was quite a special canine.

I slowly turned page after page in the book, taking in as much information as I could. Quentin Herms had been as meticulous in documenting the Quag as he had been making pretty things at Stacks. But the things he had documented and re-created in these pages were not to be taken lightly. On nearly every piece of parchment there was something that could kill you. Like a creature that was three huge bodies attached. And while you might be able to cleave them apart, the book warned that *Woe be to the Wug who forgets that destroying one part of the thing does not equal victory.*

But there were some beneficial creatures as well, including something called a Hob that would help you so long as you gave it a small gift each light. Cheeky blighter, I thought, trading kindness for coin.

I finally closed the book and peered into the fire. One smoldering log caught my attention. Its bark was reddened, nearly transparent because of the bite of flames. My grandfather and my parents — swallowed whole by fire.

But it was my grandfather who had initiated the flames. He had wanted to go. Morrigone was imploring him to stay. And he had gone anyway. And now my parents had gone too. And perhaps they had done so because they wanted to leave as well.

Which meant they had chosen to leave us. No, to leave *me*.

Well, I could not burst into flames to leave Wormwood, but I could go through the Quag to do so. For now that was my overriding obsession. To leave Wormwood and find my grandfather and my parents, because they were not dead. They were simply no longer in Wormwood. Which meant they were somewhere else. Which meant there was somewhere other than Wormwood.

Now another emotion seized me and I sat down on the cold stone floor and did something I almost never did. I started to weep. I rocked back and forth. I hurt all over. Almost like I had been swallowed by fire myself. My skin felt burned and blackened. I was gasping for breath, so hard was I crying. It was like I had saved all my sessions up to let it loose now.

I was startled when I felt it.

The big arms wrapped around me. I opened my eyes and there was Delph sitting next to me, holding me and weeping along with me.

Harry Two had awoken as well. He had sidled over to us and was inching my hand up with his snout. Trying to make me look at him. Probably trying to make me feel better. But it's hard to feel better when your entire family has left you.

And done so by their choice.

"'Tis okay, Vega Jane," Delph said into my ear, his warm breath tickling my skin. "'Tis okay," he mumbled again.

I touched his hand to let him know I'd heard. But it would not be okay.

Nothing again would ever be okay.

But come what may, I was going to leave this place.

Because I had come to learn that while Wormwood was full of many things, the truth was not one of them.

And the truth was what I needed.

I had nothing else left.

The Duelum

WHEN I LEFT for Stacks one light, there it was. The cloth banner was strung across the High Street in Wormwood, connected by metal hooks and stout ropes into the fronts of two buildings facing the cobblestones. It read:

GREETINGS, ALL WUGMORTS. THE NEXT DUELUM WILL BE HELD IN A FORTNIGHT AT THE PITCH. FIRST PRIZE FIVE HUNDRED COINS. ALL ELIGIBLE MALE WUGMORTS BETWEEN FIFTEEN AND TWENTY-FOUR SESSIONS OLD MUST COMPETE.

Underneath this was a statement that a meeting would be held in the village square this night where more information would be provided, along with a directive that all Wugmorts attend.

Duelums were twice-a-session competitions pitting strong males against one another on a broad pitch on the edge of Wormwood proper. And even though he was only sixteen sessions, Delph had won three of them, including the last.

The coin prize was startling enough. For as long as I could remember, the only prizes one got when winning a Duelum were a metal figurine of a male Wug holding another male Wug over his head and a mere handful of coins.

I wondered if Delph would win again. He and Duf could certainly use five hundred coins.

I stared up at the banner for a few moments. I would have thought, with all the work on the Wall, that it would have been postponed. Male Wugs were working hard enough without having to stop and beat one another's brains out. Yet it had little enough to do with me.

I headed on to Stacks, arriving one sliver late, but no one said anything. I changed and went to my workstation to begin my tasks. I looked around at the few other Wugs left at Stacks. I could sense in the muttering, the stealthy looks and one Dactyl flexing his impressive muscles that they had heard of the Duelum and were sizing up the competition. I was the only female there, so none of them was looking at me.

In the locker room later, when work was done, I changed into my regular clothes after the males had left. I lifted my shirt and looked down at my flat belly. Parts of the map had faded so badly that I had had to ink them back in several times now. And because Delph also had to memorize it, I had decided to copy the map back down on parchment. It was actually a little embarrassing having him stare at my bare stomach and legs. I could see sometimes that his attention was wandering more to the skin than the marks on it.

As I was passing Domitar's office, the door opened and he stepped out. This was fortuitous because I had been thinking of a question and decided that Domitar might have the answer.

I said, "Morrigone told me that her grandfather served on Council with my grandfather. I didn't know my grandfather was on Council."

"It was a volatile time in our history."

"*Volatile.* You can't mean the Battle of the Beasts I was told about at Learning? That took place long before my grandfather was even born."

Domitar looked angry for his choice of words. "Let sleeping canines lie. That's the better policy."

"To Hel with sleeping canines, Domitar. I want the truth."

He turned and went back into his office, like a rabbit into its hole. Or a rat down a drainpipe.

Later that night, with Harry Two at my side, I trudged to the village center and joined the crowd massing there. A wooden platform had been set up with stairs made from roughhewn planks leading up to it. I was not surprised in the least to see Bogle and the carriage already there. I was also not surprised to see Thansius and Morrigone seated on the platform. But I was flummoxed to see John sitting next to them. And he wore the black dress tunic of Council!

Someone whispered in my ear, "'Tis John."

I turned to see Delph standing there.

Indeed 'tis John, I thought. *And indeed 'tis not John.*

Pretty much every Wug was here. Roman Picus and his Carbineer mates, Cletus, Non and Ran Digby, were standing at comical attention with their knives and long and short mortas. I was thankful to be downwind from Digby. The niff that bloke sent off would have me barfing. As a female, I had thought about skiving off this meeting, but I was too curious to stay away.

The one Wug missing was Jurik Krone. I scanned the row of Council members seated in front of the platform, but he was not there. It was not like him to skip a public event where he could preen for the audience. I wondered when he would challenge Thansius for Council leadership. I also wondered what the other far more senior Council members thought about John sitting up there while they were relegated to being down with us average Wugs. Julius Domitar was there with tiny Dis Fidus hovering beside him. Ezekiel occupied a solitary corner of the square, resplendent in his white tunic. The Loons residents were clustered like chickens on the far side of the square.

I was startled to see Ladon-Tosh, armed to the teeth, guarding the steps up to the platform. He looked as maniacal as ever. I made sure not to lock gazes with him. For some insane reason, I thought I might disappear if I did.

All the males looked tired and dirty. All the females, while a bit cleaner by comparison, looked even more knackered. They had to work on the Wall as well, but they also had to take care of their families — cooking, cleaning and being mother Wugs. Despite all that, I sensed excitement in the crowd. And the reason was obvious. Five hundred coins. The desire for it was palpable. No one had collected the reward on Quentin Herms. But some Wug *had* to win the Duelum and with it the coins.

Thansius cleared his throat and stood. He raised his hands above his head. "Greetings, fellow Wugmorts. We have asked you here this night to announce the latest Duelum. It will begin at the second section of light a fortnight hence. The reward for the champion, as you no doubt already know, will be five hundred coins."

Whispers and murmurs zipped through the crowd. However, my gaze held steady on my brother. He was seated next to Morrigone and the two of them seemed to be having a conversation about something. John seemed happy, content. And Morrigone, well, she appeared to be like a proud Preceptor with her prize prodigy. Then Thansius said something that made my attention snap back to him.

"This Duelum will be different from all the others." He paused, seeming to gather oratorical fortitude. "This Duelum will also include all females between the ages of twenty and twenty-four sessions." And he added the stunner. "The females' participation is mandatory as well."

Now the whispers went up a thousandfold. Most males were guffawing. Females were looking confused and frightened. That included myself, although I was not old enough to have to participate. I was afraid for the females who were. I shot a glance at Delph. He wasn't laughing at the idea of females in the Duelum. I next eyed Cletus Loon. He was snickering with two of his loutish friends.

Thansius cleared his throat and asked for silence.

We Wugs quieted down. Of course there would have to be two champions, male and female, because there was no way they could expect females to fight males.

Thansius cleared this up with his next comment. "There will be only one champion." I looked up at him, stunned. He continued. "We Wugmorts have to accept the fact that there should be more equality between males and females."

Okay, I thought, if they wanted equality how about having more than one female at Stacks? Or telling males that they could cook and clean and tend to the very youngs just as well as females? Somehow, though, I didn't see getting one's brains smashed in by a far stronger male Wug as resounding evidence of a forward-thinking society.

Thansius continued. "And now here is Morrigone to more fully explain the reasoning behind this decision."

I supposed the "reasoning" behind *that* was it took a female to explain to other females why it made sense to get your brain smashed in. I watched along with every other Wug as Morrigone rose and glided to the front of the platform. She was perfectly composed and took a sliver to look over the crowd and let them feel her presence. Well, I would be composed too if I were her. She was certainly older than twenty-four sessions and therefore would not have to pit herself against males. But then again, *she* might be able to win against them.

Morrigone said, "No doubt many of you, particularly the females among us, are wondering why this decision has come about. First, let me state that all females within the age requirement who are mates with males, or mothers, or who are currently with child, or had a child within the last full session, will not have to compete."

A collective sigh of relief flowed through the crowd. There were a great many females who would qualify for these exceptions, I knew.

Morrigone continued. "As well as any females with physical disabilities or other weaknesses or infirmities. This last exception of course will apply to males as well."

I looked around the crowd of Wugs and saw a good many females who would also qualify for this exception, along with about a dozen males. They too looked greatly relieved.

She added, "But all others must fight. They will be pitted against the males. Some may say this is unfair. But times have changed in Wormwood. The Outliers surround us. They do not care who is male and who is female. They will attack us all. Thus the able-bodied and younger females among us must be prepared to fight. And the way to do that is to train to fight. To learn how to defend themselves. That is why a fortnight has been given for all eligible females to learn these skills. And professional fight Preceptors will be available for all, males and females, who desire to be trained up. I would recommend that all females competing in the Duelum avail themselves of this opportunity."

I gazed up in disbelief at her. Time to learn these skills? In a fortnight? Was she serious? When females were already killing themselves building the Wall? The males wouldn't have to waste time training, just the poor females. They couldn't suddenly put on ninety pounds of muscle. They couldn't very well turn into a male. Not that they would ever want to.

Thansius nodded at one of the Council members down below. The Wug stood and held up a cloth bag. Thansius said, "The prize of five hundred coins."

Wugs made a great fuss over this great bag of wealth. And then Thansius added, "In order to make things a bit more enticing" — he paused for effect — "if a female were to win the Duelum, the prize will be increased to one thousand coins."

There was no cheering over this from any females. They obviously could see that no female would claim it, so what was there to get excited about?

Thansius then told us that the competition rounds would

be posted soon, showing who would be competing against whom in the first round. He said that they had already calculated the number of eligible competitors, and five rounds would be necessary to declare a champion. He wished us all good luck and then told us the "meeting" was over.

As Wugs started to slowly drift away, I made a beeline for the platform. I wanted to see John. However, before I could get there, someone blocked my way.

Cletus Loon looked me up and down, a murderous expression on his face. "It's a good thing you're too young to fight. I might draw you in the first round," he said.

"It is a good thing I'm too young to fight," I replied. "A good thing for *you*. Now get out of my way, you git."

I tried to brush past him, but he put a hand on my shoulder. Before I could react or a growling Harry Two could take a bite out of him, Cletus was flying backward and landing hard on the cobblestones, his morta and knife flying away.

Before he could even attempt to get up, Delph put a huge boot on his chest and held him down.

Cletus yelled, "You take your filthy foot off me."

One of Cletus's friends came up and said, "Look at Da-Da-Da-Delph."

Delph grabbed him by the shirt, hoisted him full off the cobblestones and held him close to his face. "The name is Daniel Delphia to you, you little prat. And next time I won't be so polite in reminding you. Now shove off."

He let the Wug drop, and the git ran off as fast as he could. Then Delph removed his foot from Cletus, who was staring up with an amazed look.

"Y-you're not stut-stuttering," said Cletus in a quavering voice.

"But you are." Delph knelt down so he and Cletus were eye to eye. "You best hope I don't draw you first, Loon. And if you lay another hand on Vega Jane, you'll pray for death by garm once I get ahold of you. Now clear off!"

Cletus scrambled to his feet and raced away.

"Thanks, Delph," I said, my face full of the deep gratitude I was feeling.

"You could have taken care of that git yourself, Vega Jane."

"Maybe. But it's nice to have help." Then I remembered where I was going. John was almost at the carriage. "Good luck in the Duelum, Delph," I said. "I hope you win the five hundred coins."

I turned and sprinted down the cobblestones and reached John just as he was about to climb aboard after Morrigone.

"John?"

He turned and smiled, but the smile was . . . forced. I could tell that instantly.

"Hello, Vega," he said stiffly. But I still sensed my little brother inside. Although, maybe I just wanted it to be so.

Morrigone leaned out the door. When she saw me, she said, "John, we must go. There is last meal and then we must work on your lessons."

"It'll only take a sliver, Morrigone," I said hurriedly.

She nodded curtly and sat back in her seat. However, I suspected she was listening intently.

"What is it, Vega?" asked John. He looked down at Harry Two but made no move to pet him or even ask about him. My brother's hair was even shorter, shaved very close to his scalp. He was very nearly unrecognizable to me.

"How are you?" I said. "It seems like our last visit was a session ago."

"I've been very busy with the Wall and my lessons," he said.

"Yes, the Wall is keeping *every* Wug busy," I replied, hoping he heard my emphasis.

"But we're still behind schedule," John said. "The official timetable will not be met. We need to work harder. The Outliers may strike at any time. We *must* have a sense of urgency."

His strident tone caught me off guard.

"Uh, you look well," I said, changing the subject.

He seemed to calm, but all enthusiasm drained from his face as he focused on my simple observation. "I am very well. And you?"

"Fine." It felt like two strangers meeting.

"Have you been to the Care?" asked John.

I flinched and then my gaze darted to the carriage. "Not recently, no."

"I've wanted to visit our parents, but Morrigone says I must stay focused."

I hesitated. I was trying very hard not to jump into the carriage and have a personal Duelum with Morrigone. But I had given her my word. "I'm sure she does," I said loudly so that Morrigone was certain to hear.

Morrigone poked her head out. "We must go, John."

"Just one more sliver," I called out, staring directly at her. "And don't worry, Morrigone, I'll keep focused on what needs to be said and what *doesn't*."

She gave me a piercing look and then withdrew into the carriage once more.

"I miss you, John." Then I stepped forward and hugged him. I could feel him tense under my embrace.

I felt him mechanically patting my arm. "Things will be fine, I'm sure, Vega. You have a canine now, I see."

I stepped back and looked down at him. "I'm living in our old house."

He looked startled by this.

"Our old house?"

I nodded. "Loon won't allow canines. But it was good to go home. Very good. Reminds you of how important families are."

Morrigone looked out of the window and glared at me.

"I hope you have been enjoying your *time*, Vega."

I did a bit of a double take, as I focused on the emphasis she had placed on the word *time*.

"I'm not sure what you mean."

"You will," she said cryptically.

And for a fleeting moment, I thought I saw great sadness on Morrigone's features, but it happened so fast that I could not be sure.

She looked past me and said, "Come along, John. We have things we must accomplish this night."

John boarded the carriage.

Morrigone and I stared at each other for a half sliver longer and then Bogle whipped up the sleps and they were off.

I spun around on my heels and walked off, pushing my way through huddles of Wugs who were lingering to talk about the Duelum. I felt a sharp pain in my side and looked over to see Cletus Loon running away with what looked like a rock in his hand. I called Harry Two back because he had started to tear off after Cletus. I took a deep breath, stopped thinking about the pain and hurried on. Harry Two snorted twice and glanced back at Cletus, obviously miffed about being called off.

I reached my digs, pulled out the Adder Stone, waved it over my hurt and thought good thoughts. The hurt instantly vanished, as did the swelling.

I placed the Stone, along with Destin and the shrunken Elemental, in my cloak pocket and hung it on a wall peg. As I rubbed my side, I truly believed this was to be the last time I would ever be pain free.

Valhall

L ATE THAT NIGHT, I heard Harry Two bark. That was actually the second noise I heard. The first was my door crashing inward.

I sprang off my cot, my heart pounding painfully in my chest.

I saw Harry Two fly backward and strike the wall next to my cot. He lay there stunned even as I looked around and saw what was happening.

Jurik Krone stood before me. Behind him were Non, Ran Digby, Cletus Loon and Duk Dodgson, at twenty-four sessions old, the youngest member of Council. They all carried either long- or short-barreled mortas and they were all pointed at me.

"What is going on?" I shouted as I ran over to Harry Two and made sure he was okay. He lay there, his tongue hanging out and his breathing heavy, but nothing seemed to be broken and he did lick my hand.

"We are here to take you to Valhall, female," announced Krone.

"You are not taking me anywhere, you git. I've had quite enough —"

Krone held up the book of the Quag that Quentin Herms had authored.

His smile was as triumphant as it was cruel.

I made the mistake of glancing at the floorboard where I had hidden it.

"This was taken from your digs earlier this night during the meeting at the village square," said Krone. I winced at the utter glee in his voice. That explained why he was not at the meeting. He had been here, searching.

Krone continued. "It appears to be a book on the Quag. An illegal thing if ever there was one. Was it the Outliers that gave it to you, Vega? Does it show the routes they will use to attack us? How much are they paying you for your treachery? Or have they simply taken over your puny mind?"

· I looked at each of them, my heart pumping so fast I had to steady myself by holding on to the wall. "I don't know what you're talking about. I'm not a traitor. And I'm not working with any Outliers."

Krone drew closer and pointed his short-barreled morta at my head. With his free hand he held the book close to my face. "Then explain this book. Where did you come by it?"

"I found it."

"You found it!" exclaimed Krone. "Then why did you not report it to Council?"

"I . . . I was going to," I said lamely.

"You lie," he snapped, his features twisted into an ugly ball of fury.

He looked at Digby and Non. "Take her."

They came forward and seized me by the arms. Harry

Two started to attack them, but I ordered him back. Dodgson had taken aim at my canine's chest and I was terrified he would shoot him.

"Don't," I screamed. "He won't try and harm you. I'll come with you. I won't fight. Harry Two, you stay here. You stay!"

I was hustled out of my home and down the Low Road. All the noise must have woken up the village, because many Wugs in their nightclothes were out on the cobblestones as we reached the High Street, the buildings behind them ablaze with candle and lantern light.

We reached Valhall. Nida had evidently been forewarned and placed back on duty, because he had the cage door open. The shuck stood next to him, its ferocious eyes on me, its nostrils quivering as though it was taking in my scent in case it had to run me down and kill me later.

I was thrown inside the cage, and the huge door slammed shut behind me. Nida securely locked it.

Krone stared at me through the bars. "Formal charges will be brought against you this light. And those charges will be proved. And the penalty for treason of course is beheading."

I looked at him in disbelief. *Beheading?*

As he turned away to speak to Nida, my mind raced. It was stupid for me to have kept the book, but it did not detail attack plans against Wormwood. It was information about creatures that existed in the Quag. My spirits sank as I thought about this. How could I explain having such a book without revealing that I had taken it from Quentin's cottage? And how could I explain him even having such a book? I glanced down at my arm. I thanked Steeples that I had fallen into an exhausted sleep this night and not bothered to take off my clothes. If they had seen the marks of the Quag map on my body, they would probably tear me limb from limb here and now. I pulled my sleeve down farther and made sure my trousers were securely fastened and my shirt tucked in them.

Krone turned back to me. "You can spend the rest of this night thinking of your sins. And the punishment to come." He drew closer so that his mouth nearly touched the bars.

"And not even Madame Morrigone can get you out of this, Vega."

He cackled, turned and left.

I yelled at him and reached through the bars in a futile attempt to hit him. Then I jerked my hand back as the shuck snapped at me with his teeth. I came within an inch of losing my fingers.

Nida's club hit the bars with a powerful whack. He roared, "Never reach through the bars, female. I will not tell you this again."

I crawled to the center of the cage and sat there, dazed by what had happened. I was hoping this was simply a nightmare from which I would soon wake. But as the darkness deepened and I lay there shivering in the chill, I had to accept that this was real.

For a time, I watched Nida and the shuck patrol up and down the cobblestones. Then Nida went into his little shack, and the shuck became the sole sentry. If I moved even a muscle, it would stop its pacing, turn and make such a menacing growl that my arm and neck hairs rose heavenward.

I cried a bit because I could not help myself. Then I grew angry, thinking of how many ways I would tear Krone apart. Then I thought of what my defense to the charges might be. Then real depression set in, because I could think of no plausible explanation, not even a lie that I could carry off.

I didn't have my tuck with me so trying to pick the lock was not possible. Even if I had, the shuck would just bite me in half. I lay down on the dirt floor and ran my fingers along the ground. Prisoners before me had left their marks here in the form of holes and burrows in the dirt. I could understand that. One would want to dig into the dirt just to hide from the shame of being here.

I fell asleep three times but awoke with a start each time, either because Nida, who returned periodically to his patrol, slammed his club against the bars, or else the shuck howled at something. I wondered if this was how things usually were — the guards instructed to never allow a prisoner a sound night's sleep.

I watched the black of night turn to gray and then deepening red and then brilliant gold as the sun began its climb into the sky. I was dreading the light, for obvious reasons. Thankfully, I fell asleep again, which allowed my exhausted mind and body a bit of a reprieve. When I awoke, the sun had brightened Wormwood. I stared at the blue sky and calculated it was nearing the second section of light. My belly grumbled and I wondered if food was served here. I would not be going to Stacks this light. I hoped someone had told Domitar. I supposed this meant I was going to be sacked from my job.

And then I recalled Krone's words.

My punishment could be death. And here I was worried about not having gainful employment or food in my belly.

I blinked heavily as I saw him near the cage.

It was Delph, and he had Harry Two with him. The shuck instantly started to growl. Nida came forward and stared up at Delph.

"You will move along, male," said Nida. "And the canine too."

"I want to talk to Vega Jane," said Delph forcefully.

"You cannae talk to a prisoner. Now move along." Nida slapped the club against the palm of his hand.

"I saved your life once, Nida. And you will not grant me this?" said Delph sternly.

Nida stared up at Delph. I could see the conflicting thoughts racing across his small, brutish features.

"You have five slivers, no more. And our debt will be settled."

Nida stepped aside and whistled at the shuck, which stopped growling and drew next to his master as Delph and Harry Two passed by to the cage door.

I flung myself against the bars. "Delph, you have to help me."

"What be the charges against you, Vega Jane, rubbish though they must be?"

I couldn't look at him as I said in a low voice, "They found the book on the Quag."

He sucked in a breath and looked nervously over at Nida.

I said, "Krone is saying I'm a traitor. That the book is a way to help the Outliers attack us."

"Bollocks."

"I know, Delph. But Krone said I could be put to death for this."

He paled, though I'm sure he wasn't any paler than I was. If it was possible, I was more scared than I had been with the jabbits. I knew Krone would take great pleasure in wielding the ax on me himself.

"How did you know I was here?"

"Word got round fast, it did."

"H-how did you save Nida's life?"

"He was out on patrol with the Carbineers one night. Stupid Cletus Loon mistook him for something and took aim with his morta. I was walking past and saw what was happening. I grabbed Nida and threw him down a moment before Loon fired. Blew a hole in the side of a tree instead of Nida's head."

I nodded, but my mind had already moved back to my dilemma.

"You ain't guilty of nothing, Vega Jane. And you're going to be out of here in a sliver."

"I'm really scared," I said.

He reached out a finger and touched my hand.

An instant later, we had leapt back because Nida's club had come down on the bars, nearly crushing our fingers.

Nida barked, "Talk, not touch. Har! And your slivers are almost up, Delphia."

I looked down at Harry Two. He looked alone and scared. I said, "Delph, can you look after Harry Two?" I swallowed a huge lump in my throat. "Just while I'm in here."

He nodded. "O'course. What's one more beast to the

Delphias?" He tried to smile at his little joke but couldn't manage it.

I looked at Harry Two. "You're going to go with Delph, okay?"

Harry Two, I thought, shook his head, but I pointed my finger at him and told him again. He finally lowered his head, and his tail tucked between his hind legs.

"I have to get on to Wall building," Delph said. "I'm already late."

I nodded.

He glanced over at Nida. He was busy adjusting the shuck's spiked collar.

Delph reached in his pocket and handed me a hard roll, a bit of meat and an apple.

"I'll be back soon as I can."

I nodded again. With one more look back at me, Delph and Harry Two disappeared down the cobblestones.

I retreated to the far corner of the cage, squatted down with my back to Nida and had my meal. My belly was hungry, but my mind refused to focus on the food in front of me.

The full Council would be meeting to decide my fate. I couldn't believe they would kill me for merely possessing a book. But the more I thought about it, the worse my thoughts became. It wasn't simply any book. It was a book that described the creatures of the Quag. They would want to know how I had come by it. Would they accuse me of actually going in the Quag to learn this? Should I tell them I had nicked it from Quentin Herms's cottage? Then they would want to know why I was there. What would my defense be?

That I believed the idea of the Outliers was a load of hooey? And that the Wall was being built to keep us Wugs in and not Outliers out? Oh, yes, that would go over very well with Council. They might give me a bloody medal.

I was about to take a bite of the apple but instead I put it back in my pocket. I felt sick to my stomach; cold waves of nausea swept over me. I was not going to leave Valhall this light. I might never leave here until they took my head clean from my shoulders.

The light swept to the third section and the sun beat down on the metal roof of the cage, making it sweltering inside. I remembered the Wug McCready, who had asked me for a cuppa water when I had passed by here. I could understand his request as my throat felt like it was closing up. It was fortunate, I knew, that no Wugs had come by to see me here. Or to hurl spit at me. Or call me a traitor. How long would that last?

I looked over at Nida. He was watching me closely now, perhaps wondering how well I would handle being locked up.

I thought of several smart remarks but didn't have the courage or energy to deliver any of them.

As the light wore on, I heard the wheels before I saw the carriage. Only it wasn't a carriage. What turned the corner and headed to Valhall was a simple wagon with a cage set in the back. Two Wugs who I knew worked for Council were in the driver's box. A single old slep was pulling it, its head and tail drooping in the heat.

They stopped in front of the cage door and one of them jumped down. His tunic was not black, but green. He handed Nida a parchment.

"The prisoner is wanted at Council," he said.

Nida nodded, glanced at the parchment and then unhooked the large key from his wide belt. He unlocked the cage door and said, "Come, now!"

I stumbled forward and the Wug shackled my legs and hands. He had to lift me into the back of the wagon and I was forced into the cage, which was bolted after me.

The Wug got back in the wagon, and the other Wug whipped up the slep.

And off I went to Council.

Off I went, perhaps forever.

Council

THE COUNCIL BUILDING was located at the very
end of the High Street. It made all other structures in
Wormwood, except Stacks and Steeples, seem but a clutter of
old boards and cracked glass by comparison. It was that
grand. I had no idea who had built it or when. I had always
admired it, if from afar.

It was constructed of stone and marble with soaring col-
umns out front and grand steps leading up to it. The doors
were made of iron with intricate scrollwork that, as a Finisher,
I had long loved to gaze at. It was said that the lights in the
Council building were never extinguished and that despite
the heat or cold outside, it remained the same temperature
inside at all times.

As the head of Council, Thansius maintained his living
quarters on the second floor. I had never been inside. I had
had no reason to — until now. And I wished with all my heart
that I were not here.

They did not bring me in the front entrance. I supposed
prisoners were not given that privilege. A rear entry sufficed.
I passed other Wugs who worked at Council as I shuffled
along in the chain bindings. Most of the Wugs didn't look at

me. Those who did were fiendishly hostile. I hoped they were not part of the voting process here; otherwise I would be dead before this night.

I was led into a chamber that was nearly as large as the main room at Stacks, but far nicer. The floors were marble, the walls of stone, the ceiling a combination of the two, with enormous old worm-pitted beams crisscrossing the high space.

On a raised dais behind an intricately carved wooden waist-high wall sat the full Council. Thansius was seated in the center. He wore his robes of bloodred, which I did not take as a good sign. To his left was Krone, dressed in his usual black. To his right was Morrigone. She too was dressed in red.

Red and black would never again be favored colors of mine.

I was led to a small table with one chair. Next to it was a lectern, which the Preceptors at Learning had used when teaching us youngs.

"Remove her shackles," ordered Thansius.

This was done immediately by the two Wugs who had brought me here by wagon. Then they retreated and I heard the door close behind them.

Now it was just me and Council. I looked up at them. And they looked down at me. I felt like a mouse quivering before a garm.

"Sit down, prisoner," said Krone, "while charges against you are read."

I sat, surreptitiously tugged down my shirtsleeves and

tried to stop my heart from bursting out of my throat. From the corner of my eye I saw Ladon-Tosh seated to the side of the chamber. He was not looking at anyone or anything. I couldn't understand why he was here, but then my gaze drifted down to his waist.

There was an ax held there in a special sheath fitted to his belt.

I turned back to look at Council while tendrils of cold dread formed around me.

Jurik Krone stood with a scroll of parchment in hand. He looked triumphantly at his fellow Council members. His victorious gaze, at least it seemed to me, lingered longest on Morrigone.

"This female, Vega Jane, has long been skirting the laws of Wormwood. I have statements from Cacus Loon and his son, Cletus, as well as from Non and Roman Picus, that shows she has broken laws without consequences for some time now."

"We are here for other matters this light, Jurik," said Thansius. "So let us focus on them."

Krone nodded and glanced down at the parchment. "We found in the possession of Vega Jane a book." He reached in front of him and lifted it up for all to see. "This book gives a detailed description of the creatures living in the Quag with, in certain circumstances, ways around said creatures. It also identifies species in the Quag that may be of help to those seeking to traverse the Quag. Like —" He paused and I knew exactly what he was going to say next. I mouthed the word before he spoke it.

"Outliers," finished Krone.

On this, Council started murmuring among themselves. I noted that only Thansius and Morrigone held their own counsel and did not look at the others.

Thansius stared at a spot just over my head, although his gaze occasionally flicked to me.

Morrigone never once looked at me. I did not take that as a good sign.

Krone continued. "The only possible reason for this female to harbor a book like this is to aid the enemies of Wormwood. For such treasonous acts" — on this he gave a significant glance in the direction of Ladon-Tosh — "execution is the only appropriate punishment."

Krone looked at each of the Council members in turn and then saved his most scathing look for me.

Thansius rose and said, "Thank you, Jurik, for your, uh, typically energetic parsing of the facts." He then picked up the book and turned to me.

"How came you by this book, Vega?"

I looked around, unsure of what to do. Finally, I stood.

"I found it at Quentin Herms's cottage."

"You were never inside his cottage," protested Krone.

"I was," I said. "And I saw you there."

"Rubbish. Lies and more lies."

"'The ring is the puzzlement for me. Why would the accursed Virgil not leave it to his son?' That's what you said in the cottage, Krone. I was hiding behind the cabinet in the front room. You weren't there alone." I hesitated, and then my instinct told me to go for it. "Would you like me to say who you were there with?" I didn't know who that was, at least not for certain, but Krone couldn't know that.

"Enough!" shouted Krone. "So you were at the cottage? That merely proves that you knew of the book and took it."

"I did —"

"Did you help the traitor Herms create it?"

"I am trying to —"

"Do you expect us to believe your pathetic lies?"

"Jurik," Thansius's voice boomed.

The entire Council seemed to shudder collectively.

Thansius said, "She is trying to tell us her side of things. Your interrupting before she does so is not especially productive or a good use of Council's time."

There were murmurs of agreement on this point and Krone sat down and looked off as though he would not bother to even listen to what I had to say. I noted his crony, Duk Dodgson, sitting next to him and doing the very same thing.

Thansius looked at me and said, "Go on, Vega."

"I didn't know about the book. I went to the cottage because of the reward." A lie plus a truth was far better than two lies, at least in my estimation. In fact, it was pretty close to the truth.

I looked around the room. "That many coins means a lot to a Wug like me. Domitar told us about the reward at Stacks. Every Stacker, I'm sure, did his best to collect his reward, so why not me? I went to the cottage to see if I could find any clues to where Herms had gone."

"He had not *gone* anywhere," countered Krone, who was now once more staring at me. "Outliers took him."

"But I didn't know that at the time, did I? It was only announced later and then explained at Steeples to all Wugs."

"Then why did you keep the book?" asked Krone, a tone of triumph in his voice. "Why did you not turn it in to Council?"

"I was scared," I replied.

"Of what?" snarled Krone.

"Of Wugs reacting just like you're reacting now!" I shot back. "Even if I turned it in, I knew you, Krone, would find some way to twist it into a verdict of guilt. When you came for me last night, you said I would be executed. You'd obviously already made up your mind before the Council hearing. Where is the justice in that?"

My statement had the desired effect. Instantly, there were mutterings among the Council members. I saw two of the members give Krone harsh looks.

Morrigone stared at the wall across the room. Thansius kept his gaze on me.

Krone sputtered, "I did no such thing."

My heart was still pounding and I was still terrified, but my anger was overriding my fear.

"Then why did you take me from my digs in shackles?"

"He did that?"

We all turned to look at Morrigone, who was now staring at Krone.

"He did," I answered.

"You said you were taken last night, Vega," said Thansius. "To where were you taken?"

I stared at Krone when I said, "Valhall. I was there until I was brought here. And no food or water has passed my lips." Well, I had eaten some of what Delph brought me, but I was still starving.

"Then you must be very hungry and thirsty," said Morrigone. She clapped her hands and an assistant instantly left the chamber. He came back a sliver later carrying a platter with bread and cheeses and a carafe of water. He set it down in front of me.

Morrigone said, "On behalf of Council, Vega, I apologize. No Wug goes to Valhall who has not first been convicted." She added in a withering tone with a scathing look at Krone tacked on, "As my colleague Krone well knows."

Krone had said nothing this whole time. As I attacked my meal and drank down the water, I shot glances here and there at Council. I saw Krone looking down at his hands and no doubt wondering where his advantage had gone. I was thinking that I might even be let go in a sliver or two when I noticed the carafe had a slight crack in it. Water had dribbled out of it and onto my sleeve. A puddle of dark liquid was pooling on the table.

I stared at it for a long moment, wondering what its source was. I wasn't *that* dirty.

I didn't even know he was beside me until I looked up.

Krone was staring at the dark pool of water. Then he looked at my arm and then he looked at me. Before I could stop him, he had ripped up my shirtsleeve, exposing the marks I had made from the map of the Quag that Quentin Herms had left me.

"And what in the name of Steeples is this, I ask you," he roared. He twisted my arm and I cried out in pain.

Thansius stood. "Krone, stand down this instant."

Morrigone was on her feet too and hurrying over to us. She stopped next to me and her gaze ran down my arm. I saw her attempt to say something but then it was like the words froze in her throat.

Krone had let go of me when Thansius ordered him to, but he still held up my sleeve.

Krone said, "Unless I am much mistaken, fellow members of Council, what I perceive on this female's arm is nothing less than a map of the Quag."

I wanted to yell back at him and ask how he knew it was the Quag, but I was struck dumb by the looks on the faces of Council. Thansius alone held me spellbound. He slowly walked over to me and looked down my arm. He gently pulled up my other sleeve and looked there as well.

"Are there any other marks on you, Vega, other than these?" His voice was filled with disappointment and, even worse, betrayal.

My eyes clouding with tears, I found I could not lie. "On my belly and legs."

"And where did you come by them?"

I looked at Morrigone. She had not taken her eyes off the marks. Her expression of profound surprise was crushing to me.

"Quentin Herms left them on parchment for me," I said. "Before he disappeared."

"And did he tell you it was a way through the Quag?"

"In a way, yes."

"And where is this parchment now?"

"I burned it."

Krone broke in, "But not before copying the marks on her skin. And why do that if she were not planning to use it somehow, and no doubt against her fellow Wugmorts."

"I was not," I cried out. "I was never intending to use it at all."

"Then why keep it on your skin?"

This query was from Morrigone. She was now looking at me.

I forced myself to meet her gaze. And in holding that gaze, I decided to tell the truth. "Because it showed a way to a place other than here."

"A confession," shouted Krone. "The female has as good as told us she is working with the Outliers."

Morrigone was still staring at me, great sadness in her eyes. She looked at Thansius and said, "I believe that we have heard all that is necessary. We shall deliberate and then render our judgment."

I wanted to scream at her not to do this. That I was innocent. That they needed to hear more from me. But I said nothing. I knew beyond all doubt that I could say nothing else that would matter to them now.

She looked at Krone. "But she will not be taken back to Valhall. She will be taken to her lodgings and a guard placed over her."

Krone looked mortified at the idea. "She is a traitor. She will attempt to escape and thus avoid justice on this most serious matter. She has the map of the Quag on her. She will use it to —"

"To what, Krone?" interrupted Morrigone. "To go through the Quag? A fourteen-session-old Wug? She will be dead in two slivers. We all know what lies in there, Vega as well." She looked at me when she said this. "And she has other reasons not to leave Wormwood. These she knows as well."

Krone was about to say something, but Thansius forestalled another outburst.

"I am in agreement with Madame Morrigone. Vega will be taken to her lodgings and a guard placed there. However, before this is done, a female assistant to Council will see to . . . to the washing away of the marks on her . . . self."

Krone said, "I want a guard with her every step of the way."

Thansius looked like he wanted to strangle his colleague.

"I highly doubt Vega can escape from the Council building, Krone. But if you wish, you may go stand outside the door while the necessary, uh, organizing of the washing up is done."

Krone looked very put off by this suggestion and made no indication that he would accept this offer.

Thansius walked back to the dais and used the hilt of an enormous jewel-encrusted sword lying there to smack the wood.

"Council will take up the matter of Vega Jane immediately."

As I was led out, I looked back first at Thansius and then at Morrigone. Neither one of them would look at me.

My heart and spirits in my boots, I was led from the chamber and taken to a loo, where all the marks were washed off me with such energy that my skin was reddened and painful. But I didn't utter a sound as the marks I had kept hidden for so long disappeared from my skin. Afterward, I was taken back to my lodgings, where a very happy Non stood guard outside my door.

Delph had brought Harry Two around to me, and my canine stayed right by my side.

It was quite dark now and I lay on my cot and wondered what my fate would be.

Would they execute me?

Would they place me back in Valhall? Perhaps for many sessions?

Would they let me go free?

But I kept coming back to: Would they execute me?

I had only witnessed one execution. It was when I was ten sessions old and a male had killed his female for no cause other than he was a vile Wug. It had been intentional, or so Council had found. This Wug had also nearly beaten his youngs to death and probably would have if other Wugs had not intervened. All of Wormwood was required to attend the execution, which had taken place in the village center.

He had been led up a short stack of steps to a platform, forced to kneel; a hood was placed over his head, which was set on a block of thick wood, and the executioner, himself hooded — but who I now strongly suspected was Ladon-Tosh — had raised his ax high and with one blow had cleanly severed the head from the rest of the Wug. It had dropped into a straw pouch set in front of the wooden block. The blood had poured down the steps and I thought poor John was going to faint. I had clutched my mother's hand and felt sick. I had swayed on my feet, yet a great cheer had gone up from the crowd because justice had been served and a wicked Wug was no more.

Was that how my life was to end? With Ladon-Tosh separating my head from the rest of me? With Wugs cheering my bloody death?

I closed my eyes and tried to sleep, but it was impossible. Until I knew my fate, there would be no rest for me.

Do or Die

I T WAS THE first section of light when I heard the knock at the door. Despite my anxiety over my fate, I had finally fallen asleep. Harry Two started growling and sniffing at the door.

I staggered up, still half asleep, waves of cold dread making me feel unbalanced and sick to my stomach.

Did they carry out executions immediately after Council's decision? Would I open the door to find Ladon-Tosh there to drag me to a newly constructed platform at the village center?

I opened the door.

It wasn't Ladon-Tosh. It was Morrigone. She looked deadly pale and tired, her exhausted features neatly matching my own. Her cloak even had a few spots of dirt on the hem. I looked over her shoulder but did not see the carriage. She must have walked from the Council building to deliver the news.

"May I come in, Vega?"

I nodded and moved out of the way to allow her entry.

She sat, or rather fell, into one of the chairs. She stifled a yawn and rubbed at one of her eyes.

"You haven't slept?" I said.

She slowly shook her head but didn't really seem to have heard my query. She looked at Harry Two and held out a hand to him. He cautiously approached and allowed her to rub his ears.

"A fine canine," she said.

"He would do anything for me," I replied, sitting on my cot across from her. "Will he be denied that opportunity?" I asked cautiously.

She looked up. "You will not be executed, if that's what you're asking," she said bluntly. "Krone fought long and hard all night on that point, but Thansius and I made Council see reason."

"Why does Krone hate me so much? What have I ever done to him?"

"It's not about you," Morrigone said quietly. "Krone actually hated your grandfather."

"What?" I gasped.

"It was before my time on Council of course, but as I told you before, my grandfather was Chief of Council back then. He resigned and Thansius took his place when my father suffered his Event. . . ." Her voice drifted off; she sat there for a moment and then refocused. "Krone was only a mere assistant at the time, but his ambition was to be a full-fledged Council member. And I have no doubt he has his sights set on being chief when Thansius steps down."

"Steeples help us all if that ever comes to pass," I said fiercely.

"Well, he does have his strengths and he is fiercely devoted to the preservation of Wormwood. But I do not think he would make a very good Chief of Council."

"That doesn't explain why he hated my grandfather."

"As Virgil was leaving Council, it was rumored that Krone would take his spot. Virgil did not think much of Krone, and the two Wugs had a terrific row in the chamber in front of the entire Council. It was humiliating for Krone, I am sure, for your grandfather had an imperious manner about him that would brook no opposition, and his tongue and mind were far more advanced than Krone's. It was an oratorical slaughter of historic proportions. Another Wug was appointed to replace Virgil based, I believe, solely on that verbal dustup. And though Krone did eventually become a Council member, it was several sessions hence. I am certain he held your grandfather responsible for this delay in his career. And his hatred for your grandfather seems to have been transferred to you."

"And to my brother?" I said, looking worried.

"No. I think just to you. He was also not hateful with your parents."

"Why just me, then?" I said in a bewildered tone.

She cocked her head and looked at me with a bemused expression. "You really have to ask such a question?"

"Yes, why?"

She smiled. "It is because you are so very much like your grandfather, Vega. So very much."

"You liked him?" I thought back to Delph's description of the pair arguing right before my grandfather had left Wormwood.

"I respected him, which is even more powerful, Vega. Virgil was a great Wugmort. He has been . . . he has been sorely missed since his . . ."

She did not seem able to finish the thought.

"I miss him too," I said. "I wish he were here right now, to be with me."

Morrigone reached out and gripped my hand. "I see you have drawn the symbol he carried on your own hand. It is a strange mark, is it not?"

I had not let the female at Council wash it off. I had told her it was not part of the map and she had relented.

I had been giving this symbol a lot of thought lately. "Three hooks," I said. "Not one, or four, but three."

She stared at me, her eyes wide. "Yes, three," she said sadly. "Three can be a very powerful number. A trinity of sorts. But you don't know what the mark means?"

"I do not." I paused. "What is my fate, then? If not execution, then it must be Valhall."

"It is not Valhall."

I looked at her, puzzled. "If not execution and not Valhall, then what?"

"I will not mince words with you, Vega. The discovery of the marks on your skin was very damaging. It took all my resources and gathering support from other Council members to dissuade them from either beheading you or putting you in Valhall for the rest of your sessions."

I drew a deep breath, letting this sink in — how close I had come to dying.

I looked at her. "So what, then? What is my punishment?"

She gathered her own breath. I had never seen her look so exhausted.

"You must fight in the Duelum, Vega. You must fight your heart out. You cannot surrender or go down easily, for if you do, you will be put in Valhall for the rest of your sessions. That is the vote of Council and it is final."

"But I'm only fourteen sessions old!" I said. "I'll be fighting against fully grown males."

She rose and rubbed at her eyes again. "The fact is, Vega, they don't care. They simply don't. If you fight valiantly, all will be forgiven, your life will return to normal, and you will owe nothing else. If you won't fight, then you will be taken to Valhall immediately. And in truth, I cannot guarantee that Krone will not push for your execution. And this time he might succeed."

"Then I will fight," I said. "I give you my word that I will fight my hardest." I paused and then asked, "What happens to me until the Duelum starts?"

"You are the only Finisher left at Stacks. You can return to your work on the straps next light."

"And when I'm beaten to death in the Duelum?"

"I'm sorry, Vega. That is the best I could do. At least this way you have a chance."

"A chance," I repeated without enthusiasm. But really how much of one?

Morrigone held up a cautionary hand. "Krone and his allies are convinced you will attempt to flee Wormwood and use the map you had to lead you."

"The marks are gone from my skin," I said.

"You could have memorized them. In any event, do not think of doing so. If you were to attempt to flee, Delph would take your place in Council's eyes. And it would not simply be Valhall." She paused. "They will take his life." She paused once more and studied me intently. "And I would do nothing to block it."

"Why, Morrigone? What does Council care if a Wug goes into the Quag? If he makes the decision and dies, it's his life."

"It is not that simple, Vega. Council's job is to protect all Wugmorts, and ensure the survival of Wormwood. If Wugs started going into the Quag and dying, it would embolden the beasts there to perhaps once more take up battle against us. We might not survive a second war with them."

"And then of course there are the Outliers." I thought it enlightening that she had forgotten to mention them since we were building a bloody gargantuan wall supposedly to keep them out.

If I was expecting some barbed retort, I was to be disappointed.

Morrigone looked at me with a bittersweet expression that resembled one my mother would sometimes give me, but then her features grew hard. "I was very serious, Vega, when I said I admired you. I have no wish to see such a promising life snuffed out. But there are limits to even my feelings for you. Please do not forget that. I have my duty and I intend to carry it out. For the good of all Wugmorts and the survival of Wormwood, I cannot and will not play favorites."

With that ominous statement, she left me.

Practice Makes Imperfect

DELPH ARRIVED AT my digs right after he finished work on the Wall.

"Wotcha, Vega Jane," he called out through the door.

I opened the door and looked up at him while Harry Two jumped around our ankles.

"What is it, Delph?" I asked.

"I heard 'bout things," said Delph.

"What did you hear exactly?" I asked. I searched his face, looking for the least little hint of doubt.

"You got to fight in the Duelum."

"Yes." I slid back my sleeve and showed him the clear skin. "They found the map on me."

"We need to practice, then."

I looked at him, dumbfounded. "Practice what?"

"Practice for you to win."

"Delph, I'm not going to win the Duelum."

"Why not?"

"Because I'm a female. And I'm only fourteen sessions old."

"Very nearly fifteen," he amended. "So you're not going to even try? Don't sound like Vega Jane to me. Flying and throwing that spear thing so good-like."

"That's different."

"Is it?" he said, staring at me.

I took a step back and considered this. "How would I practice?"

"You showed me how to fly and throw. I can show you how to fight. Morrigone said females should train up. And if you have to fight, you're entitled to get trained up proper just like any other Wug. Preceptors ready to help. Well, I think I'm just as good as any Duelum Preceptor."

"I know you are. But where do we do this?"

"At my digs. Lots of privacy there."

"When?"

"Now."

It was dark as we approached the Delphias' cottage. The usual sounds associated with a beast trainer's home were no longer in evidence. There were no new beasts, as I was sure Duf had no slivers to train them. All his time was spent on the Wall.

But there *were* sounds, because the adar had seen us approach. "Hello," it said.

"Hello," I said back.

"And who might this be?" the adar asked.

"This might be Vega Jane," I answered.

It stood very tall and its great chest swelled. "Ooohhh, Ve-Vega Jane. So pr-pretty, Ve-Ve-Vega Jane. So be-be-be-beautiful, Ve-Ve-Vega Jane." It sounded exactly like Delph.

Delph roared, "Shut up, you great pile of feathers, before you end up in the pot for me sup!"

"Be-be-beautiful, Ve-Ve-Vega Jane," the adar said one last time and then gave Delph a surly glance before tucking its head under a wing and going back to sleep.

I was stunned by this outburst, but there was also an odd tingling sensation at the back of my neck. The thing was, adars only use words they've *heard*. I had no time to think about it really because as I looked over, Delph was charging straight at me full speed. I only had time to cry out and put my hands up before he had collided with me. He lifted me off the ground, raised me over his head and was about to crush me against a tree when he stopped. He looked up. I looked down.

"What in the bloody Hel are you doing, Delph?" I gasped.

He slowly lowered me to the ground. "At Duelum, there's no stopping. No rules really, neither fair nor foul. There's no point not being ready to fight at all times. Blokes come at you right from the first clang of the bell, Vega Jane. Charge, pin your arms to your sides, lift you up and smash you against the hardest thing they can find. Then you won't be getting back up. Trust me. I did it to Non last Duelum. He got careless-like, the big oaf."

I looked at the tree and then back at Delph and shivered.

"Okay," I said. "I get the point. So what now?"

"So we fight." He backed up a few paces and went into a crouch. "Now, with Ladon-Tosh —" Delph began.

"Ladon-Tosh!" I exclaimed. "He's older than twenty-four sessions. He won't be in the Duelum."

Delph shrugged. "Well, the bloke says he's twenty-three sessions."

"Bollocks," I blurted out.

"He's in the Duelum, Vega. Just the way 'tis."

"But aren't there referees?"

"O'course, but I think they're all so afraid of him. If he says he's of proper age, they're not about to challenge him, are they?"

I continued to fume. "That is the biggest load of tripe. Fine, who else?"

"Non. Ran Digby. Cletus Loon. Lots of blokes."

"But none so big as you."

"Most ain't. But it's not only the big ones you have to look out for, Vega Jane. The little blokes are quick and cagey and they pack a wallop. My last Duelum, I almost got knocked out by a bloke half me size."

"How?"

"Threw dirt in me eyes and then hit me with a board he had hidden on the pitch."

My eyes bulged. "They can do that?"

He looked at me in exasperation. "Don't you watch the Duelums, Vega Jane?"

"Well, just the championship bout. Sometimes." The truth was I could not stand to see Wugs trying to kill one another. The last time I had watched Delph win, I was violently sick as blood flowed from him and the other Wug.

He nodded. "Aye, they don't let you fight as dirty in the last round, to be sure, because the full Council is watching. But to get there, you got to expect anything."

He went into a crouch again, keeping his hands up and his arms tight to his sides. "Protect your body, Vega Jane. A blow to the belly or your side is right painful." He held his fists up higher. "And watch your head. Hard to fight with a cracked skull."

I began to feel sick to my stomach. "A cracked skull?"

"Got one two Duelums ago. Had a headache for a half a session."

My mouth had gone totally dry. "How can I protect my body and my head at the same time?" I croaked.

"Just got to keep moving." He danced around a bit on nimble feet, showing more agility than I would have allowed him credit for, given his size.

He said, "You can hit a bloke with anything. Fists, head, legs, knees."

"And boards," I reminded him.

"Now, when you get hit —"

"So you're presuming I'm going to get hit?" I interrupted.

He said matter-of-factly, "Every bloke gets hit in a Duelum. In fact, count on about a dozen times a bout. Meaning the hard shots. 'Bout fifty times total, but I don't count the little shots that just make ya wonky for a bit."

I wanted to turn and run screaming.

"When you get hit, no matter how light or hard, I would recommend you going down."

At first I rejoiced at this proposition, but then I recalled Morrigone's words. If I did not fight to my fullest, I would be going to Valhall for the rest of my sessions. But Delph's next words showed he was not planning for me to surrender.

"Going down dinnae mean you've lost the bout, Vega Jane. The bloke will just jump on you and pound you till ya can't see or hear nothing no more. It hurts," he added unnecessarily. "Now, 'tis true if ya put both your hands up in surrender, the bout is over and no Wug can hit you without getting a foul called."

"I can't surrender, Delph," I said. And I thought, *No matter how much I may want to.*

"You're nae surrendering, Vega Jane. What you do is go down in a special way. Like this."

He fell onto his back, his knees tucked up to his chest. He continued. "Just about every bloke will come at you hard soon as you go down. He'll charge head-on at you. Now, you wait till he's just a wee bit away and then you do this."

Delph kicked out with both feet with such force that I jumped back even though I was in no danger of being hit. In the next instant, he was on his feet. He leapt into the air and came down with both feet on top of his imaginary opponent. Then he jumped up again and came down with his right arm in the shape of a V and his elbow pointed downward. He sprawled on the ground with his elbow poised a quarter inch above the dirt.

"That's the bloke's throat. Elbow strike there he can't breathe, can he? He passes out. And you win. And go on to the next round. Clean and quick. Har."

I felt my own throat constrict. "But if he can't breathe, won't he die?" I said in a dry, cracked voice.

Delph rose and dusted off his trousers and hands. "Well, most blokes start breathing on their own pretty quick. For those what need a bitta help, there're Mendens standing by to come over and beat on their chests. That usually does the trick. Sometimes they have to cut open the throat to get the air flowing again, but the scar is pretty small and it don't bleed all that much."

I turned around and heaved the meager contents of my belly into a bush.

I felt Delph's big hands around my shoulders a moment later. He supported me while I finished being sick. I wiped my mouth and turned to face him, my cheeks red with embarrassment.

"Delph, I had no idea the Duelums were like this. And you winning three of them already? Well, that's about the most amazing thing ever."

His face flushed with pleasure at my praising words. "'Tain't all that special," he said modestly.

"But what you've taught me will help." I didn't believe this of course, because even if I jumped off the tallest tree in Wormwood and landed on Non's throat, I doubt he would even cough.

"This is just the start, Vega Jane. There's a lot more for you to learn. And you've got to build up your strength too."

"I'm pretty strong."

"That's not good enough."

"How do I get stronger? I work all light at Stacks building straps for the Wall. When will I have a sliver? I have to sleep."

"We'll think of a way."

"When will we know who we have to fight?"

"They'll post the first bouts seven nights before the Duelum starts," he replied.

We worked some more on various moves and strategies until I was exhausted.

Before taking my leave, I glanced over at the adar.

"Delph, that adar —"

"Dad's been having no end of trouble with the durn thing," he grumbled.

"What kind of trouble?"

Delph would not meet my eye. "Saying things we got no idea where he heard 'em. Dad says some adars have minds of their own, they do."

"But adars can't naturally stutter, can —"

"Gotta go, Vega Jane."

And then he disappeared into his cottage and closed the door tight.

A Single Care

NEXT LIGHT, I rose early. I wanted to get out of Wormwood proper before other Wugs got up.

As Harry Two and I walked down the cobblestones, we passed an old Wug I didn't know but had seen before. He glared at me and aimed a slop of spit at my boot. I hopped away and kept going, my head down. Obviously, word had gotten around about my arrest and sentencing to fight in the Duelum. It might be that the entire village loathed me now, although it was hard to fathom that Wugs could turn against me so quickly.

Out of the corner of my eye, I saw Roman Picus coming down the cobblestones. I braced myself for his insults and slurs. But he did something that bruised me even more. He pulled down his hat and cut between two buildings, apparently so he would not have to talk to or perhaps be seen with me.

I kept shuffling along, my energy sapped, and I had a full light of work ahead.

As I passed the Loons, Hestia Loon stepped out to put some rubbish in the dustbin. I tried not to make eye contact, but she called out, "Vega?"

I stopped, fearing the worst. Hestia had always been nice to me, but she was under Loon's thumb completely. I eyed the broom in her hand and wondered if she was going to take a swat at me.

"Yes?" I said quietly.

She walked over, gave Harry Two a pat and said, "'Tis a beautiful canine."

My spirits lifted a bit at her kind words. "Thank you. His name is Harry Two."

She glanced up at me, her features hardening. "It's rubbish, what they're saying 'bout you. Know that as well as I know me own frying pan."

I felt my face grow warm and moisture crept into my eyes. I hastily rubbed this away and continued to stare at her.

She looked over her shoulder back at the Loons and came forward, drawing something from her pocket. She held it up. It was a little chain with a metal disc on the end.

"Me mum gave this to me when I was but a nipper. For good luck, they say." I looked at her in confusion. She hurried on. "Luck, for in the Duelum. Heard you had to fight. Bloody mental Council is, ask me, but no Wug did." She gripped my hand and placed the good luck charm in it and curled my fingers over it.

"You take this, Vega Jane. You take this and you beat them males. I know you can do it. Bloody Outliers! Like you'd be helping them, and your grandfather being Virgil Alfadir Jane. Bloody mental, that's what they are. Barmy, the lot of 'em."

She looked down at my thin, dirty frame, and I saw her heavy cheeks start to quiver. "Give me a mo'," she said.

She nipped into the Loons and was back a half sliver later with a small cloth bag. She handed it to me. "Just between us," she said and gave my cheek a pinch. Then she was gone.

I looked in the bag and saw a loaf of freshly baked bread, two apples, a jar of pickles and a wedge of cheese and two sausages. My stomach rumbled in anticipation of devouring it.

I looked at the charm she had given me. The disc of metal was copper and had the image of a star with seven points to it. I lifted it over my head, and the chain settled around my neck. I stared back at the Loons and found Hestia peering at me from a window. She disappeared quickly when she saw me looking.

I continued on, my spirits heartened by her gesture of kindness.

When I got to my tree I stopped, dropped my tin and cloth bag, and ran forward screaming.

"No. No!" I yelled. "That's my tree."

There were four Wugs, all males, all twice my size. One of them was Non. He had an ax and was about to strike my tree a vicious blow. Two other Wugs stood ready with a long saw, while the fourth Wug had a morta, which he now pointed at me while Harry Two growled and snapped at him.

They were going to chop down my tree.

Non stopped, but still holding the ax up high, he said viciously, "Traitors dinnae get to have trees, female."

He started his downswing with the huge ax.

"No," I screamed. "You can't. You can't." I paused and then said, "You *won't*!"

Non hit my tree with a staggering blow, and the most amazing thing happened. There was not a dent or cut in the bark. Instead, the ax broke in half and fell to the ground.

Non stood there looking in disbelief at where he had hit my tree and then down at his shattered tool.

"What the Hel?" he roared. He pointed at the two Wugs holding the long saw and motioned them forward while the other Wug cocked the hammer back on his morta and kept it pointed at my head.

I just stood there, staring at my tree, willing with all my heart for it to survive this unjust attack. Even if I were a traitor — which I wasn't — my poor tree should not suffer.

The two Wugs set the saw's teeth against my tree's bark and started to cut. Or they tried to. The teeth disintegrated against the trunk.

The Wugs straightened and looked in puzzlement at their ruined saw.

Non stared fiercely over at me. "What sort of tree is this?" he demanded.

"It's my tree," I said, pushing past the Wug holding the morta. "Now, clear off."

"It's bedeviled," exclaimed Non. "You're working with them Outliers. Evil scum. They've bedeviled this tree, they have!"

"That is utter nonsense."

We all looked around and saw Thansius standing about five yards from us. He was dressed in a long gray cloak. He held a long stick in one massive hand, and I imagined he had gone for an early light walk.

"A bedeviled tree?" said Thansius as he drew nearer and looked up at my beautiful poplar. "How do you mean?"

Non shuffled his feet nervously and kept his gaze downcast. The other Wugs had all taken steps back and were studying the ground. I'm sure none of them had ever been in conversation with Thansius.

Non said haltingly, "Well, Thansius . . . sir, ax and . . . and saw don't touch it, did they . . . sir?"

"Easily explained," said Thansius, looking at me.

He rapped my tree with his knuckles. "You see, over time some trees that are ancient become petrified. That is to say their bark hardens to such a degree that it becomes stronger than iron. It's no wonder your tools fell victim to its armored husk."

He picked up the pieces of the broken ax and the toothless saw and handed them back to Non and the other two Wugs. "I would say that this tree will still be standing when we are all long since dust." He looked directly at Non. "So be off with you, Non. I'm sure you and your colleagues have labors on the Wall to perform."

Non and his cronies hastily made their way down the path and were soon out of sight.

I touched my tree's bark and then looked at the boards I had nailed into it leading up to my planks. How could I have nailed into it if it were petrified? I looked at Thansius and was about to ask this very query when he said, "It is quite a magnificent tree, Vega. It would have been a terrible shame to see it perish."

290

In his features I could tell that he wasn't talking only about my tree. He was also referring to me.

I wanted to tell Thansius that I was not a traitor and that I never would have used the map to help anything that wanted to hurt Wormwood. But he had already turned away and walked off. I watched him until I could no longer see him. I turned to my tree and gave it a hug.

I WORKED AT Stacks all light long, and after finishing, I helped transport a shipment of straps by a wagon pulled by two cretas to the section of the Wall that was currently being completed. As I helped lift the heavy straps off, I was thinking this was a great way for me to build up my strength — if I didn't die of exhaustion first.

Even I had to admit, the Wall was quite a feat of Wug craftsmanship and engineering. I did a count and there were two hundred Wugs currently working on this section. The construction was run in shifts all light and night, with the darkness illuminated by lanterns and torches so Wugs could see what they were doing. Yet there had already been injuries, some minor, others serious. One Wug had even died when he had fallen off the top of a Wall section and landed on his head, breaking his neck. He'd been buried in a special section of the Hallowed Ground now reserved for Wugs who gave their life for the Wall. All Wugs were praying there would be no more such sacrifices and that section would remain fixed forever at one grave.

As I finished unloading the straps, I stayed to look around. The Wall rose up well over thirty feet. The timbers were thick, stripped of their bark, planed and mitered. Straps that I had finished were wound around the logs and locked down tightly through the punch holes, giving the wood a strength and stability it would not otherwise have had.

The guard towers at this section were unfinished, but I could see where the Wugs with mortas would stand looking for Outliers, ostensibly. Though I now envisioned these same Wugs shooting down other Wugs trying to get over the Wall. The moats were dug but not yet filled in with water. They would be filled last, I reasoned, so the workers wouldn't get mired in the muck.

The activity was frenetic, but seemed well coordinated, with focused Wugs marching here and there with tools and materials. As I continued to gaze around, I spotted John on a raised platform with lit torches all around, overseeing the construction. Next to him were three members of Council and two other Wugs I knew were good at building things.

I had a notion to go over and speak to John but then thought better of it. What did I have to say to him that I had not already said? It was startling to me how quickly my many sessions with John had been efficiently overridden by his time under Morrigone's wing. Or *claw*, more like it. And yet she had saved my life. I was terribly conflicted about her. Was she my ally or not?

I walked over to the large holes dug for the water and gazed down at them. Another Wug came up to me, carrying some tools.

"When will the water be piped in here?" I asked.

He looked down at the hole. "They say in six more lights and nights, but I don't see how. We're behind schedule."

John's comment came back to me about the timetable. "It seems that Wugs are working as hard as they can," I said.

"Tell that to them," said the Wug, motioning to the platform where John was. The Wug looked back at me. "'Tis your brother, ain't he?"

"He is."

The Wug stared hard at me. "Then you have my pity."

As he started to walk off, I grabbed his arm. "What do you mean by that?"

"Only that he works us harder every light and night. It don't matter to him how tired or sick we are or that our families need us. He flat-out don't care, does he?"

"I thought he was just working on the plans?"

The Wug shook his head. "For a young, he acts very old. And he's mean. I know you're family and all, but that's just how I feel and I don't care who knows."

Scowling, he stalked off leaving me staring at the ground, thinking many things and none of them pleasant. I glanced back over at John, my spirits about as low as they could go. Even as I watched, he started pointing and yelling at a group of Wugs who were struggling with a heavy timber. John rushed down to them and started gesticulating at them. The Wugs looked stonily at him, any response they might have had no doubt muted by the large Wugs armed with mortas who stood behind John.

I walked up to John, who was still raging at the Wugs standing there with the log balanced precariously over their weary shoulders. I said, "Why don't you let them put it down, John, while you tell them what you want?"

He turned to me, an expression of great annoyance on his face. At first, I didn't think he even recognized me.

"We don't have time for that!" he exclaimed. "We're already behind this light, and night crew will be here in slivers."

"And these Wugs have been working hard all light. You'll be even more behind schedule if Wugs start getting sick or injured from being overworked."

"It is not your place to give orders," he said, gazing stonily at me.

"Maybe it isn't. But I'm the only family you have left."

He gave me a condescending look. "Have you forgotten the Care?"

I knew I shouldn't do it, but at this point I was no longer concerned about John's feelings. Besides, I wasn't sure he had any left. And I was destined to either get my brains bashed in fighting in the Duelum or die in Valhall.

"As I said, I'm the only family you have. There is no one you know left at the Care. I thought Morrigone would have told you by now. Our parents both suffered Events. There is of course nothing left of them."

With that I turned on my heel and marched away.

I didn't care, I just really didn't.

But, as it turned out, I should have.

For a lot of reasons.

Foes United

THE NEXT FEW lights and nights followed a uniform pattern. I worked all light at Stacks and then on the Wall. After that, Delph and I practiced my Duelum skills late into the night. He had put together a long pole with the ends weighted by bundles of rocks. He had me lift that over my head and put it on my shoulders and squat down to build up my upper and lower body. My limbs hurt so badly the next light, I cried out in pain after I tried to get off my cot. But I kept doing it. Wanting to live is a great motivator.

At first we were at his digs, then we moved to the forest and sometimes we fought inside my digs, occasionally knocking over my few pieces of furniture and scaring Harry Two half to death.

On the seventh light after Thansius had made his announcement about the Duelum, I was passing Cletus Loon and his git chums on the way to my digs after work. I stopped when Loon stepped in front of me while his chums made a crude circle around me. Harry Two started growling and the hair on his back rose as they closed in on us. I patted Harry Two on the head and told him it was okay.

Cletus said, "So you have to fight in the Duelum or else you'll rot in Valhall for being a traitor."

I stood there with as bored a look on my face as I could manage. Even his simple mind finally seemed to grasp that he would either have to say something else or shove off.

Cletus finally said, "You know what I wish, Vega?"

"I don't want to try and see inside your head, Loon; I might go blind."

"I wish that I draw you in the first round of the Duelum."

His friends laughed while I stood there staring at Cletus like he was not worth a sliver of my time.

Finally I said, "Be careful what you wish for, Loon; you might just get it."

He got right in my face. "I can't wait to see you get your arse kicked and I hope I'm the one to do it."

"I suppose you've got some brilliant moves you're itching to try out."

"You bet I do," he said, grinning maliciously.

I waited patiently for Cletus to do what I knew he was going to do. What he so desperately wanted to do.

He feinted with his right hand, swung his left to within an inch of my cheek and then pretended to knee me in the stomach.

I just stood there stoically, not even batting an eye.

His grin finally disappeared. "You best watch yourself."

"Right," I said.

He stepped to the side, allowing me to pass. I walked on with Harry Two protecting my flank.

"Thanks, you idiot," I said under my breath.

I heard Wugs calling out farther down the Low Road where it turned into the High Street cobblestones leading into Wormwood proper. Other Wugs were rushing toward that destination as well. I picked up my pace to see what was going on. I turned onto the High Street and saw that Wugs were collecting around a wooden board that was used for official announcements.

Then it occurred to me. The first Duelum bouts were being posted this night! I sprinted hard down the cobblestones and pushed my way through hordes of Wugs until I could see the long parchment strips pinned to the wood. I ran my eye down the list of names, finally reaching my name near the bottom. As I gazed across at my opponent for the first bout, my mouth twitched.

Cletus Loon indeed would be getting his wish. I had drawn him in the first round. I would have to fight and win four times to reach the championship match. Not that I expected, despite Delph's encouragement, to get that far.

Yet I knew one thing. I was going to beat Cletus Loon. That would be enough for me. I prayed the other females in the competition would survive the first round reasonably intact.

I then looked for Delph's name and found it less than a sliver later. In the first bout, he would be fighting the huge, vile Ran Digby, the patrol Wug who liked to chew his smoke weed and catch yuck in his great, filthy beard.

A hand grabbed my arm. I turned to see Jurik Krone. I pulled my arm free and stared up at him. I could sense other Wugs giving us space, but staring all the same.

"Madame Morrigone has no doubt told you of your lucky escape from justice," he snarled.

"Lucky," I said in a scathing tone. "Lucky to fight males three times my size so they can beat me to death?"

In a loud voice he proclaimed, "I would much prefer to see you in Valhall, traitor. Or with your head no longer attached. That would be real justice."

Okay, enough was bloody well enough. Now it was my turn.

"And I would much prefer to see my grandfather sitting on Council instead of a stupid git like you."

The Wugs surrounding us gave a gasp and took a collective step back.

I stepped forward. It had been a long light; I was tired and I was simply mad. And if I did not speak my piece right now, I felt like I would explode.

I pressed my finger into his chest. "My grandfather saw you for what you are and that's why he didn't want you on Council. You are a vindictive little weasel that would make a garm seem honorable. All you care about is yourself and your career and to Hel with every other Wug. I've met some pillocks in my time, Krone — some nasty, stupid pillocks of the highest order — but you, you beat them all, you lying, worthless piece of *dung*." I turned away, but only for an instant. I whirled back around and said, "Oh, and for the record" — now my voice rose to a shriek — "the only thing I'm sorry for is that your arse is not in the Duelum so I could kick it from here to the Quag. Now go straight to Hel!"

I turned around for good and stalked off. I hoped and prayed to Steeples that Krone would attack me because I was so furious that I would not only knock him to the Quag, I would knock the Wug right *through* it.

I stopped only when I saw Delph staring at me from across the cobblestones. From his stunned expression, it was clear he had seen and heard everything.

I walked over to him.

"Bloody Hel, Vega Jane," he began. "And Jurik Krone no less."

"I don't want to talk about Krone, Delph. He is nothing."

I watched as Krone and a couple of his Council confederates, including Duk Dodgson, shoved through the crowd of Wugs and headed to the Council building. Krone shot me a loathsome look and then he disappeared from my sight.

I turned back to Delph. "Did you know Ran Digby is your first opponent?"

Delph smiled. "He best hope he has teeth left to spit his slop through."

"Well, he only has three of them that I can see. I got Cletus Loon."

"You'll beat him, Vega Jane. I'll make sure of it."

In truth, I wasn't all that worried about fighting Cletus Loon. What I was thinking about was my meeting with John. I had told him that our parents were gone. I had not even waited to see his reaction. That had been so cruel on my part and I felt terrible guilt for having done it. My Duelum dilemma was a distant second to that. He was not yet twelve sessions. He might know books. But he did not know life.

Delph touched me on the shoulder and lifted me from these painful musings.

"Vega Jane? You okay?"

"I'm fine, Delph."

He drew closer. "You want to practice this night?"

I wanted to, but I shook my head. "Not this night, Delph. This night I need to rest."

He looked disappointed, then nodded, turned and walked off.

I watched him go for a bit and then set off. Not for my digs and my last meal. I was headed to the Care with Harry Two beside me. I wasn't sure why I was going, because my parents were no longer there. But something inside me was telling me I had to go.

When we arrived here, rain started pelting down. Harry Two glanced up at me a few times, probably wondering why we were out in the driving rain. It was cold and I started shivering. I finally stirred and headed to the doors. I had no idea if they would open. I had never been here this late at night. I pushed on the wood and, surprisingly, it opened. I poked my head into the darkened corridor.

My canine kept close to my shins. He wasn't growling or making any sound at all. He seemed as intimidated as I felt. I moved past all the other wooden doors with the brass plates on them. They were familiar names, but there were also a few new ones as fresh sick Wugs took the place of Wugs who had made their final journey to the Hallowed Ground from this place.

I reached my parents' old room and gazed up at the brass plate. Or where the plate had once been. Now all I could see was the outline of the brass rectangle that had once read HECTOR JANE AND HELEN JANE.

I spoke the names out loud as I had every time I had visited them for two sessions. I had grown weary of doing so, though now that they were gone, I wasn't weary anymore. I knew this would be truly the last time I would do so. But I would only be visiting an empty room.

However, when I pushed open the unlocked door I was immediately aware of the presence of someone else huddled in the corner. The room was no longer illuminated. It was as if when my parents left, they had taken the mysterious light with them. But I could still make the shape out.

It was John.

Magical Me

JOHN DIDN'T LOOK up as I walked in. I just heard his sobs. I drew closer and looked at the empty cots before returning my gaze to him. He didn't look remotely like the grand special assistant to Council who was running roughshod over the poor Wugs building the Wall. Even with his scalped hair and fancy clothes, he looked like a little male Wug who was totally lost.

I went to him, wrapped my long arms around him and held him. Harry Two sat on his haunches while I did so, all the while maintaining a respectful silence. I said things to John that I had said to him pretty much every light growing up. That everything would be okay. That he would always have me. That he should not be sad, for the next light would be better.

When I heard the door creak open about fifteen slivers later, I knew who it was before I saw her. Morrigone came into the room and walked directly over to John.

"It's time to go, John," she said without looking at me.

He stifled his sobs and nodded, wiping his eyes with the sleeve of his pristine black tunic. Morrigone put a hand on his arm, drawing him to her. I did not let go of his other arm.

I said, "Let him cry. They're gone. Let him cry."

Morrigone gave me what I can only describe as a withering look and I decided to give it right back. She leaned in close and said, "We have *you* to thank for this, Vega."

I walked away from John and stood waiting for her in a far corner. It was about time we had this out, I had decided. I'd had my say with Krone this light and now it was Morrigone's turn. She strode over to me. I must have grown a bit because I noted that without her heels, I would be taller than her. Yet even in my faded, falling-apart work boots, I was not far off her height. I stood as straight as possible, trying to match her loftiness.

"I appreciated very much what you did for me with Council, as I told you."

"You have an utterly perplexing way of showing that gratitude. John has come here every night since you told him what you promised me you would not."

I pointed at John. "It was wrong to keep this truth from him."

"You are not the one to make that sort of judgment."

"And *you* are?" I said, the skepticism as thick in my tone as I could make it.

"It seems that you have forgotten your place here, Vega."

"I didn't know that I had a place, so thank you for reserving me one."

"That sort of talk does you no credit. Not while your brother is huddled in that corner, crying his heart out night after night. It is shameful what you did."

"He *should* be crying his heart out. *I* did."

"You disappoint me. I thought you were made of stronger stuff."

"Like my grandfather?"

"Virgil had a tremendous will."

"I suppose he would have needed that to survive the fire that swallowed him on his last night here." It was as though my words had turned Morrigone to marble. I could not even swear that she was still breathing.

When she spoke, her words were like morta rounds. "What exactly do you mean by that?"

Warning signals in my head were blaring, telling me to stop talking. But I couldn't and wouldn't. I didn't care if she had saved me from beheading or Valhall. I did care that she had made me keep from my brother a truth that she never should have asked me to withhold. And she had turned a warm, loving, trusting Wug into something I could no longer recognize.

"Tell me something, Morrigone, how did it feel to watch my grandfather disappear into the flames? Despite you not wanting him to go?"

I stared at her. The look on her face was deadly.

She said in an icy tone, "You must be careful, Vega Jane. You must be very careful at this very sliver."

I had to admit that her words sent a chill up my spine. I happened to glance away and for the first time noticed that John had stopped weeping and was watching us intently.

"Morrigone?" he began.

She instantly held up her hand, and my brother fell back, his next words seemingly struck from his lips before they had a chance to fully form. This simple gesture enraged me even more.

I had no intention of backing down now.

I said, "You once taunted me with the word *time*. But I wonder if you fully understand all that I know? All that I have seen over the course of *time*?"

Again, I knew I should have stopped right there, but I wanted to stun her. I wanted to make her feel the pain I was feeling. And there was something else. Just an instant before, it had all come together in my head — the ancient battlefield and the dying female warrior. Now I knew where I had seen her before. I knew beyond all doubt.

"I met a female who looked remarkably like you, Morrigone, lying mortally wounded on a great battlefield. Do you know what she told me? What she gave me?"

"You lie!" she hissed.

"She was your Wug ancestor and she died right in front of me. She spoke to me. She knew me!"

"This cannot be true," gasped Morrigone, her calm exterior having totally collapsed.

I said, "Have you ever been chased by a flying jabbit or a creature so gigantic it can block out the sun, Morrigone? They're called colossals. It's quite exhilarating. So long as you survive it. And I did. Does that make me as special as John? Does that place me in the same league as my grandfather in your eyes?"

"You are deluded."

"She wore a ring. The same ring that my grandfather had."

Morrigone gasped and snapped, "What did she say to you?"

"What was her name?" I countered.

"What did she say to you?" she shouted.

I hesitated and then just said it. "That I had to survive. Me, Vega Jane. That I had to survive."

With a monumental effort Morrigone regained her composure and said icily, "John deserves better in a sibling, Vega. He does indeed. Consider yourself very fortunate this night."

She turned on her heel and marched off.

John said to me, "I will miss them. I will miss them greatly."

Then, before I could respond, he turned and followed Morrigone.

I stood there for a while staring at the floor. Then I finally left, Harry Two at my side. The carriage had long since gone, taking John back to his new life. I was glad he had come here each night to grieve. I was happy I had told him. It was the right thing to do, Wall or no Wall.

When I got back to my digs, I just wanted to collapse. But when I entered my room, I nearly screamed. Morrigone was standing by the fireplace, her hand on the slender wooden chimneypiece, so far less impressive than the one at her grand home. I looked around for John, but he wasn't there.

It was just Morrigone. And me. She came forward.

"Where is Bogle and the carriage?" I said.

She ignored this. "The things you said back at the Care."

"What of them?" I said.

Harry Two was growling more deeply with every step

Morrigone took toward me. I put my hand on his head to calm him but I kept my gaze on Morrigone.

"You *cannot* know such things."

"But I *do* know such things," I said.

"Those are two very different points," she replied.

In an instant I knew exactly what she meant. I couldn't be allowed to remember these things. And thus I also knew what she was about to do. It was the same thing she had done to Delph and me all those sessions ago. Her hand went up. My hand darted to my pocket. Her hand came down. My hand went up. On my hand was the glove, and in it was the Elemental, at full size. The red light ricocheted off the golden spear, struck my window and shattered all of the glass.

Both of us stood there, breathless. The look in Morrigone's eyes was truly hideous. She was no longer beautiful. She was the most ugly Wug I had ever witnessed.

Her gaze darted to the fully formed Elemental.

"Where did you get that?" she demanded in a hiss.

"From your ancestor Wug," I shot back. "She gave it to me. Before she died."

Now I took a step forward and Morrigone drew back.

"What was her name?" I asked, holding the Elemental at the ready.

"You do not realize what you have done, Vega," she said fiercely. "You do not!"

"Why not the blue light this time too, Morrigone? Why the red light? The same one you used on poor Delph."

"You have no idea what you are doing, Vega."

"I have *every* idea," I shouted back.

"I will not let you destroy us!"

"Where do Wugs go when they have their Events, Morrigone? They have to go somewhere. And I think you know. And it sure as Hel isn't Wormwood."

She was shaking her head and backing up. "No, Vega. No."

I raised the Elemental and positioned it to throw. "You know what this can do," I said. "I have no wish to harm you." Well, actually I wanted to turn her to dust, but I saw no good coming from telling her that.

"No, Vega, never," she said again.

And before I could take another step, she was gone. I blinked and looked around in bewilderment. She had simply vanished. I looked down at Harry Two. He was whimpering with his tail between his legs. When I looked up, I saw it, slight, barely visible in the darkness. It was a trail of blue light that carried out the window. As I watched, it lifted to the sky and then vanished, just as Morrigone had.

I angrily waved my hand after this trail of mist. And the most extraordinary thing happened. My shattered window flew back together and became whole once more.

Having done this, I was thrown back against the wall by some violent force and I slumped down, my energy fully spent. I looked at my hands, then at the repaired glass and wood. How had that happened? How could I possibly have done what I just did? I reached in my pocket and pulled out the Adder Stone. I rubbed it over my body and thought happy thoughts. My aches from hitting the wall ceased and my energy returned.

Eon had said that the spirit of a sorceress had been embedded in the Stone, giving it its power. Had it somehow given me some of her power by its being in my pocket?

Well, if it had, I also had no real ability to control it.

I sat there thinking thoughts that were both terrifying and exhilarating.

The Battle Begins

A**LL WUGS WERE** required to attend the opening of this Duelum. I thought that a bit interesting since we were supposedly surrounded by bloodthirsty Outliers wanting to feast on our organs. The pitch was nearly encircled by a rim of trees that had evaded inclusion on the Wall, at least for now. After eating a bit, I showed up at first section of light. I had tried to sleep the night before but couldn't. So I decided I would get down here early and see what I could see.

The pitch site was called the Peckwater Quadrangle after Ronald Peckwater, a long-ago mighty Duelum champion of Wormwood. The inside of the pitch was uneven and dented in innumerable places from large male bodies colliding violently with the dirt over the course of many previous Duelums. A wooden platform had been erected in the center of the pitch. Here would sit the VIWs, or Very Important Wugs. Behind the platform was a large board with all the names of the competitors, where the progress in the Duelum would be chronicled for all to see. There were also betting circles set up on the pitch's perimeter, where wagers would be placed. The ever-enterprising Roman Picus ran a right successful betting pool through which he had relieved many Wugs of their coin over the sessions.

I had left Destin back at my digs under the floorboards. I was terrified that during the course of the fighting, I would unconsciously take flight and my secret would be exposed.

The air was fresh and warm and the sky clear. As the time to fight drew closer, the fairies in my stomach seemed to multiply. In my mind I went over and over what Delph had taught me. I felt stronger, more nimble and tougher because of his training. I had beaten Cletus up before, but not in a Duelum. And he had grown this past session to where he was far bigger than me. Still, he was a git and I simply refused to lose to a git.

The crowds started assembling near the end of the first section of light. Some Wugs smiled and gave me encouraging words. However, others shunned me. If I were to take a poll, it seemed that Wormwood would be split right down the middle on my guilt or innocence. It wasn't that the Wugs against me really thought me bad. It was just that many Wugs accepted whatever Council told them. And, in all honesty, I had enemies here, even before I had been plunked in Valhall.

Many Wugs proceeded on to the small betting area, probably to wager coin on Cletus Loon bashing in my brains.

Delph showed up with his father in time to see Bogle and the carriage arrive. Morrigone, Thansius and John alighted and took their places on the platform along with other members of Council. Julius Domitar sat in the back of this group, along with Wugs I did not normally associate with because I was apparently not good enough.

Delph patted me on the shoulder and said, "How do you feel, Vega Jane?"

"I feel great," I lied. "I can't wait for it to start." Now, that wasn't a lie. I wanted it to start before my head exploded. I just kept telling myself that it would be terribly bad form to vomit on Cletus Loon before the fight bell had even rung. Though it would be enormously satisfying to see my sick on his shirt.

For expediency, there would be multiple bouts carried on at the same time in the quadrants of the pitch. There was no time limit on a bout. Wugs kept fighting until one no longer could. That was a stark rule and one that any sane Wug might have questioned. However, sanity seemed to be in limited supply these lights and nights in Wormwood.

I eyed the other females who would be fighting. They both looked sicker and paler than I probably did. I was not in the first set of bouts, so I sat on a small knoll overlooking the pitch and awaited Delph, who was in a first bout pitted against Digby. I was sure that most bettors had wagered on Delph, and when I looked over at the betting board, I could see that he was a heavy favorite.

Digby was in the process of removing his great, filthy shirt. I had always imagined him to be flabby and hideously dirty without clothes on. Thus, I was surprised to see him so muscular. Though I had been quite correct about the hideously dirty part.

Digby went through a series of stretches and then started running in place. His muscles rippled as he did so. Then he started to do a bit of practice pugilism, weaving and bobbing and punching. He seemed quite adept at it, very fast and very accurate. I glanced worriedly over at Delph. He had not removed his shirt and he was not stretching or pretend-boxing. He was just standing there with his gaze squarely on Ran Digby. And in his look I began to see a Delph with whom no one would want to tangle. His strong hands curled to fists and he kept looking at Digby with such fierce concentration that he reminded me of the jabbits after me at Stacks. I wanted to tell Delph good luck but I was afraid of breaking whatever trance he was putting himself in.

Thansius rose and addressed us. "Welcome to the Duelum," he said in a booming voice. "And what a fine light for it. I want to wish luck to all fighters. We all want clean bouts and I have confidence in our referees to ensure that that will indeed be the case."

I was really only half listening. My gaze flitted over to John and then away again several times. Finally, our gazes caught each other. I saw him actually smile at me encouragingly before Morrigone drew his attention away.

I caught her once looking at me. Her expression was unreadable, and all I could think about was her vanishing in a mist of blue. She could banish Wugs' memories and, in the case of Delph, damage their minds. She was an extraordinary Wug, I had to give her that. But she was also dangerous. Anyone with such powers was. And it was only an instant later that I realized I might have to include myself in that group.

Of the bouts to take place now, I cared about only one. Delph and Ran Digby entered their quadrant. Delph had taken off his shirt and I marveled at his lean, chiseled physique. There was not a smidgen of fat on him. He still looked only at Digby, who stared back at his opponent as he flexed his massive arms and worked kinks out of his creta-thick neck.

Right at the strike of the second section of light, the competition bell rang. I had to blink because I would not have thought it possible that two males that large could move that fast. They collided in the very center of the quadrant, and the sound of bone and muscles crashing together made me light-headed. It was like two cretas ramming together.

Digby got a headlock on Delph and looked like he was trying to rip his head from his torso. Delph strained to free himself with his hands and this exposed his body. Digby took advantage of this by delivering thunderous knee kicks to Delph's stomach and sides.

I cringed with each blow. I was stunned that Delph was still upright. But then with a mighty effort, he broke Digby's hold on him and the two huge Wugs faced off. Digby was breathing heavy. Delph looked calm and in control. I marveled at his composure after nearly having his head ripped off and his body wickedly slammed with blows from Digby's bony knees.

But it was over more quickly than I could have imagined. After they each threw a few punches that careened off their hardened torsos, and Digby missed with a kick, Delph got a choke hold on Digby. He lifted him full off the ground, spun around and delivered his opponent face-first into the hard dirt. There was a crunching sound and Digby lay still.

Delph let go of Digby's neck and rose. The referee checked Digby's status and then waved over the Mendens, who hurried in with their bulky bags. While they were resuscitating Digby, the referee raised Delph's hand to the sky and declared him the winner. I cheered louder than anyone. When Delph came back over, he was the old Delph again, the steely, disquieting look gone and replaced with a lopsided grin.

I gave him a hug and when I drew my hand back, it was covered with blood. I looked up in horror at him.

"'Tis Digby's, not mine, Vega Jane."

I glanced over at Digby, who was slowly sitting up, his face covered by a veil of blood and his nose cleanly broken. I had to put a hand on my stomach to keep my first meal where it should remain.

Ten slivers later the first set of bouts was over. The female had been soundly beaten by her male opponent although he had "gallantly" refrained from smashing in her brain. Yet the Mendens had still been called and she ended up being carried off the pitch on a stretcher with her mum sobbing next to her.

The bell for the next bouts rang immediately after the fighters had gathered on their respective quadrants. Twenty hard-fought slivers later, more fighters were out of the Duelum, including the only other female. She had collapsed backward after being charged by her opponent, a seventeen-session-old Dactyl who worked at Stacks. I don't believe he actually touched her. I think she simply fainted.

Part of me wished for such an option. But after my dustup with Morrigone, if I tried anything like that, I truly believed my head would soon disappear from my shoulders.

Eventually, the final set of bouts was called. I took a long breath while Delph gripped my shoulder and gave me encouraging words.

"He's a soft Wug, he is," he told me. "Loon won't know what hit him."

I smiled weakly and nodded. "We can celebrate this night," I said.

But on the inside I was scared. There was no other way to describe it. I had a plan. I really did. Cletus had taken off his shirt. He was not as flabby as he used to be, with his body growing as much as it had. I of course kept my shirt on. He was two sessions older than me, a full-grown Wug, actually. And while it was true I had bested him in the past, it had been the far past — except when I had kicked him in the belly the light I'd been confronted by the Carbineers and he'd nicked my egg. I'm sure Cletus had been training hard for this bout, no doubt learning dirty tricks from the likes of Ran Digby and Non. And I had to face that he was male and thus stronger than me.

But he was *not* tougher than me.

Loon grinned maliciously and puffed out his chest and flexed his arms while I stood rock still. Our referee appeared and told us the rules, of which there were precious few. One that did surprise me was that if you were forced out of your quadrant by your opponent, he was given a free blow to any part of your body. Why Delph had failed to mention that one, I had no idea. It was no wonder all the Wugs charged each other on the bell.

The referee stepped back. Right before the bell was to ring, Cletus said, "If you pretend to faint, I'll go easy on you. You'll be able to see out of your eyes and chew your meal this night."

"Funny, I was just about to make you the same offer."

His grin disappeared and was replaced with a determination I had seldom seen on his features. So much for my bravado.

I glanced over his shoulder and was not surprised to see Delph gazing anxiously at me. But I was surprised to see that my brother was staring just as anxiously from the platform. To my left stood Cletus's parents. Cacus Loon looked very confident. Hestia looked like she might be sick.

My heart was beating so fast I was afraid it might break a rib. I had no saliva left in my mouth. I felt like I had forgotten how to breathe. Before I realized it, the bell had rung and Cletus came charging at me. I managed to block most of his first blow, but my arm instantly started swelling. I fell back, giving up precious ground of which Cletus took full advantage.

He swung a kick at my midsection that I just barely managed to avoid. But I was near the edge of the quadrant and if Cletus got a free shot on me, I seriously doubted I could withstand it. At the last instant I ducked under his blow, whipsawed around him and stood back up on the other side of him. He whirled and came at me.

"What's the matter, Vega, afraid to fight?"

I would have said something clever back, only my mouth was so dry all that came out was "Aaaghmllff-prat."

We danced around for a bit, each probing the other's defenses. I threw a few awkward punches, which he easily blocked. His confidence was growing by the sliver, I could tell. I swung a kick that he derisively flicked away. He laughed.

But I had my plan and I bided my time. And then it came. He feinted with his right hand. I kept the grin from showing on my face as I pretended to block this blow. When he threw his left, I had already struck. I slammed the top of my head into his face, a move that Wugs quaintly termed a Wormwood kiss. As Cletus had done when I tricked him into revealing his fighting maneuvers, he brought up his knee, aiming for my belly. However, my blow to his head having staggered him, Cletus drifted to the left, allowing me time to hook his leg with my arm. With all my strength I ripped upward on this limb. He flipped over backward and landed on his head.

That was all I needed. I pounced and was on him like the black shuck on an escaped prisoner from Valhall. Scissoring my long legs around his torso and pinning his arms to his sides, I pounded away with my fists until Cletus, teary and wailing like a hungry baby Wug, screamed out that he was surrendering.

The referee quickly stepped in. When he tried to help Cletus up, he pushed him away, nearly causing the referee to fall. The referee lifted my hand in victory at the same time that Cletus punched me full in the face. I fell backward and carried the referee down with me.

Cries of "Foul!" and "Valhall for him!" came from the crowd of Wugs.

Cacus Loon grabbed his enraged son by the arm and dragged him off the pitch while Delph raced over and lifted me off the ground.

"Are you okay, Vega Jane?" he asked anxiously. He aimed a glare at Cletus and yelled, "You shameless pillock!"

I rubbed the blood off my mouth and nose and checked to make sure my teeth were all still there. They were, but I felt my eye swelling already. Despite all that, the biggest grin spread across my face.

"I won, Delph," I gasped.

"I know you did," he replied, grinning back.

With his help I staggered off the pitch. The first round was done. Only four more to go. With this thought, the grin slipped off my face. But only for a sliver. I had won after all. The first female to ever do so in a Duelum.

As I looked up at the platform, I saw John standing and clapping while Morrigone put her hands together once and then stopped. As we passed the betting circle, I saw Roman Picus giving a what-for to Cacus Loon while Cletus stood there with murder all over his features, although tears still stained his face. My victory had apparently cost Roman dearly.

I was surprised when Delph went over to Roman and held out a tiny slip of parchment. Roman eyed him with unfriendly eyes and then proceeded to count off ten coins and handed them to Delph. "Lucky first time," Roman said bitterly.

"She won fair and square," replied Delph. "No luck about it. Har!"

As we walked off, I said, "You bet on me?"

"Course I did."

"I didn't know you wagered."

"Every Wug takes a flutter now and again and I ain't no different, am I?" he said casually.

"What if I'd lost? Did you have the coin to lose?"

"I put it on credit. Besides, I knew you were going to win," he said flatly.

"But what if I didn't?"

"Well, then I might have had a wee problem with Roman Picus, mightn't I?"

"Delph, you're mental, you really are."

"And we're also winners this light, Vega Jane."

We were winners, both of us. I hadn't felt this good in a really long time.

Even with a bashed-in face.

LATER, DELPH USED his coins to treat us to a meal at a shop on the High Street called the Starving Tove. I had never eaten a meal in a shop before. It was not something that a working Wug like myself could ever have considered. To pay another Wug perfectly good coin to sit leisurely at a table and be served a fancy meal seemed barmy.

I absolutely loved it!

Before we went, Delph and I had cleaned up and I had put on the only other set of clothes I owned — a wool skirt that nearly reached the ground and a long-sleeved shirt made from amaroc hide that had belonged to my mother. I even found an old hat of hers from a pile of odds and ends in the corner. It was wide-brimmed and faded and looked, I'm sure, hideously old-fashioned. But I wanted to wear it that night more than anything I had ever owned.

I had run cold water from the pipes over my eye, but it was still so puffy I could barely see out of it. I had decided against using the Adder Stone to heal it. Wugs might get suspicious with such a speedy recovery.

We sat at a table in the back of the Starving Tove. Other Wugs sat at several tables nearer the front. I didn't know if that was because we weren't dressed as nicely, but it probably was. The other Wugs eating there — two of whom were members of Council — occasionally glanced over at us and then had whispered conversations. I tried to ignore it, but it wasn't easy.

Delph, who had obviously noted this, said, "Everybody knows you now, Vega Jane."

I focused on him. "What?"

"Beat a male, didn't you? First female ever to do it in a Duelum. Famous you are."

I thought about this for a sliver or two and looked around at some of the Wugs who were staring at me. A couple smiled and nodded encouragingly. Maybe Delph was right.

When our food came, I couldn't believe the abundance of it. I didn't even pick up my fork. I just looked at the heaping plate in front of me. I whispered to Delph, "Do we just take a bit and then pass it on to the other tables?"

"'Tis all yours, Vega Jane."

"Are you sure?" I said incredulously.

"Yup."

"But you've never been here, have you?"

"Once."

"When?" I demanded.

"After I won a Duelum. Roman Picus took me here."

"Why would that lout take you anywhere?"

"It was me first Duelum. I was the underdog. Picus bet many coins on me and won. So he treated me to a meal. Only thing I ever got from that great git, o'course."

I looked down at the cornucopia of meats, vegetables, cheeses and breads, and licked my lips like a hungry canine.

Which reminded me, I had to save some of this for Harry Two, who was patiently waiting outside.

Thirty slivers later, I set down my fork and knife. I had my berry juice topped off and took a last long draught and rubbed my full belly. I then let out a long sigh and stretched like a feline after a nap. Delph grinned at me.

"Good eating," he said.

"You shouldn't have, Delph. It cost a coin apiece. I saw the menu board out front."

"Coins you won me, so there."

Well, I couldn't really argue with that. And I had the bruises and bloodletting to show for it. I got a small bag from the server and put the rest of my meal in it for Harry Two. As we were walking out, a well-dressed female Wug rose from her table and shook my hand. "I am very proud of you, my dear Vega Jane," she said.

I had seen her before. Her mate was on Council. He sat there in his great black tunic and stared up at me with a disapproving expression. I imagined he might be one of Krone's allies. He didn't put out his hand for me to shake. But then again, he wouldn't, would he? Some of my dirt might rub off on him.

Her mate pulled her back to her chair and looked at her reproachfully.

"Thank you," I managed to mumble and then hurried on.

I heard them start arguing as we reached the door.

Outside, I gave Harry Two his meal right there on the cobblestones. As he gobbled it up, I turned to Delph.

"Thanks for the meal."

He smiled. "It was a good light."

"It was a *great* light. When will the next Duelum round be?"

"Two lights."

I groaned. I thought there would be a longer interval.

"When will we know who we have to fight?"

"Next night."

We walked back to my digs and sat in front of the empty fireplace.

It was night now and my eyes were heavy.

Delph noted this, rose and we said our good-byes. I watched him walk off down the Low Road until I could see him no longer. I closed the door and lay on my cot, Harry Two next to me. And then I did the only thing I could do. I closed my eyes and fell asleep.

Hall of Truth

THE NEXT LIGHT at Stacks began with Newton Tilt, a tall, muscled eighteen-session-old Cutter coming over to me to congratulate me on my victory. He was nice, very good-looking and I had always considered him quite slithy. In fact, I would sometimes snatch a glance while he worked away.

"I'm glad you beat that git Loon," he said, dazzling me with a wide smile. He lowered his voice. "You have a friend in the Tilt family, Vega, never fear. Done me heart good to see you tell Krone off like that."

I smiled and thanked him and watched him walk off, my heart growing warm.

The next round of competitors would be posted at the first section of night. I was both anxious and leery to know. If I had drawn Delph, I didn't know what I would do. I thought about us making a run for the Quag now. That would prevent them from taking my punishment out on Delph. Yet something held me back. Well, it was quite clear what was holding me back. I had given my word that I would fight my hardest in the Duelum. That had been my deal with Morrigone. She was not my favorite Wug. But a promise was a promise. I didn't mind lying occasionally, particularly when it helped me survive. To go back on my word, though, that was something my grandfather never would have done. And neither would I. It would be a taint on the Jane name.

I usually couldn't care less what other Wugs thought. But this was different. I would never forget the look Thansius had given me when the marks were revealed on my skin. I just wanted to show him that, well, that I was an honorable, if not overly clean, Wug.

I looked up quickly when I spotted his shadow across my workstation.

Domitar was staring at me. I glanced up at him expectantly.

"You did well last light, Vega, very well indeed."

"Thank you, Domitar."

"I won twenty coins on you, in fact," he added in a giddy tone, rubbing his fat hands together.

I was very surprised by this, and my features must have revealed that.

He waved this look off. "I knew you would win. Cletus Loon is an even bigger idiot than his father." He toddled off, chuckling to himself.

I went outside at the mid-light meal to bring water and some food to Harry Two. As I sat in the high grass, I stared up at Stacks. I had been to the top floor twice now. Once I had found Destin and the other time my past.

But was it the top floor?

I continued to gaze upward as Stacks soared on and on. It had to be taller than two floors. Which meant I had more of the place to discover. This was a ridiculously dangerous thought, I knew. I was one slip at the Duelum from going to

Valhall for the rest of my sessions. But the sword hanging over my head had also given me true clarity of mind, perhaps for the first time in my life.

I was tired of so many questions on my part and no answers in return. Could I perhaps find some answers in Stacks, which seemed to have more secrets than any other place in Wormwood? Every time I had gone in there, I had come away with something of value. Could I try my luck once more?

When the bell rang for the end of work, I changed my clothes and waited outside for the other Wugs to leave. I was surprised to see Delph run up, his shirt soaked with sweat from his Wall work.

"What are you doing here?" I asked.

"Duelum practice," he answered.

"It'll have to wait."

"Why?"

"Because I'm sneaking back in Stacks after everyone has gone. I've been to the second floor. Now I want to go higher."

"Are you nutters, Vega Jane?" sputtered Delph.

"Probably," I answered.

"Krone'll be looking for any chance to throw you back in Valhall. What if his blokes are watching us right now?"

"I thought of that," I said. "I'm going to come back here a little later and sneak in the side. It would be pretty much impossible for anyone to spot me then."

"Why go in a'tall?"

"I've been in there twice now and I've gotten out okay each time. And every time I have, I've learned something important. That's where I got Destin," I added, pointing at the chain, which sat around my waist. "And the Elemental and the Adder Stone."

"But you said that was from the little room on the second floor. Now ya want to find a way to go higher, you said."

"Right."

"And I can't talk you out of doing this?"

"No."

He gazed up at Stacks. "So how do we do this?"

"*We* aren't doing anything. I'm going in. You can take Harry Two to your digs and wait for me there. I'll come by after I'm done here."

"Either I go in with you, or I go and tell bloody Domitar what you're planning to do. Bet he nips off to tell Krone."

"Delph, you wouldn't!" I said in a shocked tone.

"The Hel I wouldn't."

We stared at each other for about a sliver. He said, "I'm not letting you go into that place alone."

"Delph, you don't know what I've faced in there. It's very dangerous and —"

"There's Domitar leaving now. Shall I go have a chat with him?"

I looked over and saw Domitar and Dis Fidus leaving. I turned back and glared at Delph, whipping my hair out of my face.

"All right, but if you get killed, don't come complaining to me."

"Har," he shot back.

Then a thought struck me. No, it was more a truth. I had

given my word to fight in the Duelum, as hard as I could. If I did that, Morrigone said everything would return to normal. I would owe Council nothing. But I had no intention of staying in Wormwood after that. My parents were gone. My brother was lost to me. Morrigone had said that if I tried to leave, they would punish Delph. Well, our original plan of fleeing together solved that dilemma. And if Delph was going with me into the Quag, he had to learn, firsthand, how to handle himself in the face of things that a Wug was not used to confronting. Perhaps this night would be a good opportunity for Delph to be initiated into what lurked inside Stacks.

I looked up at him. "Delph?"

"What?" he barked, obviously ready for another argument.

"After the Duelum is done and you've won the thing, I'm leaving Wormwood. I'm going through the Quag. My mind is made up."

"Okay," he said, his features calming, but there was a heightened anxiety in his eyes, which I did not like.

"Are you still coming with me?"

He didn't say anything for a long moment. "Are you a nutter? Course I am."

Before I knew it, I had reached up on tiptoes and kissed him.

"Vega Jane," he said, his face red with embarrassment over the unexpected snog. And in truth, I had surprised myself.

I hunched over defensively. "Just to seal the covenant, Delph," I said quickly. "That's all," I added firmly.

LATER, WE SNUCK around the side of Stacks after leaving Harry Two at my digs. We had taken a meandering route here and even practiced some for the Duelum, which was perfectly legal if anyone was watching. Then I had led Delph down a forest path, which I knew was a shortcut to Stacks. I defeated the lock on the same door as before with my tools while Delph looked on admiringly.

"Right good touch, Vega Jane," he said.

I opened the door and we stole into Stacks. I knew which way to go, which was fortunate. Even though it was still light outside, it was dark and shadowy in here.

I felt like I could hear Delph's heart beating behind me as I gripped his hand and led him along. We reached the second floor with no problem. I was listening for the sounds of the jabbits coming, but the only things I heard were my breathing and Delph's heart hammering. As I'd suspected, the jabbits didn't seem to come out until dark.

We walked along the second floor and I reached the wooden door. On the other side was the little door with the crazy Wug doorknob. I didn't want to go that way again.

I turned and led Delph in the other direction. I heard no slithers, no footfalls other than our own. I said, "There is at least one more floor up. The only way I can see it being is down here."

Delph nodded, though I knew he was too nervous and fearful to be thinking clearly.

All we found was a solid wall with no evidence of stairs leading up. However, as I leaned out a window, I could see the floor above us. There had to be a way up.

I shut the window and turned back to Delph, who was standing in front of the blank wall probing every crevice with his strong fingers.

"Delph," I began. And then I could no longer see Delph. My mind filled with vapor, as if a fog had rolled through my head. When it cleared, I still could not see Delph. What I saw was a staircase leading up. I shook my head clear and Delph reappeared in my sight line. I rubbed my eyes, but the image of the stairs did not come back.

"Delph," I said. "Stand back."

He turned to look at me. "There is nae stairs here, Vega Jane."

"Step back."

He moved away. I put on my glove, drew out the Elemental, thought it to full form, cranked my arm back and threw it as hard as I could at the wall.

"Vega Ja —" Delph began, but he never finished.

The wall had disappeared in a cloud of smoke, leaving a gaping hole. The Elemental returned to my hand like a trained prey bird.

Revealed in the hole was a set of black marble stairs, just like in the image in my head. I had no idea how I had seen it. But I was awfully glad I had.

I stepped through the hole, and Delph followed. We cautiously made our way up the steps. At the top of the stairs was a large room with words carved into the stone above the entrance.

HALL OF TRUTH.

I looked at Delph and he stared blankly back. We stepped into the room, stunned at both its size and beauty.

There were stone walls, marble floors, a wooden ceiling and not a single window. I marveled at the craftsmanship that had gone into the creation of this space. I had not seen stone carved so elegantly, and the pattern on the marble made it more resemble a work of art than a floor to walk upon. The beams overhead were darkened with age and were heavily carved with symbols I had never seen before and which, for some reason, gave me a moment of seized terror in my heart. And along each wall were enormous wooden bookcases filled with dusty, thick tomes.

I reached for Delph's hand at the same moment his reached for mine. We walked to the middle of the room, stopped, and gazed around like two just-born Wugs first discovering what was outside the bellies of our mums.

"Lotta books," noted Delph quite unnecessarily.

I had no idea there were these many books in existence. My first thought was that John would love this room, followed by a pang of depression. He was not the same John, was he?

"What do we do now?" asked Delph in a hushed voice.

That was a reasonable question. I supposed there was only one thing to do. I stepped toward the closest bookcase and slid out a book. I wish I hadn't.

The instant I opened the book, the entire room transformed into something as unlike a room as it was possible to be. Gone were the books and the walls and the floor and the ceiling. Replacing them was a hurricane of images, voices, screams, slashes of light, vortexes of movement, Wugs, winged sleps, an army of flying jabbits and the vilest creatures dirtbound. Garms and amarocs and freks hurtling over and through piles of bodies. And then there were non-Wugs, colossals, warriors in chain mail, things with peaked ears and red faces and blackened bodies, and shrouded shapes lurking in shadows from which streams of light burst forth. And then came explosions and kaleidoscopes of flames and towers of ice plummeting into abysses so deep they seemed to have no bottom.

My heart was in my throat. I felt Delph's fingers fall away from mine. In this maelstrom of Hel, I turned and saw him running away. I wanted to flee too, but my feet seemed rooted where they were. I looked down at my hands. Still there was the open book. Out of the pages was pouring everything we were seeing.

I am not so brilliant as my brother, but simple problems sometimes have simple answers. I slammed shut the book. When the two halves smacked together, the room was once more just a room. I stood there out of breath, though I had not moved an inch.

I turned to see Delph bent over gasping for air, his face pale as goat's milk.

"Bloody Hel," he yelled.

"Bloody Hel," I said more quietly, in agreement. I wanted to yell it too, actually, but my lungs lacked the capacity to do so.

"The Hall of Truth. All these books, Delph. Where did they come from? They can't all be about Wormwood. It just isn't that, well —"

"Important," Delph finished for me. He shrugged. "Dunno, Vega Jane. Can't make head nor tail of it. But let's get outta this place." He started for the stairs.

And that's precisely when we heard it coming. Delph retreated to stand next to me. By the sound it was making, we were not about to be confronted by jabbits.

I thought this a good thing. Until I saw what came through the entrance.

Then all I could think to do was scream. And I did.

I would have preferred the jabbits.

A Case of Cobbles

WHEN THE CREATURE stepped into the room, the vast space seemed too small to contain it. I knew exactly what it was. I had seen a drawing and description of it in Quentin Herms's book on the Quag. His illustration did not do it terrifying justice.

It was a cobble.

Not nearly as large as the colossals I had been pitted against, it was still horrifyingly huge. And it looked to be made of rock. But that was not the most alarming element of the thing. It had three bodies, all male and all attached, shoulder to shoulder. It had three heads and three sets of tiny wings growing out of its muscular backs. And when I looked down at its hands, I saw three swords and three axes. When I looked at the three faces, they each held the same expression: hatred fueled by fury.

"You trespass here," one of the mouths said. Its voice was like a shriek crossed with a thunder-thrust.

I would have said something back, only I was so scared, words would not form in my throat.

Another mouth pronounced, "The punishment for trespassing is death."

The cobble took a step forward, its immense weight threatening to crush the marble floor. I barely had time to jerk Delph downward before three axes soared over the spot where our heads had just been. They flew across the room and embedded in the far bookcase, knocking it and two of its neighbors over. As books toppled to the floor and flew open, the room was once more engulfed in the fury unleashed from their freed pages.

I grabbed Delph's hand and jerked him to cover behind one of the fallen bookcases. For a sliver, I ignored the images cascading around us, although it wasn't easy. A banshee screamed away in my ear. That creature too had been in Quentin's Quag book.

One of the cobble's swords sliced the bookcase we were hiding behind in half; the blade stopped an inch from turning me into two Wugs. Delph started hurling books at it, but the cobble crushed the bookcase under its two middle legs as I flung myself away from it and slid across the room, crashing into another bookcase and causing a multitude of tomes to rain down on my head. Creatures great and small, long-dead Wugs, and creations I had no way to even recognize poured out of these fat volumes. The room could not hope to contain this maelstrom of mayhem.

I slipped my gloved hand in my pocket, drew out the Elemental, willed it to full form, drew my arm back, aimed and fired it directly at the middle of the cobble. It connected and disappeared in a huge wall of smoke. When the smoke cleared, the middle body of the cobble was no longer. I breathed a sigh of relief and relaxed slightly. However, the other two bodies, freed from their mate, were still standing. Well, actually, they were running directly at me.

I looked wildly around for the Elemental. Then I saw it. The spear had taken a long arc around the room and was now heading back to me. Then a sword thrown by one of the cobbles collided with it, knocking it violently off course. It slammed with great velocity against a wall of bookcases. They tumbled down and, to my horror, the Elemental became trapped under them. As one of the cobbles surged straight at me, his sword held high for the killing stroke, I saw a blur of motion to my right.

"No, Delph!" I screamed.

Delph either didn't hear me or didn't want to hear me. He slammed into one of the cobble's thighs. The creature was so massive that as big and strong as Delph was, he was like a bird crashing against a solid wall. Delph slumped to the floor, the senses shaken clean from him. Before I could move, the cobble had lifted him off the ground and flung him through the air as if he were a bit of parchment. I watched in horror as Delph sailed the entire length of the room and crashed into another wall of bookcases.

I started to run toward him, but I was blinded by a fiery image that had come soaring out of one of the books flying past my face. I tripped and fell to the floor. On the way down, I turned and saw a sword slashing through the air where I had been standing.

The cobble was now right over me. It raised the sword above its head and was just about to plunge it downward and separate my legs from the rest of me when I soared straight upward and shot past it. This was my true advantage against my massive opponent.

Under my cloak, Destin was warm to the touch. I zipped along the perimeter of the wall, heading toward Delph. I wouldn't make it. I had lost track of the other cobble until it reared up directly in front of me. I had forgotten about the ruddy wings on the monstrous back. It seemed impossible that a set of fragile wings could lift such an enormous weight. But I was nimble while the cobble was not.

I flew under its arm and then around its back. It spun around, trying to keep me in sight. I kept flying in circles, faster and faster, pushing Destin and myself harder than I ever had. The cobble kept spinning too and started resembling the bonce I would rotate on the ground when I was a very young.

I shot downward as the cobble continued to spin. I pushed a bookcase out of the way, gripped the Elemental and flung it as hard as I could. The cobble came out of the rotation just as the Elemental found its mark.

The cobble exploded.

As the Elemental flew back toward me, Delph screamed, "Look out, Vega Jane."

I partially ducked but was still knocked heels over bum and landed hard against a wall. As I slumped to the floor, the remaining cobble swung its great fist back to batter me once more, this time surely into the Hallowed Ground. I had forgotten the warning in Quentin's book: *Woe be to the Wug who forgets that destroying one part of the thing does not equal victory.*

I was too wonky to fly. The Elemental was not yet back in hand. And an extremely large fist was coming right at my head. At the last instant, I sprang up and smashed my own fist into the cobble's belly.

The cobble was lifted off its massive feet and flew backward through the air, where it struck the wall opposite so hard it exploded into fragments. I just stood there for a sliver or two looking at what remained of the cobble and then at my fist. I had no idea what had just happened. The Elemental arrived in my gloved hand and I closed my fingers around it.

I looked once more at the remains of the cobble and then my mind went back to that night at the Care when I had struck Non: My hand was injured delivering the blow. Striking the rocklike cobble, my poor bones should have shattered. There was only one explanation. I lifted my cloak and looked down at Destin. It was an ice blue. I touched it and then hastily withdrew my finger. It was molten to the touch, although all I could feel around my waist was a heightened sense of warmth.

"Wo-wo-wotcha, Ve-Ve-Vega Jane?" the voice called out.

"Delph!" I had forgotten about him.

I ran to him, used my newfound strength to throw off the bookcases that covered most of him. He was bruised and bloodied.

"Can you stand?" I asked.

He nodded slowly and said weakly, "Th-think so."

I gingerly helped him up. He was holding his right arm funny and he couldn't put much weight on his left leg.

"Delph, hold on to me."

I willed the Elemental to shrink, placed it in my pocket and then lifted him up and over my back. He gasped in amazement at this, but I had no time for explanations. I leapt into the air and flew out the doorway, down the stairs, and didn't land until we were at the door we had come through. I was giving the jabbits no chance to get us. I smashed open the door, flew through it with Delph on my back and we soared into the nighttime sky.

I didn't land again until we were at Delph's cottage. As I set him down, he said in a dazed voice, "How did you lift me like that, Vega Jane?"

"I'm not sure, Delph. How bad are you hurt?" I asked anxiously.

"Busted up pretty good," he admitted. "Cobbles," he added.

"You *did* read the book."

"Dinnae figure on meeting one of them on this side of the Quag, though."

"Can you walk?"

"I can limp."

I slapped my forehead. "I've got the Adder Stone. I'll sort you out in no time."

I reached in one pocket. Then my other. I frantically searched every crevice of clothing I had. Then I groaned. The Stone was gone. I looked at Delph with a miserable expression.

"I must have lost it back at Stacks. I can go and —"

He gripped my arm. "You are nae going back there."

"But the Stone. Your injuries."

"I'll heal, Vega Jane. Just take a bit of time."

Then another thought seized me. "The Duelum!"

He nodded sadly. "Can't fight with one arm and leg, can I?"

"Delph, I'm so sorry. This was all my fault."

"In this together, Vega Jane, ain't we? I chose to come, insisted on it, actually. And you saved me life."

I helped him into the cottage. Duf was not there. Probably working at the Wall, I reckoned. I got Delph into his cot after cleaning up his cuts and icing his bruises with cold water from a bucket his father kept in the little cave. I fashioned a sling for his arm and found a thick cudgel he could use to help him walk.

"I'm sorry," I said again, tears forming in my eyes.

He smiled weakly. "No dull times round you, is there? Har."

A Wager to Win

THE NEXT THING I knew, it was light and I was waking up on my cot. I was tired, sore, out of sorts and my head mired in the events of last night. Something licked my hand and I sat up and patted Harry Two on the head. When I looked outside my window, I saw Wugs streaming past in large numbers.

I took a sliver to realize what was going on. The Duelum! It was at second light. I was late. I jumped off my cot, nearly scaring Harry Two to death, and scrambled into the clothes I had let fall to the floor the night before. I stopped, looked down at Destin where I had dropped it on the floor. With that I could defeat any Wug in the Duelum. I was torn. One thousand coins. It was a lot of wealth, more than I would ever have. But it wasn't the coins that mattered. Other Wugs would think highly of me if I were champion crowned — the female in the Starving Tove and plenty of others. Like Delph said, I was famous. Wugs knew me.

Still I made no move to pick up Destin. I finally used my foot to edge the chain under my cot. I didn't have to win the bloody Duelum. I just had to fight my hardest. And part of me was afraid if I used Destin and its power, I might unintentionally kill a Wug. I did not want that on my conscience. I also wanted to win fair and square. I was a liar, a sometime thief, a pain in the arse on more than a few occasions, but apparently I had some moral tendencies left.

As I passed other Wugs streaming toward the pitch, it occurred to me that I had not checked the board last night to see who I would be fighting. I arrived as the bell sounded and looked quickly around. Was I in this set of bouts? I spotted the betting board and rushed over to it.

"When do I fight?" I cried out breathlessly to the Wug there collecting coin and doling out parchment in return. His name was Litches McGee and he had the reputation of being scrupulously honest with his bets and being an ugly git in all other aspects of his life. He was Roman Picus's chief competitor when it came to the betting business, which was reason enough for me to deal with McGee. The lesser of two pillocks, as it were.

He looked at me. "Second set of bouts, Vega, for the good it'll do you," he said snidely. Then I looked up at the betting board and saw there were fifty bets placed on my match. And not a single Wug had picked me to win. My gaze went across the wood to see who I would be fighting. When I saw the name, I realized why the odds on my victory were so poor, well, nonexistent, to be precise.

Non. I was fighting blithering, bleeding Non.

McGee smiled at me. "Nae Cletus Loon this light, female. Say good-bye to that thousand coins, or me name's Alvis Alcumus."

I trembled with rage at his words. I stuck my hand in my pocket, pulled out the only coin I had and held it out to him.

He nodded approvingly. "You're betting on Non, o'course. Make up for having your brains beat outta you. But with the odds so in favor of Non, it won't be much you win."

"I'm betting on Vega Jane to win," I said with far more confidence than I felt. Actually, I felt no confidence at all. Why in the Hel had I left Destin back at my digs? Why did I think it was smart to be honorable? To fight fair?

"You're joshing, o'course," McGee said in an incredulous tone.

"Give me the parchment with *my* name as winner," I said between clenched teeth.

He sighed, gave me a patronizing smile, wrote it out and handed it to me.

"'Tis your coin. But like taking it from a nip of a Wug."

"Exactly what I was thinking about you."

I turned and rushed off before I barfed in front of him. That coin was my last. I had nary a bean to my name after that.

The first bouts this light went by more slowly than in the first round. The competition had gotten harder as the weakest fighters had already fallen. This gave me time to work myself up into a ball of nerves so tight I found I couldn't even speak.

It didn't help that word had gotten around that Delph had withdrawn from the Duelum because of unspecified injuries. I knew his absence from the field would make Non a favorite to win, as he had narrowly lost to Delph in the last Duelum. This would only give that oaf more incentive to crush me, not that he needed any. I looked down at my fist.

Without Destin, it was just a fist, a female fist and nothing more.

I walked around the pitch, swinging my arms and trying to keep loose. I wasn't paying attention and knocked into something so hard that I fell back on the ground. When I looked up to see what I had hit, Non was staring down at me. And behind him was Cletus Loon, with his face all bandaged, several friends of Cletus, and Ted Racksport, who had already won his match this light by quickly beating senseless the muscular Dactyl who worked at Stacks. I had watched the match and come away impressed. Racksport was stronger and more nimble than he looked and had turned the Dactyl's muscle against him and given the bloke quite a pasting. He smiled at me through crooked teeth.

But I wasn't focused on him. I was looking at Non. He seemed huge. As big as the cobble last night. He wore his metal breastplate, which I didn't think was even allowed in the Duelum, not that he would need it. The dent that I had put in it was still there. As I looked at him, his gaze drifted down to the dent and then back to me.

He smiled and bent down so only I could hear him when he spoke.

"Luck dinnae strike twice, Vega. If I were you, I'd see to a bed at the Care before you step in the quad with me." He put a knuckled fist in my face and said in a loud voice, "Be sure and count all your teeth. That way you'll know how many you have to pick up when I'm done with ya."

Racksport, Cletus and his chums thought this the funniest thing they ever in all their sessions had heard. They roared with laughter even as I picked myself up and walked off on jelly legs. I was wondering if I had time to go back to my digs and retrieve Destin when the bell for the second set of matches rang.

My mouth as dry as the bank of a dead river, I headed for my assigned quad. I had not previously looked up to the spectator platform, but now I did. Thansius was there, but there was no sign of John or Morrigone. Well, at least Morrigone wouldn't have the satisfaction of seeing Non beat me senseless.

Harry Two followed me to my quad and I had to tell him in no uncertain terms that he could not attack Non while we were fighting. Then I whispered in his ear, "But when he finishes me off, have at the bloke and don't leave much behind."

Harry Two was now nearly ninety pounds and none of it was fat. And his fangs were nearly as long as my longest finger. He looked at me with what seemed like the greatest understanding. I believe he even smiled. I dearly loved my canine.

As I stepped into the quad, I glanced to my left and saw Delph shuffling up with his arm in the sling and his bad leg supported by the cudgel I had given him. He smiled encouragingly, but when he glanced at Non, who had stepped into the other side of the quad, I could see his encouraging look fade to a morose resignation.

I swallowed hard as the referee gave instructions. That's when I noted that Non had not taken off his metal. When I pointed this out to the referee, he looked at me like I was quite barmy.

"Unless he takes it off and beats you with it, female, 'tis well within the rules of the Duelum."

"And if he hits me with it and kills me?" I said angrily.

"Then he will be appropriately penalized."

Non laughed. "But you'll still be dead."

"Non!" admonished the referee, a small, wizened old Wug named Silas. I suspected he had very poor eyesight, because he had looked at my belly button when addressing me and had looked to Non's left when addressing him. "Let's have a good, clean fight," Silas added, now staring at my knees.

Non cracked his knuckles. I tried to crack my knuckles but succeeded only in bending one of my pinkies back so far I cried out in pain. Non laughed.

The fight bell was rung and Non hurtled straight at me. I instinctively backed away, sidestepped Non at the last instant and poked one of my long legs out. He tripped over my shin, sending shock waves up and down my entire body, and he fell like a great tree to the dirt. I skirted away from him as he rose and whirled around, blood in both eyes. He came at me again and once more I dodged him. I wasn't sure how long I could keep this up. At some point I would be out of puff. One punch and I had little doubt I would go down. I once again lamented leaving Destin behind.

"Stop mucking about, female," snarled Non. "You're here to fight, not run like a skittish baby slep." But as he said these words, he was also breathing heavily. It finally dawned on me. The lout's metal breastplate was very heavy, no doubt. Wearing it and having to chase me was tiring him out faster than he had anticipated.

He lunged at me again and I let him get within a gnat's whisker before I leapt out of the way. My laboring with the bundles of rocks that Delph had made for me was actually paying off. I felt very light on my feet. And strong even without Destin.

Non dropped to one knee to regain his breath and I took the opportunity to slam my boot into his arse, driving him headfirst into the dirt.

Delph yelled, "Atta female, Vega Jane!"

When Non regained his feet, I could see he was in a paddy, nearly foaming at the mouth. If his eyes could have harmed me, I would have been blown into a million bits. But, as with Cletus Loon, I now had a plan. It seemed that on the field of combat, I was becoming good at keeping my wits and employing my tactics on the fly.

Non continued to chase me and I continued to keep just out of reach. I got a bit overconfident once, though, and his backhanded blow swiped across my head and knocked me more than three feet into the air. I tasted my blood as a great gash was opened over my left eye. I also believed I felt my brain bounce off both sides of my skull. When I landed, I rolled just in time to avoid Non coming down on top of me with his elbow pointed down, like Delph had once demonstrated. Instead of colliding with my neck, his bony arm hit the hard-packed dirt and he howled in pain and toppled forward on his belly. This time I did not let him get back up.

I tucked my hands inside the opening of the breastplate around his neck and pulled with all my strength. The breastplate came halfway off and did what I had intended it to do. It pinned his arms helplessly straight up in the air and his head was now inside the metal, so he was also blinded. I leapt up and came down on the back of the breastplate with both boots. Even though I was far smaller than he was, I still carried a big wallop when I struck. Non's face was propelled not into the dirt but, instead, into the far harder metal of the breastplate. I did this four more times until I heard something crack and he screamed.

I jumped off him, grabbed the breastplate, pulled it completely off and coshed him on the head with it. There was a sound like a melon dropped from a great height hitting the dirt and Non became very still.

Silas hurried to examine him and then waved the Mendens over. I stood there, my breath coming in short bursts, my head bloody and swollen where his fist had connected and my legs nearly numb from stomping on the metal. As the Mendens worked away on Non, Silas glanced at the breastplate, looked in my general vicinity and then glanced at the breastplate once more. He tapped his fingers against his chin. "I will have to look this up in the rule book," he said. "As I told you, the breastplate cannot be used as a weapon."

"By *him*," I blurted out. "He chose to wear it. It's not my fault if he was stupid enough to let me get it off him and use it against him, is it?"

"Hmmm," he said as he considered this.

"She's right, Silas," said a voice.

We both turned to see Thansius standing there. "Vega is right," he said again. "Oh, you can look it up. Section twelve, paragraph N of the *Duelum Rules of Combative Conduct*. Anything that an opponent wears into the quad can be legally used as a weapon against him by his opponent. In other words, he who brings into the quad what can be weaponized does so at his peril." He glanced at the prostrate Non. "An apt description in this case, I would think."

"Quite right, Thansius," said Silas. "No need to look it up. As a past Duelum champion many times over, your knowledge on the subject is far better than mine," he added to a spot a foot to the right of the great Wug. I really thought they needed to get younger referees or at least those who could see properly.

Silas turned and held up my hand in victory.

I just stood gaping as six Wugs lifted a groaning Non onto a stretcher and carried him off. I hoped he later would be delivered to the Care, where no one would ever come and visit him. When Silas let my hand drop, I stayed there, unable to move. My paralysis was broken by Thansius, who gripped my shoulder. I turned to look up at him.

"Well done, Vega, well done indeed."

"Thank you, Thansius."

"Now, I think we best leave the quad. The next bouts are about to commence."

We walked off the pitch together.

"Your fighting skills are quite ingenious," Thansius commented. "You sized up your far larger and stronger opponent and used his own strength and tools against him."

"Well, if I had fought him toe-to-toe, I would have lost. And I don't like to lose."

"I can see that."

The way he said it, I wasn't quite sure if he thought that a good or a bad attribute.

He pointed to my face. "You might want to get a Menden to tidy you up a bit."

I nodded and wiped at the blood. What with the dirty shot to the face I had taken from Cletus and now these fresh wounds, it was a wonder I could even see.

"So on to the third round with you," he said pleasantly enough.

I stared at him, wondering why he was even bothering to talk to me.

"Do you really expect me to keep winning?" I said.

"I can't say, Vega."

"Why would you even care?"

He seemed startled by the bluntness of my question. "I care about all Wugmorts."

"Even those accused of treason?" I asked.

He flinched with this comment. "Your frankness is often spellbinding, Vega."

"I'm not a traitor. I had the book and the map, but I would never use either against my fellow Wugs. Never."

He searched my features. "You're a fine warrior, Vega. If all Wugs could fight as well as you, we would have little worry in case of invasion."

"Or Morrigone could simply exercise her considerable powers and vanquish the so-called Outliers in a sea of blue mist with one sweep of her graceful hand."

I had no idea why I had said this. And I did not know what his reaction would be to my words. But his response was unexpected.

"We have many things to fear in Wormwood, Vega. But that is not one of them."

I gaped at him, trying to decipher his words precisely.

He said, "Now, don't forget to have your injuries sorted out. We need you at your best come the third round."

He picked up his pace and was soon well ahead of me. I slowed my walk, eyed something, grinned and bolted to the betting circle. There was a long queue, but this light I had a patience that was inexhaustible.

When I reached the front of the queue, I held out my parchment to Litches McGee. I expected him to be very angry, but he wasn't. He gleefully counted out a great many coins from a very fat bag of them and handed them to me. I stared down at them in wonder. I had never held more than one coin at any one time, and then only briefly as it would quickly go to pay a bill or two.

McGee said, "I made a small fortune this light, seeing as how every Wug wagered against you."

"Not every Wug," said a voice.

I turned to see Delph holding out his parchment.

As we put our coins in our pockets, I said to McGee, "So you'll be changing your name now?"

"What say you?" he asked with a puzzled look. "Change me name to what?"

"To Alvis Alcumus, you prat."

I walked off chortling with Delph.

"On to the third round," said Delph eagerly as Harry Two sidled up next to us. My canine looked a bit sad that he had not been able to take a few chunks out of Non.

I rubbed my bloody, swollen face and looked at Delph out of the only eye I could. "I'm not sure I'll last."

"Just three more times and you're champion," he said, smiling broadly.

Only I wasn't sure I had many tricks or strategies left.

We were both hobbling along on our gimpy legs when a Wug named Thaddeus Kitchen, who worked in the Mill with Delph, came running up. He was breathless and his face pale.

"Delph, you need to come quick!" he gasped.

"Why, what's wrong?" asked Delph, the smile struck from his face.

"It be your dad. He's terrible hurt down by the Wall."

Kitchen turned and rushed off.

Delph threw aside his cudgel and, bad leg and all, ran full tilt after him, with me and Harry Two right behind.

All Fall Down

TERRIBLE HURT.

That's what Kitchen had said about Duf.

It still didn't prepare either of us for what we saw.

Duf Delphia lay on a patch of dirt in front of the great and ugly Wall that to me now seemed as grotesque and evil as any vile creature I had yet faced. Delph raced to his father's right side while I knelt on the other. We at once realized that Duf's lower legs were smashed nearly flat at the knees. He was delirious with the pain and writhing wildly even as two Mendens worked feverishly over him with their instruments, bandages and salves.

Delph gripped his dad's hand. "I'm here," he said, his voice breaking. "I'm here, Dad."

"What happened?" I asked.

Thaddeus Kitchen was standing behind me.

He pointed to the Wall. "Section of timbers fell, caught him at the knees. Blood and bone, 'twas everywhere. Never seen nothing like it. Mawky it was. Why, 'twas like the most disgustin' bitta —"

"All right, we get the idea," I said, my worried gaze on Delph.

I looked over at a gaping hole in the Wall nearly thirty feet up.

"How the Hel did they fall?" I asked.

"Strap failed, what done it," replied Kitchen.

I jerked so badly I nearly fell over.

A strap failed? My straps?

Kitchen said in a loud, patronizing tone, "If I've said it once, I've said it a dozen times, haven't I? We're all rushing around like we're mad for it, and now we're a right pig's ear, ain't we? Cut Wugs. Smashed Wugs. Dead Wugs. And for what? A bunch of stacked wood that will no more keep away the Outliers than me female could waving her knickers at 'em. One cookie short of a picnic was the Wug thought that up, ask me."

"Well, nobody did ask you, Thaddeus Kitchen!" I exclaimed.

I shot a glance at Delph. He was looking directly at me, his features a jumble of emotions including confusion, but the only one that really stood out for me was disappointment. Disappointment in my straps. I was so focused on Delph that I never heard one of the Mendens say that Duf needed to be taken to hospital.

A cart and burly slep was brought around and Duf, now no longer conscious, was hoisted into it. I helped lift him along with some other Wugs, while Delph just stood there helplessly. I finally gripped his arm and pushed him into the cart with his father.

"I'll be there shortly," I said.

As the cart headed off, I turned to the Wall and walked over to the section that had given way. Several Wugs were inspecting the pile of splintered wood, but I focused my attention on the metal strap. I had etched my initials into each of the straps and I could see the letters of my name clear as first light. The strap was in two pieces, one large, one smaller because it had torn. I couldn't conceive of how that could have happened. Everything had been planned out so carefully in the specifications. And I had carried out those details as meticulously as I had ever done on a job at Stacks, for the simple reason that I well knew how much weight the straps would be supporting.

As I squatted down for a closer look, my jaw eased lower. Two holes had been added at the bottom of the strap, and then these additional holes had been widened considerably. By about four inches was my rough judgment. The tear had come right in the middle of one of the extra holes. It was crystal clear to me that by adding holes and making them bigger, someone had considerably weakened the strap.

"You can see right there where it done give way," said Kitchen, who had followed me over and was pointing at the tear in the strap.

"Who added the holes and made them bigger?" I asked, gazing up at him.

He drew closer and gathered his focus. "Blimey, them pair *are* bigger, ain't they?"

"They were not done like that at Stacks. How did they get that way?" I demanded.

Another Wug joined us. He was a bit taller than me, with a bristly beard, gangly limbs and a self-important look. I had seen him before in Wormwood proper but didn't know his name.

355

"Design change," he said.

"Why?" I asked.

"Holes lower like that, they can load more timber with each one that way. Simple, see. We made the fresh cuts right here on-site."

I said, "But by doing that, you also made it weak. It was never meant to hold that many timbers," I said, pointing at the splintery mess on the ground. I rose and eyed him severely. "The specifics of the straps were not to be changed."

He puffed out his chest and hooked his thumbs behind the length of braided cord riding over his shoulders and keeping his britches up. "What do you know about it, eh, female?"

"I punched the holes in the straps at Stacks," I shot out. "I'm the *Finisher*." I looked up at the Wall. "How many more of the straps did they do this to?" He didn't answer. I grabbed him by the collar and shook him violently. "How many more?!"

"Blimey, you the female in the Duelum, ain't ya?"

"She beat Non this light," added Kitchen, looking nervously at me.

"How many more?!" I screamed.

"A great many more," said the voice.

I turned and she stood there before me, in her resplendent cloak, a sheet of white in a sea of dung. Morrigone said, "Please let poor Henry go, Vega. I don't think he deserves to be throttled for simply doing his job."

I let "poor" Henry go and advanced on her. "Do you know what happened to Duf?" I asked. My head felt like it was fracturing right down the middle.

"I was fully apprised of the unfortunate incident. I will go to see him in hospital."

"If he's still alive," I shot back.

Another Wug came up to her with a scroll and an ink stick. She looked at the scroll and then took the ink stick from him, wrote some notes on the scroll, and I watched as she signed her name in an elongated motion that took up nearly half the page. She motioned for me to join her as she moved away from the two Wugs.

"So what exactly is your grievance?" she asked.

"Whoever changed the strap design is responsible for what happened to Duf." My pointed finger hovered near her perfect chin. "The pillocks should be in Valhall."

She glanced to her left and said, "I am surprised that you of all Wugs would advocate for him to be sent there."

I followed her gaze, and my eyes alighted on my brother standing on a raised platform and working away on a tilt-top desk, massive plans on scrolls laid in front of him. For the second time in a very few slivers, my jaw dropped.

"John changed the design on the straps?" I managed to say, my confidence and, with it, my voice having nearly vanished.

"He worked out the numbers on it and pronounced it sound," she said smoothly, as though she were merely recounting a recipe for cookies.

Her smug attitude brought my anger roaring back. I pointed to the mess of timbers. "Well, there's your proof of how *sound* it is. John may be brilliant, but he has never built anything before in all his sessions." My voice rose. "You can't expect to just thrust him into something like this and have no mistakes made. It's unfair to ask it."

"On the contrary, I do not ask it. In an undertaking like

this, mistakes are certain to be made. We must learn from them and move on."

"And what of Duf?"

"All that can be done will be done to ease Mr. Delphia's situation."

My anger swelled. "He's a beast trainer. How can he do that with no legs!"

"He will be supported by Council. Injury wages shall be paid."

"And what of his self-respect? What of his love for his job? You give him a few coins and tell him to be happy with what he no longer has?"

Tears were welling up in my eyes because all I could think of was Delph staring at me. The disappointment in his face. As though I had let him and his father down. As though *I* had taken his father's limbs and maybe his life along with them.

"You're emotional, Vega. It is not sound to try and think clearly under those circumstances."

As I watched her queenly, condescending chin slowly descend, followed by a pair of eyes that seemed to define haughtiness as something far more than a word or a look, I did calm. Remarkably, my reason did return amid all the chaos festering in my mind.

"I saw *you* emotional, Morrigone," I said in speech as smooth as her own. "With your lovely hair all awry, and your pretty cloak stained, and your eyes full of not simply tears but fear. Real fear. I saw all that and more, much more."

Just the barest of tremors clutched at her right cheek.

I continued primarily because I couldn't stop. "And in case you hadn't noticed, I repaired the window at my digs.

After you left on your trail of blue mist of course. I just waved my hand, thought it, and it happened. Was that how it was for you, Morrigone? Because Thansius really didn't elaborate on your powers when we spoke."

I thought she was going to raise her hand to strike. But instead, she spun on her heels and walked away. If I had had my Elemental, I very much felt that this light would have been Morrigone's last. And I very much regretted not having my Elemental.

I looked over at John as he used his ink stick to jot notes and redesign plans and come up with the most wonderful Wall of all. His enthusiasm was as beautiful as it was terrible to behold. I walked back over to Kitchen and Henry.

"If he tells you to make more holes, you will not obey. Do you understand?"

"And who are you to be giving orders, female?" said Henry indignantly.

He looked at my grimy clothing and still bloody and bruised face. Kitchen took a few steps back. He no doubt saw the murderous look in my eyes. My rage was such that I felt tremendous energy coursing down to what seemed my very soul. It was all I could do to contain it: I drew closer, made a fist and presented it an inch from Henry's chin. When I spoke, my voice was low and even but radiated more power than a thousand gospels from Ezekiel.

"Non is in hospital this light because I smashed his head so hard I heard his skull crack." Henry swallowed so slowly, it appeared he thought it would be his last gulp as my gaze threatened to split him in half. "So if I find another section of Wall has bellied up because of extra holes in *my* straps" — I pushed my fist firmly into the side of his bony, whiskered face — "I will come to your home and do four times to you what I did to Non. Do I make myself understandable to you, *male?*"

Henry tried to speak even as Kitchen let out a low whistle and seemed poised to run for it. Finally, Henry just nodded his head. I removed my fist, turned and headed to hospital as fast as my shaky legs could carry me.

HOSPITAL WAS A quarter mile from the Care, the theory being that unfortunate Wugs often went from one to the other. It was a stark, flat-faced building, gray and foreboding and set at the end of a dirt road. Even if one had hopes of survival, it was doubtful they would remain after seeing this awful place.

That was why Wugs tended to their own families for the most part. Cuts, bruises, broken bones, sick and other ailments were largely handled at home and hearth. Thus, the most severe injuries were the only ones dealt with here. If a Wug had to come to hospital, it was very possible his or her next stop would be the Hallowed Ground.

As I passed through the large double doors that were carved with a serpent and a feather symbolizing who the Hel knew what, a Nurse dressed in a gray cloak and domed white cap came forward. I explained who I was and why I was here. She nodded, her look sympathetic, which I did not think boded well for Duf's prospects.

As I followed her through the narrow, dark corridors, I heard moans and the occasional scream. As we passed one room with the door open, I saw Non lying in a cot, groaning and holding his bandaged head. Roman Picus and Cacus and Cletus Loon were gathered around. I heard the white-cloaked Menden at his cot side say, "No permanent damage, Non. A few lights' rest and you'll be good as new."

I clenched my jaw and kept going, although I was sorely tempted to go in there and finish the bloke off.

Duf's room was at the end of the hall. I heard quiet sobs coming from inside. My heart shuddered and I felt a bit queasy. I thanked the Nurse and she left me. I stood just outside the door and tried to steel myself for what I was about to encounter. I told myself that whatever it was, Delph and I would face it together.

I gently pushed open the door and went in. Delph was leaning over the cot, his face littered with fresh tears. Duf lay in the cot, his eyes closed and his chest rising and falling unevenly. I crept forward until I was next to Delph.

"How is he?" I asked in a bare whisper.

"Me-Me-Mendens just in. Say they got to co-co-come off."

"What? His legs?"

Delph nodded, his features an oblivion of misery. "Say 'tis th-th-that or he's next for the Ha-Ha-Hallowed Ground. Don't underst-st-stand it all, Ve-Ve-Vega Jane. But that wh-wh-what they say."

I could well understand his stammering returning, what with all he was feeling. I closed my hand around his arm and squeezed lightly.

"When will they do it?" I asked.

"So-so-soon," he replied.

I gripped his arm harder. "Delph, I'm going to get the Stone." He looked at me quizzically. "The Adder Stone," I said in a low voice. "I can heal him in no time with it."

He looked alarmed. "No, Ve-Ve-Vega Jane. N-no."

"I'm going to make this right, Delph."

"I'll c-come t-too."

"You have to stay here with Duf." As I looked down at the poor Wug, my mind raced ahead. "If the Mendens come for him before I get back, just try and stall for a bit."

"But they say he could di-die."

"I know, Delph," I snapped. "I know," I added in a calmer voice. "Just try and give me a few extra slivers. I'll do my best."

I ran from the room, principally because I felt unworthy to be around the pair of them.

Looking Glass, Looking Glass on the Wall

I KNEW I HAD not many slivers to get this done. The Mendens might come at any time to take Duf and lop off his legs. And I doubted whether Delph would have the where-withal to stand up to the medical Wugs. I sprinted back to my digs on the Low Road, retrieved Destin and the Elemental and ran back out, leaving Harry Two behind. I was not going to risk another Wug's or beast's life through my actions. As soon as I was clear of the village, I ran flat out and soared into the sky. I knew it was a risk, but saving Duf's legs and maybe his life was more important than my being seen flying.

Stacks was closed this light because of the Duelum. I alighted within twenty yards of the rear of the place, hurried to the same side door and used my tools to open it. It was light outside, but that was no comfort. It had been light out-side last time, and the cobble had still come to try and smash us to nothing.

I retraced my steps on the main floor but found nothing. I took a sliver to check out Domitar's office in case he had found the Stone. I hurried up the stairs, ran to the end of the hall and saw, not surprisingly, that the wall I had pierced with my Elemental was now all repaired.

I put on my glove, pulled the Elemental from my pocket, thought it to full size, took aim and the wall once more blasted open. I willed the Elemental to shrink and put it back in my pocket, but I kept my glove on. I took my time going up the steps, thinking that I might have dropped the Adder Stone heading up or coming down them. Only there was nothing there. And the white rock would have stood out starkly against the dark marble.

At the top of the stairs, I stopped and took a long look at the words carved into the wall above the entrance to the room: HALL OF TRUTH. I didn't care about the truth right now. All I wanted was the Adder Stone.

I hurried into the room, stood in the middle, and looked goggle-eyed around the vast space. There wasn't a single book because there wasn't a single bookcase on which to put them. In their place was a series of floor-to-ceiling looking glasses hung on the walls. I couldn't believe my eyes. I looked at the frames on the looking glasses, all ornately carved with twisty, slithering creatures. They seemed familiar to me.

With a start I refocused. I scoured every crevice of the room for the Stone. I rose from the last corner, mired in defeat. It was then that I glanced at the first looking glass. Nothing could have prepared me for the image I saw there.

"Quentin!" I screamed.

Quentin Herms was in the looking glass seemingly running for his life. As I observed his surroundings, I knew at once that he must be deep in the Quag. There were no trees, vegetation or terrain like that in Wormwood. I glanced to the left and saw what was after him. My heart skipped a beat.

It was not one but a pack of freks, huge wolflike beasts with long snouts and longer fangs. They were fierce creatures. I had seen one slain by a morta after it had attacked a male Wug near the boundary of the Quag. Not only were the fangs sharp, apparently their bite drove one mad. The bitten Wug had thrown himself out a window at hospital four nights later and died.

I yelled at Quentin to run faster, faster, but no Wug could outrun a frek. Then he turned and looked toward me.

He had *both* his eyes!

If this image was real then what Thansius had told us at Steeples had been a lie. Although I already knew that to be the case, it was nice to have confirmation. Even Thansius had seemingly admitted it when he had told me on the pitch earlier that while we in Wormwood had many things to fear, Outliers were not among their number. But was the image I was seeing now real?

An instant later the glass went back to being just a looking glass. I saw my reflection in it and gasped as I whirled around, thinking I was now trapped inside there and a frek might be just behind me. But I was alone in the room.

Poor Quentin. I saw no way for him to survive. This made my heart sink. And then I stiffened.

There it was, in the glass, barely inches from my hand. The Adder Stone!

The dazzling white rock was simply resting on the marble floor. I whirled around again because I thought what I was seeing was a real reflection of it in this room and the Stone was just behind me on the floor. But there was nothing there.

I turned back. I suspected some sort of trap because Stacks had been none too kind to me in that regard.

Still, I thought of Delph hovering over his terribly injured dad, waiting for the legs to come off. I could not go back and face Delph unless I had tried everything Wugly possible to save Duf's limbs.

I reached out tentatively, my fingers lightly touching the glass. I jerked them back, although nothing had happened. I decided I was just being a git. I touched the glass again. It was hard, like glass should be, and impenetrable, unless I smashed it. I wondered if I should use my Elemental to do so. But what if the Elemental also smashed the Stone? I couldn't take that chance.

Then I recalled what I had done in fixing the window in my house. I wasn't sure how I'd done it exactly, but I looked at the glass and imagined that it was simply a wall of water. I focused all my thoughts on transforming glass to water.

I reached out again and my hand passed through the glass. A satisfied smile filled my face. I had done it! Maybe I was becoming like that sorceress thing Eon had mentioned being in the Adder Stone.

As my fingers closed around the rock, hard and cool in my palm, my smile was immense. Until something seized upon my wrist and pulled me off my feet and headfirst through the looking glass. I landed on something rough and warm to the touch. Momentarily stunned, I quickly picked myself up and stood ready to defend myself. The darkness was all around me, quite a change from the well-lighted room I'd just vacated.

I thrust the Stone in my pocket and stiffened when I heard something coming toward me from out of the black. I took out the Elemental and willed it to full size. Yet, for the first time ever, nothing happened. When I glanced down at my gloved hand, the Elemental remained as small as a long splinter of wood. I thrust it back into my pocket and tried to take to the air. But Destin seemed as powerless as the Elemental inside the glass and I fell back to the floor. I pushed down the lump in my throat and faced what was coming with none of my special tools.

A vague silhouette a shade lighter than the darkness around it emerged into my line of sight. As it drew closer and I could see it better, I gapsed in shock.

It was a very young, only it wasn't a Wug, or at least none I had seen before. It was dressed only in a cloth diaper. It had a few hairs on its head, and its skin was as pearl white as the Adder Stone in my pocket. Its features were as angelic as any I'd ever seen. But I was still on my guard, for sweetness could quickly transform to wickedness. The image of Morrigone appeared in my mind.

It closed to within a yard of me and then stopped. It looked up at me and I looked down at it. I felt my heart go out to the tiny creature because its mouth drooped and its eyes narrowed and tears dribbled out from them. Then it gave a little bit of a cry and then something truly remarkable took place.

Its features softened and turned Wug-like. When it was done, I could only stare transfixed. It was my brother, John, at age three sessions. He started to cry once more. When I instinctively put out my hand, he immediately drew back.

"It's okay, John," I said in a hushed voice. "I'm going to get you out of here." I knew none of this made any sense. John could not be here, and he certainly couldn't be three sessions old. But my mind wasn't working very well in here. I put out my hand once more, and once more he shrank back. His distrust eased my suspicions and I lunged forward and gripped his hand tightly.

John looked up at me, his tears now stopped. "Vega?"

I nodded. "It'll be okay. I'll get you out of here."

I could only think that Morrigone had somehow imprisoned John here to get back at me. As I turned to look around for a way out, I let go of his hand. Or at least I tried to. I looked down at my hand and what I saw made me more than slightly sick. His fingers were now part of my fingers. They had somehow grown together. I jerked my arm back, but all that did was lift John off the floor. His other arm reached out and gripped my shoulder.

Instantly, I felt a weird, invasive sensation. I looked down and his hand and arm were now growing into my shoulder, right through my cloak. And when next I looked at his face, John was no longer there. What was there was the most odious, foul creature I had ever seen. It was like a moldering skeleton with bits of skin dangling in odd spots. And there were no eyes in the sockets, only ripples of black flame. With each dark flicker I felt pain course through my body. Its teeth were black and grinned at me like some savage demon that had just triumphed over its prey.

I screamed, turned and ran. All this did was allow the thing to wrap its small legs around my waist. I felt the invasive feeling again but I kept running. I just wanted to go back through the looking glass, yet I had no idea how. I could feel the thing melding onto my back. And then the most extraordinary thing happened. I suddenly felt like I weighed a thousand pounds. I couldn't remain standing. My legs buckled. I fell to my knees, and then forward onto my face. I felt my nose shatter and my already injured eye swell even more. A dislodged tooth fell out of my mouth. I spit up blood.

The thing was on my head now. I could feel fingers like tentacles encircling my skull. And if I thought this was the worst it could possibly get, I was about to be proved wrong. In my mind grew darkness so profound, so overwhelming, that I felt paralyzed. I thought I had been struck blind and moaned in anguish. And then something vanquished the darkness. What I saw next made me wish the darkness would return.

It was every nightmare I had ever had times a factor of a thousand. From my earliest memories to seemingly the last sliver of my life, every painful fragment of memory I had ever experienced exploded onto my consciousness with the force of a million colossals crashing on top of me.

And then, even surpassing those horrible visions, were images I had never seen before, but which now flooded my brain.

Everyone I had ever loved — my parents, Virgil, Calliope, John — was running away from me. When I tried to go after them, a serpent came out of a dark hole in the dirt, wrapped itself around my ankle and started pulling me down. I cried out for help, but my family simply ran away from me faster. In another nightmare, Krone was lifting the ax high above his head and when it came down, two heads rolled off the block — mine and Delph's. Our heads lay there staring life-lessly at each other.

And then I was reaching out to my parents on their cots in the Care. But in my hand was an open flame. When I touched them with it, they burst afire. They screamed at me, tried to escape, but couldn't. Their flesh turned black and then fell away until there was only bone left and then that too vanished. Their screams, however, continued to ring in my ears, each burst like a knife between my ribs.

The last image was somehow the worst. I was on a flying steed, dressed all in chain mail, like the female I had seen. I was fighting. I had a sword in one hand and the Elemental in the other. Bodies were falling all around me as I cleaved and thrust my way through a horde of attackers. And then it hit me directly in the chest. The light entered me in the front and left me in the back. The pain was unimaginable.

I watched myself look down at the wound. The mortal wound. The next instant I was falling through the sky, down . . . down . . . down. . . .

I tried to scream but nothing came out. I felt the creature on my back tightening its grip around me. I swung my arms back and tried to hit it. But in hitting it, I was only striking myself. I had thought fighting in the Duelum was hard. I would take a thousand Nons trying to crush my skull over this. This was so awful, all I wanted was to die.

The thing was gripping me so tightly I could barely breathe. My chest was rising and falling in increasingly constricted space. I knew at some point soon it would have no more latitude to operate. But I didn't care. Right now I had no desire to live. The nightmarish images became darker, smaller, but their potency somehow grew immeasurably with each passing moment. I was being dissolved from the inside out.

I'm not sure how it came to me because I don't really remember doing it. My hand reached down to my waist. My breathing was so labored now that any upcoming breath could very well be my last. I managed, despite the crushing weight I felt, to slip Destin free.

I gripped it in both my hands, which of course were now part of the creature's hands. I flipped it upward over my head and felt it settle around the creature's neck. I crossed my arms as fiercely as I could. This, in turn, made Destin replicate that movement. It encircled the creature's neck and then tightened. If this didn't work, I was truly lost. I pulled with all the strength I had left.

I heard a gurgle, the first sound the creature had made since it stopped crying.

The next thing I saw struck me first with horror and then with relief as the chain grew lax. The thing's head hit the floor in front of me, bounced once and then lay still. Slowly, an inch and a sliver at a time, I felt the grip of the thing begin to ease and then fall away. In three excruciatingly long slivers, it was gone. My mind cleared. I rose on wobbly legs.

I didn't want to because I thought it might have turned back into John, but I finally had to stare down at the evil thing that had very nearly killed me. It was turning black and was shriveling up before my eyes.

I turned and ran as fast as I could. Only this time I knew where I was going because the darkness inside wherever I was had started to lift. It was as though the evil dead thing was absorbing all the blackness in here into itself, allowing the light to shine once more.

When I saw my reflection just up ahead, I sped up and leapt, my hands outstretched. I flew through the looking glass, tumbled to the hard marble floor, and was up in an instant. I turned to stare back at the looking glasses. All of them were starting to fade. In less than a sliver, they disappeared. But I had glimpsed once more the intricate designs on the wooden frames. And this time, I remembered where I had seen them before.

The Adder Stone safely in my pocket, I raced down the steps and out through the side door of Stacks. Freed from the place, I soared into the air, Destin in fine working order after being freed from the glass. I had to get back to hospital as fast as possible.

Slivers Too Few

SLIVERS LATER, I landed as near the place as I dared. I sprinted the rest of the way, pushed through the doors and raced down the hall. Another sliver passed and then I was back in Duf's room. Breathing hard, I skirted around the sheet that hung from the ceiling giving the space some privacy.

Then I stopped dead. The cot was empty. The room was empty. Delph and his father were gone. I rushed back down the corridor, thinking only terrible thoughts, the next worse than the previous one. There were no Nurses or Mendens in the passageways, so I started poking my head in each room I came to.

Wugs in various states of ill health or injury peered back at me from their cots. Heads bandaged, faces red and swollen, lungs hacking, legs bound in plaster, arms tethered to bodies — none of them was Duf. I had to believe many of them had been injured on the Wall construction, yet none so badly as Duf.

When I came out of one room I heard the scream. I looked wildly about because I recognized the voice. I hustled toward the sound, rounding one corner and then another. The screams kept coming and then they abruptly died out. I reached a set of double doors, pushed them open and hurtled into the room, panting from being out of breath, my broken nose pouring blood and throbbing. I slowly straightened and looked upon the horror in front of me.

Duf lay on the table, a sheet covering the top of him. As I looked down below, my stomach gave a lurch. There was nothing there. His legs below the knees were gone. Duf was covered in sweat and unconscious, something for which I was dearly grateful.

Delph was just standing there, his big hands tucked into fists, his great chest heaving, the tears spreading over his cheeks as he peered at what was left of his father. I looked at the Menden who stood there with blood smeared across his white gown and a vicious-looking saw in one hand. A Nurse stood next to him, staring anxiously at Delph.

I drew closer to the cot. Where Duf's legs had been were just stumps. I could barely find the breath to keep my lungs going.

"What happened?" I asked breathlessly.

"Cu-cut 'em off," said Delph. He was teetering. "Just cu-cu-cu —"

I gripped his hand and looked at the Menden. "When did you do this?"

He was staring at my injured face, but then focused on my question.

"Finished about a sliver ago. Delph didn't want it done, but it had to be done. Otherwise, we'd have a dead Wug."

"A sliver?"

The Nurse pulled me away from Delph and said in a low voice, "He tried to stop the Menden." She pointed to his torn gown and battered face. "It took five Wug orderlies to man-age him while the Menden performed the amputation. He said you were coming with something that would help Duf. And we did wait, for a bit, although we knew that was non-sense. You never came back, so we had to get it done. You understand. Medical matter."

I couldn't find the breath to speak. My mind was so full of things that it was impossible to form a response.

A sliver. A bloody sliver. Why did I take so long? Why did I lose the bloody Stone in the first place?

Duf's legs were gone. I didn't think even the Adder Stone could help. Still, I slipped it from my pocket, thought of Duf with his legs fully healed and then waved the Stone over his stumps, disguising the movement by pretending to straighten the sheet.

I held my breath, waiting for the legs to be regrown. And I kept waiting. And nothing happened. Finally, sick to my stomach, I let go of the Adder Stone and it fell to the bottom of my pocket.

The Menden came over and studied my face. "What hap-pened to your nose?"

"Duelum," I said absently. I doubted whether he would have known this was a lie or not. And I really didn't care.

"Do you want me to attend to your injuries? I can reset your nose."

I shook my head. "It's nothing," I said in a hushed tone. And it *was* nothing. "You just . . . you just tend to Duf."

I went back over to Delph. "I'm so sorry," I said. "So very sorry."

He sniffled and rubbed his eyes. "You tried, Vega Jane. I

know ya did. Just ran out of slivers, didn't we? Just ran out of . . ." His voice trailed off.

"But he'll live," I said.

"If you can call it that!" said Delph in a sudden rush of anger. He calmed just as quickly and looked tenderly at me. "Glad you made it back safe." He saw my face and gaped. "Vega, you're hurt bad. You need to —"

I gripped his arm tighter. "It's nothing, Delph. It's really nothing. I'll be fine."

My mind heaved like I had been wrenched upside down. *I am nothing, Delph. I failed you. I am nothing.*

Delph nodded sadly. "The thing is, you tried. For that I'll always be grateful. Did you run into —" He lowered his voice. "Into, you know? Your face and all?"

"I tripped and hit some stone. Just stupid of me. That's all."

He looked vastly relieved by this. "Do you mind if I have a mo' with me dad?" I nodded quickly and hurriedly left the room.

I waited until I was well down the dark and dank corridor before I sank to the cold floor and sobbed uncontrollably.

WHEN I FINALLY rose, my tears were gone, my sadness replaced with a smoldering anger. I raced from hospital and took to the air. Slivers later my feet hit crushed gravel. My skin still ached where that awful thing had pinned itself to me. My head reeled from the impressions of a lifetime of nightmares bundled into one continuous dark vision.

I knew what the creature was, because it, like the cobble, had been in Quentin Herms's book. I hadn't recognized it before it struck because it was impossible to recognize.

It could assume any shape it wanted. I knew what it was because of what it had done to me.

It was a maniack, an evil spirit that attached to your body and then your mind and drove you irreversibly insane with every fear you've ever had. And yet as I stood there, my mind cleared and my body stopped hurting so much, though my broken nose ached like blazes. I hadn't even thought to pull the Adder Stone to heal myself. And I didn't take the time to do it now.

I hurried up the walk, pushed open the gates and sprinted to the massive doorway. I didn't bother to knock. I just opened the door and stormed inside. William, the pudgy Wug in his sparkling clean uniform of the dutiful servant, came into the hall and looked at me in surprise.

"What are you doing here?" he exclaimed.

I knew I must be a sight. One eye nearly closed. My face bloody and bruised from my fight with Non. I had no idea what discernible residue the maniack had left on me. I knew I was missing a tooth, and my nose was broken. But I didn't really care.

I said, "William, please get out of my way. I just need to see something."

He continued to bar my path. "Madame Morrigone is not here."

"I don't want to see her," I barked.

"Neither is Master John."

"Or Master John," I snapped.

"She told me of no visitors. And so no visitors will be admitted —"

He stopped because I had hoisted him off the floor and

hooked the back of his collar over an unlighted torch holder set on the wall. With Destin around my waist, William was as light as air.

"Just stay there," I said. "I'll let you down when I'm done."

Blocking out his cries of protest, I rushed down the hall to the library. I threw open the doors and entered. No fire was lit. The sunlight streamed in through the windows. The books were all still there. I stepped up to it: the looking glass that hung on the wall above the chimneypiece.

I had seen it when John and I had first supped here, back when I thought Morrigone was a good, decent Wug. Before she had stolen my brother from me and made him into something that he was never meant to be. My gaze drifted to the ornately carved wooden frame. It was the exact same design as the looking glasses back at Stacks. As I peered closer, I could clearly see the carved frame was made up of a series of interlocked serpents that formed one continuous, foul beast.

As I stepped back and took in the whole glass, I knew without doubt that this looking glass and the ones at Stacks were identical. I had no idea what power Morrigone had that allowed her to do this, but I knew that she had somehow taken this mirror and replicated it many times over at Stacks as a way to trap and then kill me.

Well, two could play that game.

I drew my Elemental, willed it to full size, took aim and hurled it dead center of the mirror. It blasted into tiny pieces that sprayed all over the beautiful and, up to that moment, immaculate room. As the debris settled over all her pretty things, I allowed myself a grim smile.

I rushed back down the hall and lifted the still-sputtering William off the torch holder and set him gently down. He looked at me indignantly and smoothed down his ruffled clothes. "Rest assured that I will inform Madame Morrigone of this most inexcusable trespass as soon as she returns."

I said, "That's exactly what I want you to do."

As a parting shot, I ripped from the wall the silver candle-holders I had made and took them with me. When I was high up in the air, flying on a seam of wind, I flung them as far away as I could manage. And all I wished was that I could fling myself just as far from this place.

A Bit of Mischief

DUK **D**ODGSON WAS the youngest member of Council and a protégé of Jurik Krone's. He was also my next opponent. He was tall and strong but had never won a Duelum because, at least to my mind, he was too cocksure to acknowledge that he had weaknesses on which he should work. He was handsome, though his mouth was cruel and his eyes arrogant. His ambition was the black tunic, not the small figurine, even if it did come with five hundred coins. I had seen Dodgson in the Council Chamber. He had been seated next to Krone and followed his lead in every way. He clearly loathed me because his master did. And I just as clearly loathed him because he was a spineless git.

I was very glad I had drawn him in the Duelum. Getting even was not just fun; sometimes it was all you had.

Delph had beaten Dodgson in the last Duelum. He had told me that Dodgson would hang back and not attack right away, and that he had a bad habit of keeping his fists too low, which made his neck and head vulnerable. This gave me an idea, and I had snuck into hospital the night before the next round and nicked a book. I pored over the pages and pictures late into the night, learning what I needed to learn in order to carry out my plan good and proper.

At the next first light, I was up early and slipped on my cloak. I left Harry Two at the digs. I was afraid if I started losing, my canine would attack Dodgson, and Jurik Krone would use that as an excuse to kill Harry Two.

When I got to the pitch, I saw on the betting boards that odds were running fairly even, meaning as many coin had been placed on me to win as on Dodgson. I'm sure that was not sitting well with the ambitious Council member. I was on at the second bell this light. I placed my bet and then turned and nearly bumped into him.

Krone wore his black tunic like it was a halo of gold. When he spoke his tone was one of derision.

"Do you like to lose your coin?" he said. "You can't have that much."

"Excuse me?" I said in an indifferent voice.

"You wagered on yourself. My esteemed colleague barely lost to Delph in the last Duelum. You won't stand a chance. Why not just surrender and we can take you away to Valhall where you belong." He made a show of handing Litches McGee twenty-five coins wagering on his "esteemed colleague" to beat my brains out.

"Why don't you simply give me the coins now," I said. "It'll save McGee the trouble of handing them over to me when I'm finished with your precious little Wug."

Before he could respond I turned on my heel and stalked away to the pitch.

I watched Ted Racksport skillfully dispatch a quivering Wug who worked at the Mill in just under five slivers. As his hand was raised in victory, Racksport eyed me and smiled wickedly. He pointed at me as if to say I was next.

My pleasure, I thought.

The second bell sounded and I marched toward my quad. Dodgson stood across from me, his shirt off and his muscles flexed in an intimidating manner. When the referee called us in for instruction, Dodgson eyed me, his gaze coming to rest on my broken nose, which was swollen and hurt so badly it made me queasy.

"What happened to your nose?" he asked. "Don't remember you getting *that* banged up in the Duelum."

To this I said nothing.

He finally shrugged and said, "Well, I won't hurt you too bad." He smiled with those cruel lips, but the smile never reached his eyes. He next spoke in a voice only I could hear. "That was a lie. I am going to hurt you very bad. You should be in Valhall. It is Krone's wish and I serve him well." I didn't respond to this either. Instead I turned to look at Krone, who stood right on the edge of the quad to cheer on his Wug. I held up five fingers and opened and closed my hand five times representing his twenty-five wagered coins, and then pointed to myself.

I turned back to Dodgson. He had seen this exchange and his face was full of fury.

He flexed his muscles. "No mercy for you, female. None!"

"I don't remember asking for any," I said in a deadly calm voice.

My face, with all its wounds, I knew, looked awful. Even scary. And right now I was perfectly fine with that. Because, as I continued to stare over at Dodgson, I could see something I had yet to see in one of my male opponents.

I saw fear.

The bell rang, our bout began and I charged straight at Dodgson. As Delph had said, he liked to hang back and he *did* keep his hands too low. I leapt and wrapped my legs around his torso and arms, locking my ankles together as I had done with Cletus in my first bout. By being forced to carry my weight too, he was thrown off balance just enough that when I twisted my body to the right, he toppled over. I squeezed my legs tighter, trapping his arms by his side. I gripped his neck and pinched the throbbing pipes of blood that ran up to his head. He struggled to break my leg lock, but I was a lot stronger than I looked and my legs were far stronger than my arms.

He did succeed in ramming his head against my face again and again until I thought I might actually pass out. I felt fresh blood run down my lips and I tasted it in my mouth. I thought I felt my cheekbone crack and my good eye puff up. But I held on. I was not going to let this Wug go.

As the blood going to his head was constricted by my grip, his eyes fluttered once, twice, he stopped struggling and his arrogant eyes closed. I released my grip and stood. Dodgson remained where he was, senseless.

The book I had nicked from hospital had explained this little medical fact and I had employed it to full measure. Dodgson would rise shortly and be no worse off for it, except for his wounded pride and a splitting headache. The referee checked Dodgson's status and then raised my hand in victory.

As I stood there, bruised and bloodied, with my hand overhead, I found Racksport's gaze on me. I could tell by his amazed look that he had lost coin on the bout. Well, it was the git's own fault. If I could dispatch Non, any sane Wug should realize that the likes of Dodgson might bloody me, which he had, but would not best me. Of course, I was female, which was the great antidote to all reason. How could a female beat a male not once, not twice, but thrice? It was not possible. I read those thoughts in Racksport's beady, disturbed eyes. But like when I had first confronted Dodgson in the quad, I stared dead at Ted Racksport. Then I rubbed a bit of blood off my face and pointed my reddened finger at *him* until he gave a nervous, hollow laugh and turned away.

And then I turned to Krone. I didn't smile. I didn't laugh. I didn't say a word. I simply stared. And then I held my five fingers up five more times and pointed to myself.

His face filled with hatred, he stalked off, leaving precious Dodgson unconscious on the dirt.

So much for "esteemed colleagues."

After this round was completed, there would be only four combatants left standing. And after that, only two. I meant to be one of the two. And then the one of the one: the champion. I had never won anything in all my sessions. Now I was determined to win the Duelum.

I collected my winnings and walked down the High Street with many slivers on my hands, wondering what best to do with them. There was no work at Stacks because of the Duelum and it was still not yet the fourth section of light.

As I passed the Witch-Pidgy Pub, Thaddeus Kitchen ambled out, looking the worse for a pint of flame water or two or three.

"No work on the Wall this light?" I said.

He glanced at me and in that look I could tell something was wrong.

He hiccupped and said, "Me and Henry got sacked, thanks to your lot."

"My lot?" I replied, stunned by this.

"Cause of the Wa-Wall (hiccup) tumblin' down on D-Du . . . that bloke whatsis."

"I didn't make the Wall fall. *Your lot* doctoring the straps did. Who sacked you?"

His face filled with anger as though he was only now seeing me clearly for who I was. "Your brother, that's who." He belched.

"John sacked you? I thought he was the one who made the design change?"

"He bloody well did. But what matter is it to mister (hiccup) high-and-mighty Wug that he is? And I got me a family to su-suppo . . . take care of, now don't I?"

"I'm sorry," I said, though I really wasn't. "But Duf Delphia lost his legs. You can always get another job."

He wobbled about on his feet before regaining his balance. "Oh, can I now? Not with a bad reference from him, I can't, the little g-g-git."

"My brother sacked you because you made something weak," I said angrily. "I'm sure when he found out what happened, he was furious with himself. He took it out on you and Henry. I'm not saying it's fair, but that doesn't make him a git."

Kitchen drew closer and leaned into my face, so I could smell the flame water full-on. "He sacked us, female, 'cause we took *you* at your word and didn't punch no more holes in them fancy bloody straps-a yours. When he found out, *that's* when he sacked us. He didn't care a thing for poor D-Du-whatsis. Now, in my book, that's a *git*." He hiccupped again.

I said nothing to this because I could think of nothing to say.

Taking my silence for acquiescence, Kitchen belched again and said, "A pox on the house of Jane, I say. What good are you?" He stumbled a bit and then refocused on me, a silly grin spreading over his face. "But I got a coin or two on you in the next round, Vega, so (hiccup) don't let me down, luv. Har."

He staggered off, leaving me to think hard about what he had just told me. At least I wanted to, but I heard the foot-steps on the cobblestones and I turned to see who it was. Roman Picus looked none too pleased. With him were Cletus, Ran Digby with his nose bandaged and, bringing up the rear, Non, who looked as bad as I felt. They made a semicircle around me, armed to the teeth with their mortas and knives.

"Good light, Roman," I said. Before he could answer, I added, "And if you want a piece of advice, I would stop wager-ing coin against me."

Digby of course aimed a slop of smoke weed at my boot but missed. Cletus hissed. Non growled. Roman, however, just eyed me steadily.

"Gotta question for ya, Vega," he said at last.

"Don't keep me in suspense, Roman," I replied with a smile.

"You've beat three males, including Non here. And you done this in your very first Duelum. You done this while almost losing to Cletus here, who's a fine Wug but not in the league-a Non or even the lad you fought this light." He rubbed his chin with his greasy hand. "Now, tell me, how can that be?"

"I'm a quick learner and I got better."

"And stronger. And faster. And everything, it seems. Non here tells me you laid him out with one blow. And put a dent in his metal."

I looked up at Non, whose face still held the marks of the beating I had given him. If expressions could slaughter, I would be buried in pieces in the Hallowed Ground. "I guess he doesn't match up well with me in the Duelum."

Cletus snorted, which drew as condescending a stare as I could possibly make. "If you want a second go at me, Loon, I've no issue with that." I made a little lunge in his direction and he fell backward on his arse on the cobblestones.

Digby laughed out loud at this before catching himself and then aiming another chunk of slop at my boot and, again, missing his target. Cletus scrambled to his feet, his face a sheet of red.

Roman was still staring at me. "Curious and curious," he said, rubbing his chin so hard I thought he would take skin and whiskers off. "I think I'll have a talk with Council. 'Tain't right for no Wugs to have unfair advantage in a Duelum."

"I completely agree," I said. "So the next Wug who out-weighs me by more than a hundred pounds with arms bigger than my legs can just stand on his hands while I hit away."

"You're missing my point, female."

"Then try explaining it in a way that an intelligent Wug can understand."

"I think you're cheating!" he snapped. "And so does every other Wug. A female beating the likes-a Non, why, I ask you."

The fact that I had beaten all of my opponents without the aid of my special weapons made my face flame with indignation. "I'd say the likelihood is one hundred percent, since it happened." I turned to Non. "And next time you walk into a quad for a Duelum, you might want to remember how I used your own stupid breastplate against you. I didn't have to employ tricks to beat you, you creta's arse, when I used your own heavy metal to tire you first and then knock you senseless. All I needed was your being an idiot."

I stared Non down until the oaf turned and strode angrily off. With him no longer there anchoring their defense, Cletus and Digby picked up their heels and were soon disappearing in the distance.

"I still say you're cheating," Roman said.

"Then take it up with Council. I'll see *you* to collect my winnings after the Duelum is over. Why should I let Litches McGee have all the fun?"

"You sound pretty confident of victory," he said suspiciously.

"If I can't believe in myself, who can?"

A Matter of Parchment

I STOPPED BY MY digs, picked up Harry Two and together we walked to the Care. Since Non was no longer guarding the place, I hurried in and found Duf's room. I was surprised because they had put him in my parents' old quarters. I read the nameplate on the door twice to make sure.

I eased the door open and peered in. As I suspected would be the case, Delph was perched on the edge of his father's cot, rubbing Duf's head with a wet cloth. I opened the door all the way and Harry Two and I strode in. Delph looked up.

"Duelum?" he said.

"I won."

"Who'd you fight?"

"Doesn't matter. How's Duf?"

I drew closer to the bed and looked down at him. He seemed to be sleeping peacefully. I stole a glance at his legs, or where his legs used to be. The sheets lay flat against the mattress there, them having nothing of Duf to cover.

Delph replied, "Okay I guess. Timbertoes coming next light."

I nodded at this. With timbertoes, Duf would be able to hobble about, but that would be all. No more beast training for him. Sometimes, no matter how good he was, a trainer had to run for his life. And you couldn't do that on timbers.

"I'm so sorry, Delph," I said.

"'Tain't your fault, Vega Jane. Accident. Happens."

I struggled with what to say next. How could I tell him that my brother had redesigned the straps and that had caused them to fail? Would he go and attack my brother and be thrown in Valhall for his troubles?

In the end I said nothing. Delph's eyes searched my face for a moment and then he looked away and started mopping his father's brow once more. I looked from father to son.

"Delph?"

He turned again to me.

"The Quag?" I said in a low voice. "After the Duelum?"

I could see the range of emotions flitter across Delph's face. He looked from me to his father. From me again and then back to his father. And his gaze symbolically held there. He lowered his head.

"S-sorry, Vega Jane."

I turned away as I felt the tears climb to my eyes. I patted him on the back and said, "I understand, Delph. It's the right choice. It's . . . family."

I wish I had some left.

I headed to the door.

"Good luck in the Duelum, Vega Jane."

I turned to see him staring at me.

"I hope you win it all," he added.

"Thanks," I said. I left him there with his father. As I walked out into the warmth of the light, I had never felt such cold in my heart.

MY NEXT STOP was the Council building. I trotted up the steps, passing several Council members who were heading down them. I ignored their surprised looks at traitorous me and opened one of the massive doors that were carved with eagles and lions and what looked to be a slain garm.

This was the first time I had come in the front entrance. My only other visit here had been through the back, in shackles.

I walked in to see a great chamber with soaring ceilings, lighted torches and a temperature that felt about as perfect as was possible. Council members and their staff, more humbly dressed Wugs, most males but some females, were walking to and fro. I had always wondered why such a small place like Wormwood even required a council and along with it a building of such size and opulence. Yet like most of my queries, that one too had remained unanswered.

I walked up to a marble-topped counter where a short, prim-looking female stood dressed in a gray tunic, her white hair pulled so tightly into a bun that her eyes were catlike. She turned her nose up at me and said in an officious voice, "Can I help you?"

"I hope so," I said. "Is Thansius here?"

Her nose turned even more upward so I could actually see down both nostrils.

"Thansius? You are seeking Thansius?" she said imperiously.

Her tone implied that I might as well be here for a consult with the Noc.

"Yes, I am."

"And how are you called?" she asked in a perfunctory voice.

"I am called Vega Jane."

There was a flicker across her face that indicated she recognized my name.

She said in a friendlier tone, "Course you are. The Duelum." Her gaze ran over my battered features and she clucked in pity. "Oh my Steeples, your poor face. I've seen you around Wormwood, come to think of it. And you *were* so pretty too. So sad."

A mixed compliment if ever I'd heard one. "Thanks," I mumbled in reply. "So is Thansius in?"

She instantly looked more guarded. "And why do you need to speak with him?"

"A personal matter. As you know, my brother is a special assistant —"

Her lips formed a frown. "I know all about young John Jane, thank you very much." She pondered my request. "Half a mo'," she said and slipped out from behind the counter. I watched her scuttle off down the hall, twice casting backward glances at me.

I waited patiently for her return. I looked up at a painting of our founder, Alvis Alcumus, which hung over the doorway. He looked kind and scholarly, but there was a dreamy look in his eyes too, which I found interesting. His beard was so long it rested on his chest. I wondered where he had come from to found Wormwood. Through the Quag? Or did the Quag not exist back then? Or had he sprouted up from the dirt like a mushroom? Or was he the figment of some Wug's imagination?

I was beginning to think that our history was far more fiction than fact.

I wandered over to the massive paintings on the long walls that made up a side hall of the building. They were mostly scenes of warfare involving beasts and Wugs outfitted in armor. This must be the Battle of the Beasts that we had been taught at Learning. How our ancestors had defeated the creatures and driven them back into the Quag was the stuff of Wormwood legend.

As I grew closer to one of the paintings, I saw a scene depicted that was very familiar to me. It was a warrior in chain mail on a slep, carrying a golden spear and leaping over something. I observed the silver glove that the warrior wore on the right hand. I examined the spear and saw that it was identical to the one that was, right this instant — albeit in reduced form — residing in my pocket. The warrior was undoubtedly the female who had expired on the battlefield, but not before bequeathing to me the Elemental.

Yet the thing she was leaping over was a small rock. Such an obstacle would not require a leap at all. And the beast she was after was a frek. There had been no freks on the battlefield that light. She had thrown her spear, destroyed a charging male on a *flying* steed, leapt over *me* and soared into the air when her slep sprouted wings, in order to do battle in the sky with another figure on a giant adar. I knew I had seen all this. I could never forget it.

I realized that this painting could have been about a battle where I had not been present at all. But everything else was so exactly as I remembered it that I did not think this was the case. What had been erased was myself and the male on the flying steed, with the frek added in its stead. And the shield of the warrior was down when I clearly remembered she had raised it, allowing me to see that she was a female. Perhaps Morrigone did not want others to make the connection that her ancestor had been such a warrior. And there were certainly no colossals in the painting because to all Wugs except me, there were no such things as colossals.

I stepped back from the painting when I heard rapid footsteps coming down the hall. The prim Wug was returning, her face a bit flushed, I thought.

"Thansius will see you," she said breathlessly, her eyes bulging at this prospect. "By all merciful Steeples, he will see you right this sliver."

"Is that unusual?" I said.

"No, not a'tall. If you think asking an amaroc over for tea and cookies is *usual*."

She led me down the hall to a large metal door that stood at the end. She timidly knocked and a loud "Enter" was heard. She opened the door, pushed me through, slammed the portal shut, and I could hear her heels clickety-clacking back down the marble floor.

A bit breathless, I turned and took in the large room filled with innumerable objects. Then my gaze fixed on the large Wug sitting behind a desk that seemed too small by half for him or this room. Thansius rose and smiled at me.

"Vega, please come and sit."

I came forward with as much confidence as I could muster, and I had to delve awfully deep to find any. I sat in a fragile-looking chair opposite his desk. I heard it creak when I placed my full weight on it and I was terrified it would collapse. But it held firm and I relaxed.

Thansius had resumed his seat and was staring at me expectantly. His desk was littered with letters, rolled scrolls, reports and Wall plans, along with blank official parchment of Council. Before I could speak, he said, "I don't remember you breaking your nose in the Duelum."

"Stacks," I said casually. "Bit careless. It's healing. Just takes time." I self-consciously rubbed at the black eye the break had given me. My other eye was still swollen, though it too had turned black.

"I see," he replied in a way that told me he knew I was telling an untruth.

I cleared my throat and said, "I won my bout this light."

He held up a sheet of parchment from the piles on his desk. "I know you did. The report came a sliver after you so quickly subdued Mr. Dodgson. That is quite an achievement. He's strong and has good technique. But if he has a weakness —"

"He's too conceited to admit he has weaknesses on which he should improve."

Thansius nodded thoughtfully. "Precisely."

"Well, maybe it's harder for near-perfect Wugs to acknowledge they have problems. Me, I have so many shortcomings, I try to work on them all the time."

Thansius smiled. "I think that would be a good lesson for us all, perfect or not."

"I bet on myself to win," I said, rattling the coins in my pocket.

"The laws of Council forbid my wagering on any Duelum. However, if I were to have a flutter, I would have fluttered on you, Vega."

"Why?" I asked, suddenly very interested in his answer. "Dodgson was a formidable and experienced opponent."

His eyes narrowed, but his smile remained. "There is strength here," he replied as he held up a massive arm and flexed. I saw a muscle pull hard against the confines of his robes. "And there is strength here," he continued, touching his chest. "You have a great deal of strength, I think, here, which is where true power resides."

I said nothing but continued to stare at him curiously.

He added, "One more victory and you battle for the right to be champion."

"And a thousand coins," I added.

He waved his hand dismissively. "What does coin really have to do with it? I fought in many Duelums and never was coin part of the prize. I think —"

Here he broke off and I think I know why. His gaze was taking in how thin I was. How dirty my cloak was. How old my brogans were. And how filthy was my skin.

He looked down for a moment. "As I was saying, I think that a prize of coins is a good thing, actually. It can help Wugs . . . and their families."

"Yes, it can," I said. "But I come to you on another matter."

"Oh?" he said expectantly, seeming delighted with the change in topic.

"Duf Delphia?"

He nodded. "I know his status. I saw him at hospital last night before he was moved to the Care. It is quite tragic."

I was surprised that he had visited. Delph hadn't said. But then again, Delph had a lot to think about now.

"Morrigone said that Duf would be taken care of by Council."

"That is quite correct. He was struck down while on Council work on the Wall. He will receive life wages and timbertoes at our cost."

"That is very generous," I said. "But what of his occupation?"

"You mean as a beast trainer? I have never seen a finer one in all my sessions, but now, with no legs? You can well see the difficulty."

"I can. But if he is paired with another Wug who has an interest in beast training? Duf could teach him, for Wormwood will need another one of course. The Wug could act as Duf's legs while he is properly trained up."

Thansius added, "And that way Mr. Delphia could have not just coin with which to live on, but a proper purpose for his remaining sessions?"

"Yes," I replied.

I saw his eyes crinkle and his mouth widen into a smile. "I think it a sound idea. I will make preparations for doing just as you advise. Did you have anyone in mind?"

I gave him the name of a Wug who I thought would be a fine beast trainer. He turned to take up his ink stick and put on his specs to write the name down. As he did so, my hand shot out and scooped up a blank piece of parchment with Thansius's name and the official seal of Council on top of the page. By the time Thansius turned back around, the parchment was safely in my pocket.

I watched closely as he wrote the name in a particularly stiff hand, so unlike the flourish with which I had seen Morrigone write and with none of the curlicues of which Domitar was fond. I thanked Thansius and hustled out.

I passed the prim Wug on the way out. "Oh, thank the Steeples you've come out in one piece, luv," she said with obvious great relief.

I looked at her in surprise. "What, did you expect Thansius to do me harm?"

She looked horrified at the thought. "O'course not. I just thought you might, well, that you might simply combust from the honor of being in his exalted presence."

"Well, I didn't. Har!" I said crossly and made my way out.

Going down the steps, I patted my pocket where the official parchment sat. I had seized an opportunity that had presented itself. I smiled because I knew exactly what I was going to do with it.

I was going to write a letter.

This light was a very special one for me. I was going to make the most of it.

Vega Down Under

I WALKED DIRECTLY BACK to my digs, where Harry Two was waiting not so patiently for me. The plan had more fully come together in my mind as I was traveling here. I pulled the chair over to my table, took out my ink stick, filled it and then set to my task with the parchment. I had to see out of one eye, but I knew what I wanted to write.

I had seen Morrigone write on the report that a Wug working on the Wall had given her. Thus, I'd had a good gander at her handwriting. I knew now that all the parchment at Stacks that had constituted my instructions in building the pretty things for two long sessions had been written in *her* hand. I did not think my fury at the female could have increased, but it had. She had me work my fingers to the bone for low wages and all the pretty things had ended up in a hole.

Yet it was not Morrigone's handwriting that I would be replicating this light. It was Thansius's. And I, had seen several examples of Thansius's penmanship on his desk at the Council building. The letter was composed slowly as I took great pains to make the recipient believe that the missive had come from the Chief of Council, using words that I had heard him employ many times.

I set the parchment aside after it was completed. My stomach was rumbling and I looked in my larder, which, unfortunately, I found to be empty. As I stared at the barren space, I put my hand in my pocket and found the coins that I had won from Litches McGee. I had never done this before but I decided now was as good a time as any. I started to head out, but then I looked down at myself. I was battered, bloody and filthy.

I went to the back of my digs with a bit of suds and spent ten slivers rubbing the dirt off with water from the pipes. I had taken off every stitch of clothes I had on, right down to my skin only. I dried off and went back inside. My hair was wet but clean and I could stand the smell of myself for once in a great while. I again looked at the coins in my hand and an idea occurred to me.

It was an impossibly silly idea, but I thought, *Why not?*

I found a too-short pair of trousers and a too-small sweater my mum had knitted for me sessions ago, from the stack in the corner that I had failed to finish sorting through. I squeezed my long feet into too-tight shoes from three sessions ago. At least these things were clean, or anyway, far cleaner than my usual clothes.

There was a shop on the High Street called Fancy Frocks that sold female clothing. I had passed it often with never a thought to going inside. When I opened the door, a bell tinkled and a shop's assistant, a plump female about forty sessions old, quite nattily attired, came out from the back. She looked at me with a severe eye.

"Can I help you?" she asked in a way that told me she believed me beyond assistance.

I was suddenly tongue-tied and my confidence, shaky at best in situations like this, dropped through my feet and directly onto the floor. I mumbled, "I was hoping for some new things."

"What was that?" she said in a loud voice.

"Some new things," I said halfheartedly. I had about made up my mind to turn and walk back out. Wugs like me just didn't do things like this. Our clothes came as hand-me-downs when they came at all.

"Well, why didn't you say so, dear?" she said. "I suppose you've got coin?" she added inquisitively. I held out a palm full for her to see. Her face brightened. "More than enough." She put on a pair of thick specs. "Now let me look at you."

Her eyes behind the glasses widened. "Why, you're that lass in the Duelum. Vega Jane."

"Yes, I am."

She looked me up and down. "You're tall and slender and you've nice wide shoulders and long legs. Clothes will hang well on you, my dear."

"They will?" I said in a perplexed tone. Clothes hanging well was something I knew nothing about.

"Now, let me just nip some things out and we'll see what we'll see, shan't we?"

Many slivers later and many garments tried on, some discarded and others settled upon, she had packaged my new clothes while I now wore the one she had fitted me with because, well, I fancied it the best. The clothes I had come in with went directly into the dustbin.

Now I wore a blue frock, white stockings and shoes that had heels on them and made me even taller.

She gazed in admiration at her handiwork. "Well, I'll be. I knew there was something under there, dear. We just had to dig for it, didn't we?"

"I guess so," I said in a half whisper.

"Now what about your hair, luv?" said the kindly if exuberant Wug who had long before introduced herself as Darla Gunn. There was a looking glass mounted on the wall. I stared at myself in it.

"What *about* my hair?" I asked.

Darla eyed it with what I thought was a professional appraisal. "Well, it needs a bit of sorting out. Tidying up, like. Maybe a cut or two or three, if you know what I mean. Nothing too drastic, well, maybe just a wee bit drastic." She sighed and added in an apologetic tone, "It does need some *work*, dear."

I gave a few stabs at it with my hand and it settled back down just as unruly as before. "How?" I asked.

"Oh, there are many ways. And seeing as how you've surely spent a good many coins this light, I'll throw the tidying-up in for free."

"Will it hurt?"

Gunn laughed. "Crikey! And you being in the Duelum and all."

I smiled and touched my battered face.

She said, "Saw you best Non, Vega. Cheered like a mad female, I did. Just didn't want to go on about it when I recognized you. You're like, well, a celebrity now, aren't you?"

I flushed at these words.

"But your poor face. Your eyes, that nose. Well, I'll

402

see what I can do to tidy them up till they heal good and proper."

She was as true as her word. The things she did to my hair and how she doctored my face were totally foreign to me. When she was done and had laced a white ribbon with a bow through my newly done tresses, I looked in the glass and caught my breath. It seemed that I had disappeared and been replaced by another female.

She took out a little bottle with a tiny hose attached to it and a round inflated part at one end. She squeezed on the inflated part and some liquid misted on my neck and cheek. I flinched and she just laughed.

"Take a wee sniff, Vega," she said.

I did so and the most wonderful aroma entered my nostrils. "Lavender," I said.

"With just a touch of honeysuckle. Made it myself." Darla gazed at me, and her face crinkled into a smile. "Very nice, Vega. Very nice indeed. Now, once your face heals up proper-like, what a stunner you'll be, luv."

A stunner? Part of me was certain this would be a dream from which I would awake and have to deal once more with filthy duds and grubby hair. I paid over my coin and took my packages and walked out of the shop, feeling things I had never felt before.

Two Wugs whom I knew were passing by as I came out. One was a young Tiller named Rufus, the other was Newton Tilt, the Cutter at Stacks who I always thought was so slithy. Rufus gaped and ran into a post supporting the roof over the walkway and knocked himself to the cobblestones. Newton simply stood there looking me up and down with a silly grin on his face.

"Vega, is that really you down under?" said Newton.

I hurried on, my face reddening. *Down under?*

I had one more shop to go to and one more item to purchase. I paid my coin and had it wrapped in pretty paper and then hurried on. I had shopped more this light than I ever had before. Which wasn't saying much because I had *never* really shopped before.

I got back to my digs and threw Harry Two for a loop. It seemed that at first my canine didn't know me, and his hackles rose and he bared his teeth. But after he sniffed around me for a bit, he seemed satisfied I was actually his owner after all.

I found a scrap of looking glass that had once belonged to my mother. I managed to angle it so that I could see my face and hair. I again shook my head in disbelief. But my eyes were still swollen and the skin blackened, my nose broken and my cheek bruised and swollen as well. It sort of ruined everything.

I sighed and then a wistful desire crept into my head.

I found my hand going into the pocket of my frock and pulling out the Adder Stone. I held it in front of my face and thought good thoughts and the blemishes instantly vanished. My eyes were normal, the swelling was gone and I could feel my nose reset and mend immediately. I slowly put the Stone away and then set off.

I checked the falling sun and believed the time to be right. I walked quickly, for my energy had returned with my physical transformation.

The trip to Morrigone's went quickly and I was able to sneak up to the front door and push the parchment through the slit there. I knew that Morrigone would not be home yet, nor would John. But I was certain the ever-faithful William would ensure that *Madame Morrigone* would receive it.

That errand complete, I hurried on to my next destination. The Care.

A Special Night

AFTER LEAVING HARRY Two to wait outside, I spoke with a Care Nurse I found in the corridor. A coin was passed after I told her what I wanted. As I thought, Delph was perched on his dad's cot. He looked up when I opened the door.

"Vega Jane? What are you doing here again?"

"I've arranged for a Nurse to sit with Duf."

"What?" he said, looking puzzled.

"When was the last time you had a proper meal, Delph?"

As I came fully into the curious light provided in each room, I could see Delph's eyes widen in amazement. It actually sent a chill up my spine and I found myself smiling like a silly young.

"Vega Jane, whatta ya . . . whatta ya done to yourself?" he sputtered.

"Just . . . just tidied up a bit," I said shyly.

He rose and walked over to me. "Tidying up? Is that what you call it?"

"What would *you* call it, Delph?" I asked bluntly, and then wondered why I had.

This query caught him off guard. He scratched his head, looked unsure.

"Uh, I think I'd call it . . . Well, you do look quite tidy, now that you mention it. Quite tidy indeed." Then his face turned crimson.

I smiled. "I'm here to take you to meal."

He started to say something but then shook his head. "Dunno, Vega Jane, just dunno." He looked over at Duf. "What 'bout me dad?"

"That's why the Nurse is coming."

"You look so, well, you look so, you know and . . . and I don't." He ran his gaze down his dirty self.

I hooked my arm through his. "I think you look perfectly respectable. And I'm going to eat a meal at the Starving Tove and I want you to come with me."

He suddenly grinned. "What's the occasion?"

I decided to just tell him. "It's my birthlight. I'm fifteen sessions old, Delph."

He looked dumbstruck. "But I ain't done nothin' . . . I mean I didn't know. . . ."

"There's no need for you to do anything other than accept my offer to join me for a meal to celebrate my coming into Wormwood fifteen sessions ago."

With one more anxious glance at his dad, which was vastly alleviated when the Nurse I'd paid walked in and announced herself ready to look properly after Duf, we set off.

Wugs watched goggle-eyed as we passed by on the High Street, Harry Two bringing up the rear. Delph was so very tall, and me in my heels was in good proportion to him. He wasn't dressed as fancy as me, but I had caught him wetting his hand with his tongue and using it to drive his wild hair a bit into place. And he had stopped at the pipes outside the Care to wash his face and arms and rinse some of the grime off his clothes.

"Been meaning to do it for some lights," he explained sheepishly. "Just ain't got round to it is all."

We were seated at the Starving Tove at a table not in the back this time but up near the front. Every time I looked around, I caught Wugs staring at me. Females seemed irritated with their mates and kept hooking them by the chin and pulling their attention back to their own table.

Delph said, "Every Wug's watching you, Vega. 'Specially the males. Har."

"Well, they'll get over it. Can't make silk out of a sow's ear."

He gazed at me blankly. "Do ya hear yourself? Sow's ear, my eye. You're, you're . . ." He took a deep shuddering breath. "You're beautiful, Vega Jane."

Now he turned so very red in the face that I thought he was choking.

"Thank you, Delph," I said quite sincerely, although I was also blushing. The only Wugs to ever call me beautiful were my parents and my grandparents, and I had always believed they had done so out of a sense of duty.

We ordered and had the best meal I had ever had. Later, our bellies so full I could not pack one more thing inside mine, I managed to do so anyway. It was a bit of cake that we ate together as Delph wished me a light and night of happiness.

"I am happy, Delph," I said. "Very happy to be with you."

He tried to stop me, but I paid for the meal with my coin. "I should be giving *you* something," he protested. "Not the other way round."

"You have given me something."

"I have not," he said firmly.

I reached over and gripped his hand. "You've given me the pleasure of your company on a very special light."

He smiled bashfully and squeezed my hand back. "Wouldn't want to be no other place, Vega Jane." He paused and his lips quivered. "'Cept maybe with me dad."

"I know," I said quietly.

He seemed to read my thoughts. He leaned forward and lowered his voice. "Now, 'bout the next round of the Duelum."

I reached over and put my fingers over his lips, quieting him. "Not this night, Delph. This night let's just . . ."

He nodded as my voice trailed off. "Okay, Vega Jane. Okay."

I walked him back to the Care and left him there with his dad.

I looked to the sky and calculated the time. I made it back to my digs, changed my frock and heels and stockings for my new trousers, sweater and boots. I picked up Destin, wrapping it around my waist and under my new cloak. I also pocketed the Elemental and the package wrapped with pretty paper, and then I set off.

I hurried along until I was well away from Wormwood proper. I reached my predetermined hiding place at the exact sliver I wanted. The carriage rattled out from Morrigone's home two slivers later. I knew Morrigone was inside. I knew she was going to meet with Thansius at the south portion of the Wall near Stacks at the second section of night. I knew this because I had written that request in Thansius's hand on his official stationery. I had chosen the south side of the Wall because it was the farthest away from Morrigone's home and would give me time to complete my task.

When the carriage was well past, I hurried up not to the front door but to the back. I took out my tools and soon the lock gave way and I slipped into the house. I looked around quickly for any sign of William or the maid I knew also worked here.

The only Wug I wanted to see was John. I silently mounted the stairs, counted down the doors to his room and knocked quietly. I stepped back as footsteps came. I knew they were John's by his gait.

The door opened and there he was. He seemed to have gotten a bit taller and his frame had continued to fill out. His clothes were beautiful, but this time so were mine. And I would wager coin that this night I was as clean and smelled as nice as he did.

He looked at me curiously and I suddenly realized he didn't recognize me.

"John, it's me, Vega."

His mouth fell open slightly. "Have I changed that much?" I said in amusement.

"What happened to you?" he asked.

"Some new odds and ends."

"What are you doing here?"

Now my face paled. There was no warmth in that query. There was only suspicion tinged with impatience. "I came to visit you."

"Morrigone has told me what took place between you. She saved your life before Council. Your life, Vega! And you repay her kindness with betrayal."

"You did not say this when we were at the Care. When you were crying your eyes out over our parents being gone. You were glad I told you. You said so."

He waved this away. "I have had more time to think of it. Yes, I needed to know about our parents. But you still betrayed Morrigone." He stopped and stared darkly at me. "What do you want, Vega? I have much to do this night still."

I collected my composure and said in a softer tone, "I came to visit. I wanted to before now, but I've been so busy. And I know you have too with the Wall."

I sucked in a breath and silently cursed myself. I saw his features darken even more at the mention of the Wall.

"You told my workers to disobey my orders," he said sharply.

I thought to myself, Your *bloody workers?* "They were weakening the straps by punching more holes in them. You know what happened to Duf Delphia. He lost his legs."

He made a dismissive gesture with his hand. "Morrigone reported this to me."

She reported this *to you?* I thought.

He continued. "He will be taken care of. Timbertoes. Sticks. Injury wages. He will have no reason to complain."

"He will have no reason to complain?" I said incredulously.

"With his legs gone? How would you feel if you were getting the timbers and sticks and not him?"

"He is a *worker* Wug, Vega. Injuries to those types happen. But they will be taken care of. And their families. We are grateful for their service for the greater good."

We are grateful for their service? Since when did John start talking in the third Wug about himself?

"*I'm* a worker Wug," I said. "What if my legs or arms got lopped off while I was performing for *you* and the greater bloody good?"

He stared up at me, his expression unchanged by my blunt words.

I looked past his shoulder and into his room. Every inch of every wall was covered with scrolls, and on them were languages and symbols and drawings that made me gape. Some of them were hideous things, foul things. There was one creature whose head was a mass of slimy tentacles, and another whose legs were those of a spider and whose mouth was literally lined with fangs.

I shot him a bewildered glance tingled with the horror I was feeling. He quickly closed his door, blocking my view.

"What are those things, John?" I said, my voice tipped with disgust.

"Many of the things we will be pitted against are horrible, but that does not mean we cannot learn from them. In fact, the more we know, the better prepared we will be."

"I just don't want you delving into things that may . . . overwhelm you, John."

"I'm up to it, Vega, I can absolutely assure you."

I swallowed and finally said what I had come here to say. "John, would you consider coming back to live with me? At our old home? We could —"

But he was already shaking his head. "Impossible, Vega. Wormwood needs me doing what I am doing. Morrigone assures me that I am absolutely indispensable."

All the hopes I had carried with me here instantly vanished. Before I could say anything, John hurried on. "You should not be here," he said. "Morrigone will not be pleased. She had to go out to meet with Thansius, but she'll be back this night."

"I'm sure she will. What has she been saying about me to you? Other than my betraying her?"

"Nothing, not really."

Now John the young had returned to me, but with a significant difference. He was lying. And he was not good at it because of having had no practice. Unlike me.

"Did she mention that we did battle?" He blinked rapidly. "Did she tell you that she wrecked the window at my digs and then vanished?" He blinked more rapidly. I pointed over his shoulder toward his room. "What are those things on your walls?"

"Just things I am learning."

"They look foul and evil. Is that what Morrigone wants you to learn about?"

"My studies are no concern of yours!" he said defiantly.

"Do you think our parents would want you knowing about such things?"

"They are gone. I must continue to live. The more I know, the better."

"You might want to ask yourself, why does Morrigone want you to know such things? For the greater good? How likely is that?"

I let the silence linger. I wanted him to really think about what I had just said.

"You . . . you're still in the Duelum."

"I know I am. I'm surprised you're even aware of it."

"I . . . I hope that you win."

"Thank you."

"You should go now."

I reached in my pocket and pulled out the package wrapped in pretty paper and handed it to him. "Happy twelve sessions, John."

He registered surprise as he looked down at the package. My brother and I shared the same birthlight. He looked up at me with guilty eyes. "But that means . . . I lost track . . ."

"It's okay. As you said, you've been very busy." I was gratified to see that under a shell that was hardening with each passing light, my brother was still in there somewhere. But for how much longer?

"Open it," I said.

His fingers dispatched the pretty paper. It was a journal inside.

"You've read so many books, John, that I thought it quite unnecessary to give you another. But as smart as you are, I thought you might want to start writing one of your very own."

He looked up at me with tears in his eyes. Slowly, we both reached out for the other and embraced. I squeezed John as tightly as I could and he did the same to me.

"I love you, John."

"You best go," he said anxiously.

I nodded. "I best," I replied.

And so I did.

As I left Morrigone's beautiful home, I doubted I would ever see John again. In truth, I had come here to see if he would leave Wormwood and go through the Quag with me. That was obviously not to be. So now that Delph no longer could go, it was just me.

I would go through the Quag alone.

The Blow from Nowhere

THE NEXT ROUND of the Duelum pitted the last four combatants against one another. My opponent was Ted Racksport. I arrived at the pitch early, in my other set of old clothes. The betting this time showed me to be a slight favorite. I put two coins on me to win, with Roman Picus. He snarled in response and threw the parchment at me.

"How are the Carbineer patrols coming, Roman?" I asked. "I haven't seen you blokes around much lately."

"We're there, female, you can be sure-a that." He sniffed the air. "What's that smell?" he asked, his gaze quizzical.

"Lavender and honeysuckle," I answered. "If you like the scent, you can buy it at Fancy Frocks on the High Street."

His jaw collapsed. "Are you doolally? Fancy Frocks? How likely is it I'd put even one of me toes in that place, eh?"

"You never know, Roman. If you want a female as mate, you might want to smell like something other than flame water and smoke weed."

He gaped at me and I smiled sweetly at him, and then I walked over to the quad. Since there were only two matches scheduled, Racksport and I would battle first. The second bout would take place directly after. The crowd was growing larger by the sliver. As I looked toward the raised platform, it seemed that many more Council members and their mates were there. I also thought I saw a glimpse of Thansius.

Silas, the aged Wug referee, headed over and I readied myself. I was taking no chance with Racksport. I had seen up close how tricky and resourceful he was fighting. I could not use the same move I had employed against Duk Dodgson, for Racksport would be ready for that. So I had something else up my sleeve. While it was true I could have defeated him easily using Destin, I had already proven that I could win using my wits and what other talents I actually possessed. And I wanted to beat Racksport fair and square.

But it was not to be.

Silas came up to me and raised my hand in victory. I looked at him, puzzled, as a groan went up from the crowd of Wugs who had been all set to see some blood.

"What happened?" I asked him in bewilderment.

"Win by default is what," he answered promptly, looking at my left ear.

"Why? Where's Racksport?"

"Shot himself in the foot with one-a his blasted mortas, that's why," barked Roman Picus, who had drawn close to the edge of the quad. "Just now heard. Can't fathom how lucky you are, Vega. Ted's a right good fighter."

"Really?" I said. "I was just thinking how lucky Racksport was. A shot in the foot with a morta is nothing to what I was going to do to him."

Roman looked at Silas. "And I ain't paying off on no bets. Not with no bout."

"Naturally," replied Silas. He cleared his throat and in his weedy voice said, "Section forty-two, paragraph D, of the *Duelum Rules of Combative Conduct* plainly states that —"

"Oh, bugger off," bellowed Roman as he turned on his heel and stormed away.

Grinning, I turned to watch the other match that would now take place immediately. The grin fell off my face quick as a heartbeat.

Newton Tilt, the slithy Cutter from Stacks, was stepping into the quad. I had watched two of his other bouts and knew how strong he was, especially his grip. He was a good, capable fighter. Still, I feared for him. Because stepping onto the quad to face him was Ladon-Tosh. I had lost track of the remaining combatants, and on the betting board I had always focused only on my own bout. But the simple fact was, I would be facing the winner of this round. And when I looked at Ladon-Tosh, I had little doubt it would be him.

I drew closer, along with pretty much every other Wug out here.

The referee gave instructions and Tilt put out his hand for Ladon-Tosh to take. He didn't. Tilt grinned at this sporting insult and retreated a few yards, his arms raised, his shoulders squared and his jaw set.

Ladon-Tosh took nary a step back. He just stood there staring off like he always did at Stacks. The bell sounded. Tilt came rushing on, his fist cocked back, his other arm up as his guard.

He had drawn within a foot of Ladon-Tosh, who still hadn't moved, when it happened. I'm not sure I even saw the blow fall. No, I am sure. I didn't. All I saw was Tilt rise up in the air and hurtle backward far faster than he had ever rushed forward. He landed in a crazy pile of arms and legs a good twenty feet out of the quad and didn't move again.

The referee rushed over to his prostrate body and I saw him grimace painfully at the state of Tilt. He frantically waved over a team of Mendens. They rushed forward with their bags and huddled around the fallen Wug. We all held our collective breath. All except Ladon-Tosh, who had merely walked off the quad and left the pitch. I stared after him, dumbfounded. When I turned back to the Mendens, I saw with horror that they were placing a sheet fully over Tilt, including his face. I turned to the old male Wug standing next to me.

"Is he . . . ? He can't be . . ." I said shakily, all my limbs tingling and trembling.

In a quavering voice he said, "'Fraid he is, Vega. Ladon-Tosh has killed that poor lad with one blow. I can't believe it neither."

They hoisted Tilt up on a stretcher and carried him off. His sobbing mother came rushing up and grabbed the hand of her dead son that dangled off the side of the stretcher. She walked beside him, overcome with the grief of it all.

I looked around at other Wugs and they were as stricken as I was. Even Roman Picus stood over by his betting circle with his eyes wide as teacup saucers. As I continued to watch, bits of parchment dribbled unnoticed by him out of his clenched hand and littered the ground around his boots.

I felt something touch my arm and I looked down.

I was surprised to see that it was Hestia Loon. She gripped my wrist firmly and said in a fierce whisper, "You are not to step one foot inside the quad with the likes of Ladon-Tosh. Not one foot, mind you, Vega. Your poor mum. Why, she would never have allowed it. And since she's not here to speak up for herself, I will. I'll talk to bloody Thansius himself if I must, but you are not fighting that . . . that *thing*."

She stormed off, leaving me openmouthed. As Wugs began to disperse, more and more of them came over to me. They knew I was next up for Ladon-Tosh. And, like Hestia Loon, not a single one of them wanted me to fight him.

As I was leaving a few slivers later, Roman Picus came over and handed me back my two wagered coins. He eyed me nervously and then said in a subdued tone, "Listen, Vega, you saw? I mean you *saw*?"

"I saw," I replied quietly.

I could see his hands were trembling and his lips quivered. "It's not like you and me have always seen eye to eye on things, o'course."

I managed a brief smile. "No, we haven't. In fact, you accused me of cheating."

"I know, I know," he said miserably. He gazed over my shoulder at the pitch. "But I liked your mum and dad. And Virgil too, truth be known. And there weren't a finer Wug than your granny, Calliope. And o'course John and all his good work."

"What are you trying to say, Roman?"

"The thing is . . . ya see, the thing is . . ." He suddenly pulled me closer. "Ain't enough coin in all of Wormwood to get yourself killed for it, that's what."

"You think Ladon-Tosh can beat me?"

He looked at me as if I had a chimney growing out of my

head. "Beat you, female? *Beat* you? He'll knock you into the Quag. They'll be not a bitta you left to put in the Hallowed Ground, which is where poor Newton Tilt is headed. You can't fight him, Vega. He'll kill you just like he done that strapping lad."

"But I'm a combatant. I have to fight unless I'm injured like Racksport."

"Then I'll shoot you in the foot this night with one of me mortas and Ladon-Tosh can win the damn Duelum!"

"I can't do that, Roman."

"Why in the name-a Steeples? Why, female? Not for the bloody coin. You got by all this time without it."

"You're right, it's not about the coin."

If I didn't fight, I would be right back in Valhall. And now without Morrigone's support, I would probably end up beheaded. And if I tried to escape through the Quag, they would go after Delph, who was now staying behind. I was trapped, and I knew it. My only way through this was to fight. Then I could worry about escape. And the thing was, I wanted to fight. I wanted to win. And if I had to beat Ladon-Tosh to do it, so be it. I had never considered myself a warrior female, but right now, that's exactly how I felt. Like Morrigone's ancestor, the courageous female on the battlefield from so long ago. She had given her life fighting against something, something that I could sense was evil and wrong and, well, terrible. I wondered if I had the courage to die for such a cause.

Roman gripped my shoulders tighter, tearing me from these thoughts. "Vega, for the love of your mum and dad's memory, please don't do this."

"I am touched by your concern, Roman. I really am." And I really was. "But I have to fight; I have to finish this." I paused. "I am a Finisher after all."

He slowly let me go, but his gaze held me until he abruptly looked away and then walked off, his head hanging, his arms swinging aimlessly at his sides. I felt tears in my eyes and had to put up a hand to whisk them away.

As I walked off the pitch, I noted that the combatant board had just been updated. In three more lights, there would be one more bout and then a champion decided, crowned and coined. And perhaps the loser laid to rest in the Hallowed Ground with an eternity to think about the quality of her choices.

Vega Jane, age fifteen sessions (just), versus Ladon-Tosh, exact age unknown but definitely older than twenty-four sessions. And who had just killed a Wug twice my size with one unimaginably powerful blow that had been struck with such speed that I had never even seen it delivered.

My throat started to dry up a bit as I walked back toward my digs. I passed the High Street to get there and thus had to traverse pocket after pocket of Wugs talking about one thing only. Well, maybe two. Newton Tilt dying. And me being next.

Darla Gunn stood at the door of her shop. Her sad, heavy face told me that she knew what had happened. And her deep look of fear aimed at me also told me she was well aware I was next up for Ladon-Tosh, the killer, now.

I reached my digs, took off my cloak and lay down on my cot. Harry Two jumped up next to me and put his head on my chest, as though he could sense something was not quite right. I stroked his fur and thought about what was to come.

I would have three lights to think about this. That, in itself, was a horror. I wished I could fight right now and be done with it.

I didn't think Ladon-Tosh had ever fought in a Duelum before. The rumors of the dead gonk at Stacks who'd tried to get to the second floor came rushing back to me. I had spoken very bravely in front of Roman, but I was hardly feeling such courage right now. I had seen the look in Ladon-Tosh's eyes. He knew that he'd killed poor Tilt as soon as he struck. And the thing was he didn't care. He just didn't care. Where had a bloke like that come from?

I sat up and repeated this question again. But it wasn't just a question. It was a possible solution too. And I knew just the Wug to ask.

I had three lights left to find a path to victory and probably save my life. And I meant to take it.

I WAS TWENTY slivers early to work at Stacks the next light. This was something unusual for me, but these were unusual times. And I had an excellent reason for my superior punctuality.

"Good light, Domitar," I said somberly as I stood in the doorway of his office.

I thought the Wug was going to fall over dead in his boots.

As it was, he overturned the Quick and Stevenson ink bottle on his tilt-top table.

He clutched his chest and stared at me. "Hel's bells, female, are you trying to plant me in the Hallowed Ground before my time?"

"No, Domitar. I just had a question."

"What is it?" he said suspiciously.

"Where does Ladon-Tosh hail from?"

He was clearly surprised by this query. He came around the corner of his desk to face me. "Would this be because you're facing him in the final bout of the Duelum?"

"It would. And because he killed poor Newton Tilt with one blow."

Domitar bowed his head. "I know," he said, his voice shaking. "'Tis a terrible, terrible thing. The Tilts are fine Wugs. Fine Wugs. For this to happen, well . . ."

I ventured farther into Domitar's office.

"You look different, Vega," he noted as he glanced up.

"I've lost weight. Now, about Ladon-Tosh?"

Domitar moved closer to me. "'Tis complicated."

"Why?" I said reasonably enough. "Isn't it easy to tell where Wugs come from?"

"In most cases, yes. In Ladon-Tosh's case, no."

"So why is that?"

"I inherited him, as i'twere."

"You mean he was here before you were at Stacks?"

"That is precisely what I mean."

I snapped, "So how can he compete in a Duelum restricted to Wugs no older than twenty-four sessions?"

"A reasonable question you must take up with Council, I'm afraid."

"Many Wugs have come up to me and told me not to fight Ladon-Tosh."

Domitar dropped into his desk chair and looked at me.

"And Racksport shot himself in the foot with one of his mortas? Curious. Curious indeed."

I perked up at this change in subject. "Why? He runs a morta business. Accidents happen."

"He has been running that business for nearly five sessions and had yet to shoot himself."

I took this in and said slowly, "Meaning it might have been done so I would face Ladon-Tosh in the last bout?"

"The truth is, Vega, you've made enemies. And now the price for that is coming due." He hesitated, glancing away and then seeming to make up his mind. "Though not on Council, I have learned a little of your situation."

"Then you know why I must fight?"

He nodded. "And perhaps your ally is now your enemy?"

I nodded in return. "Morrigone, like Ladon-Tosh, has quite the mysterious past."

"I cannot deny that."

"Words and events have passed between us, many of them unpleasant."

"She is a formidable Wug, Vega. Perhaps the most formidable of us all."

"How do I beat Ladon-Tosh, Domitar? For that is why I am here. I believe you know how it can be done. And I need you to tell me or else I will surely perish in the quad."

Domitar looked away for a sliver. When he turned to face me, his expression was truly strange. "You already know how to defeat him, Vega."

I gaped. "I do? How can that be?"

"Because you've done it before."

Dust to Dust

A T MID-LIGHT MEAL I didn't go into the common room with the others. Quite frankly, we were all mourning the loss of Newton Tilt and I did not want to sit with the other Stackers and talk about his death. Soon I would be facing the Wug that had killed him.

Instead I sat on the marble steps leading up to the second floor. I sat on the exact spot where Ladon-Tosh would stand when he was the guard here. Perhaps I felt that whatever answers I needed about the sinister Wug would be conveyed to my poor brain merely by my close proximity to his former presence.

When I finished my work that light, I met Harry Two outside and walked back to my digs. I had a bit of food, changed into my blue frock and heels and headed back out. My destination this night was not one of pleasure. All of Wormwood was heading to the Hallowed Ground. This night we would be putting Newton Tilt into the dirt.

I had not been to the Hallowed Ground since they had buried my grandmother Calliope. It was a peaceful place, granted, but not a happy one. And there was enough unhappiness in Wormwood without adding to the burden by plunking yourself down in the middle of more. I moved through the rusty iron gates with the image of a mother and a very young on them. Crowds had already started to gather around the hole.

As I drew closer, I saw the long, plain wooden box with Tilt's remains inside. His mum and dad were sobbing next to it. Tilt had three brothers and one sister. They were all there, all crying just as hard. Tears were constantly wicked off the faces of all Wugs here because the Tilts were a kind and good family that did not deserve such a tragedy as this.

I stopped drawing closer when I saw Morrigone sitting in a chair next to Thansius as he stood by the hole that would quite soon become a grave. She was dressed not in white this night, but in black. The far darker color seemed to suit her better, I thought. Yet I had to admit I had never seen a Wug more stricken than Morrigone. Her face was a hard knot of rigid pain. She looked sessions older. Lines on her face I had never seen before now were bared to us all. Tears stained her cheeks and, while she was doing her best to hide it from us, every so often her body shuddered.

From time to time, Thansius placed a large, supportive hand on her shoulder and spoke quietly to her with words I could not hear. What was going on between those two special Wugs would take a great deal more thinking than I could give it right now.

As I continued to look around, I noted that there was one Wug conspicuously absent. Ladon-Tosh was nowhere to be seen. I wondered if charges were to be referred against him. What he had done was murder in my eyes, plain and simple. He could have beaten poor Tilt easily and with no need to kill him. It was an evil act, but then again, I wondered if the rules of the Duelum exempted combatants from any such punishments. If they did, the rules should be changed.

Wrong, after all, was wrong, no matter in what venue it might have occurred.

Everything had a moral hitched to it if one bothered to look for it.

I was surprised to see Delph slowly coming up the path. He was still limping and still holding his arm funny, yet he seemed to be getting stronger with each light and night. However, I was stunned to see Duf walking next to him, wearing his new timbertoes and using his new stick, which he gripped in his right hand. He seemed to have adapted to it well and it was hard to tell who was supporting whom more, injured son or legless father, because each had an arm around the other.

I hurried over to them and hugged first Duf and kissed him on the cheek, and then I embraced Delph, who was as cleaned up as I had ever seen him. I think he had actually used some of his winning wager to buy new clothes at the male shop next to Herman Helvet's confectionery.

"Heard 'bout your last round, Vega Jane," said Delph. "But we need to talk," he added solemnly.

I shushed him as Ezekiel came forward, the only sparkle of white in a sea of dark.

He prayed out loud and then led us through another. We sang. He committed the body of Newton Tilt, a fine Wug struck down long before his proper time, to the dirt.

Then Thansius rose and said some comforting words, his huge frame quivering with emotion. All of Wormwood was distraught, but I had heard no protests that the Duelum should be canceled before the last bout was held. Our collective empathy apparently had certain limits.

After Thansius finished speaking, all heads turned to Morrigone, figuring that she would close the sad ceremony with some appropriate female commentary, but that was not to be. She never rose from her chair and never looked up at any of us. She just sat there as though cast in unyielding marble. Her grief seemed even greater than the stricken Tilt family's.

Later, as the box was lowered by some sturdy Wugs into the grave, the crowd started to disperse. I was surprised to see Morrigone leave her perch and walk over to the Tilts. She put her arm around Tilt's parents and started speaking to them in a low voice. They nodded and cast tearful smiles and seemed consoled by her words. She was evidently evoking kindness and sympathy and support. A more inscrutable Wug I had never encountered, because I was certain she had used her powers to try and kill me in that looking glass. Anyone who could control a maniack in order to murder was not someone I wanted as a friend.

Then I turned to Duf.

"You seem to have taken to the timbertoes and stick very quickly, Duf," I said encouragingly. "You're getting around like your old self."

He seemed pleased by my words but in his gritted teeth I saw the pain behind his smile. And I noted how his hands kept clenching and unclenching. "Takes a bit of gettin' used to, I'll grant you that. But I'm gettin' there, I am." He added with a lifeless chortle, "And I'll never have to worry 'bout me bad knees no more, will I?"

"No," I said with a smile, admiring greatly his attitude but feeling awful at seeing his obvious discomfort.

"Still, I probably shoulda kept to me bed this night," said Duf, his face suddenly contorted in pain. He gasped and held on to Delph for support. Then he righted himself and added weakly, "But known the Tilts for ages. So sad. Couldn't not come, could I? Wouldn't be right. Can't believe little Newtie's gone. Held him in me arms when he was just a wee Wug. Never gave no one a lick of trouble. A good lad. A fine lad." A tear trickled down his face even as he gave a sharp cry and grabbed at his right stump.

I was becoming more and more bewildered by this. I thought with the legs gone and the timbertoes on, there would be no more pain for him. When I looked over at Delph questioningly, he explained, "They had to burn the ends of his legs, Vega Jane, to get the stumps ready for the timbers."

His father said admonishingly, "This pretty female don't need to hear no rubbish talk like that, Daniel Delphia." He smiled back another bout of suffering that crossed his face and said, "Now, that is the loveliest frock I believe I've ever seen, Vega," he commented. He nudged his huge son. "Ain't it, Delph? Eh?"

Delph nodded shyly and said, "'Tis, Dad. 'Tis."

I reached in the pocket of my frock where the Adder Stone lay. After nearly losing it I'd decided to always keep it with me. I palmed the Stone so it could not be seen by either of them. Maybe it could not regrow limbs, but I knew it could make pain vanish. When they turned and spoke to some other Wugs who inquired how Duf was doing, I surreptitiously waved the Stone over what remained of Duf's legs and thought as good thoughts as I could. The change in Duf was almost instantaneous. I had just put the Stone back in my pocket when Duf turned to look at me, the most serene expression on his face.

"Are you okay, Duf?" I asked innocently.

He nodded. "Okay? I'm like a new Wug, ain't I?" He slapped his thigh.

Delph saw this and exclaimed, "Cor blimey, don't do that, Dad."

Duf slapped his other thigh and stood totally erect without his son's help. "Lookit that, Delph. No more pain. Bloody miracle, i'tis."

Delph eyed his father's legs and then he turned to me, suspicion all across his features. He knew. I could just tell he knew what I'd done. When Delph glanced away, I passed the Stone over him too. He turned once more to stare at me. His leg was now fine. His arm no longer hung funny. He was healed too. I was a git for not thinking of doing this before. But I was happy, and some of my guilt melted away.

We parted company on the High Street. Delph and Duf were headed back to the Care. But Duf felt he could head home soon, especially with the pain gone.

I heard the carriage wheels long before I turned. I was on the Low Road now and the carriage shouldn't have been. I finally looked back to see Bogle pulling his sleps to a halt next to where I stood.

As she stepped from the carriage, Morrigone still looked awful, which made me feel immeasurably better, despite the grief she had shown at the Hallowed Ground, despite her consoling words to the Tilts. Her gaze searched mine. I merely stared back quizzically. I did notice with unconcealed relish that with my heels on, I was now taller than her. She had to look up to *me*.

She said, "I was glad to see Duf here this night. The timbertoes seem to be working for him."

"I think they'll work just fine now," I replied tersely, watching her closely.

"And I have spoken with Delph recently. He . . . he seems far more assured in his speech than he once did."

"He is," I said. "It simply took him remembering something that others did not want him to recall."

"I see."

"So you can stop paying him coin, Morrigone. He doesn't need your *pity* or your coin anymore to recompense for what you did to him."

I had finally figured that one out too.

"Is that what you thought it was, pity?"

"Wasn't it?" I challenged.

"You have much to learn, Vega. However, I came not to speak of Delph but of the Duelum," she began.

"What about it?" I said.

"You versus Ladon-Tosh."

"That's what the competition board says."

"He didn't mean to kill poor Newton Tilt."

I shook my head stubbornly. "I was there. I saw what happened. He didn't need to hit him that hard."

She looked down and I thought I saw her lips tremble. She looked back up and her features were tight and composed. "I think he sees that now."

"Lucky for me, since I'm next. Where is he, by the by?"

"I asked him to stay away. I didn't think it would be . . . appropriate."

"Why is he even in the Duelum?" I asked.

"Why shouldn't he be?" she said warily.

"He's clearly older than twenty-four sessions, for starters."

"Not according to his records."

"I'd like to see those records. Just to confirm where the Hel he came from."

She looked at me with a degree of incredulity that I found pathetic under the circumstances. "He came from Wormwood. Where else would he have come from?"

I shook my head again, plainly showing my disappointment with her response. "Well, if he is a Wug, he's a most unusual one. I've never even heard him speak. And the rumor about him killing that Wug at Stacks . . . you have to admit, it's all a bit dodgy."

"It is a bit dodgy" was her surprising reply. She had lowered her eyes again, but then she raised her head and looked directly at me, her green eyes glowing as though they had been ignited. "You don't have to fight him, Vega."

"Then I'll end up in Valhall, won't I?"

"I can meet with Krone. I can work something out. Any sentence in Valhall would be relatively short. But there would be another condition."

I folded my arms over my chest. "What?"

"You know far more than is good for a Wug."

"You mean I know the truth," I shot back.

"The condition is that you will not be allowed to remember such things anymore."

"So the red light, then?" I remarked coolly. "I think I've figured that out. Red must be more powerful than blue. Delph was much bigger than me, even back then. The blue light was sufficient to wipe my thoughts nearly clear, although I could still remember the scream, Morrigone. And the blue light."

"What?" she said, clearly astonished by this.

"I thought it was just a nightmare. And Delph eventually remembered, with a little help from me. That's what I meant when I said he no longer stutters. He remembers, Morrigone. All of it."

We stared at each other in silence. I finally said, "So I'll take my chances in the quad, thanks anyway." I added firmly, "You're not messing with my mind ever again."

"I am well aware that you dispatched your other competitors with relative ease."

"Except for Racksport. He shot himself accidentally. Or so they say."

"What do you mean 'or so they say'?"

"What I mean is that a suspicious Wug, namely me, would think that Racksport was got out of the way so I would have to meet Ladon-Tosh in the final bout."

She said, "If true, that would be a very evil thing to do."

"I completely agree," I replied, staring back at her. "I also know that our last few encounters have ended badly, very badly."

"And I also know that you have visited my home twice now while I was away. May I ask why?"

"Once to confirm something."

"What?"

"Your taste in looking glasses."

We once more stared at each other in silence. I could tell that Morrigone was appraising me in a whole new light and she wasn't sure what to do about it.

"And the other time?"

"To wish my brother a happy birthlight. And to give him a present."

She looked down. "That was thoughtful of you, very thoughtful, considering the circumstances."

"He is my brother, Morrigone. No matter what happens, he will always be my brother. And I love him. Unconditionally. Far more than you ever could."

I said all of this in a loud voice because I just knew that John was in the carriage listening intently.

"I can understand that," she said. "Blood is blood."

"As to the Duelum. Why are you suddenly so concerned about my welfare? You said I had to fight my best. Well, I'm fighting my best. And if I die, so be it. I die for the right reasons. I die with the truth in my heart. Not like the adars that Wugs have become, just parroting back what they're told. Not understanding who they really are. Where we came from. What Wormwood really is."

"And what do you think Wormwood is, Vega?" she said, giving me a deadly stare.

"Well, speaking for me — it's a prison."

"I'm sorry you feel that way."

I cocked my head, studied her. I was comfortable doing so, because now, more than ever before, I was seeing myself in a different way. I was seeing myself — as her equal. Or better. "I saw you at the Hallowed Ground. I believe your tears were very real."

"They were. I was crushed by what happened. It was unthinkable."

"I'm curious that you had a chat with Ladon-Tosh, and you said he understands he was in the wrong?"

"That's right."

"So he *does* talk, then?"

She seemed caught off guard by this. "Yes, I mean, he . . . communicates."

"But only with . . . you?"

"I can't really speak to that. I'm not with him for much of the time."

"I see. Well, put in a good word with him for me, will you?" I said casually.

She suddenly gripped my arm tightly. "Do not take this lightly, Vega. Please do not. If nothing else, think of your brother. You would not want to be lost to him, would you?"

I glanced at the carriage. I thought back to my last encounter with John. To the things I had seen on the walls of his room.

"I think *he* might already be lost to *me*," I replied slowly. "So you see, there is really nothing left for me here. Nothing at all."

She released my arm, stepped back and looked down. "I see."

"Do you really see, Morrigone?" I asked.

She glanced up sharply, her gaze probing, almost menacing. "I see far more than you realize, Vega."

I squared my shoulders and stared down at her. "If I fight, I was told I would be free. I intend to fight to the end. And if I survive, I intend to be free. Really free," I added. Then I turned and walked off. As always, it was a good idea to keep moving in Wormwood.

And so I did.

I had two more lights. Perhaps to live.

A Hodgepodge Plan

I WAS JUST THINKING of crawling into my cot and pulling the covers over me when someone rapped at my door. Harry Two barked and started clawing at the wood. I walked to the door and said, "Who is it?"

"Wotcha, Vega Jane."

I opened the door, stepped back and let Delph pass through. He knelt to pet Harry Two, who was jumping all over him and trying to lick every exposed piece of skin Delph had. I closed the door and motioned him to the chair by the empty fireplace. I perched on the cot, my hands in my lap, and stared at him.

"What do you want?" I asked.

He gave me a furtive glance. "You okay?"

"Well, let me see. I just went to watch a Wug being planted at the Hallowed Ground. I no longer recognize my brother. My parents are gone. In two lights, I'm probably going to die in the Duelum at the hands of a murderer. So, spot on, I'm definitely *not* okay."

He bowed his head and I felt bad for having said what I had.

"I'm sorry, Delph. None of this is your problem."

"But 'tis my problem. You dying? Can't let that happen, can I? I mean, I just *can't*."

"I have to fight Ladon-Tosh," I said. "And nothing you say will make me change my mind."

He nodded at this, which surprised me. "So the thing is, you got to not get killed."

"Trust me, that point I understand."

"How you going to do it, then?"

I stared at him. It had just occurred to me that as much thought as I had given to my upcoming bout with Ladon-Tosh, I had given no thinking time to how I was actually going to win. Or at least survive. "I've been thinking," I said slowly, allowing myself time to actually "think" of something.

"Well, I been thinking too," said Delph forcefully. "And some blokes told me what he done to poor Tilt."

I sat forward, suddenly feeling engaged. "The thing is, Delph, I never even saw Ladon-Tosh strike. That's how fast the blow was. It knocked Tilt completely out of the quad. He weighed over two hundred pounds if he weighed an ounce. He was dead before he hit the dirt. Killed with one blow. I've never seen anything like it." This all came out in a rush of fear that had been welling up inside me ever since Tilt had struck the ground.

"But look what you done to that cobble at Stacks," he pointed out. "That thing weighed more'n Tilt, I'll tell you that. And you didn't just kill it. You exploded it."

"That was because I had Destin."

"And you'll have Destin when you fight Ladon-Tosh."

"That would be cheating."

"Bollocks!! Do you really think Ladon-Tosh is a normal Wug? Something's going on there, Vega Jane. You having Destin when you take him on won't be cheating. It'll be making the fight fair, way I see it."

I sat back and thought about this. What Delph was saying made perfect sense. I had won all my other matches on my own by a combination of luck, planning and instinct. But I knew in my heart that none of those would allow me to prevail against Ladon-Tosh. He had killed a Wug with one blow. That was not possible; only it had definitely happened.

"Okay, I guess I can see that," I finally said.

He looked vastly relieved by my acquiescence on this critical point. "So it comes down to you landing your blow before Ladon-Tosh can land his."

"Like I said, I never even saw him hit Tilt. I might have killed that cobble with one blow, but I was nowhere near as fast as Ladon-Tosh."

"Then we have to come up with a way that you're even faster. Or else you have to make him miss with his first strike and finish him off before he can try again."

"And how exactly am I supposed to do that?" I said incredulously.

"'Tis why I'm here. Fought in enough Duelums, haven't I? Know my way around the quad, don't I?"

"Okay, what suggestions do you have?"

"Watched Ladon-Tosh's second round. He dinnae kill no Wug that time, but there are some things I noted."

"Like what?"

"He don't move on the bell, not up or back."

"That's right, he didn't move against Tilt either."

"He lets you come to him, then he strikes."

"Faster than the eye can see," I groused.

"Where's the chain?"

"Why?"

"Want to see something."

I fetched Destin from under the floorboard and put it around my waist. Delph stood and put up his hands. "Put yours up too." I did so. "Now I'm going to throw a punch, and I'm not going to say when —"

He snapped a blow at my head. I easily flicked it away.

He smiled, but I didn't. "That wasn't nearly as fast as Ladon-Tosh's," I said.

"Back up to the wall over there."

"What?"

"Wanta try something else."

I did as he asked, reluctantly. From his coat he pulled out a long strip of rubber with a small square patch of leather attached. On the patch he placed a stone he'd taken from his trouser pocket. He started to spin the rubber, which I now saw as a shotslinger, faster and faster.

"Can you see the stone?" he asked.

"Barely."

He spun it faster. "How about now?"

"Just a glimpse."

He whirled it even faster. "Now?"

"Not at al —"

Before I finished speaking, he had fired off the stone right at me. When I looked down a sliver later, I saw the stone cupped in my hand.

I looked up in amazement. "How did I do that?"

Delph grinned and pointed at Destin. "Reckon the answer lies there."

"But it lets me fly. And it gives me strength. But —"

And now Delph was about to shock me.

"I think what it does, Vega Jane, is give ya what i'tis you need at the time you need it."

I gazed openmouthed up at him. This was stunning. Not what Destin could do, although that *was* amazing. No, it was that Delph had thought of it and I hadn't.

"Do you really think so?" I asked hopefully.

"Fly when you need to? Give a pasting to a cobble when it needs doing? Stop a stone from hitting you in the face?"

I touched Destin. It felt warm, as though it had just had a bit of exercise.

"But that's not all, Vega Jane."

I looked at him with wrinkled brow. "What do you mean?"

"Chain is a big help, no doubt. But you got to have more than one way to beat Ladon-Tosh. He's big, strong, fast. Can't count on taking him with just speed."

"What, then?"

"You got to move. Wear him down. Let him punch." He paused. "And if you got to take to the air, Vega Jane, take to the bloody air."

I stared wide-eyed at him. "Okay, up to that last statement, you didn't sound mental at all. But you want me to fly? In front of Council? In front of every Wug?"

"Would you rather be headed to the Hallowed Ground for all of eternity instead?"

What irritated me most about this exchange was that Delph sounded the far more logical one of us. "A bit of me says yes. Most of me says no."

"Listen to most of you, then."

"What else?"

"At the bell you don't move either. It'll confuse the lout. Make him come to *you*. He'll throw a punch. Then you'll move away. Hit him if you can. Taps at first. Let his confidence build."

"I think he has plenty of confidence already."

"You know what you done with that other cobble at Stacks?"

"I didn't know you were watching."

"Oh, I was. You spun him like a top. Got him all jargoled, didn't ya?" He pointed a finger at me. "Now, I reckon with Ladon-Tosh, you do the same. You'll get one shot to get 'er done. You got to bring all ya got. All you and the chain got."

I looked down at Destin and felt once more guilty.

Delph must have read my look, because he snapped, "Don't be barmy. Like I said, you think something dodgy's not going on with Ladon-Tosh? Bloke don't even talk. And he ain't younger'n twenty-four sessions, I'll tell you that. I'm not sure he's even a Wug, tell the truth. Har."

"I guess you're right," I said slowly.

"Course I'm right. Now, what we're going to do is practice right and proper every sliver we can till it's time to fight."

"You really think I can beat him, Delph?"

"You're *going* to beat him."

"Thanks, Delph."

"Thank me after you win the Duelum, Vega Jane."

EVERYWHERE I WENT the next lights and nights, Wugs came out of all corners of Wormwood to wish me well or, in some cases, to say their good-byes. Pieces of parchment were slipped under my door. Most were kind and encouraging. However, one was particularly nasty. But I recognized Cletus Loon's poor scrawl and I didn't take any heed.

Delph and I had practiced his strategy over and over until I could do it in my sleep. It lifted my spirits. I felt as if I had a fighting chance, which is all one is entitled to in my view.

Thansius visited me on the night before the Duelum's final bout. He came not by carriage; I would have heard that. He simply walked up to my humble door and knocked. I of course asked him in. Harry Two let Thansius scratch him on the head before settling down by my cot. I insisted Thansius take the more comfortable chair while I perched in the other. At first, Thansius remained silent, his face brooding and his long fingers slowly stroking his beard. Finally, seeming to have reached a decision, he leaned forward and focused on me.

But I broke the silence first. "I'm fighting Ladon-Tosh. So please don't bother trying to talk me out of it."

"I never intended to. I believe you must fight him."

This stunned me. I sat back, gaping at him.

"You're surprised by my statement?" he said unnecessarily, for my mouth was still hanging open.

"I am."

"So many of our fellow Wugmorts never manage to see past the sole light facing them. Past the borders of

Wormwood or their own narrow minds. For our borders are indeed narrow, Vega."

"You put it far more eloquently than I could have, Thansius."

"I understand that you and Morrigone have had words on a number of occasions. Harsh words."

"If she said so, I don't deny it."

"You believe her to be evil?"

"No. I *know* her to be evil. What do you consider her to be?"

"Her history is an interesting one. A sterling Wug family. Good upbringing. Brilliant at Learning."

"She has lots of books. Most Wugs don't."

"That is very true."

"And her house is probably the most beautiful home in all of Wormwood."

"Doubtless it is."

"And the things she can do? Where did that come from?"

He paused and gave me a stare so sharp that I thought I would bleed. "You mean the things you also can do?"

"How did you —"

He waved away my surprise. "Every Wug has a job, from the lowest to the highest. Now, my job is to know things, Vega. I don't know all, but I know close to all. And I know that the powers with which Morrigone has been endowed are showing themselves in you. There is, however, a critical difference, I think."

"And what is that?"

"Simply that your powers are greater."

I turned away from those penetrating eyes. "I have no idea what I'm doing. She does."

"On the contrary, I think you do. You recall your tree?"

I turned back to him. "What about my tree?"

"It wasn't petrified of course," said Thansius matter-of-factly. "But I knew that explanation would suffice for the likes of Non and his followers."

"Didn't you harden my tree and protect it?" I asked. Because this is what I had thought had happened.

"No, indeed. I don't have the means with which to do so. You, Vega, you saved your tree."

"How?"

"By, I believe, simply willing it to survive. I saw your face. I could easily realize what was in your heart. Thus, your beloved tree became hard as rock. And it survived."

I slowly took this all in. "And my grandfather?"

"I think you know the answer to that. These things are handed down in Wug families. Only a few possess it anymore. It seems that the passage of time has diluted it to almost nothing for most of us."

"But what is *it*, Thansius?"

"Power, Vega. And power is a funny thing, for handled by different Wugs for different reasons, the very same power can look very different."

"I think I can see that." And in my mind's eye, I saw Morrigone using Ladon-Tosh as a lethal puppet to kill me.

"Your grandfather possessed it in abundance. It is the reason he is no longer among us."

I looked at him eagerly. "So you know where he's gone? You said you know all, or at least almost all."

"He is gone from us, Vega. To another place, most certainly. A place assuredly beyond the Quag."

"And why did he go?"

"It was his destiny to do so," Thansius said simply. "And please do not ask me more than that, because I will have no answer for you."

I looked away, disappointed. "So what is Wormwood, then, Thansius? And please, don't answer my query with a question or a riddle."

He didn't respond right away. When he did, his speech was slow and measured. "For most Wugs, Wormwood is their home, the only one they'll ever have. For some of us, it is our home but not our destiny, like Virgil." He gazed off for a sliver and then glanced back at me. "Was that too much of a riddle for you?"

"We have always been taught that this is all there is."

He looked around. "Taught, perhaps. Yet that is not the same as belief or, more significantly, truth, is it?"

I shook my head. "No, it's not."

He nodded, seemingly pleased that I understood the difference.

"Why do you stay here, then, Thansius? You are a mighty and special Wug. Surely your destiny cannot lie simply in Wormwood."

"Oh, indeed I think that it does. And Wormwood is my home. Wugs, my brethren. Those concepts should never be taken lightly."

"And what of the Outliers? The Wall?"

For the first time I could ever recall, Thansius, mighty Thansius, looked embarrassed, even ashamed.

He said, "There is a sense of duty sometimes, Vega, which compels even the most honest of Wugs to do things that lack that very honesty."

"So it's all a lie, then?"

"Lies are sometimes given for the very best of intentions."

"Do you think that's the case here?"

"On the surface, unequivocally yes. When one reaches more deeply?" He shook his head sadly. "Then it merely becomes an act of dishonesty for which there is no sound basis."

"My grandfather once told me that the most bitterly awful place of all is one that Wugmorts don't know is as wrong as wrong can possibly be." I grew silent and looked at him questioningly.

Thansius studied his large, strong hands for a few moments before looking up at me. "I would say that your grandfather was a very wise Wug." He rose. "And now duty calls and thus I must be off."

At the door, he turned back. "Good luck, Vega, next light." He paused and seemed to stare off for a moment before looking back at me. "And beyond. For I knew this time must come at some point."

And then Thansius was gone.

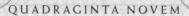

To the Death

T HAT NIGHT IT was no surprise that I found it difficult to sleep. At the fourth section, I gave it up as a bad
job. I pulled out my cloak and, using strong thread, sewed
Destin into the garment's sleeves and across its shoulders.
This would hide my chain from view and also prevent it from
being torn off me too easily. I put the Stone and the Elemental in my pocket, and set off with Harry Two.

I had fashioned a harness and a cradle of sorts, using
scraps of leather and metal from Stacks. When we were safely
away from Wormwood proper, I tied the shoulder straps
around me, placed Harry Two in the cradle and buckled him
in against my chest. I had bound him up like this before and
he had taken to it good-naturedly.

I took a running start and soared into the air. This might
be my last chance to leave the ground and feel the wind in
my face, let it lift my hair. This light could very well be my
last one. That made a Wug think.

I flew along for a great many slivers with Harry Two dangling happily underneath me. I don't know which of our grins
was bigger. But there was a melancholy behind my smile, for
obvious reasons. And as I looked down at Harry Two from
time to time, I could sense the same with him. It was as though

what was in my heart was magically transferred to his. Canines were indeed curiously marvelous beasts.

We landed on the dirt, and I freed Harry Two from the harness. I had a cookie in my pocket, and I broke it in half and gave my canine his share, which he wolfed down while I took my time with mine. I chewed methodically, probably because I wanted to slow every sliver down now. It was all very morose and I wished I didn't feel this way, but I did.

Many things passed through my mind. I wondered if it hurt to die. I thought back to how Tilt looked when the blow from Ladon-Tosh had hurried him on to the Hallowed Ground. To tell the truth, I don't think Tilt ever realized he had died. It had happened just that fast. So maybe there was no pain. But you were still dead. So the consolation was not simply small, it was nonexistent. At that moment, I happened to look up at the sky and felt a sudden thrill when I saw it.

A shooting star. It raced across my point of view while all the other winks of light remained stationary. It had soon left them all behind. A sudden thought occurred to me.

It seemed lost, that star. And alone. In such a big place as the heavens, I guess this was always a possibility. I harkened back to what my grandfather had said. When you see a shooting star, it meant change was coming for some Wugmort. I had to believe that the change was finally coming for me. Whether it would be my death or my escape from here, only this coming light would tell.

I couldn't take my eyes off the shooter. The little tail of fire kept going, powering the thing to, I'm sure, unimaginable speeds. I had never really believed my grandfather, just as youngs often don't believe their elders when they're trying to teach something. Yet now, sitting here, I somehow knew that Virgil had been entirely literal when telling me this. Change would come. It just would. Maybe he knew that one light, it would come for me. I kept sitting there and kept staring at the little pulse of brilliance. Since I had never glimpsed one before, I had no idea how long it would be visible. For some reason, in my head, I desperately wanted to keep it in sight. If it disappeared, it seemed to me, then so might I.

And it was there, for the longest time, until something came to dispel it for good. Or at least from my eyes. The break of the first section of light.

When the glow finally vanished, I rubbed my eyes and stretched my limbs. I picked up Harry Two and settled him into his cradle. I soared into the sky, performed a long dive and then came swooping back up into the lightening sky. Harry Two seemed to love this maneuver and barked happily.

I landed on the outskirts of the Delphias' property. I didn't wake them, though they would be up soon enough. I had brought a bit of parchment with me and used my ink stick to mark a few words down and then slipped it inside the Delphias' door.

I bent down and gave Harry Two a long hug. It was hard to leave Wugs. It seemed just as hard to say good-bye to a beloved canine. I told Harry Two to stay with the Delphias. That the note would be read and they would understand.

In the note I had asked Delph to take in Harry Two if I was killed this light. I knew he would. My canine would make a wonderful addition to the lives of Delph and Duf and that was a good thing. And I didn't feel bad about this. Harry Two had given me much happiness in the brief time I'd had him. I hoped I had at least done the same for him. Other than Harry Two, I really had no instructions to give. I had nothing left that anyone would care about. John was provided for. My parents were gone. My digs would go back to being empty. Another Finisher would take my place at Stacks. Life in Wormwood would go on, just like it always had.

I didn't fly back to my digs. I walked. By the time I got there, it was nearly time for me to go to the pitch. I would get there neither early nor late but rather right on the sliver. I was surprised to see some flowers that Wugs had left in front of my door with parchments attached containing hopeful words. I took them all inside and placed them on the table, where they looked awfully fine.

I sat alone in my chair in front of the empty fireplace and counted off the slivers in my head. I turned to the window when I heard footfalls outside. Wugs were headed to the pitch. I waited a bit more and then rose and checked to make sure Destin was securely sewn into my cloak. As I touched the chain, it was warm. I took that as a good sign. I'm not sure why. Then I reached my hand in my pocket and touched first the Stone and then the Elemental. For luck? Again, I wasn't sure.

I went around the room and touched everything I had found here. The stacks of clothes and papers. And the drawings I had made as a very young. I looked over every square inch of what used to be my home and was once more where I dwelled. As I opened the door to leave, I took one last look around. Then I stepped outside, closed the door and headed to the pitch.

It seemed that every Wugmort in Wormwood was here this light. I had truly never seen the pitch fuller. When I looked over at the betting boards, I was stunned to see not a single wager had been placed. Litches McGee and Roman Picus did not seem especially bothered by this. In fact, they were together mumbling things, their hands free of parchment bits.

When Wugs saw me coming, something truly extraordinary happened. They started to clap. Just a few at first, but then others took it up and within a sliver, the pitch was thundering with the sounds of hands coming together. As I continued to march forward and the sea of Wugs respectfully parted so I could pass, I felt my face redden and my eyes moisten.

Selene Jones, who ran the Noc Shop on the High Street, stepped forward and said excitedly, "Did your future reading last night, Vega. And guess what."

I looked at her expectantly. "What?" I finally asked.

"Well, let's just say I see bloody stacks of coins in your future, luv."

I smiled appreciatively, yet her words did not hearten me much. To my knowledge, Selene Jones had never made one correct prophecy in all her sessions.

Darla Gunn came up seemingly from nowhere and wrung my hand. "You are so brave, Vega, so brave. But I still wish you weren't doing this. I mean, we just got your hair looking so nice, didn't we?"

I laughed and it did my spirits good. "*You* got my hair looking nice, Darla. I had nothing to do with it."

I looked away when tears filled her eyes. I was not going

to let myself cry. Ladon-Tosh would probably just kill me harder.

Since there was only one bout this light, I was directed to the very center of the pitch where a special ring had been laid out. It seemed so small that I wagered Ladon-Tosh could simply stand at one end and kill me with one blow without either of us moving our feet. The strategy Delph had laid out was a good one, but right now it seemed absurdly inadequate. My confidence had totally deserted me.

The referee was old Silas, whose eyesight had apparently worsened over the last few lights and nights, because he was standing at one end of the ring and looking the wrong way for the last two combatants to arrive. He remained that way until Thansius emerged from the crowd and gently pointed him in the correct direction.

I next watched as Bogle and the carriage rattled up, and out stepped not just Morrigone but John. I caught her gaze for an instant but then she looked away. John's eyes lingered on me. I had hoped to see something in them, something that told me . . . I wasn't exactly sure what. But he dutifully followed Morrigone onto the platform and took his seat while the other members of Council sat in a row below.

Krone was seated at the end of this row with Duk Dodgson next to him. They both seemed self-satisfied, as though my fate had already been decided.

Their superior smiles made every muscle in my body tighten. Ladon-Tosh might end up killing me, but the lout would know he had been in a fight.

Delph showed up a sliver later. He had Harry Two next

to him. He caught my eye and held my canine up as if to say firmly, *I've got him till you come to take him back.*

I smiled and then had to look away before the tears started to fly. I was here to fight, not cry. The clapping for me had continued all this time and then it abruptly stopped. A moment later, I knew why.

Ladon-Tosh came striding down the path to the ring. He had on a plain shirt and a pair of old, dark trousers. He was barefoot. His eyes looked neither right nor left. Wugs pushed against each other trying to get out of his way. As I watched him approach, I felt Destin start to grow cold against my skin and I panicked. Was my chain abandoning me at this critical time?

The official bell rang. Silas beckoned both Ladon-Tosh and me to the center of the ring so he could deliver his instructions. I stepped forward although my legs seemed unwilling to follow the command of my mind to move. Ladon-Tosh stepped right up to the center as though he were going for a stroll. He didn't look at me, and I could manage only to shoot glimpses at him. My heart was pounding so fiercely in my ears that I could barely hear Silas's by-now-familiar words.

"Fair fight. Keep it clean. Penalty if one of you falls out of the ring." Here Silas stopped and seemed to remember what had happened to Newton Tilt. He glanced at me and for the first time I think the wizened old bloke actually *saw* me. His look of fear for me was not very encouraging. And then from the corner of my eye, I saw Ezekiel stride toward the crowd in his flowing white robe. I assumed he was here to measure me

455

for the box and an appropriate prayer when all was said and done.

Silas stepped back, but before the second bell for the start of combat was sounded, Thansius came forward.

He said, "This bout will determine the champion of this Duelum. As you all know, tragedy struck last time and we all hope that it does not do so again."

He looked at Ladon-Tosh when he said this part, but the latter's gaze rested on a spot about six feet above my head. I even looked that way to see what he was staring at, but there was nothing there.

Thansius continued. "If Vega Jane wins, she will be the first female champion ever and more than entitled to the one-thousand-coin reward." He looked at Ladon-Tosh again, but since the git obviously wasn't even paying attention, whatever else Thansius was going to say, he apparently decided not to. "Let the bout begin," he said, and stepped clear of the ring.

Silas motioned Ladon-Tosh and me to opposite ends of the ring and I obeyed with alacrity, naturally wanting to put as much space between us as I could.

Right before the bell sounded, I looked over and saw Domitar. He was staring directly at me. I could swear he was saying something to me. I tried to hear the words.

"All before. Done it before" was all I could make out.

Then my attention snapped back to the bout. The bell rang. Neither Ladon-Tosh nor I moved. For all my feelings of hopelessness, I had my strategy — well, actually Delph's strategy — and I intended to carry it out.

For two long slivers, we simply stood there staring at each other. My heart continued to beat like a runaway slep as time ticked by. The crowd was holding its collective breath. No one was moving there either.

And then it happened. I have no idea how or when. It just happened.

I saw the fist coming at me so fast it seemed impossible to avoid its crushing impact. But as the knuckles raced at me, I flipped sideways in the air and came down on both feet. The crowd screamed as Ladon-Tosh was suddenly now on my side of the ring.

"Oh my holy Steeples," screamed Darla Gunn.

I circled away from Ladon-Tosh as he straightened up and looked at his fist as though he couldn't quite fathom how I was not dead.

He turned toward me. I went into a crouch and studied him. And then another amazing thing happened. Everything, and I mean everything, slowed down. My breathing, the movements of the crowd, the birds in the sky, the wind and even the sounds. They all seemed to be moving at a mere hundredth of their normal speeds. I watched one Wug sneeze and it seemed to take him a sliver to accomplish. Another excited Wug was jumping up and down and it seemed as if he was suspended in the air before he began his descent.

But most important of all was the slowing down of Ladon-Tosh.

The next punch came, but I saw it so well in advance that I had already moved, it seemed, before he even threw it. In fact, I leisurely watched it go by at the spot I had been a moment ago. He whirled around and looked at me. Yes, now Ladon-Tosh was looking at me. I was glad the git had finally condescended to actually see *who* he was trying to kill.

Though when I saw the eyes, I wished he hadn't. They were terrifying, to be sure. But they were also something else.

They were *familiar*. I had seen them before, I just didn't remember where.

I heard a scream. I had lost my focus and I spun out of the way in the nick of time as a fist screamed past me with so much force that it seemed to carry a wake of turbulent air with it. This time I struck. I slammed my fist into my opponent's back with such violence that I was convinced I had punched a hole right through him.

Pain shot all the way up my arm and burst into my shoulder. I had never hit anything so hard in my life. Not even the rock cobble had been that hard. And I had exploded him. I hadn't exploded Ladon-Tosh, though I had accomplished the seemingly impossible.

I had knocked him flat on his face. A great cheer rang from the crowd.

But as I stood there, my right arm dangling like a limp rope, I had nothing much to cheer about, for Ladon-Tosh was getting back up. I had hit him as hard as I possibly could and he was getting back up with no signs of permanent damage. I had forgotten Delph's instructions. Tap-tap. Don't hit him hard at first. But I had. And it was an enormous mistake.

I had an instant to glance toward the platform and shuddered as I saw Morrigone staring directly at Ladon-Tosh, as though she were willing him to stand. And then I knew I couldn't win. I knew that Ladon-Tosh had an ally I couldn't defeat.

He came at me again. With my right arm totally useless, but my senses otherwise intact, I easily sidestepped him.

Instead of hitting him with my good hand — since it would be good no longer — I spun around, supported by my one able arm, and flicked my feet against his buttocks as he flew past me. This propelled him out of the ring and into the crowd. Wugs ran hither and thither trying to get out of his way. He was like an enraged creta, only a hundred times more powerful and a thousand times more murderous.

Old Silas toddled forward and said, "Wug out of ring. Penalty against Ladon-Tosh. Free blow for Vega Jane. Well done, lass."

Fortunately, Delph snatched Silas out of the way before he was crushed by Ladon-Tosh leaping back into the ring to attack me.

He was now throwing punch after punch with astonishing speed. I dodged them all and then I started to employ my other tactic. I started to race in a circle around him. He spun too, punching at me but landing nothing. I told myself that he had to tire at some point.

When I glanced over at Morrigone, she still had her gaze fixed on Ladon-Tosh, yet I could see the rising panic in her eyes. She was upset that I was not yet dead. She was afraid I might win. Well, I just might.

I ran one more circle around him and then leapt and kicked him in the head with my left foot. Again, the shattering pain swept down my limb. Again, he went down hard. I noted with satisfaction that he took longer to rise this time. But rise he did.

And I had made another even more egregious mistake. I could run with one arm. I could not with one leg. "Damn!" I screamed, so furious was I with myself.

Then I smacked myself in the head with my good arm.

The Stone. The bleeding Adder Stone. I snatched it from my pocket and, concealing it in my hand, I swiftly ran it up and down my damaged limbs.

They were damaged no longer, but I once more lost my focus. I heard the crowd collectively scream and I felt the blow hit me across my shoulders. I was knocked fifty feet into the air and crashed hard well outside the ring.

Ladon-Tosh did not wait for me to reenter it. He leapt and came down hard with his elbow pointed downward right on top of me. Or where I had been an instant before. He struck the ground so hard, it dug a hole in the dirt three feet deep, and about twenty Wugs toppled over from the ground, shaking with the impact.

I raced back to the ring, turned and breathlessly waited for him to come. I knew the only thing that had saved my life when the blow had struck was Destin. Its links still felt ice-cold to the touch as though it had absorbed almost all the energy of a blow that a few lights ago had easily killed a fully grown male Wug.

If I couldn't hit my opponent without crippling myself, how could I win? If this kept up much longer, one of his blows would land squarely on target and it would be over. Despite my tactics, he was not growing tired.

But I was. My lungs were heaving and my heart, I believed, had reached its maximum pumping capacity. I could not last much longer.

Ladon-Tosh stood there frozen, but I could sense the tremendous building up of energy coming from him. He was about to put everything he had into one blow that would hit

460

me so hard, there might be nothing left. I felt my heart in my throat, and my stomach gave a sickening lurch.

I glanced over at Morrigone. Her gaze was only on Ladon-Tosh. I had never seen her face look so hard, so . . . unrelenting. She had obviously made her decision. I was to die. And Ladon-Tosh was the tool with which she would kill me. Newton Tilt had doubtless been a mistake for which she had grieved mightily. I doubted she would be nearly as saddened by my passing.

I looked back at Ladon-Tosh and knew the moment had come.

And yet as he made his final charge, it occurred to me exactly what I had to do. I had to end this. And I had to end it now. He was trying to kill me. Well, that was a two-way path.

Not a natural killer, I steeled myself to become one.

I slipped off my cloak. Underneath I had on a shirt and trousers. But in my cloak was Destin. I gripped the chain at both ends and waited.

When Ladon-Tosh struck with a speed that was beyond a blur, I had already somersaulted over him. When he sailed past me, I turned in midair and flung the cloak and with it Destin around his neck. I landed on the ground, set my feet and pulled with every bit of strength I had.

The giant Ladon-Tosh was lifted off his feet, flew backward over me and, as he went past, I crossed my arm and thus the chain, as I had with the maniack in the looking glass.

The result was not the same as in the glass. In fact, it was not anything like it.

I heard the screech before I *saw* anything.

I was instantly paralyzed with fear by the sound. But what I then *saw* made the sound seem as nothing.

Ladon-Tosh was rising slowly. Actually, Ladon-Tosh was coming apart at the seams. His head was gone but his body was now upright. Bloodcurdling screams came from up and down the crowd. Both females and males fainted at the sight.

"Bloody Hels" cascaded through the air like flocks of frightened birds.

But that was not the worst part. I knew the worst part. It was about to happen.

Ladon-Tosh's body burst open, half his torso going left, half to the right.

"No," screamed a voice. I looked up in time to see Morrigone yelling this over and over. "No! No!"

I searched the crowd and saw Krone. He was racing away with Dodgson, his face filled with panic and dread. Krone even ran over a very young in his escape. The bloody cowards.

The crowd had turned as one to run. Now they turned back for an instant to see what Morrigone was screaming at. I already knew. The screeches were ear-shattering.

The two jabbits that had nearly killed me at Stacks catapulted from the husk that had once been Ladon-Tosh. How creatures so large had been compressed into the space of one Wug, albeit a big Wug, I couldn't fathom. They hit the ground so hard that the pitch seemed to whipsaw under our legs. Then five hundred heads and with them one thousand eyes looked at all the Wugs so perilously close, and I could almost see the lustful hunger in the monsters' sinister orbs.

Every Wug ran for his or her life. Parents snatched up their youngs and very youngs. Screams kept coming, but they came nowhere near to drowning out the screeches that heralded a slaughter of Wugs about to occur.

I glanced once more at Morrigone. To her credit, she had not run away. Indeed, she was waving her hands and it looked like, as difficult as it was for me to believe, she was trying to will Ladon-Tosh back together again. But it was clear that she had not been able to control the creatures with Tilt and it was just as clear that she would not be able to stop them now. As I watched, she glanced at me. Tears were in her panic-filled eyes. She looked desperate.

Cries of "Outliers, it's the Outliers come" sprang up and were repeated from Wug mouths everywhere.

I looked for Thansius and found him trying to fight his way forward through the sea of Wugs and toward the jabbits. He drew something from under his robe. It was the same sword he had used at the Council hearing. He said he had no special powers, but what the Wug did have in abundance was courage. Yet I didn't think he would get a chance to use his blade in time.

I thought this because both jabbits had risen up, their innumerable fangs exposed, and they were just about to launch themselves against the nearest Wugs. It would be a bloodbath not seen here for hundreds of sessions.

I looked back once more at Morrigone. She was staring dead at me. Her mouth was moving. She was yelling something. Finally, I could make it out over the screams of the crowd.

"Help me, Vega! Help me!"

I don't remember reaching in my pocket and slipping on my glove. I really don't. I willed the Elemental to full size, sprang upward into the air, twisted my body to the left — and the golden spear launched from my grip with as much torque as I could place upon it.

It shot through the air just as the jabbits struck. They attacked in parallel, as I knew the beasts did, which made it perfectly perfect for me. The Elemental hit the first jabbit, passed through its body and collided with the second jabbit a moment later.

There was a tremendous explosion and the shock wave struck me while I was still sixteen feet off the ground. I was propelled forward like a fish by a great wave. It seemed that I flew a long, long way before hitting something extraordinarily hard.

And then everything was gone.

The Duelum Champion

I OPENED MY EYES quite suddenly and tried to sit up, but a hand pushed me back down. I looked to my right and was not unduly surprised to see Delph there.

"Wotcha, Vega Jane?" he said, his voice weary but now filled with relief.

I blurted out wildly, "Where am I? Hospital? The Care? The Hallowed Ground?"

He touched my forehead as though to test for its warmth. "You jargoled?"

"Where, Delph?" I persisted.

"Your digs."

I looked around and saw that this was so. "How did I get here?"

"Carried you."

"I remember hitting something really hard."

"Spot on, that was *me* you hit."

I sat up slowly to see a welt on his forehead the size of a hen's egg.

"How did I hit you? I was thrown far away from all Wugs."

"Well, I sort of ran to . . . to catch you when you got blown."

"The jabbits?" I said, my face paling at the mention of the name.

"Dead and gone. You took care-a that."

"No Wugs hurt?"

"Just the ones who trampled each other getting away like. They'll be okay."

"Ladon-Tosh had jabbits inside him," I said slowly, as though trying to make myself understand what I was saying.

Delph grimaced. "Well, what I'd say is jabbits had Ladon-Tosh *outside* of *them*."

I turned on my side, rested my head on my arm and gazed at him. "I guess that's one way to look at it." Something else came back to me. "My cloak? The Elemental?"

"Don't wad your knickers. There and there," he added, pointing.

On a peg on the wall was my cloak. I could see the bulge of Destin inside it. Standing in one corner was the full-size Elemental.

Delph said, "Almost forgot to put the glove on before I picked it up."

My next words carried a heaviness that I found nearly unbearable. "Delph, Wugs had to see what I did."

"What Wugs saw was two jabbits coming out another Wug. After that, they didn't see nothin'. 'Cept you killing the pair of 'em. And they ain't too clear on how you done it. But I don't see no Wug holding that against ya."

"So what do the Wugs say about it all?"

"Outliers. They was shouting it when it was happening. 'Outliers got Ladon-Tosh. Got inside-a him.' That's what they said."

"That's mental!"

"Course i'tis, but that don't mean they don't believe it."

I sighed and sat back. I was just so tired.

"You feeling up to snuff, Vega Jane?"

I glanced over at him. "Why?"

"Well, they're waiting, ain't they?"

"Who's waiting?" I said suspiciously.

He held out a hand, which I slowly took and rose off the cot. He led me over to the window. I peered out and my jaw dropped.

"*They* are," said Delph, smiling.

When Delph opened the door to my digs and I stepped out, the cheers started and hats were flung high into the air. It looked like every Wug was in attendance.

"Ve-ga Jane. Ve-ga Jane," they started chanting over and over.

I heard a canine bark and looked down to see Harry Two next to me. He apparently had been guarding my privacy. I stroked his head and then gazed up at Delph.

"What is all this?" I asked in bewilderment.

"Are ya serious? Time for the prize. You're champion, you silly goose."

I had forgotten that with the defeat of Ladon-Tosh, I *was* the champion.

"Quiet, please. Quiet."

The voice belonged to Thansius. As the crowd parted and became silent, he came forward holding two objects. One was a metal figurine. The other a woolen bag with a cord tied firmly around its neck.

Thansius motioned to me. "Vega, please step forward."

I let go of Delph's hand and walked toward the Chief of Council with hesitant steps. I was still a bit wonky, but I couldn't not go, could I?

Thansius turned to the crowd and proclaimed, "I officially declare Vega Jane the champion of the Duelum."

A cheer went up again. As I looked out on the masses of Wugs, I saw many tears and smiles and only the very occasional sour look from the likes of Ran Digby, Ted Racksport — on sticks because of his morta-shot foot — and Cletus Loon, who, as usual, looked murderously at me. And when I glanced to the right, I saw Krone and Dodgson staring daggers.

As the crowd quieted, Thansius said, "I now present you with the trophy."

He handed me the figurine. They must have made it special because it was a *female* holding a *male* over her head. Thansius bent down and said in my ear, "The young Dactyl Jasper Forke, one of your fellow Stackers, made that for you. Just in case," he added.

I took it and held it and my smile widened to my ears. I looked and found Forke in the crowd and thanked him with my eyes before he glanced shyly down at his feet.

I held the figurine over my head, and the crowd cheered again.

When they had settled down, Thansius said, "And now the one thousand coins." He handed me the wool bag. "As the first female champion in the history of the Duelum. And on a job exceptionally well done." He peered at me. "Exceptionally well done. Where not only a prize was won but many Wug lives were saved." He put out his hand. "Thank you, Vega Jane. All of Wormwood thanks you."

As I shook his hand, the crowd truly went mad this time. I looked over at Delph, who was smiling, it seemed, with his whole body. A tear trickled down his face.

When I looked back at Thansius, he was smiling broadly as he turned to face the crowd. "Drinks are on me at the Witch-Pidgy. And for those younger wugs, there will be pink ginger ale. And food for the bellies all around. Off you go."

A great cheer went up from the Wugs as Thansius finished and a stream of them headed off to the pub, with the very youngs jumping and twirling and making noise.

When we were alone, I touched Delph on the arm. "Can we go see your dad?"

"Don't you want to go to the pub and celebrate, like Thansius said?"

I looked down at the bag of coins in my hand. "Let's go to see your dad first."

DUF DELPHIA HAD stayed at his cottage because one of his timbertoes had developed a crack. This Delph had told me on our walk there. Duf was sitting out on the steps with the bad timber off and a stick bowl between his teeth when we appeared in his view. He knocked the dottle out, replaced the smoke weed and lit the bowl. He hailed us as we walked up to him. I saw that his corral was empty of beasts.

Duf grinned and pointed at me. "I knew it," he said. "You done did it. You won the bloody thing, didn't-cha? Course you did. Knew it, didn't I?"

"How did you know?" I called out, though I couldn't keep the grin off my face.

"'Cause you ain't dead, that's why."

"Dad!" exclaimed a mortified Delph.

"He's right, Delph," I said. "I'm not dead, ergo, I won."

"What you be doing here, then?" asked Duf. "Should be, I don't know, celebrating, eh?"

I walked up to the steps and sat next to him. Harry Two, who had come with us, let Duf scratch his ears.

"Right good canine there," said Duf. "He was here this light, weren't he, Delph?"

"He was," said Delph. "But now he's back with Vega Jane, right and proper."

I said, "How are the timbers coming? Delph said one has a crack."

"Aye, but it'll be fine, don't you know. Getting used to the things, I am."

I took the bag of coins from my cloak and held it up. "The winnings," I said.

"Har," he said. He pointed the lip end of his stick bowl at it. "Now, that's some winnings, I tell you. Thousand coins. Right, Delph?"

"Right."

"Well, it's *our* winnings," I said.

"What?" said Delph, looking gobsmacked.

"Delph helped train me up, Duf. Never would've won without his help."

"G'on with yourself," said Duf. He puffed on his stick bowl and studied me curiously.

"And since I've no head for coin, I want you and Delph to take it."

"Vega Jane, are you nutters?" exclaimed Delph.

"You'd be doing me a favor, actually," I said. I looked around the land. "Where are the beasts?" I asked. "The adar and the young slep?"

Duf slapped his timber and for the first time, I saw the hopelessness in his expression. "Gone, ain't they?"

"Gone where?"

"To a Wug can train 'em up proper, that's where. And that Wug ain't me."

"What Wug?" I said.

"Crank Desmond."

"Crank Desmond! He doesn't know a slep's arse from the other end, does he?"

"Be that as it may, he got two good legs and I got none. Har."

I held up the bag of coins higher. "Then what we're going to do is bring a young Wug here, pay him a proper wage and train him up." I looked around at the empty corrals. "And we can turn it into a business."

"Bizness? What'd you mean?" asked Delph.

"I already talked to Thansius about this. I gave him a name of a Wug who I know likes beasts. He said he was all in favor of it." I paused, thinking through my next words as Duf and Delph continued to stare at me, openmouthed. "They sell beasts around here, young ones, don't they? Cretas and sleps and whists and adars and more. And Wugs with coin want them. Need cretas and sleps at the Mill and the Tillers. Wugs like Roman Picus need the whists. And who wouldn't want to pay good coin for an adar that can keep 'em company and carry messages and the like?"

Duf sat a bit forward. "But Wugs just give me the beasts to train up."

"So now you can sell 'em the beast along with the training. Bet it'll be worth more coin to Wugs if you supply a handpicked beast too."

"We don't know nothin' 'bout no bizness," protested Delph.

"You know beasts, don't you?" I pointed out. "That's what's important."

Duf's eyes twinkled. "She makes a right good point, Delph."

Delph still looked confused. "Then you got to share in the coin we make."

"Oh, you bet I will," I lied.

I must have said this too quickly, because Delph eyed me funny. I gave the bag of coins to Duf, rose and said my good-byes. As I walked off, Delph caught up to me.

"What was all that chuff back there?" he asked.

"Duf and you can really make a go of it. You just needed a bit of coin."

"Okay, but we need to talk about this."

"We will. Next light. Now I just need some rest."

I would never have that conversation with Delph.

Because I *was* going to leave Wormwood and enter the Quag. And I was going to do so this very night. I walked on.

Answers at Last

STACKS LOOMED AHEAD of me like a castle without a moat outside or a king or queen inside. While I knew other Wugs were managing a pub crawl with only the one pub, I had decided to come to my place of work for the last time. It was not for nostalgic purposes.

I opened the large door and peered inside. With the two jabbits dead, I wasn't afraid to go inside, certainly not while it was still light. I knew now that Ladon-Tosh had guarded this place both light and night, just in different forms.

Domitar sat in his little office at his tilt-top desk. There was no scroll or ink bottle there. But there was another bottle present: flame water.

"I was hoping you might come by" was his surprising greeting as he waved me in. He poured a glass of flame water and took a sip. "Trounced the blackguard."

"You saw the jabbits?"

He smacked his lips. "They were a wee bit hard to miss."

I could tell from his expression that he knew what my next question would be.

"How did you know?" I asked.

He feigned surprise, though I could tell he didn't mean it.

I said, "You said I'd done it before. Beaten Ladon-Tosh. But you really meant I'd beaten the jabbits before."

"Did I?"

I ignored this. "That could mean one of two things."

He set the glass down. "I'm listening," he said amiably.

"One, you knew of my coming to Stacks at night. And of my being chased by the pair of jabbits to the little room on the second floor."

"Dear me, dear me," said Domitar.

I kept going. "Though I really didn't beat them. I simply escaped from them."

"Same as in my book, but please continue," he said when I paused.

"Or you saw me destroy a flying jabbit on a great battle-field many sessions ago."

I had expected him to look startled by this second possibility, but Domitar remained unshaken. "I will admit to the first, but not the second." He tapped his glass against his chin. "Quite a mess you made here too," he said. "Many pieces to pick up. Not really my job, but there you are."

I felt myself growing warm. "So you knew about the jabbits in here?"

He finished the flame water in his glass. "Don't know why I drink the stuff," he said. "Becomes a habit, I suppose. So much of life does, doesn't it?"

"The jabbits!" I cried out.

"All right, all right, but no Wug is supposed to come in here at night, are they?"

"Is that your answer?"

"Do I need another?"

"You bloody well do. *I* almost was eaten by those vile creatures."

"Let that be a lesson to you, then."

"Domitar, they were *jabbits*."

"Yes, yes, I quite get the point, thank you. Hideous things." He shivered.

"And what of the room with the blood? And going back into the past? And books that explode in your face? And the looking glasses with demons?"

He looked at me blankly. "I think perhaps the Duelum has affected your mind, Vega Jane. Do you need a lie-down?"

"So you're saying you don't know about those things here? You said this had always been Stacks."

"I said this had been Stacks since I came here," he corrected.

I folded my arms over my chest and continued to stare at him.

"What does Stacks look like to you?" he asked.

"Magic, sorcery, devilry, call it what you will, it's strange."

"I mean what does it look like from the *outside*?"

I thought about this. "Like a castle I saw once in a book at Learning. But that was fantasy, not real."

"Who says so?" he asked pedantically.

"Well, I mean." I drew a long breath. "It's all rubbish, I know."

"Well done."

"So whose castle was it?"

"I am not the one to answer that because I don't know."

"If you know it was a castle once, how can you not know whose castle it was?" I demanded.

"One can possess some shallow perspective without the depth of true knowledge."

I fumed over this for a sliver. "All right. So has the Quag always been the Quag?"

He refilled his glass, sloshing the flame water onto the surface of his desk. He took a quick drink, dribbling a bit down his chin. "The Quag? The Quag, you say? I know nothing of the Quag for the simple fact that I have never been in the Quag, I will never be in the Quag, and I thank the holy Steeples for that."

"So in Wormwood, you are destined to stay and die?"

"As we all are."

"Not Quentin Herms."

"No, the Outliers got him."

"Now who is talking rubbish?"

He set his glass down. "Do you have proof otherwise?" he asked sternly.

"I aim to get it."

"Vega, if you're planning to do what I think you're —"

"I think that she is, Domitar. I most assuredly do."

I whirled around at this voice. Little Dis Fidus stood in the doorway, a rag and a small bottle of liquid in hand.

"Hello," I said, not understanding what he had meant by his words. How could little, old Dis Fidus know anything of my plans?

He shuffled forward. "I am happy for your victory in the Duelum this light."

"Thank you, but what did you mean —"

However, he had shifted his gaze to Domitar. "We knew this moment would come of course. We needn't a Selene Jones prophecy to know that."

I looked at Domitar as he slowly nodded. "The time *has* come, I suppose."

Dis Fidus held the rag to the bottle and doused the cloth with the liquid. "Hold out your hand, Vega," he said.

"Why? What's that stuff on the cloth?"

"Just hold out your hand. Your inked hand."

I glanced at Domitar, who slowly nodded at me.

I tentatively held out my hand. My gaze was drawn to the blue skin on top, the result of two sessions of having Dis Fidus stamp my hand for no reason.

Dis Fidus said, "This will not occur without some discomfort. I'm sorry. It is unavoidable." I drew back my hand and looked at Domitar, who would not meet my gaze.

"Why should I endure the pain?" I asked. "What result will come of it?"

"It will be much less painful than what's in the Quag if you have the ink on you."

"I don't understand."

"Nor should you," said Domitar. "But if that is your plan, it is essential that the ink comes off." He shut his mouth and turned to the wall.

I looked back at Dis Fidus. I held out my hand once more, half closed my eyes and prepared for the pain. He touched the top of my hand with the rag and I felt like a thousand flying stingers had attacked the surface. I tried to jerk my hand back but I couldn't. When I fully opened my eyes, I saw that Dis Fidus had gripped my wrist with his hand. He was surprisingly strong for being so small and old.

I moaned, clenched my teeth, bit my lip, screwed my eyes shut and swayed on my feet. When it got to the point where I could stand it no longer, Dis Fidus said, "'Tis done."

He let go of my wrist and I opened my eyes. The back of my hand was scarred and pink and sore. But there was not a trace of blue on it. I looked up at him as I rubbed it with my other hand. "Why did that need to be done?"

"You have of course wondered why I spend my lights inking hands here," said Dis Fidus. I nodded. "Well, now you have the answer. Simply put, to go through the Quag with an inked hand is a death sentence."

"So Quentin Herms, then?" I said bitterly.

I looked from Domitar to Dis Fidus. Each shook their heads. Finally, Dis Fidus said, "If he went through the Quag with his hand as 'twas, I fear for him."

"So you don't believe that Outliers took him, then?" I said, a sense of triumph in my words.

Dis Fidus's look told me that was unnecessary. "Surely, you have moved on from that theory," he said in a voice I had never heard from him before. Gone was timid, bowing Dis Fidus. He still looked old and feeble, but there was a fire in his eyes I had never seen before.

"I have," I answered.

"Then let us waste no more time speaking of it," said Dis Fidus with finality. He corked the bottle and handed it and a fresh cloth to me. "Take this."

"But my hand is clean of ink."

"Take it nonetheless," he urged.

I put them away in my cloak. "So what is the ink, then? How is it harmful to us?"

"In the Quag, it is like honey to stingers," answered Domitar. "Or the scent given off by a female slep in need of a male."

"So it draws the beasts right to the Wugs," I said fiercely. "A death sentence clearly," I added accusingly. "And you knew about it!"

"Wugs are not supposed to go into the Quag," said Domitar defensively. "And if they don't, the ink marks are meaningless to them."

"But what if the beasts come out of the Quag?" I said. "A garm came after me, chased me up my tree. And now I know why, because of the marks on my hand."

Domitar looked guiltily at Dis Fidus before continuing. "No system is perfect."

"And whose system was it?" I asked.

Surprisingly, Dis Fidus answered. "It has always been so, that I know. And there is no Wug alive whose sessions tally to mine."

"What of Morrigone? Or Thansius?"

"Even Thansius is not so old as Dis Fidus. Now, Morrigone is a special case, you understand," said Domitar.

"Oh, she's special all right!" I exclaimed.

"She's not an evil Wug, strike that right from your mind right this sliver," said Dis Fidus with startling energy.

"I'll think she's evil if I want to, thank you very much," I retorted.

"Well, you would be wrong, then," said Domitar wearily

as he sipped from his glass. "Wugs and Wormwood are not so easily categorized."

I exclaimed, "What are we, then?"

Domitar answered. "In one sense we're Wugs, plain and simple. What we might have been before, well, it's for our ancestors to say, isn't it?"

"They're dead!" I shot back.

"Well, there you are," said Domitar imperturbably.

"You talk in a circle!" I exclaimed. "You tell me Morrigone isn't evil and expect me to believe that. She was controlling Ladon-Tosh. She was the reason those jabbits were inside him. She couldn't control them. She had to beg me for help in slaying them."

To my astonishment, this did not seem to surprise either of them.

Dis Fidus merely nodded, as though I were simply confirming what he already suspected.

"Yes, it would be difficult for her," said Dis Fidus in a nonchalant tone.

"For her?" I shouted. "What about me?"

"Some Wugs have duties passed down," explained Domitar. "Morrigone is one of them. Before her, it was her mother's responsibility to see to Wug welfare. And that is what she was doing this light."

"By trying to murder me?"

"You are a danger to her and to all of Wormwood, Vega, do you not understand that?" said Domitar in exasperation.

"How am I a danger to her? She pretended to be my friend. She let me think Krone was my true enemy. And she was trying to kill me in the Duelum. Why?"

480

"That is something you must discover for yourself."

"Domitar!"

"No, Vega. That is my last word on the subject."

I looked at them both. "So where does that leave us?"

Domitar rose and corked his flame water. "Me still safely in Wormwood and you apparently not."

"You don't think I'll make it past the Quag, do you?"

"Actually, I believe that you will," he said in a whisper, and bowed his head. "And then may Steeples help all Wugs."

When I looked at Dis Fidus, he had bowed his head too.

I turned and left Stacks. I would not be coming back.

The End of the Beginning

I WENT BACK TO my digs and packed up everything I owned — which wasn't much — and placed it in my tuck. In the pocket of my cloak went the Adder Stone and the shrunken Elemental. I placed my tuck under my cot and decided to spend one of the coins I had in my cloak pocket on a last meal in my place of birth.

The Starving Tove was where Delph and I had eaten twice before. As I walked toward it on the High Street with Harry Two at my heels, I could hear the cries of celebration still swirling from the Witch-Pidgy. Wugs had spilled out onto the cobblestones to pull on their pints and whittle down bits of meats, breads and potatoes.

Roman Picus seemed quite on the other side of the sail, as did Thaddeus Kitchen and Litches McGee. The three of them staggered about like Wugs on ice singing at the top of their lungs. I next saw Cacus Loon leaning against a post. His face was as red with flame water as the bottom of Hestia Loon's frying pan coming off the coals.

I ducked around to the Tove before any of them could get a gander at me. I wanted food. I did not desire company. The Tove held no Wugs except the ones working there because of the free food at the pub. I held out my coin, as a matter of course, to let them know I could pay for my meal, but the big, flat-faced Wug who seated me waved this off.

"Your coin is no good here, Vega."

"What?"

"On us, Vega. And what an honor i'tis."

"Are you sure you can do that?" I asked.

"Sure as you beat that wicked Ladon-Tosh to nothing."

When he brought me the scroll with the food items on it, I said I would have one of everything. At first, he looked surprised by this, but then a silly grin spread across his face and he replied, "Coming right up, luv."

I ate like I never had in all my sessions. It was as though I had never had a meal before. The more I ate, the more I wanted, until I could gorge no more. I knew I would probably never have a meal like this one again. I pushed back the last plate, patted my belly contentedly and then refocused on what was coming. I glanced out the window. The first section of night was here.

I would wait until the fourth section. That seemed as good a time as any to tackle the Quag. I figured going into the darkness *during* the darkness was a good plan. There was danger to be faced, and confronting it head-on and as soon as possible seemed more sensible to my mind than trying to forever avoid it. I needed to know if I had the mettle to make it or not. Why dither about?

I also doubted quite seriously if one could wholly navigate the Quag during the brightness. I just knew that one had to go through the blackness of the shadows to get to the gold of the light. That sorry thought was about as poetic as I was ever going to be.

I had brought some food out with me to give to Harry Two. This was my other concern. Food. We had to eat while we were in the Quag. I looked down at the few remaining coins I had. I went to another shop and spent it all on some basic provisions for my canine and me. It wasn't much, and part of me was glad of that. I couldn't be bogged down with pounds of food if I was running from a garm. I had no idea how long it would take to get through the Quag.

The food I had purchased clearly would not last us that long. And I would have to bring water too. But water was also heavy and I could not carry enough of it to last half a session. The truth was I had to be able to locate food and water in the Quag. I was somewhat heartened by the fact that beasts, no matter how vile, also needed to eat and have water to drink. I just didn't want their food to be us.

It was now the second section of night and I had just reached my digs when I looked up and saw it coming.

Adars are clumsy-looking beasts when ground-bound. In the air, though, they are creatures of grace and beauty. This one soared along, flying far better than I ever would.

It drew closer and closer and finally descended and came to rest a few feet from me. As I looked more closely at it, I realized it was the adar Duf had been training up for Thansius. And then I also observed it had a woolen bag in its beak. It ambled toward me and dropped the bag at my feet.

I looked down at it and then up at the tall adar.

"A present from Thansius," said the adar in a voice that was remarkably like the Wug himself.

I knelt, picked up the cloth bag and opened it. There were two items inside.

My grandfather's ring.

And the book on the Quag.

I looked at the adar. I had to close my eyes and reopen them. For a moment I could have sworn I was staring into the face of Thansius.

The adar continued. "He says take them with faith and the belief that the courage of one can change everything."

I slipped the ring and book inside my cloak. I thought I was done with the adar, or he with me, but that was not the case. His next words froze me, but only for an instant. Then I was running full tilt to the door of my digs, where I frantically retrieved my tuck. I burst out of my door and ran down the cobblestones with Harry Two bounding next to me.

The adar had already taken flight and I watched it soar overhead.

Its last words came back to me. Indeed, I knew I would never forget them.

They are coming for you, Vega. They are coming for you right now.

HARRY TWO AND I did not stop running until we were well out of Wormwood proper. I looked to the sky and blinked. There were no stars up there save one. And it was moving. This was the second shooting star I had seen and it seemed identical to the first one I had glimpsed. But that was impossible. Besides, they were so far away, how could a Wug tell from all the way down here? It seemed to be following me as I hurried along the path to the point where I would confront the Wall.

I thought to myself that it seemed lonely, that star. Lonely and perhaps lost, as I had thought before. It was shooting across a sky of nothing but black, going somewhere or at least trying to. But if you don't know where you want to go, I suppose any path will get you there.

After a quarter mile, I stopped and pulled some things from my tuck. I had built these from scraps at Stacks over a period of time. I knelt down in front of Harry Two and told him to be still and quiet. I slipped the small breastplate over his chest and fastened it with the leather straps I had fashioned. It was lightweight but strong, just as I had designed it. I then clipped a metal cap I had made over Harry Two's head. My canine took all of this fuss and bother perfectly stoically and wore the contraption like he had been born to it. I rubbed his ears and thanked him for being so good. I then strapped the harness around my shoulders. I would load Harry Two into it when we grew closer to the Wall.

Then I dropped to the ground and listened.

Whatever was coming did not care about stealth. It was making so much noise, I became alarmed. Predators unafraid of what lay ahead made noise. Prey kept quiet and in the shadows. I slipped behind a large bush and waited to see what it was.

I donned the glove, drew the Elemental and willed it to full size. And waited.

The noise was drawing closer. In less than a sliver, I would know what I would be confronting.

"Delph!"

He was hurtling past where I lay hidden. At my voice, he pulled up short and stared around in bewilderment until I rose up so he could see me.

"What are you doing here?"

"Thansius's adar told me they were coming. He said he'd told you too. So's I took off."

"Took off for where?"

His face turned to a scowl. "You're asking me that, you prat?"

I gaped at him. Daniel Delphia had never called me such a name in all the sessions I had known him, which was basically all of my sessions.

"A prat?" I said in astonishment. "You called me a prat?"

"What kind of a Wug do ya take me for? Prat I said and prat I meant," he added huffily.

I walked over and was about to slap him. My hand was reared back to strike when I noticed that he had a tuck over his shoulders.

"What's that?"

"Me stuff. Same as you got there, ain't it?" He indicated my tuck. He looked down at the armored Harry Two and said, "Blimey, that's right fine." He looked back up.

"Where are you going?" I asked.

"Same place you're going."

"No, you're not."

"Yes, I bloody well am."

"Delph, you are not coming with me."

"Then you're not going."

"You think you can stop me?"

"I think I can try."

"Why are you doing this?"

"What we planned all along, right?" he said.

"But your dad — I thought —"

487

"He and me talked it out, didn't we? Told him stuff. He agreed I should go. You got ridda his pain. And . . . and he said to thank you for, well, putting me back right with me head and all. He wanted to tell you himself, but he kept blubbering in front of me when he talked of it. 'Spect he'd never be able to say it to you directly."

"I, well, I'm very touched by that."

"And he got coin and a bloke to train. A bizness, like you said."

"But I meant for the two of you to run it."

He shook his head stubbornly. "Can't let you go in the Quag by yourself, Vega Jane. Just can't."

I stood there looking up at him and he stood there looking down at me. I was going to say something back to him when I happened to glance at the sky. That's when I saw it.

Two shooting stars racing side by side. It was a lesson, I supposed, not to focus only on oneself. Delph, I'm sure, wanted to escape the confines of Wormwood too. There were other Wugs besides me whose destinies lay outside this place.

I looked at him and gripped his hand. "I'm glad you're here, Delph."

His face brightened. "You are? Really?"

I went up on tiptoes and kissed him.

As he went all red in the face, I said, "I'd have to be a nutter to want to go into the Quag without you, wouldn't I? And I am many things, but a nutter is not one of them."

"No, Vega Jane, you're no nutter."

And then he picked me up off the ground and kissed me back so hard I felt my breath leave my body so fast I thought

I would pass out. When he set me back down, both our eyes were closed. When they opened, nearly simultaneously, Delph and I just looked at each other for what seemed a handful of slivers.

Finally he said, "So what now?"

"The Wall," I said. Something struck me. "How did you know I'd be here?"

"Didn't. Been running all over the place trying to find you."

"A while back I picked a particular finished spot on the Wall. I think it's our best shot to get through."

"Wug guards on the towers," he said anxiously.

"I know that. But the distance in between them leaves a gap."

He eyed my cloak. "Got your chain?"

I nodded. "You ready?"

When we reached my planned breach point, we hid behind a bush and looked up at the Wall. Two hundred feet on either side of this spot were lantern-lighted watchtowers with Wugs carrying mortas stationed in them.

I hooked up Harry Two with the harness and he dangled from my chest. With Destin across my shoulders providing me strength, he felt no heavier than a couple of pounds.

"Wrap your arms around my shoulders, Delph, like we did before."

He never got a chance to.

"There they are!" yelled a voice.

At the sound, my heart sank.

I looked to the right and saw a cluster of Wugs rushing toward us, mortas in hand. My heart sank even more when I saw who it was. To our left was Ted Racksport hobbling on his gimpy foot, Cletus with bloodlust in his wicked eyes and Ran Digby with his ugly beard and filthy face.

To our right was Jurik Krone and Duk Dodgson.

And leading all of them was Morrigone. "No, Vega!" she screamed. "You will not leave Wormwood. You cannot."

They were each cocking their mortas and starting to take aim.

I grabbed Delph by the hand and ran, Harry Two banging against my chest with each stride. We were within fifty yards of the Wall when I left my feet, pulling Delph with me. It was an awkward balance and I veered to the side Delph was on before righting my path of ascendance.

I turned in time to see Morrigone aim her hands at us. The full Elemental was in my hand a moment later and the deflected beam of red light she hurled at us struck part of the Wall and blasted a hole in it. We soared on.

"Fire!" shouted Krone.

The mortas roared. I felt something race past my head. I heard Delph cry out and he went limp. I gripped his arm tighter.

"Delph," I shouted.

"Just go, go," he said in a strained voice. "I'm okay."

But I knew he was not okay. I banked to the left and then back to the right as the mortas fired again. Harry Two barked and then howled and then whimpered. Then he fell silent. I felt something wet against my face.

Harry Two had been shot as well. I shrunk my Elemental, put it away and supported Harry Two with my free hand while my other clutched Delph.

"Stop firing!" I yelled.

I didn't think they would, since they had already hit two of us. I just wanted an instant to do what I was about to. I banked hard right, flew around a tree, cupped Harry Two with my elbow, ripped off a branch as I raced by, and when I came out of the turn, I was facing the Wugs.

I threw the branch, scattering them, and it plowed into the dirt right where they had been standing. I turned once more and aimed for the top timber of the Wall.

The mortas were quieted for the moment. But I knew I didn't have much time. Delph was moaning. And, even more frightening, Harry Two was hanging limp in his harness, not moving at all. I headed right for the Wall at speed, but I was having immense trouble gaining enough lift with Delph and Harry Two.

When I looked back I froze in fear.

Jurik Krone, the finest shot in all of Wormwood, had his morta pointed directly at my head. I could not pull my Elemental because I was holding on to Delph with one hand and I was supporting Harry Two's body with the other.

I could see Krone smile as he started to pull the trigger that would send a morta round directly into my head. And all three of us would fall to our deaths.

And then something hit Krone so hard that he was knocked sideways for thirty feet. He tumbled and rolled and his morta flew from his hands.

I looked to see what had just saved my life.

Morrigone was lowering her hands, which were pointed at where Krone had been standing. She turned and looked at me. For an instant I imagined a metal helmet around

Morrigone's face, the shield raised, and how she looked so much like the female on that battlefield from so long ago. Then she lifted her hands once more and I felt an invisible force, like an iron tether, grip my leg. When I glanced at her, Morrigone was moving her arms as though pulling a rope toward her. I felt my momentum stop and, with a jerk, I felt us being pulled backward, downward.

This was it. This was the moment. If I could not do this, then everything would have been for nothing.

With a scream that seemed to go on for slivers, I summoned every ounce of strength I had. I felt energy surging through me. I kicked with my feet and I could feel the invisible tether loosen. I kicked harder and bent my shoulders forward as though I were laboring under an impossibly heavy weight. And then with one more long scream and my muscles so tense I thought I was paralyzed, I broke free, soared over the top timbers — Delph's boots actually scraped across them — and we were past the Wall.

As I looked back once more, I saw Morrigone on the ground, spent, dirty and defeated. Our gazes locked.

She raised one hand toward me — not to try and stop me — but, I realized, simply to say farewell.

The next quarter sliver we cleared the filled moat below and passed into the Quag. We sailed over the first stand of trees and bushes. And then it became so dense I had to quickly drop to the ground.

It was good that I did. I already had snatched the Adder Stone out of my cloak pocket. Delph was slumped on the ground, holding his arm, and blood had saturated his shirt. I ran the Stone over it and the wound vanished and the pain on his face disappeared. He straightened and gasped, "Thanks, Vega Jane."

But I wasn't listening to him. I had unhooked Harry Two from his harness. He lay limply on the ground. He was barely breathing. His eyes were closed.

"No," I whimpered. "Please, no!"

I pulled off the breastplate and saw where the morta metal had pierced it. I rubbed the Adder Stone over the wound on his side where the morta metal had struck him. He was so badly hurt I thought that touching the Stone to his body would make the wound heal faster. I kept rubbing, pressing the Stone into his fur and passing it over the wound. Still nothing. The tears streamed down my face as Delph knelt next to me.

"Vega Jane."

He put a hand on my shoulder, trying to draw me away. "Vega Jane, leave him be now. He's gone."

"Shove off!" I screamed and pushed him so hard he flew backward and sprawled in the dirt.

I looked down at Harry Two and thought every good thought I could think of.

"Please, please," I moaned. "Please don't leave me again." In my despair, I was merging the two canines in my mind. My vision was blurred by my tears.

Harry Two didn't move. His breathing was slowing down to where I could barely see his chest rise.

I couldn't believe this. I had lost my Harry Two. I turned to see Delph picking himself back up. That's when something nudged my hand. I snatched it away, thinking it was a creature of the Quag testing my flesh for eating.

Harry Two touched my hand again with his wet nose. His eyes were now open and he was breathing normally. He rose on his paws and shook all over, as though throwing off his near death good and proper. I think he even smiled at me. I was so happy I shouted for joy and hugged him tightly.

In return he licked my face and barked.

Delph knelt next to us. "Thank the Steeples," he said, scratching Harry Two's snout.

I smiled and then I stopped smiling. I was staring at Delph's hand.

Delph's ink-stamped hand from all those sessions at the Mill.

That's when I heard the growls on either side of us.

I slowly turned.

There was a garm to the right and an enormous frek on our left.

The blue ink: like honey to stingers.

I didn't wait an instant longer. I drew the Elemental and thought it to full size. I threw it even as the frek leapt at Delph. It struck the frek dead center of the chest and the beast disintegrated.

But the garm had lunged forward, its own blood pouring down its chest and its odious smell searing my lungs. And bursting from its powerful jaw was that awful sound it makes when on the hunt. I knew the next thing leaping from its jaws would be a chest full of fire that would cremate us.

I snatched the jug of water from my tuck and hurled it at the creature. It struck it full in the snout, the jug cracked open and the water splashed in the garm's face.

It only gave me a moment, but a moment was all I needed. As soon as the Elemental touched my hand on its return from destroying the frek, I flung it onward.

The Elemental passed right through the garm's mouth and burst out its backside. The creature turned a burning orange and flamed up, as though all the fire on its inside couldn't reach the outside. A moment later, it exploded in a cloud of black smoke. When the smoke cleared, the garm was no more.

"Bloody Hel," exclaimed Delph.

I couldn't have agreed more.

We had no time to celebrate our victory. I grabbed Delph's inked hand and snagged the bottle and cloth Dis Fidus had given me from my pocket.

"What's that?" he asked.

"Just shut up and know this is going to hurt like the blazes."

I poured the liquid on the cloth and then pressed it on his hand.

Delph clenched his teeth and to his credit didn't utter a sound though his body shook like he was having the heaves after eating bad creta meat.

When the liquid had done its job, the back of his hand was as pink and scarred as mine. But all the ink was gone.

"Is this a good thing?" he asked, wincing and shaking his hand.

"It'll make it harder for those beasts to track us."

"Then it's a good thing," he said with conviction.

We grabbed our tucks where they had fallen.

"We need to keep moving, Delph."

I went first, with the fully formed Elemental ready in my hand, Delph second and Harry Two covering our rear flank.

We cleared the trees and thick vegetation, and then the most astounding thing happened. The Quag opened up to a flat expanse of green fields with small stands of towering trees that allowed us to see many miles in the distance. Far off to the west was a wide fog-shrouded river full of black water. To the east was a rocky slope that led up to somewhere. Far ahead of us to the north was a towering forested mountain that in the uneasy darkness looked not green, but blue.

There was only one problem. Before we could reach the flat expanse where we could see danger coming at us from a long way away, we had to get past the next obstacle. We were right on the edge of a cliff. I looked down. I figured the drop to be nearly a full mile. I looked at Delph and he looked back at me.

"Are you ready?" I asked.

He gripped my hand and nodded.

I lifted Harry Two into his harness and gave his head a pat. I had come so close to losing both of them so soon in here that a part of me wanted to go back to Wormwood. But a bigger part of me knew I couldn't. Not now. Perhaps one light.

We heard the sounds behind us and they were coming fast. From the quantity of noise, I figured three or four garms and what sounded like a whole herd of freks. They had no doubt been alerted to our presence by the previous battle.

They burst from the dense forest, which lay behind us. I looked back. I had been wrong. It wasn't four garms, it was ten. And they weren't freks. They were amarocs. And if anything, they were even more terrifying than the freks.

I turned and looked ahead to the distant blue mountain that somehow I knew was where we needed to go. Just beyond that, in the sky, were the stars, the lost stars as I thought of them now. Lost, like we were. Would they ever find their way? Would we? Perhaps not. Perhaps we would simply flame out. But at least we would have tried.

I looked once more at Delph, attempted a smile that died before it reached my face, and then we jumped. The three of us were suspended in air for a long moment as the wicked beasts sped toward us.

And then we soared downward, now fully embraced by the Quag.

FROM THE AUTHOR OF THE #1 *NEW YORK TIMES* BESTSELLER *THE FINISHER*

DAVID BALDACCI

THE KEEPER

Freedom begins with survival.

What lies beyond the Quag?

THE KEEPER

Sneak Peek

Harry Two started growling. I looked down at him. His hackles were up, his fangs bared, and I quickly gazed around to see what was causing this reaction in my canine. But there was nothing in the darkness, at least that I could see.

I looked at Delph. He said, "What's got into 'im?"

And then it struck me. My canine was breathing heavily through his snout. He wasn't seeing the danger—he was *smelling* it.

And in my experience, foul smells usually led to foul beasts.

I took a whiff of the air, wrinkled up my face and glanced sharply at Delph. "Do you smell that?"

He took in a chestful of the air and then exhaled it. "No."

I thought rapidly. I knew that scent, or at least something close to it.

And then the clouds in my mind slowly cleared.

Poison.

"What is it?" he asked nervously.

"I'm not exactly sure," I replied, and I wasn't. But I had smelled that sort of concoction before, back at Stacks, the factory where I was employed as a Finisher.

I pointed to the left. "Let's try that way."

"Shouldn't we maybe fly?" said Delph. "Get there faster, won't we? Let us . . . let us maybe see what's coming,

before . . . before it *gets* us," he finished breathlessly.

We would get there faster flying. But something in the back of my head said to leave our feet firmly on the ground. At least for now.

I was one who tended to follow her instincts. They had served me more right than wrong over my sessions.

And that's when I happened to look up, and saw it. Or rather, *them*.

A flock of birds was racing in perfect formation across the Noc-lit sky. This surprised me because I did not think that birds flew at night, but perhaps things were different in the Quag. As I watched the birds soar along, something very strange happened. From out of nowhere appeared a cloud of bluish smoke.

The birds turned sharply to avoid it, but a few could not make the turn in time. And when these birds passed through the smoke and came out the other side, they were no longer flying.

They were falling.

Because they were dead.

I stood there, paralyzed. Then I felt something grip my arm. It was Delph.

"Run, Vega Jane," he yelled. "Run!"

DAVID BALDACCI is a global #1
bestselling author. His books are published
in over 45 languages and in more than 80
countries; over 110 million copies are in
print. His works have been adapted for
both feature film and television. He is
also the co-founder, along with his wife,
of the Wish You Well Foundation®, which
supports literacy efforts across America.
David and his family live in Virginia.